AND
SO IT
BEGINS

Rachel Abbott

AND SO IT BEGINS

WILDFIRE

First published in 2018 by WILDFIRE
An imprint of HEADLINE PUBLISHING GROUP

1

Cataloguing in Publication Data is available from the British Library

Hardback ISBN 978 1 4722 5489 4
Trade Paperback ISBN 978 1 4722 5490 0

Typeset in Dante MT 11.25/15.25 pt by Palimpsest Book Production Limited,
Falkirk, Stirlingshire

Printed and bound in Great Britain by Clays Ltd, Elcograf S.p.A.

Headline's policy is to use papers that are natural, renewable
and recyclable products and made from wood grown in sustainable forests.
The logging and manufacturing processes are expected to conform to the
environmental regulations of the country of origin.

MIX
Paper from
responsible sources
FSC® C104740

HEADLINE PUBLISHING GROUP
An Hachette UK Company
Carmelite House
50 Victoria Embankment
London EC4Y 0DZ

www.headline.co.uk
www.hachette.co.uk

Prologue

I

So this is how it ends.

It is clear to me now: one of us has to die.

Some deaths are inevitable. Others can be prevented. And then there are those tragedies that are driven by their own momentum, that once begun will gather force, causing harm after harm, loss after loss.

Yes. It is time to end this.

II

Finally it was quiet in the car. Stephanie had managed to silence Jason by telling him that if he didn't stop talking she would pull over and throw him out. He could walk back to the station. It wasn't a comfortable silence, and Stephanie gripped the steering wheel tightly. She opened the window a crack to let out some of the hot air and breathed in the moist sea breeze, catching a vague scent of the waves crashing onto the rocks below.

Relax, a voice in her head said. *It won't be like last time.*

'So you think it's a domestic then, Sarge?' Jason said, his voice intruding into her thoughts. 'It's a bit posh up here for that, isn't it? They can't be rowing about money, that's for sure.'

Jason folded his arms as if that said it all, and Stephanie wanted to ask if he had listened to anything during his training. She hated taking probationers out, particularly when they were as opinionated and misinformed as this one.

'There was a 999 call and a woman was screaming for help – that's all we know. Then the line went dead. The security company that keeps an eye on the place says it's like bloody Fort Knox so it's unlikely anyone's broken in.'

Stephanie knew all too well what that meant. Whoever the woman needed saving from was known to her.

'The security patrol car is at the scene already and their guy's waiting to let us in, so we'll find out soon enough,' she said.

Too soon. She wasn't sure she wanted to know.

The gravel of the track crunched beneath the tyres, the bright light of a full moon illuminating the shrubbery that lined the narrow driveway as the clouds cleared. As she turned the corner she saw a long white wall ahead of them, about twenty feet high with a huge double wooden doorway in the centre.

'What the hell is this place?' Jason asked, his voice quiet as he took in the unusual sight.

'It's the rear wall of the house.'

'There aren't any windows. Why would you build a house without windows?'

'Just wait until you get inside, Jason.'

Out of the corner of her eye she saw his head swivel towards her. 'You know this house, then?'

Stephanie nodded. She didn't want to think about the last time she was called here and was hoping and praying that tonight wasn't going to be anything like it. But a cry for help was never a good sign, and despite its beauty this house gave her chills.

She pulled the car to a halt next to a vehicle with the badge of a security company on the side. A skinny young guy with a severe case of acne jumped out.

Oh Lord, she thought. *Two babies for the price of one.*

'Sergeant Stephanie King,' she said. 'Have you got the key?'

The young man nodded. 'I'm Gary Salter. From the security firm.'

Nothing like stating the obvious.

'Did you try ringing the bell?' she asked. Gary's eyes darted nervously from left to right.

'I didn't know if I should or not.'

'Probably the right decision,' Stephanie said. 'We don't know what's going on in there, and you'd have been vulnerable all on your own. Get back in the car, Gary. Until we know what's what we can't have you trampling all over the place.'

Stephanie pressed her finger hard on the bell and bent her head to listen for any sign of movement inside. It was completely silent. She tried once more for luck and then pushed the key into the lock and turned it.

She heard Gary jump out of the car behind her.

'There's an alarm,' he said. 'Code's 140329.'

Stephanie nodded and pushed the door open. The alarm box was inside the porch, but it wasn't armed. She opened the inner door and stepped into the house, Jason hot on her heels. The corridor was dark, and there wasn't a sound. The silence had the thick quality of a heavily insulated house, and as she called out her voice seemed flattened, dead.

A fragment of light spilled through a partially open door that led into what Stephanie knew to be the main living room of the house. With one hand on the wall to guide her, she inched forward, calling out, 'Hello? Police!' as she went. She pushed the double doors at the end of the hall fully open and suddenly they were out of the gloom.

'Bloody hell!' Jason said, and Stephanie knew exactly what he meant. The impact of the view in front of her was every bit as staggering as the last time she had seen it. There may have been no windows on the entrance side of the building, but the far wall of the vast living space was a single sheet of glass. Bright moonlight was reflecting on the black sea far below and it felt as if the house was suspended high above the ocean.

'No time to look at the view, kid. Hello!' she shouted again. 'Police. Anyone home?' There wasn't a sound. 'Come on, Jason, let's check the place out.'

The whole of the cavernous space they were in was open plan, with an ultra-modern kitchen, a dining table for about twenty people and an array of sofas. Just then the moon went behind a cloud and Stephanie reached out to switch on the lights. Nothing happened.

'Shit,' she muttered. 'Go and get the torch – and be quick. I'm going downstairs to the bedrooms. Come and find me.'

Jason turned back towards the door and Stephanie slowly made her way to the top of the stairwell and grasped the smooth steel bannister for support. It was cold under her fingers.

'Police!' she shouted. 'Mr North – are you here?' She could hear the lack of confidence in her voice, and cursed her memories of this place. 'Mr North?' she shouted again.

Although the caller had been a woman, the only name Stephanie had was North's and to the best of her knowledge he hadn't remarried.

The moon suddenly reappeared, drawing her gaze to the mesmerising sight of its reflection on the dark water, but she turned back to the stairs and drew her baton in her right hand. Holding tightly to the bannister with her left she stepped carefully down the glass staircase, calling out as she went.

Something had happened here. She could feel it.

She knew the bedrooms were on this floor, and at the far end of the corridor there was another staircase that led to the basement. She didn't want to have to go down there again.

She heard clomping feet behind her and turned into the full beam of a strong flashlight, lifting her arm across her eyes to protect them from the glare.

'Sorry, Sarge.' Jason's voice sounded slightly uneven, as if he was either scared or excited. She didn't want to know which.

Stephanie called out again into the silence. She remembered where the master bedroom was. Last time she was here the door had stood open and North had been sitting on the bed, his head bowed, his shoulders shaking.

She reached out with her foot and gently pushed the door open.

They didn't need the torch. Moonlight flooded through the room's floor-to-ceiling windows, supplemented by the flickering yellow glow of a dozen candles strategically placed around the room.

'Jesus!'

Jason's whispered blasphemy said it all. The bed was a mass of tangled sheets wrapped around the legs and arms of two people – Stephanie couldn't tell whether male or female from where she stood. The metallic smell confirmed what she was seeing. Both bodies were still, and the white bedding was drenched in thick, dark blood.

Despite the warm night, Stephanie felt a shiver run across the back of her neck and she swallowed hard. What the hell had happened here? She felt an abrupt urge to run from the room, away from the brutal sight in front of her.

Forcing herself to take a deep breath, she turned to Jason and quietly asked him to go back upstairs and call it in. She didn't need a mirror to know that the round-eyed look of horror on his face was a reflection of her own.

As he left the room, Stephanie heard a sound that made every hair on her arms stand on end. It was the cry of a very young child. She spun towards the door, trying to work out where it was coming from. She needed to find the child, but it didn't sound like a cry of pain or distress, and before she could leave this room, there was one thing she had to do. She was going to have to walk over to the blood-soaked bed and touch both bodies to check if they were dead, although in her mind there could be little doubt. The spatter pattern on the wall resembled a weird abstract painting and viscous red splodges decorated a larger than life black and white photograph of a blonde-haired woman, hanging in pride of place above where they lay.

Stephanie took a deep breath and forced herself to put one foot in front of the other, inching towards the bodies.

At first she thought she was seeing things. A leg twitched. Then a moment later the distant sound of the crying child was accompanied by a lower, deeper sound. It was a groan of pain. And it was coming from the bed.

One of them was alive.

PART ONE

Three Months Earlier

It began with small acts of cruelty. A foot outstretched, a cry of pain as a knee hit the ground. He developed a taste for it. The moments became more frequent, the acts more brutal. The pleasure, it seemed, greater with each callous deed.

1

I see the photograph from across the street. It fills the window of the gallery, suspended on thin wires so it appears to be floating mid-air. It's the black and white image of a girl's face, her body little more than a shadow against a black background. The contrast has been heightened so that each raised surface of skin – a cheekbone, her nose, the end of her chin – glows a dazzling white, while every hollow seems dark and secretive.

I stop dead on the pavement and stare. The gallery is small – no larger than the shops on either side, one selling fancy cakes, the other displaying the kind of rubbish people buy on holiday that has no purpose once their fortnight in the sun is over: blow-up sharks, beach balls that will pop the first time anyone kicks them, lurid pink lilos and fancy kites that probably will never fly.

The gallery is sophisticated in comparison, its grey fascia adorned with nothing more than two words painted to the far right, almost as if they're apologising for their presence: Marcus North.

I don't know how long I've been staring, but the photograph reaches out to me. I don't even notice the chaotic traffic as I cross the narrow road to stand outside the window. For a few long moments I am lost in thoughts of the past but finally I push open the door and take a step inside. It's a stunning space stretching far back, the walls a sombre grey. Every few metres a brick pillar punctuates the dark plaster on which the photographs are hanging, discreetly lit from above and, despite the lack of colour, glowing with life.

One picture draws me to it, and I slowly take the three steps down into the body of the gallery, my eyes fixed on an image of two young children, one black, one white, playing together. A black hand seems to be stroking a white cheek, while a white hand rests on a black leg. Again, the contrast is pitched high, and the smiles of baby teeth are captivating.

On each of the brick pillars is a small brass sculpture: a pig's head, a wizened hand, a dancer's leg bent at the knee. And hanging from each sculpture is a piece of the most original and beautiful silver jewellery I have ever seen. A long necklace with undulating waves hangs from the wing of a bird, a jewelled earring sits in the pig's nose.

I sense someone behind me and I turn my head.

In stark contrast to the monochrome of the gallery, the woman is wearing a short, sleeveless dress in fuchsia pink. Her hair is cut close to her head, cropped almost, and dyed a startling white. Her eyes seem to grab me and won't let go. Pale grey, luminous and huge, they watch me.

I know who this is. Cleo North.

'Can I help you,' she asks, 'or are you happy to browse?'

She's smiling, but it's the professional smile of a salesperson and it holds little genuine warmth. I clear my throat, angry at myself for my jittering nerves, but I remember why I'm here and the anxiety ebbs as I walk back up the steps towards her, stretching out my hand. Hers is cool to the touch.

'Evie Clarke,' I say. 'I was interested to see whether Marcus North's photography is as good as I've been led to believe.'

The grey eyes narrow slightly. 'I'm Cleo North, Marcus's sister. I think you'll find it's probably better. Can I ask how you came across his work?'

I smile and twist a strand of my long blonde hair, which seems an almost gaudy yellow next to the pure white of Cleo's, between my fingers.

'I've been doing a bit of research recently and there was an article in a local paper about Marcus. You were named as his business manager.'

'Are you local, then?' she asks, a puzzled frown suggesting she should know me if that were the case.

'No, I'm from London. But a friend was on holiday here and brought back a copy of the newspaper. I was intrigued and decided to take a trip to check the photos out for myself. I'm looking for someone to take a series of pictures of me.' I smile at Cleo, knowing this sounds terribly vain. 'They're for my father, but if left to his own devices we'd probably end up with some stuffy posed portraits, so I asked if I could choose the photographer.'

I see a flash of concern in her eyes which she disguises with another smile. 'I'm not sure if Marcus is taking on that kind of portrait work at the moment. He's been focusing more on reportage photography, capturing pictures that tell a story. These,' she says, indicating the portrait shots in the gallery with her hand, 'are mainly examples of his earlier work.'

I nod, as if I understand. 'Look, why don't I talk to him, tell him what I'm after. My father's well connected, and if he's pleased with the outcome I'm sure he'll be only too happy to spread the word.'

I can see indecision in her eyes. She has aspirations for her brother – the newspaper article made that clear – and I need to find a way to win her over.

'If it helps, I'm not specifically looking for studio images. I'd love to have a number of photos taken over time with different moods and a range of locations. I don't want something obvious or too staged.'

Cleo looks vaguely affronted that I might think Marcus capable of the mundane.

'Well I think you can see his pictures are never boring. He's highly sought after, as you can imagine.'

It takes another ten minutes of subtle persuasion, with the unspoken lure of enhancing Marcus's reputation, before she thaws and I begin to see a flicker of excitement. I'm sure she has greatly exaggerated the current demand for his work – he's been virtually a recluse for the past eighteen months – and I can see ambition in her eyes. Not for herself, but for Marcus. I know she's on my side now.

'How would you like to take this forward?' she asks, her smile genuine for the first time since I arrived. I hadn't thought of it before, but after what happened to Marcus maybe people sometimes come into the gallery to try to catch a glimpse of him, to see if tragedy is written all over his face. But it seems Cleo believes my interest is genuine.

'I need to meet Marcus to understand how he works, to see if his ideas match mine and – a potentially much more difficult challenge – meet my father's expectations.'

'Oh, I'm sure they will. Let me have a word with him, and I'll get back to you.'

I pull a face. 'I don't want to hang around for too long. If he's not interested I'd prefer to know now rather than waste time. I'd like to meet him today, if that's possible.'

I can see this idea worries her, but finally she agrees to speak to him there and then to arrange an appointment, and picks up the phone. I can tell from her expression that he's not happy about the idea. I turn away, as if I haven't noticed. She tries to keep her voice smiley and cheery, and I wander down the gallery so she can work her magic on her brother in private.

Finally she hangs up and gives me a smile. 'He knows you want to see him today, and he's agreed. He gets quite engrossed in his work and sometimes can seem a bit aloof, but that's all part of the artistic temperament, I suppose.'

She's making excuses for him before I've even met him, but I give her an understanding smile as she hands over the address.

I say my goodbyes, knowing it's far from the last I'm going to see of Cleo, and decide to walk to Marcus North's home to give myself time to get my thoughts under control and plan how I can convince him to take this commission.

As I climb the steep track that leads to his house, I look down at the beach. Children are playing on the sand, laughing and screaming as they go into the chilly sea, splashing their more cold-averse mums and dads. I am envious of their carefree spirits. I don't remember ever feeling like that as a child.

I plod up the incline over rough gravel until I see the huge expanse of white wall that is Marcus North's home, although I know it's not his photography that has paid for it. There isn't a window in sight, but I am sure that on the other side of the wall it will be a different matter. The house is perched on the edge of a cliff, and the views will be stunning.

I approach the big wooden door and raise my left fist to knock. I beat down on the door, and the pain in my hand is excruciating, *unbearable. And yet I keep knocking and screaming at the same time. I know I need to stop – to hold my hand safe. But I can't and the more I hit the door, the more agonising my hand becomes.*

As the fierce pain drags me out of my drug-induced sleep, taking with it the last remnants of the dream, I realise that nothing except the agony in my hand is real. I'm not standing outside the door of Marcus North's house. Instead, I'm inside it – lying in bed in a dark room with a huge window overlooking the sea. From wrist to fingertip, my left hand is encased in plaster and it hurts like hell. The drugs must have worn off and I feel an aching throb and a desire to scratch an itch on skin that I can't reach.

My eyes feel sticky. I must have been crying in my sleep as I remembered that day. Every second of my dream was a rerun of a day nearly two years ago, accurate up to the point when I raised my hand to knock on the door. At that moment the stabbing pain that is now making me gasp became one with the dream, the sensation embedding itself into the story, disrupting the final moments.

I want to dive back into that moment – to remind myself of what happened next and convince myself that all the decisions taken since that day were the right ones. But the gossamer threads are snapping one by one and I know that even if I could fall asleep again there is little chance that I would be back outside that door, waiting for it to be answered. The dream has floated away.

'Evie?' The voice, usually so confident, sounds hesitant, worried.

'I'm awake. You can come in.' I keep my eyes closed. I don't want to see Cleo's perfection when I know how I must look. 'Is Lulu okay?'

'She's fine. She's having a nap, but she's been as good as gold. What can I do for you?' She walks over to the bed and I can feel her hovering above me, but still I don't look at her. 'Your eyes are all gummy – where's your cleanser? I can clean you up a bit, if you like.'

'Bathroom.' Speaking suddenly seems hard work and now I know that Lulu is okay I just want Cleo to go.

'I can't see it,' she shouts from the other side of the door.

'It's called soap,' I answer.

I don't need to see her face to know that she will be tutting, appalled at my low standards. Sometimes I just like to wind her up.

Cleo wears her perfection as armour, like the hard, shiny cowrie shell I picked up on the beach for Lulu last week – impenetrable, but beautiful. Everything about her on the outside is bold, bright – from the bleached white hair and perfect makeup to the vivid colours of her clothes. I've seen people stare at her in the street, wondering who this flawless creature can be, not realising that, however hard they tried, they would not be allowed to get close. Only the chosen few are permitted access to the real Cleo – and I'm not one of them.

I can hear her moving back across the room towards the bed.

'I've got some damp cotton wool. That should do the trick.' She wipes my eyes gently, and I hold myself still. I don't want her to touch me. We'll never be close but we do our best to pretend, and right now I can feel her genuine concern. She sits

17

gingerly on the edge of the bed and pauses before asking the question I knew was coming.

'Are you sure you don't want me to call Mark?'

At the mention of his name, I am back in my dream – outside the tall door in the long white wall, rapping on the wood. This time I'm there in my memory, though. Sadly, I'm wide awake and I wonder where the time has gone. How much of all that has happened since have I blocked from my mind?

The man who answered the door that day looked a wreck – grubby, dishevelled, with three or four days of beard growth that owed nothing to style.

'Marcus North?' I said.

'No I'm not. My name is Mark. With a K. Always has been – always will be.'

I'd already known that, but hadn't realised he wasn't part of the whole pretence at a background more prestigious than the reality.

'I'm sorry,' I said. 'Mark North, then, I presume?'

He rubbed a hand over his greasy hair, making it stand on end. 'Sorry. My bloody sister thinks being called Marcus makes me sound more interesting. I thought it was the quality of my photographs that mattered, but there you go.'

My brief memory of that day is disturbed again as Cleo pushes me to respond to her question about whether she should call Mark. Even she's stopped calling him Marcus now, because in the end he refused to answer to it.

'No, of course you shouldn't. You know he'd find any excuse to come straight home, and you worked hard to get him this commission. I can manage.'

18

Cleo stands up from the bed, and walks towards the floor-to-ceiling window, looking out over the view to the sea. She glances back at my hand and turns away again.

'I don't understand how you did it, Evie. It doesn't make sense to me.'

For a moment I picture my hand, held firm on the lower weights of the multi gym, six blocks each weighing five kilograms hovering high above. I see another hand, holding the bar that keeps the blocks in the air. The hand lets go, and in the split second it takes for thirty kilos to shatter my bones I'm waiting for the pain, knowing I will probably have broken carpals, metacarpals and phalanges. I know the names of most of the bones in the body.

'I told you. The bar slipped out of my fingers at the wrong time. Stupid, but they say most accidents happen in the home.'

'But it could only have been moments after Mark left. Why didn't you call him to come back?'

I sigh at this. I can't think of a sensible answer, or not one that Cleo would believe.

'It's done now. There's no point bringing him back. If you don't mind helping a bit with Lulu, we'll be fine. I'd rather he didn't come back.'

She looks at me sharply.

'Don't, Cleo. You know he'll be stressed by it and I can't deal with that right now. By the time he's back I'll be feeling much better – much more able to cope.'

And I will be. I have to be.

2

When I first met Mark, I tried to make Cleo like me. Her influence over him in those days was so great that I couldn't afford for her to be my enemy, but when the balance of power shifted in my favour I could feel her resentment, and there developed a relationship of superficial tolerance. Mark is immune to it all. He sees me welcoming Cleo to our home, inviting her to eat with us, never appreciating how much she detests the fact that her welcome is at my behest.

She will do her duty, now that I'm hurt, knowing what Mark will expect of her – but I'm relieved to have an hour or so of respite from her ministrations while she takes Lulu out. I can see she's worried. Am I so clumsy that I shouldn't be left in charge of her brother's child? Because Cleo knows it's not the first time I've had a painful accident. The obvious answer is one that she's not even prepared to consider.

More and more often I catch a glimpse of her looking at me as if she's not sure why I'm here, trespassing in their lives.

I close my eyes. Until the painkillers kick in again I have no chance of sleeping, and even when I do I know I won't be back in my dream. But I can remember and wonder at the way fate works its magic.

That first day, when Mark opened the door in the long white wall looking as if he had just got out of a bed he had been buried in for several days, he was angry. He was too thin; it made him seem even taller. His eyes, grey like his sister's but twice as cold, glared at me. He said he'd had time to think about it, and decided he had nothing to give, so I should leave and not come back.

It wasn't the best start but neither was it unexpected. I went back to the gallery and explained what had happened. I had no intention of giving up, but I wasn't going to let Cleo know that.

'I'm so sorry,' she said. 'Would you consider giving me a bit of time to see if he might reconsider?'

I'd raised my eyes to the heavens as if thinking deeply about it. 'Okay, but my dad's keen for me to confirm the details. If I can't have Marcus, I'll have to find someone else.'

It had taken Cleo twenty-four hours, but she finally managed to persuade him to at least talk to me, so the next day saw me trudging up the track again. This time, though, it was wet and windy, the summer weather typically changeable, as it often is in the south-west of England. A few people were on the beach, trying to fly kites without much luck, but most families were probably either hanging out in the amusement arcades or in one of the numerous cafés.

I couldn't believe Mark was the same man when he opened the door. His hair, which yesterday had looked thick and dark, was newly washed and a warm russet brown, and he had shaved off most of the fuzz. His eyes had lost their fury, and now looked almost mystified – as if he had no idea how he had been talked into this. It wasn't until months later that I discovered Cleo had threatened to close the gallery and move away if he refused to take on new commissions.

He held out his hand to shake mine.

'I'm sorry about yesterday,' he said. 'I'd been working on some pictures and they weren't going well.' He dropped his hand and looked me in the eye. 'Actually, that's total bollocks. I was just being obnoxious and I apologise.'

I liked him in that moment, and I wasn't sure if that was a good thing or not.

He lifted an arm to welcome me to his home, and I stepped in front of him through the huge wooden door in the blank white wall.

'Oh . . . my . . . God!' I walked forwards slowly, staring at the spectacular sight in front of me. I knew this was the upper level of the property – nobody would call it a house – and it appeared to float above the ocean with a massive rain-splattered sheet of glass forming the only barrier to the wild sea below. Even on a day like that the view was breathtaking.

Mark showed me to a sofa that faced the window, and I could barely concentrate on what he was saying as he talked about his pictures, his influences, his approach to each new subject and the techniques he would like to use for my photographs. I was constantly distracted by the view: by the sight of a gannet soaring above the sea, or the waves crashing onto a rock that protruded high above the water in the bay.

He offered me a cup of coffee and walked over to the kitchen, set along one wall of the living space. There was the sound of beans grinding and the air was filled with the delicious aroma of freshly ground coffee.

I glanced around the rest of the room, which until that point had hardly registered with me. I turned my head in all directions, expecting to see more huge photographs like those in the gallery. But there was only one, hanging on the wall behind me, facing the window where I realised it would catch the changing light of each day. It was a portrait of a woman with short dark hair brushed back from a thin face dominated by thick pale lips. But it was the small, slightly narrowed eyes that drew me. They seemed to watch me, judge me, and as I turned away I could feel them on my back.

While I sipped coffee from the china mug that Mark handed me I tried to block those eyes from my mind and engage him in conversation. I needed him to like me. To trust me. I tried to draw him out, to smile at his attempts at wit and his obvious belief that he had to charm me, if only to keep his sister quiet. I didn't fool myself that it was anything more. At least, not then.

We agreed that he would start the project by working on six photographs, each taken on separate days, at different times so the light would vary. He had the idea of taking one shot of me amongst a mass of holiday makers, but only my image would receive the high-contrast treatment, the others faded to shades of grey so I would stand out – quite literally – from the crowd. He had another location in mind, where I could hang over the ramparts of an old derelict building, and it seemed as if, now he had accepted the commission, he was beginning to get excited.

When I could think of no valid reason to extend my visit, I

stood up to leave. But I couldn't go without asking him about his home.

'It's so incredibly well designed. It must have taken years to build. Have you lived here since it was first built?'

His face closed down. 'No.'

The eyes in the photograph were watching me, driving me to be reckless, and suddenly I was behaving as badly as any motorway rubbernecker.

'So there's another level below here – the bedrooms, I presume?'

His jaw was rigid. I knew what I was doing, but I couldn't stop. I knew the lower levels were cut into the rock, and like this room, the windows faced out to sea.

'Another two levels, actually.' His eyes didn't meet mine as he spoke.

'Gosh – is your studio in the basement?'

For a moment he didn't speak. 'No. There's a pool and a gym down there. But they're closed.'

He picked up both empty coffee mugs and they clunked together.

'You don't use either of them?'

'I don't go down there.'

I raised my eyebrows. 'Not haunted, is it?'

'Probably. It's where my wife died.' Mark's eyes flicked to his left, to where the portrait was hanging.

I looked shocked and apologetic, as if I – unlike everyone else who knew the name Marcus North – didn't already know what had happened. I could feel the narrowed eyes of the portrait judging me.

It's twenty-two months since we had that conversation the first time I came to this house, and more than eleven months since I moved in. Even now I do everything possible to avoid the gaze of Mia North, Mark's dead wife.

3

Cleo reversed into the steamed-up glass door of the café, pushing it open with her back and pulling Lulu's buggy behind her, trying but probably failing to hide her surprise when a teenage boy with too many piercings jumped up to help her.

'Thank you,' she said as the boy bent down to smile at Lulu, who seemed totally unfazed by the sight of all that metal sticking out of his face.

She glanced around the half-empty room, her eyes seeking out the comfortable shape of her best friend, Aminah Basra. In a couple of months' time the café would be overflowing with holiday makers and neither she nor Aminah would come near it, but this early in the season it was a pleasant and convenient place to meet. A mop of unruly black hair caught Cleo's eye, and Aminah raised her arm in an enthusiastic wave.

Pushing the buggy over to the far corner where her friend was sitting nursing a cappuccino, Cleo returned her wide grin.

'Your face!' Aminah said as Cleo sat down. 'That's what comes of pre-judging people.'

'I know. I'm ashamed of myself. My natural reaction was to stop the poor lad getting too close to Lulu. How awful is that?'

Cleo leaned across the table and grimaced. 'But I can't understand how he blows his nose,' she whispered. 'Anyway, it's good to see you. No Anik today?'

'I left him with his granny, who will be trying to teach him some manners as she believes I'm far too indulgent with my children. It's supposed to be the other way round, isn't it? Grandparents being all-forgiving? And how come you've got Lulu, not that it isn't delightful to see her?'

A bored-looking waitress sauntered over to take Cleo's order before she had a chance to answer, and it gave her a moment to consider her reply. Aminah had spent quite a bit of time with Evie over the past few months and had once or twice suggested that Cleo was a little hard on her brother's partner, so she had been at pains since then to make sure she kept any hint of criticism from her voice.

'Evie's had another accident. But don't worry – she's okay now. I've left her doped up with stuff from the hospital and she's sleeping.'

Aminah looked horrified. 'What happened? Does Mark know?'

'He'd only just left when it happened. She's asked me not to call him, but she's in a lot of pain. She managed to trap her hand and she's broken some bones.'

'Trap her hand in *what*, for God's sake?'

Cleo didn't want to describe Evie's accident. It filled her with horror to imagine the weights crashing down onto her fingers, but she knew Aminah wouldn't stop asking until she had all the details.

'She said she was doing some lat pulldowns in the gym.' Cleo saw Aminah's look of confusion and gave her a brief smile. 'Don't worry – you don't need to know what that means. Anyway, she leaned forward to adjust the weights, while still hanging onto the bar. Her hands must have been slippery with sweat and she let go of the handle when her other hand was between the weights. A stupid accident that should never have happened. It must have been over in seconds. She's going to be fine, though, and she doesn't want me to call Mark.'

'The gym.' Aminah looked Cleo steadily in the eye. 'Again.'

Cleo looked away, fussing with Lulu's pushchair, stroking her niece's silky hair.

'I know,' she said, keeping her eyes on the child. 'Mark still won't go down there – not since Mia died, as far as I know – and Evie's probably scared he'll have the whole place locked up if she tells him what happened to her. She'd hate that – she takes Lulu in the pool with her all the time. She says if you live that close to the sea it should be a criminal offence not to teach your children to swim.'

'She's got a point.'

Cleo sighed. Everything Evie said seemed sensible but she had been so accident-prone of late.

'What's going on in that head of yours, Cleo?' Aminah asked. 'Come on. I know that face.'

Cleo lifted her head and met Aminah's eyes. 'I don't know what to think, and I know you'll say I'm being ridiculous – which is why I'm hesitating about saying anything.'

The waitress brought over the order of sparkling mineral water for Cleo, still water for Lulu and a second cappuccino for Aminah and plonked them down in the middle of the table without a word. Neither of the women paid any attention to her. Aminah was staring at Cleo, waiting for her to carry on.

'The thing is, Aminah, it's not the first accident she's had, is it? And it always happens within hours of Mark leaving. Like that time when she managed to pour boiling water all over herself? She said she'd sneezed as she was tipping the water from the kettle into her mug and she'd splashed herself, but I saw under the bandage and it was more than a splash.'

'So what are you saying? That she's attention-seeking – or that she's just plain clumsy? If it was for attention, she'd want Mark to come home immediately, surely?'

'I don't know. But something's not right.'

Aminah snorted. 'Bloody hell, Cleo, you said that about Mia too. You didn't like her either, and you didn't trust her an inch.'

'Are you surprised? She was so much older than Mark, and she thought his photography was just a hobby.' Cleo put on an affected American accent. 'Mark's married to me now, so he doesn't need to be successful. I'm successful enough for both of us and we have all the money we need – just let him have fun.'

She pulled a face at Aminah, who laughed.

'You know, my lovely, there's a lot to be said for just having fun. You want Mark to be famous, but is that what *he* wants?'

Cleo poured some water into Lulu's sippy cup and pushed the lid on.

'There you go, sweetie.' Lulu was such a placid little thing. At nine months old she was already starting to look like Mark, with hair the same reddish-brown as his.

'You're ignoring me, Cleo,' Aminah said softly.

'I've always had to look out for Mark – you know that.'

'Bollocks. I've said this before, but I'm going to say it again whether you like it or not. You treat Mark as if he's your seven-year-old son, instead of your thirty-seven-year-old brother. I know you took care of him after your mother left, but he's an adult now and he can make his own mistakes, if that's what Evie is – and I honestly can't see why you would think that. She's okay, you know. I like her, but more to the point, Mark seems to love her, so why not do yourself a favour and relax a little. Maybe it's your turn to be looked after and made a fuss of.'

Aminah spoke the final words gently, and for a split second Cleo felt the urge to let go and allow life to take its course without feeling the compulsion to control it. She'd had her chance, though, and made her choice. But she wasn't about to admit that to Aminah.

Her moment of introspection passed as a plate of cakes arrived at their table. She shook her head at Aminah in mock dismay.

'What?' Aminah said as she bit into some sort of chocolate confection that made Cleo shudder. 'I like cake – it's one of the joys in my life. I'm your best friend and I love you, but where does *your* joy come from? You spend your days trying to keep Mark motivated and working hard to maintain that admittedly fabulous shape of yours. But at what cost? Why not have a drink, eat a chip, find some guy and make wild, passionate love on the beach in broad daylight?'

Aminah grinned at Cleo, who was tempted to admit how often she wanted to do as her friend suggested. But she had always been afraid that if she let her guard down, even a fraction, everything would fall apart.

'You're not far off forty, Cleo. A fine age, and one to be relished. But are you happy? Because that's all I want for you.'

Aminah reached across the table to touch Cleo's hand, but this conversation had to be deflected.

'Never mind me. I'm fine, honestly, and let's face it, I've heard all your wonderful advice before.' Cleo smiled to take any sting out of her words. 'Just tell me what I should do about Evie. Do you think, given her accidents, that it's safe for her to look after Lulu?'

'Sorry, love. It's not your call. If you so much as suggest to Mark that Evie's not fit to look after their daughter because she's had a couple of accidents in the home, you'll drive a massive wedge between the two of you. You very nearly did that when he was married to Mia, so don't make the same mistake again. You were quite devastated last time when he shut you out.'

Cleo was silent. Aminah was right – she hadn't liked Mia and had tried to make Mark see that his wife was stifling both him and his talent. But Evie was different. She appeared to support Mark wholeheartedly, so why did she fall apart every time he left the house?

Cleo could feel that Aminah wasn't one hundred per cent on her side. She and Evie had a lot in common – they both had children, and according to Aminah they shared some of the same bad habits. Cleo couldn't help worrying that their budding friendship might gradually, over time, push her own relationship with Aminah into second place. Only the previous week she had walked past the café and glanced in to see the two of them enjoying a slice of chocolate cake, laughing together at something. She hadn't gone in to join them. She felt she might have been intruding.

There were only three people in Cleo's life that mattered to her now – Mark, Lulu and Aminah – and at that moment, it felt as if Evie was fast becoming the pivot around which all three of them revolved, with Cleo on the sidelines, watching but not participating.

4

As Cleo bumped Lulu's buggy up the rough track to Mark's house she tried to drive Aminah's words from her thoughts. It was true that she had disliked Mia – both for her arrogance and for the fact that she made Cleo feel like a fool for being so enthusiastic about Mark's photography. Coming from such a wealthy background, Mia had an air of entitlement about her. She treated Mark more like a recalcitrant teenager than a husband, smiling rather benignly when he spoke, and Cleo had made the mistake of saying as much to her brother. It had nearly caused a rift that couldn't be mended until, reluctantly, Cleo had apologised. But she blamed herself entirely for pushing Mark and Mia together.

Just like Evie, Mia had come to the gallery one day looking to commission a photographer – in her case to take pictures throughout the different seasons of her stunning new house with its all-glass wall overlooking the sea. Cleo had fought hard to win the job on Mark's behalf, and for a year he had trotted up there every few weeks to spend days waiting for the weather or the lighting to be right. It had never occurred to Cleo that her brother would be interested in this thin

American woman with her almost gaunt face, and she hadn't realised they were becoming close until her brother announced that they were getting married.

And now there was Evie – different in so many ways. Why couldn't Cleo like her more than she did? She had Evie to thank for dragging Mark out of the dark cavern into which he had slunk after Mia's death, but she couldn't help feeling a twinge of resentment that Evie had succeeded where she herself had so comprehensively failed.

'I'm just a bad-tempered middle-aged woman, Lulu,' she said to the child in the pushchair, safe in the knowledge that she would neither understand nor be able to repeat anything she heard. 'But I love your daddy so much, and all I've ever wanted was for him to be happy. I don't think your mummy likes me, though.'

She sighed, knowing it was the truth. She had been living in the house with Evie for the past week, taking care of both her and Lulu. It should have brought them closer, but although Evie was polite, Cleo never felt that together they were a family. There was Cleo and Mark, or Evie and Mark – and Lulu of course. For the child's sake if nobody else's, she had to keep Evie close. The chances of Cleo having children of her own were getting more and more remote each year, and she needed to pour all her maternal love into Lulu.

For a moment she thought of the love she'd had, but had rejected. Turning her back on Joe was one of the hardest things she had ever done, but there were too many sacrifices to make. Not just for her, but for Joe too.

'Let's get you home, sweetie. It's time for your nap,' she said, ignoring the prickle of tears at the back of her eyes.

Reaching the long white wall of the house, Cleo headed towards the garage. A little-used door beyond two parked cars opened onto a private garden that ran along one side of the house, its far boundary overlooking the sea and giving a terrifying view over the cliff to the two lower floors of the house, built into the rock. Cleo had her own key to the front door, but Evie knew nothing about that and she didn't feel that now was the time to reveal its existence.

For a second she remembered the day over three years ago when she had come up here, uninvited, to see Mia. She had let herself in, certain that Mia neither knew nor would approve of the fact that she had a key but wanting to precipitate an argument – an excuse to unleash her anger at the way Mia treated Mark.

Cleo took a deep breath in an effort to drive the thoughts of that day from her mind. The nightmares had all but stopped now, and it was better not to remember.

As she walked through the back door of the garage and into the garden, Cleo glanced through the long window that looked into the kitchen area of the vast living space. She could see Evie sitting at the breakfast bar, her posture slumped, her head resting on folded arms. Was she crying? Had something else happened?

She hurried to the door and pushed it open, pulling the buggy in behind her.

'Evie, is everything okay?' she called.

Evie lifted her head. Her eyes were red-rimmed, but dry. 'I'm fine. Just tired.'

Cleo pushed the door closed and lifted Lulu out of the buggy. 'Why don't you go and lie down again?'

35

'I don't need to, honestly. If I sleep now, I won't sleep tonight.'

'Don't the pills help?' Cleo asked, shrugging the coat off a struggling Lulu.

'A bit, but if I fall into a deep sleep I roll onto my arm, and then it hurts like hell.'

Cleo popped Lulu into her rocker chair and passed her a couple of her favourite toys. She was so good at amusing herself and loved anything that made a sound or played a tune.

'I'll make you a coffee,' Evie said, sliding off the high stool.

'Sit down. I'll make it. I'm here to look after you both.'

'Cleo, it's kind of you and I appreciate your help, but I'm fine. I can manage everything but Lulu. And anyway, all I have to do is press buttons – I only need one hand for that.'

Cleo stared at Evie's back. Even after the enforced living arrangements this week they continued to dance around each other mouthing platitudes. Evie had become more withdrawn over recent weeks and Cleo knew perfectly well why she didn't try to get closer, to ask Evie more questions.

It was because she didn't want to hear the answers.

5

Mark is due home at any moment, and I can feel the blood fizzing in my veins as the pressure builds inside me. Cleo is still here. She's been here since I was hurt last week, staying overnight, taking care of Lulu. I think she'd like to take Lulu back to her house where she could lavish attention on her and pretend she is her own child. But that's not going to happen.

We get no warning of Mark's arrival. The walls are so thick that we can't hear the approach of a taxi, and I jump when I hear the front door open.

There's a thud as he puts down his bag, but I have my back to him and I don't turn round. I'm nervous and Cleo can sense it. I don't know what he's going to say, or what he expects me to say, but I can't make any mistakes. Not now.

'Hi, Mark,' Cleo calls, bouncing a beaming Lulu up and down on her knee. Lulu loves her daddy and she does a better job than anyone at raising a smile from him. Which makes it all the more terrible, really.

'Hi, Cleo. What are you doing here?' he asks, walking down the two steps from the entrance hall into the living room. He knows how unusual it is for Cleo and me to enjoy each other's company when he's not around.

He walks up behind me and leans down to kiss me. That's when he sees my left wrist and hand encased in plaster.

'Jesus, what's happened, Evie?'

I'm watching Cleo as he speaks to see who she looks at – me, or Mark. I want to read her expression, but she looks away and fusses over Lulu as if she's giving us a moment.

'Evie?' Mark repeats.

'I trapped my hand. It's fine, darling. More of a nuisance than anything else,' I say, smiling and lifting my chin slightly so that I can see his face hovering above me, his strong, bristly chin and the black void of his nostrils. I can't quite make out his eyes so I don't know what he's thinking.

His hand comes down heavily on my shoulder and grips me firmly. 'Why didn't either of you call me?'

Cleo raises her eyes to Mark's then and I watch her give him an apologetic smile. 'I wanted to call you, but Evie wouldn't have it.'

She's like the school snitch, but it's what I expected. If Mark's going to be mad at anyone, it had better be me.

The hand on my shoulder suddenly seems heavier, as if he's resting his weight there. I shrug and sit forward, mainly to shift his grip, but I turn it into a move to stand up.

'Come and sit down, Mark. I'll get you a drink.' I don't need to ask what he would like. It will be a glass of red wine.

I can't avoid his gaze any longer. 'No, *you* sit, Evie. I want to know why nobody called me. I'd have come straight back.'

The truth is that Mark would happily find any excuse not to

go away at all. He hates commissions, even when they're worth thousands like this one. Cleo's done a good job for him since he's come out of purdah. His latest client lives in Paris but has a house at Cap-Ferrat and he wants Mark to take a series of photographs to form some incredible mural for one wall. He's very demanding of Mark's time and insists on regular visits to discuss themes. The client, Alain Roussel, has made his money through a string of casinos, and he likes to parade Mark like a prize bull to impress his newly acquired acquaintances amongst the nouveau riche of France.

Cleo sees this commission as a real coup, telling Mark that he'll have people queuing up for the latest Marcus North photographs in no time at all. Cleo's vivid description of a future in which Mark will be feted everywhere he goes seems to get to him, and somewhere under his dismissive exterior I feel certain there is a germ of ambition. It's not about the money – it's about the recognition of his talent.

But each time he leaves this house I'm certain he remembers the time he left his wife here, and returned to find her dead.

I already knew about Mia before I met Mark. I knew who she was and how she died – it wasn't a secret around here. I shouldn't have pushed him to explain his reluctance to go into the basement that first day, but I wanted to test his reaction, to get a feel for the man, and Mia's eyes in the photograph seemed to be goading me.

On one of the rare occasions that Mark has talked about his wife, he said he blamed himself for taking the commission that meant he had to leave her alone in the house. There was no logical reason for his concern – she had lived here alone when he first met her. He just felt strangely uncomfortable about the idea.

The commission had been arranged by Cleo but Mark hadn't been interested in the subject. He'd felt torn, struggling with the opposing views of the two women in his life – Cleo, who urged him to fulfil his potential, and Mia, who wanted him to treat his photography as a hobby.

Of course in the end he had succumbed to Cleo's persuasion, and he and Mia had rowed about it before he left – something he never admitted to the police because he said it was irrelevant. He had tried to call her from the airport to apologise, but she didn't answer. At first he wasn't concerned, but he called again when his flight landed, and when she didn't answer for a second time he asked Cleo to pop round. She found Mia's broken body at the bottom of the stairs on the hard stone floor.

Mark told me that it was a dreadful time, but the police managed to piece together what had happened. They concluded that Mia had fallen down the stairs about forty-five minutes after Mark left the house. She must have run downstairs to go into the gym. She tripped and fell, a loose lace on one of her trainers being blamed for the accident. The thinking was that she must have trodden on it and gone headlong down the stairs. Her watch was shattered and had stopped, which was how they had been able to assess the time so accurately.

I always knew that there was something missing from that story – some small detail that Mark had chosen to omit. In the end, he told me the rest of it, or at least, the version he believed to be the truth.

I suddenly return to the here and now with a jolt. The only sound in the room is that of the waves crashing onto the rocks below, but both Mark and Cleo are staring at me. Mark must have asked me a question and I haven't answered. Cleo, I know, has expressed concern about my ability to shut out the world while my mind explores some other place, some other time. But she has no idea where I go to. I don't think she would like it there.

'Is someone going to tell me what happened?' Mark is looking from me to Cleo, sensing that he might get more of an answer from his sister.

He knows why I didn't call him, and I wander into the kitchen to put the kettle on. I don't drink alcohol often these days, and Cleo never touches anything that might put poison into her bloodstream, so I grab a single glass to pour Mark some wine. I hear him talking in a low voice to his sister. They know full well that I can hear them speaking, if not the words they're saying. It's a big space, and Lulu is producing the strange humming noise she makes when she seems to be trying to sing. The kettle is gurgling away as the water boils, but conveniently it clicks off at the exact moment that Lulu stops murmuring. Just in time for me to make out Cleo's words.

'What shall we do?'

6

I'm relieved when Cleo leaves. The evening has passed without incident, although I could feel the tension sizzling round the room.

Mark has been worried since he walked through the door and found Cleo here. He doesn't know what I'm thinking. I could see he was unsettled, unbalanced, and he hates that. He worries that he might be sinking back into the depression out of which he believes I dragged him, and tonight isn't the way he would have planned his triumphant return. I feel a pang of regret for what might have been.

Cleo watched the two of us all evening, trying to understand the dynamic and wondering why I was moving away from Mark if ever he came too close. I pretended I hadn't heard what she said earlier. I knew what she was trying to do. Since Mark and I got together, there has always been the danger that Cleo will try to worm her way between us, and I think she might see this as her opportunity. 'What shall we do?' puts her and Mark on one side, with me on the other. It makes *me* the problem – my accidents, my clumsiness.

Alienating Cleo is not the answer though, so I insisted that she stay and eat with us as a thank you for all her help over the past week. Even one-handed I managed to griddle three steaks and Cleo chopped the salad ingredients.

I wasn't ready to be alone with Mark. We both needed time to settle first, and I wanted Cleo to spend a little time with us both, to get a sense of how things are between us.

But she's gone now, and we can't avoid the conversation any longer. For once, I decide to have a large gin.

Mark sits down opposite me and leans back against the soft sofa cushions, watching me sip my drink.

'How are you really?' he asks, suspecting that I had put a brave face on things for Cleo.

'I'm fine. It was painful – it's still painful. But it's done now.'

'I should have come back.'

How can I tell him that I didn't want him to? I know this is hurting him too.

'Can we change the subject?' I ask. 'I haven't been able to do any more writing, I'm sorry to say.'

I'm talking about his blog, which I'm supposed to update regularly to help promote him. I'm supposed to be contributing to his career and the online marketing has become my province. It's my own fault – the blog was my idea in the first place.

The original commission for a series of photographs by Marcus North had done little more than introduce me to the man. I had been expecting long sessions in his studio, sitting for him as he tried to capture me on camera, getting to know him, getting close to him. But only one photograph was a studio shot, and that took no more than a couple of hours. The others were in settings of his choosing – each and every one dramatic

43

in its own way. But I was instructed to meet him at the location, and while he was firing off shots his mind was only on his camera and giving me instructions.

'Lean a little more towards me. No – just your upper body.' Or, 'Throw your head back and then bring it forward again.' The camera would be clicking on continuous shooting mode as I turned, jumped, or balanced. There was no opportunity to talk while these works of art were being created.

And then we were done. The pictures were finished and he had to perfect each of them on his computer to turn them from the mundane to the extraordinary.

It was after I received an email from Mark asking me to go and view the final images that I had to share my tragic news with him. I arrived at his door in floods of tears.

'Mark, I'm so sorry. I don't know what to say.'

'What is it? What's happened?'

'It's my father. He's dead!'

I sobbed out the words, and despite looking perplexed and unsure of what he should do, Mark invited me in, sat me down and gave me a glass of water.

'What happened?' he repeated.

I rested my elbows on my knees and buried my head in my hands.

'He had a heart attack. It was instant, which is great for him but crap for the rest of us.'

I cried some more, and Mark opened a bottle of wine thinking that might help, all the while looking as if he knew he should be doing something for me, but didn't quite know what.

'I don't know what to say to you. All Dad's money is tied up in probate, and it's going to be so bloody difficult to unravel. He's got too many dependents and his ex-wives are all clamouring over what's theirs – which should be nothing, but I don't know how it works. They reckon it will be at least six months until some money is freed up, and then the whole lot will no doubt go to my witch of a stepmother.' I kept my head down, afraid to face him. 'I don't know how I'm going to pay you, Mark. I'm so very sorry.' I spoke quietly, the shuddering shoulders stilled.

He let out a bark of relieved laughter, as if I might have been expecting something more of him. This, however, was something he could handle.

'God, that doesn't matter, Evie. It's only a pile of photographs, and I hardly need the cash. I'm just sorry for *you* – did you live at home with your dad?'

'Sort of. I had my own apartment in the house, but now that will have to be sold of course, so I'm going to have to move out.'

Mark topped up my wine glass. 'Do you have somewhere else to go?'

'No.' I let that lie for a while and took a gulp of wine. 'I was thinking of moving down here. I can work from anywhere, and I've liked what I've seen of this part of the world. Beats London anyway. I only stayed there to be near Dad.'

He moved around the kitchen, giving me some space, I think. Or maybe he had run out of words of sympathy.

'I should go.'

'No – it's fine. Stay a while and look at the sea. I always find it soothing.'

We chatted, off and on, and I did as he suggested. It had turned dark and there must have been an electric storm out at sea, because every few moments the sky lit up and the bright white light reflected off the rippled surface of the water. Finally, Mark asked about my job and why it was that I was able to move around freely, and I told him that I create and manage blogs for customers.

'I did a degree in creative technology at Kingston University,' I told him. 'A bit too far from home to travel daily, but close enough that I was able to get back most weekends.'

Mark feigned interest in my course, but I already knew that he thought design done solely on a computer didn't count for much.

'I've had an idea,' I said suddenly, looking up at him, enthusiasm bursting from me. 'I'll create a blog for you – for free, of course – as a kind of payment for your time on the photos. It'll give you a presence on the internet, and you need that. I'll set it all up and then it just needs updating every so often. I could do that too. Can I? Please say yes.'

'Why would anyone be interested in me?' The amazement on Mark's face hadn't been faked. 'I've hardly done anything worth blogging about, surely? What on earth could I talk about?'

I had to persuade him that he was wrong; that he was a beacon of hope for young artists in all fields. He was a young man with his own successful gallery, living what many of his contemporaries would consider the dream.

'Oh, come on!' he said, his eyes wide with astonishment that I might think this. 'I married an American heiress, for God's sake. That's the only reason I have the house and the gallery. Mia paid for the lot.'

That had been hard to argue against. I wasn't ready to walk away from him, but I could feel Mia's eyes watching me as I spoke.

'How you got here doesn't matter. It's *your* art people are buying – not hers.'

Mark had shaken his head and run his fingers through his hair – always a sign of confusion – leaving him looking slightly wild.

'People go into the gallery mainly because of Cleo's jewellery. She's an artist too, but she won't take any credit. They go in looking for a £200 bracelet and she breaks her neck trying to sell them a £2000 photograph, or an even higher-value commission.'

I told him that was an excellent point. We could put Cleo's jewellery on the site too, emphasising how he couldn't have done any of it without her.

'Have you always been close?' I asked.

'She looked out for me. She's two years older than me, and when I first went to secondary school I was the butt of a few jokes because all I wanted to do was take photographs. I was bullied for being different. One boy in particular was a complete bastard to me.'

'What did you do?'

'Nothing.' Mark glanced away from me for a second and I couldn't read his expression. 'In the end, the problem went away. Cleo was on to him, but . . . it's a long time ago.'

I could see in his face that he was ready for me to leave. My tears had long since dried, and I stood up, turning to him as I reached the door.

'Look, I'm going to try to find a place around here this week to rent for a month or so. When I'm sorted, why don't you join me for dinner one night? I'd ask Cleo too, but maybe it's better if you make the decision about the blog yourself, because you know what Cleo will say.' I was standing close to him and I raised my face and smiled at the idea of Cleo's excitement, my breath caressing his chin. 'Perhaps we should make our plans and we'll tell her when we have a clear idea of what we're going to do.'

It was the first move I'd made to place myself with Mark. The two of us together, facing Cleo.

And so it began.

'Where would you like me to take you to dinner?' I hadn't paused for his answer, carrying on with enthusiasm. 'Ooh – I've got an idea. This might be a bit off the wall, and if you prefer something grander, please do say, but I discovered this brilliant little crab shack down the coast. It's a bit rough and ready, but the food is to die for – if you like crab, of course. What do you think?'

His face lit up. 'How did you find it? It's a gem of a place. I haven't been for ages. I used to go a lot before Mia but it wasn't her kind of thing. I'd love to go there again.'

I had somehow managed to raise a spark of interest in a man who had thought he was emotionally dead, and I set in motion a chain of events that led us to where we are today. I spent nearly every day with him after that, claiming I had to make recompense for my failure to pay for the photographs, working on the blog but often offering to make him lunch, dinner. I became indispensable. The blog – my excuse to be around him – did bring him business, commissions that took him away from me. But I stopped working as soon as I became pregnant, claiming I was struggling to concentrate.

I have only recently started to post articles about Mark again, mainly because Cleo kept going on about it. But now – with my hand in plaster – I'm not able to continue, and I apologise again.

There is a flash of irritation on Mark's face. 'I'm not the one who cares about the blog. You know that. It's the least of our problems.'

We end the evening with a mountain of unspoken words between us, and Mark decides it's time for bed.

'I'll be with you in a while,' I tell him. I don't want him to see me struggle to get undressed and I don't want him to help me. I don't want to be needy. 'I'm going to sit with Lulu for a bit. You go ahead.'

'Evie, I'm sorry. I shouldn't have lost my temper before I left. And I should have called you to apologise. Will you forgive me and come to bed?'

'In a while,' I say, with neither anger nor forgiveness in my voice. But I feel my heart break a little more at the look in his eyes.

He's disappointed. Despite the friction, Mark is a man of routine. His rituals keep him focused, and tonight's his first night back after a trip. We should be making love, but we won't be. I've disrupted his plans, unsettled him. He won't like that.

7

One of my pleasures in life is watching my daughter sleep. It takes me away from reality and gives me peace. When she sleeps, all I can see are the naked features of her face, as if the sea has washed over her skin and taken away everything but the pure beauty of her tiny nose, her pink lips and the bluish tinge of her eyelids.

I reach out a finger and stroke her soft cheek. I made this child with Mark, and I want to enjoy every moment I can with her before the inevitability of what is to come.

I wonder if it could have been different, if I could have taken an alternative path? I'm always fascinated by the thought of how one single decision can alter the course of not just one life but potentially so many. How might things have turned out if Mark hadn't chosen that night – the night that Lulu was conceived – to talk to me about his childhood? Would we ever have become a couple? We had known each other for a few months, and with each passing week Mark had begun to reveal more of himself. I knew he found me attractive, but I also knew I had to let him make the first move.

I had been working hard for him that day, and had cooked

him a simple, but tasty, home-made pizza for dinner. He took great delight in eating food that would have made Cleo run for the door. He wouldn't tell her about it though; that would mean telling her how often I cooked for him, and he wasn't ready for that. Not yet.

We'd finished eating, and had moved to sit in comfort while we shared another glass of wine. Mark encouraged me to talk about my father as he assumed my grief was still raw, but I deflected the conversation and asked him about his own parents. He told me he and Cleo had an unsettled childhood – not quite on the scale of my own, but difficult enough.

'I barely remember my mother. She left when I was just seven, and I've never known why. My dad wouldn't talk about it – we weren't allowed to mention her name. All I know is that Cleo and I came home from school one day and Dad said, "She's gone." I do remember that we never needed to ask who. I ran upstairs, crying, but I stopped when I reached the doorway to my room. There, in the middle of my bed, was her camera. She'd left it for me. The only memory I have of her is the three of us on the beach. She was laughing at Cleo and me pretending to be pirates, fighting with swords made from pieces of drift-wood, and she was snapping away with her camera like crazy. But I don't remember much else. She loved that camera and after she'd gone it was the only thing I had left of her.'

I perched on the edge of the sofa, leaning towards where he sat on an adjacent armchair, hanging on his every word. I felt my pulse quicken. Tonight was going to be the turning point. I heard a voice in my head, 'Walk away, walk away.' It was my last chance, and I didn't take it.

'Dad tried his best, but he was lost. When Cleo and I finally left home, he gave up the battle and took his own life. I don't think he'd ever recovered from Mum leaving. Cleo saved me after that. I wanted to look for Mum, but Cleo said she'd made her choice years ago and we had each other. We didn't need anyone else. I realised at quite a young age that I need to live by a set of rules, routines. I felt as if life had always been outside my control, so Cleo told me what to do. Not in a bossy way, but because she understood that my head was – and still is – a jumbled mess. Mia took over from Cleo, but when she died the rules were broken and life seemed too difficult. That's why I was so depressed – not just the thought of losing her, but the thought that I had no structure to cling onto.'

I reached out both hands and grasped one of his, smiling gently at him. He could read this as the caring touch of a friend, or he could see it as something more. His eyes met mine and I knew he wanted me. I edged forward on the sofa and I felt a slight tug on my hands. It was all I needed. I dropped to my knees in front of him, letting go of his hand so that both of mine were free to rest on his thighs. He gripped my upper arms with his fingers, harder than was necessary but not because he wanted to inflict pain. It was more to do with his uncertainty. I moved closer, my hands sliding up to his hips, urging him towards me, and he slipped his hands around my waist and lifted me into him.

The following days were exciting. I felt as if my life was slotting into place and I was right where I wanted to be. Mark was keen that Cleo knew nothing of what was happening – at least for now – and I was happy with that. I knew she would cast doubt on my suitability and question my motives.

Mark asked me many times to stay with him for the entire night, but I refused, rising in the early hours to drive my clapped-out old Fiesta back to my small rented flat. He couldn't understand my reluctance, but I said that, like him, I needed to feel I was in control of my life. I didn't want him to take me for granted.

Mark liked to know when I would be there, how long I would stay, what time we would go to bed, and I knew for him it was a battle to cope with my unpredictability. But I wasn't going to be slotted into a Tuesday and Saturday night routine.

One of Mark's rituals was to go to Cleo's for dinner every Thursday night. I knew this of course, so when on one Wednesday night about three months after we had first slept together he said he was going to struggle to wait until Friday to see me, I told him I was planning to go to London on Friday.

'I won't be back until Monday or maybe Tuesday,' I said, as I snuggled down on the sofa next to him. 'I can't believe I'm not going to see you for nearly a week. Shame we can't see each other tomorrow.'

Mark was silent. 'Maybe I could ask Cleo to change the day?' he suggested, somewhat half-heartedly.

'It's up to you,' I said.

After a couple of minutes, he eased himself off the sofa and went for his phone, giving me a grin as if we were co-conspirators, which in many ways we were. I followed him as he pressed the screen to place his call and I wrapped my arms round his waist from behind, sliding my hand under his t-shirt to stroke the soft hairs on his flat stomach.

I couldn't hear what Cleo said, but I could sense her disappointment as Mark made some excuse. I was more focused on him than her, and I slid the tips of my fingers under the waistband of his jeans, moving to his side so I could see his face. He turned hot eyes on me, and ended the conversation abruptly, leaving Cleo hanging.

I quickly dodged away, laughing, running round the other side of the kitchen island.

'Call your sister back now – invite her to dinner on Monday. I'll come straight back from London and I'll cook, but don't tell her. It can be our surprise.'

Mark knew what I was saying. It was time that Cleo knew we were a couple. He looked slightly wary, but I raised my eyebrows, my face offering a challenge I knew he wouldn't resist.

He made the call. I could hear notes of surprise down the line, and Mark said, 'It's not a special occasion. Just us.'

Cleo hadn't understood then that 'just us' included me.

It seems like a thousand years ago now, and as I look at my beautiful daughter I know that it has to end soon, but not quite yet.

Slowly I make my way to our bedroom, where I know Mark will be waiting.

8

The discreet buzzer told Cleo that someone had come into the gallery, so she placed the strip of silver she had been working on back on the workbench and switched off the buffing machine. Giving her short hair a quick ruffle, she painted on her professional smile and walked out of her workroom and into the gallery.

'Oh, it's you,' she said, her smile widening as she saw the visitor was Mark. 'I wasn't expecting you this morning.'

'Do I need an appointment to come to my own gallery?' he asked with a grin that didn't quite reach his eyes.

'Sorry – I was concentrating on a particularly delicate task, but it's good to see you. Have you come for some special reason, or were you just passing?'

Mark came to the gallery as rarely as possible. He didn't want to get involved in conversations with customers who asked him too many questions about the technical aspects of his photos. He felt uncomfortable justifying his creativity, so he came to hang his pictures mainly when the gallery was closed.

'Any chance of a coffee?' he asked, pulling out one of the

visitors' chairs from opposite the small desk where all transactions took place.

'Of course. It would be good to take a break, to be honest.'

As Cleo went into the small kitchen that sat between the gallery and her tiny workroom, she could hear Mark calling out to her.

'Do you still enjoy doing the silver work, Cleo? Any time you want to stop, you know, we can sort out your income.'

Cleo smiled to herself as she poured boiling water onto the ground coffee. Mark thought she made jewellery for the money, but he couldn't be more wrong. He had no idea how boring it could be sitting in this gallery day after day with only the occasional visitor interested in the photographs. The silver brought people in and it made the place a bit quirky – different. People liked that. And it gave her something to do when the shop was quiet.

She took the cafetière and a mug through to the gallery and, perching herself on the edge of the desk facing Mark, poured his coffee.

'That's very generous, but I need a purpose in life, and if I don't have to earn a living – whether that's commission on sales of your pictures or income from my jewellery – what would I do with myself?'

'Probably spend more time enjoying yourself?'

'Oh don't you start.' Cleo laughed. 'I get that from Aminah all the time. I'm okay. I've got my work, my best friend, a gorgeous niece, and you. What more could I want from life? You'd be the first person to know if I wasn't happy.'

Mark took a sip of coffee and Cleo could see he was waiting to say something.

'Are you over him?'

She hadn't expected that. Mark almost always avoided emotional conversations. He had never spoken of how he felt about Mia's untimely death, although locking himself away for the best part of eighteen months had said it all. But he rarely asked Cleo how she was feeling.

'I'm fine.'

'That's not what I asked. Look, I know you loved him and you thought he loved you.'

Cleo clenched her bottom lip between her teeth for a second to get herself under control.

'He *did* love me. But that's not the point, is it?'

Mark raised his eyebrows. 'Some would say it's the *only* point.'

Cleo laughed. 'Oh yes. Don't I know it. Love conquers all, and all that bollocks. I'm not the only one who loves him, though, so what right have I to put my happiness before someone else's – especially when that someone else is a child? How can our love for each other be more important than the love of two little boys for their dad?'

'Is that you speaking, or Joe?'

Cleo looked over her shoulder, as if mention of her lover's name was going to be overheard. They rarely said it out loud. In fact, they rarely spoke of him at all.

'It's not him. It's me. He would have left his wife, his family, but I wouldn't let him. You can't build true happiness on someone else's misery and he's not the kind of guy who could walk away without a backward glance. If he had been, I wouldn't have wanted him. So how long would it have been before he started to subconsciously blame me for his unhappiness?'

57

'So why not carry on what seemed to have been working fine between the two of you for the last year?'

Cleo felt her eyes fill with hot tears and she brushed them away with the back of her hand. 'He couldn't. He said it was too painful – he either had to leave, or he had to commit to staying. We agreed he had to stay.'

Mark stood up, and putting his mug down on the desk he reached out his arms to his sister.

'Come here.'

Cleo felt the rare comfort of her brother's arms. He found spontaneous affection difficult and had always been wary of giving it freely. She blamed their mother. Mark had adored her, and she him. She would sing and dance at any opportunity, even in the kitchen when concocting a plate of fish fingers and frozen peas, which was about the limit of her culinary skills. But there was something of the wild bird about her, and during the months before she left there were days when she had become angry – shouting and crying as often as she sang. Mark couldn't remember it, but there were many nights in those final few weeks when he had crawled into Cleo's bed, his little body shaking with distress.

Cleo was the one person in his life on whom he could rely one hundred per cent. Mark was safe with her and right now, having him hold her close, she knew theirs was a bond that nobody could break. She put her arms round his waist and hugged him back.

'You haven't told Evie about Joe, have you?' she whispered against his neck.

There was a pause which was a beat longer than she would have liked.

'Of course not. Does Aminah know?'

'I'm sure she suspects and she digs from time to time, but I can't tell her. She thinks I should be shagging half of the county for entertainment, so she'd probably force-feed me a vanilla slice and tell me to just get on and have some fun.'

Cleo laughed at the thought of her friend and wished, not for the first time, that she could be more like her.

The brief emotional moment passed quickly, and Mark finished his coffee while they discussed a few possible commissions.

'Your French chum, Alain Roussel, seems to have been bragging about you, and we've had some interest from an acquaintance of his in Croatia. He's just bought a sizeable motor yacht, and he seems to think a photo montage by you in the master stateroom would make his life complete. He wants you to take a look.'

Cleo had to smile at the look of dismay on Mark's face. Most people would have been thrilled by the idea of an all-expenses-paid trip to Croatia.

'Where's the yacht moored?'

'It's in Zadar, but the skipper could sail it down to Split if that's easier for you, and he'll meet you there. Don't look so miserable, Mark. Go for it. Split's a lovely place, I'm told.'

Mark grumbled about it being a bloody long way to go when he could just as easily come up with some ideas based on an internet search. He only needed to go there for the final photography session.

'If I do it, I'm not going until Evie's hand's better – I can't leave her like this.'

Cleo preferred not to think about Evie's accident. It raised too many questions in her head.

'Why don't you take Evie with you?' she said. 'I could have Lulu.'

Mark wouldn't meet her gaze, and not for the first time Cleo wondered what was going on with her brother and his partner. She had found it hard to adapt to Mark having another woman in his life. She wanted him to be happy, but with Evie by his side he didn't need his sister so much any more. And that, Cleo knew full well, was the reason she had fallen so hard for Joe. He had filled the vacuum that Evie had created.

After a few moments of silence, Mark lifted his eyes. 'I'm not going to take Evie, but will you make me a gorgeous piece of jewellery, Cleo? Something extra special? I know all of your stuff's beautiful, but I'm talking a big-budget item.'

'Of course. Do you want to tell me more?'

He nodded. 'It's for Evie, obviously. Is there any chance it can be ready before I go to Croatia?'

Cleo thought about the commissions she already had. Realistically, Evie's hand was going to be in plaster for another three weeks at least so that gave her plenty of time.

'What kind of piece are you looking for?'

'Something that reflects her personality – you're so good at that,' Mark said, and Cleo knew that it was true, usually. But she wasn't sure that in this case it would work out the way Mark wanted.

'Tell me how *you* see her,' she said.

Mark put his head back and closed his eyes, as if summoning up a vision of Evie.

'Beautiful, of course, and totally undemanding, but that's not helpful. She's clever, creative, but there's something elusive about her. I sometimes feel she's just out of reach.'

As she watched her brother's expression, Cleo wished she hadn't asked. He opened his eyes wide and looked at her.

'I can't lose her, Cleo. You do see that, don't you.'

She leaned towards him and squeezed his arm.

'You're not going to, are you? I think I've got the idea of what you're looking for. Is it for something special? I know it's not her birthday.'

Mark dropped his gaze again and rested his forearms on his thighs, clasping his hands together.

'I want her to know that, despite everything, I love her.'

Cleo felt her hackles rise. 'Despite *what*?'

Mark sighed, but didn't look up.

'I'm not easy to live with, you know that.'

'That's nonsense. We all have our foibles, Evie included. I think she's unbelievably lucky to have you.'

'Not really. And anyway, she clearly doesn't feel *that* lucky.'

'What on earth do you mean?'

'I asked her to marry me again this morning.'

'And?'

Mark spoke softly. 'She said no. But I need her to know that she's still mine, and even if she won't wear my ring or bear my name, she has to understand that as far as I'm concerned we're for keeps.'

Cleo was silent. For so long she had wanted to tell her brother of her suspicions – that Evie had been after Mark from the minute she met him. She must have heard of him, known of

61

his wealth and unhappiness. He was the perfect candidate for a young, attractive woman who wanted to better herself. Yet Evie refused to do the one thing that would guarantee her future. She refused to marry Mark, and that made no sense at all to Cleo.

9

'No, Anik, you can't have an ice-cream. We're going to Granny's for tea and she'll be cross if you don't eat up everything on your plate.'

Aminah would happily have let her three-year-old son have an ice-cream if he wanted one, but her mother-in-law didn't approve of Aminah's 'lax ways' with the children. Why it was considered better for the child to eat the chocolate cake that Granny baked before each visit she didn't know, but she wasn't interested in a battle of wills. It was too beautiful a day to be spoilt with unnecessary tension.

She bumped the pushchair over the cobbles to the other side of the road and took in the view. Lifting Anik out of the push-chair, she held him up so that he could look over the sea wall. He kicked his little feet and she let him stand on the top. She held onto him tightly with both hands – the low railing offered some protection, but not enough. Anik loved the sea as much as she did, and they both watched as the gentle waves washed onto the rocks below.

'Hi, Aminah.' She heard the voice before she realised that Evie was standing right next to her.

'Hey! Great to see you out and about,' Aminah said. 'How's the hand?'

'Bloody awful, if I'm honest.' Evie cast a quick look of concern at Anik. But he was too excited by the waves to notice what she had said. 'It's not so bad that I can't push Lulu around to give her a bit of fresh air, though.'

Lifting an indignant Anik from the wall and ignoring his shouts of protest, Aminah bent down to smile at Lulu. She was a delicate-looking child with fine bones and pale skin, her dark wispy hair falling in loose curls over her ears. She gave Aminah a sweet smile, and Aminah couldn't help thinking how different Lulu was from her own rumbustious offspring.

'She's the cutest thing,' she said, looking up at Evie's pasty cheeks.

'Thank you. I know I'm biased but she's such a good little girl.' Evie crouched down and gently kissed the top of her daughter's head. 'You're Mummy's little darling, aren't you?'

'You still don't look too great, though,' Aminah said. 'Are you sure you're okay?'

Evie pulled a face.

'Trouble sleeping, that's all,' she said. 'I'm not quite sure where to put my hand but it always ends up being somewhere painful. Maybe I should adopt your attitude to exercise in the future – it certainly seems a lot less dangerous to steer clear altogether.'

The two women shared a smile while an impatient Anik tried, without success, to scramble back up the wall. Aminah lifted him onto the top and wrapped her arm tight around his waist while she talked to her friend.

'I can't drag him away from the sea. God knows what's going to happen when I can't hold onto him any more.'

As if to give credence to her words, Anik shouted out a laugh and tried to jump up and down, pushing against his mother's arm.

'Stop it, Anik. I'm not going to let you go. It's dangerous.'

She turned back to Evie, who if anything was looking even paler than she had a couple of minutes before. She was staring out to sea, as fascinated by the waves as Anik, it seemed.

'Has Cleo ever told you that a boy died here?' Aminah said, keeping her voice low.

Evie didn't turn towards her but Aminah could see the frown between her eyes.

'She hasn't mentioned it,' Evie said. 'What happened?'

'I'm not sure. Some kid – a boy of about eleven or twelve – was showing off walking on the wall in a howling gale. Cleo said she was shouting at him to come down, but he wouldn't. Then a massive wave swept him off and down onto the rocks. It must have been terrible. I suppose that's why they put the railing along the top, but you know what it's like when it gets rough here. The waves come right over.'

She had the feeling that Evie wasn't listening and had gone somewhere else in her mind. There was sometimes a sadness about her that Aminah had tried, and failed, to get to the bottom of, and she seemed so isolated. Even though Evie never said a bad word about Cleo, she would be in no doubt that Mark's sister didn't like her, and that was a shame. Everyone needed family.

Aminah looked at Evie now as her frown deepened, and it

65

was a moment before she seemed to realise that Aminah had stopped speaking.

'Sorry, Aminah. I just had a bit of a pain spasm. I can't wait to get this stupid thing off.' She raised a hand to scratch around the edges of the offending plaster. 'Which reminds me. I have a favour to ask. Is there any way you could drive me to hospital when I have to go and have it removed? It won't be for a couple of weeks, but I don't know if Mark will be here and I don't like to ask Cleo because she would have to close the gallery. If I know I've got a lift it would be great. I'll have to bring Lulu, of course, so if it's a problem I can arrange a taxi.'

'Course I'll take you. The other three are at school, and this little horror . . .' she squeezed Anik tightly, '. . . can stay with Granny, or Zahid if he's not working. Just give me a day's notice if you can so I can sort it.'

Evie nodded her thanks, but she still looked distracted.

'Listen, Evie, we're on our way to see Granny, but she always makes a mountain of food. Why don't you and Lulu come along too? She wouldn't mind – I'm sure of that.'

Evie leaned forward and gave Aminah a quick hug.

'Thanks, Aminah. You're a gem, but I need to get back. Mark gets a bit restless if I'm out for too long.'

With a weak smile, Evie turned Lulu's pushchair around. 'Bye, Anik,' she said. But he ignored her, still bouncing up and down each time a gentle wave washed the shore.

Aminah watched her go and not for the first time wondered what it must be like to live with a man who was so needy.

10

The weeks since I hurt my hand have dragged. Mark has been attentive, and Cleo has never been out of the house. Thank God she has to be at the gallery for a chunk of each day, because when she's here she watches me as I play with Lulu. I know she thinks I'm accident-prone, but I'm careful with my daughter.

I've missed my swimming sessions with Lulu. We love playing together in the pool, and she was becoming quite a water baby. But I can't persuade Mark to take her and Cleo doesn't want to upset her brother by having fun in the basement. He tells me that he's over Mia, that her death doesn't hurt him any more, yet he still claims he can't go down there, where she died.

I had plucked up the courage to ask him about it just before he went away to France. It's the reason we argued.

'Why do you pretend that you'll never darken the depths of your beautiful basement again?' I asked as I pulled on my workout kit. 'You've been down more than once – I know you have – so what's the big deal?'

Mark has the most expressive eyes I've ever seen, and at that moment they reminded me of the sea on a stormy day as a flash of lightning rips through the air and fleetingly reflects off the water's wild black surface.

'I go when I need to. When I want to get a few things straight in my head.'

I sat down on the bed and leaned back on my elbows, trying to look relaxed – as if this was just a normal conversation. Mark was collecting the clothes for his trip and shoving them into a holdall.

'It must have been hell for you when Mia died,' I said. 'I understand that. But it was an accident and maybe you'd find it easier to live with if you didn't treat part of your home as a no-go area.'

Mark seemed frozen to the spot. He had his back to me still and was gripping the top of the chest of drawers. I could see how white his knuckles were.

'I see her every time I go down there. In my head, I picture her body sprawled on the tiles, face up, eyes staring. I know what she was wearing, just as I always know what you're wearing when you exercise. I see you getting ready, just as I saw her getting ready.'

'Don't you think that if you went up and down there every day, used the gym, used the pool, those visions might fade?'

He spun round and marched over to the bed, grabbed my hand and pulled me forward.

'Right. Let's see if that works, shall we? Come on. We'll go to the basement, and you can see for yourself what it does to me.'

I tried to resist, but he's always been too strong for me.

He was right, though. There was no mistaking the impact

the basement had on him, and I'm never going to suggest it again. He left me down there once he'd proved his point and I didn't see him again until he came back from France.

Mark has a photographic studio on the middle floor next to our bedroom. It's a huge space hewn out of the cliff face, with windows to the north. Even though he's a photographer and not a painter, he loves to use natural light wherever possible for his studio shots. I never understood why a north-facing room mattered so much to an artist until he took my photograph in there. It was a hot day, but I realised that the sun's rays couldn't penetrate the room – couldn't throw shadows or change the colour of the walls. The level of light could alter depending on the weather or the time of day, but it was never yellow or tinged with the red of a sunset.

He's been working down there all morning on the French commission, and he seems quite happy with how it's going. I expected him to be there until this evening but I hear the heavy door close with a thud and I know he's on his way upstairs to me and Lulu.

'Cup of tea?' he asks, walking over to the kitchen. It's surprising how normal things can appear on the surface.

'No thanks. Have you finished for the day? I've got to go and have my plaster cast removed, and if you're not working I thought you might look after Lulu.'

He grabs a mug from the cupboard and plonks it down on the worktop.

'Course I will. What had you planned to do with her?'

'I was going to take her with me. Aminah's driving me there.'

Mark switches off the kettle and walks across to perch on the arm of the sofa. 'Evie, why didn't you ask me? I would have taken you. Surely you know that?'

There is no answer I can think of that won't sound like I'm being difficult.

'I thought it would be easier, and I've not seen Aminah for a while. But as you're here, I know Lulu would enjoy some time with her daddy.'

Lulu is crawling around on her play mat and Mark falls to his knees to tickle her. She giggles and grabs his hand.

I look at them both and wonder, not for the first time, if I'm doing the right thing. Should I leave him, take Lulu and disappear so Mark can get on with his life? But I can't do that. It's hard, but I'm not about to give up. Not after so long.

My phone buzzes and I know it is Aminah telling me she is outside.

'I've got to go. Are you sure you don't mind?'

Mark jumps to his feet, picking Lulu up and spinning her round. He pulls her close and brings her across to me.

'Kiss Mummy goodbye, Lulu.'

He smiles at me, and for a moment I see shades of his sister in his face. It strengthens my resolve.

I kiss my daughter's velvety cheek and Mark's rough one before I leave.

11

'Thanks for doing this,' I say as I lower myself into the passenger seat of Aminah's sports car. It's surprising how difficult some tasks are with one useless hand, but it's not for much longer. I can't help wondering where she thought we were going to put Lulu if Mark hadn't agreed to look after her but she answers that question without me having to ask.

'It's my pleasure and it's good to see you. Zahid has the people-carrier to pick up the kids, so I get the mean machine. Special treat. Thought we could use yours if Lulu was coming, but as she's not . . .'

Aminah puts the car into gear and roars off down the track sending shards of stone flying. She drives like she does everything else – with total abandon. At this point I usually reach for the grab handle, but I can't today so I clutch the edge of the seat with my good hand.

'Sorry I haven't been to see you recently,' she says as we hit the main road. 'I came down with tonsillitis the day after I saw you down by the sea wall. *Tonsillitis!* I thought only kids got that, but I can tell you it bloody hurt. I felt as if my throat was full of razor blades and I couldn't eat a thing. I lost nearly a stone in a week!' She laughs at this idea. 'Not a problem, though. A few cakes and a bar or two of chocolate and it will all be back where it belongs. What joy.'

I can't help but smile when I'm with Aminah, and I can never work out why she and Cleo are such good friends. Cleo is so controlled, so uptight. They couldn't be more different. Maybe it's the whole yin and yang thing, because they appear to have totally opposing values.

'I didn't want to come round and infect you with my bugs,' she said. That's the other thing about her. She never stops talking and it makes life so much easier. I don't have to think about what I'm going to say, because I rarely get a chance.

'So, how've you been?' she asks. 'Okay, scratch that. You've been shit, I know. I can tell, and Cleo sent me a few messages saying how difficult you were finding things – especially with Lulu.'

I bet she did.

'How's Mark taken it? He's bloody paranoid about that stupid basement – I tell you, Evie, if you've got to go and hurt your-self again, can you please make it in another part of the house?' She glances sideways at me. 'Cleo says Mark's off on another trip soon – Croatia, I think she said. Do you think you'll be able to cope, because I can always call round to help you out?'

I wait, fully expecting her to answer her own question. For once, she doesn't.

'I'll be fine. Cleo's always happy to help with Lulu if I'm stuck.' I say that because I know it's what a good sister-in-law would say, but Aminah hears something in my voice and briefly turns to me, her eyes slightly narrowed.

'She loves Lulu, you know.' There's another pause and I'm thinking what to say when she saves me the trouble. 'Cleo should have had kids of her own, then maybe she wouldn't obsess about Mark and Lulu. She'd be best suited to one child, I think. Some people are . . . I'd have another at the drop of a hat – or something like that.' She chuckles.

'Why don't you, then?'

'Zahid put his foot down. He already thinks four is irrespon-sible, but Anik is only three, so I'll give it a while then have another go at him. He usually caves.' She grins. 'What about you? Plans for more?'

That's not going to happen, but I'm not sure how to answer.

'It's too soon,' I say. It's a short answer and I feel I should give more. Despite giving the appearance that she doesn't listen to anyone else, Aminah is perceptive and I don't want her to read anything into my silence.

'How's Mark doing as a dad, then? He's been the focus of attention with his sister and then Mia for so long, I wasn't sure how he would stand up to the competition.'

I have to admit that Mark is good with Lulu. The man that I met – the totally distracted, muddled character who wanted to keep the world at bay – would not have known what to do with a child. But being a father has changed him – at least when he's with his daughter.

'How long have you known Cleo, Aminah?' Last time I asked I was told 'forever' but I want to know more than that.

'We met when I moved here. I was fifteen and quite bolshy. I felt I had to be, because there were so few Asians living in this part of the world and it was hard to integrate. Cleo was in my year and a bit of a loner herself – she was always fussing over Mark and making sure he was okay and the other kids used to take the piss out of her, accused her of treating him like a baby, that sort of thing. So she was stroppy, unpopular, and then I came along. It wasn't that we chose each other so much as neither of us had anyone else. And we came to rely on each other.'

That made sense. The difference was that Aminah had moved on. She had a husband and four children, plus a host of friends. She and Zahid entertained regularly in their own haphazard way and their home was noisy, loving and fun.

Cleo, on the other hand, had only Aminah as a friend. She told me once that she didn't need anyone else, because she would always have Mark. I know for a fact that she would do anything for him, would turn a blind eye to whatever he did, right or wrong. And Mark knows it too.

12

It's a week now since the plaster came off my hand, and it's a huge relief. I can pick Lulu up again and dance her round the house to her favourite music. She's not a fan of nursery rhymes but she seems to have developed a baby crush on Ed Sheeran and she loves it when we dance.

Tomorrow, Mark's going away again. It's the research trip to Croatia and he's been moaning about it for days.

'Why do I have to see the yacht? Surely all they have to do is tell me the dimensions they'd like and I can take it from there. This is absolutely ridiculous and I don't know why Cleo doesn't tell them that this is *not* how I work.'

I do my best to calm him down, but I know it's all noise. He's going to go, just as he always does.

Cleo came round earlier, saying it wasn't too late for me to go with him, but I said I don't want to leave Lulu. I do find Cleo-watching to be a fascinating pastime, though.

I remember when we told her about the blog. I hadn't seen her in the three weeks since I had confessed to Mark that I wasn't going to be able to pay for the photos, but I knew he had told her my father had died. We weren't a couple then, but

I was beginning to understand Mark, and I thought it might have been the first time he had ever done anything without consulting Cleo. I discovered later that evening that I was wrong.

He asked Cleo to call in for a drink on her way home from work, to chat about the gallery and his commissions. It was clear from the minute she walked through the door that she had no idea that I was going to be there.

We all sat on the sofas, Mark and I next to each other and Cleo facing us, trying to look relaxed but failing. Her eyes were so like Mark's – so grey and expressive – and I knew she was confused by my presence. I was just a client, wasn't I? And one who couldn't pay the bill, at that.

Mark waffled on a bit about the gallery and I could see he was biding his time, almost as if he was afraid of his sister's reaction. But eventually he broached the subject of the blog, how we had been working on it for a couple of weeks and how excited he was by the idea. I had my iPad next to me so I pulled up the site on screen and turned it round to face Cleo. She was stunned. Not by the designs, though.

'Why have you been hatching this plan behind my back?' she asked, her brows joined together in a frown.

'We've not been *hatching* anything,' Mark said, rolling his eyes. 'For God's sake, Evie wanted to do something to help because of the problems with her dad's money. She offered and, although I wasn't sure about it to start with, it looks great and I thought you'd be pleased. It's supposed to be a *good* surprise. You're always on about better promotion, and this looks pretty damn good to me.'

Cleo turned her head towards me, and I could see she was

weighing me up. Was I trying to come between her and Mark, or was I just some poor young woman who had recently lost her father? She still hadn't responded to Mark's enthusiasm for the blog, and he was starting to get cross.

'Take that look off your face, Cleo. This is costing us nothing, and it's good publicity. Evie wanted us to keep it as a surprise until the design was done, and I thought that was a great idea.'

She was still giving me a puzzled look, and I gave her what I trusted was a hopeful smile.

'I tell you what,' I said. 'Why don't I leave you for a few moments then you can chat. Mark, is it okay if I take some photos of your studio as long as I don't touch anything? I know I'm no professional, but for the blog we need shots of where you work, and you can always replace them with something better when you have the time.'

He gave me a distracted nod, staring at his sister as he tried to control his irritation, but I could see he was close to apologising – although for what, I wasn't entirely sure.

I wandered off with my iPad to take the pictures, leaving behind the silent living room. Cleo was obviously waiting until I was out of earshot.

I walked down the stairs until I reached the door to the studio, opened it and let it swing closed with a thud. I stood still in the hall. I could hear every word.

'Mark, I know this is a small thing. It's only a stupid blog, when all's said and done. But you need to be careful of Evie. I don't trust her.'

I heard the wine bottle go down rather too heavily on the table.

77

'For God's sake, Cleo. What on earth is wrong with you? She's not charging us a penny, and it would probably have cost as much as the bloody photos if we'd had to pay someone to do it.'

'You've been so much better these past weeks, and I know some of that is down to the work you did on Evie's photographs. But I don't want you to be taken in by another woman, that's all.'

There was the type of silence you could cut with a knife. I had no idea what Mark was going to do and say next. In the end his voice was so low I could barely hear him.

'What, precisely, does that mean?'

'You know what it means. You never told me how you felt about Mia until it was too late, and I don't want you making any more mistakes with your life.'

'Too late? For whom, may I ask?'

There was a deadly note in Mark's voice. I had rarely heard him angry with his sister, but I could feel it even at the bottom of the stairs. It didn't deter Cleo, though.

'She wasn't good for you. She didn't have any faith in you, in your work. She didn't encourage you, and she thought your photography was a hobby. Look, it's nearly two years since she died, so surely you can finally see what a negative influence she was?'

The silence intensified.

'Cleo, if you're saying that I'm better off without Mia – are you also saying it's a good thing she's dead?'

There was a gasp. 'Of course not! I wouldn't ever say that.'

'What would you say if I was the one who believed that? If

my apparent grief was actually guilt – because I knew how bad she was for me and perhaps I think I'm better off without her? What would you say?' There was a pause and then the rasping sound of a chair being pushed violently backwards on a solid floor. 'I'm going to find Evie. I suggest you leave before one of us goes down a path from which there's no return.'

Silently I pushed the studio door open and just as quietly I closed it behind me.

13

Mark's gone now. He spent most of yesterday looking for an excuse to stay at home with us. He's not comfortable doing what he calls 'sucking up to the rich guys' and although he's no longer the recluse he was, he still doesn't enjoy it.

This afternoon I am supposed to be on duty at the charity where I volunteer. It's my turn to man the phones. I haven't been for weeks because I couldn't drive, and today I'm going to have to cry off again. I feel guilty, but I know I'm doing the right thing. I'm going to have to call Harriet to make an excuse.

The first time I saw Harriet James she was on the local news, standing outside a courtroom speaking on behalf of a client. A slight woman with sleek dark hair pulled tightly back into a ponytail, her brown eyes shone with fervour as she explained why the judge had made the wrong decision. There was an intensity about Harriet that silenced those around her and I was so impressed with the way she spoke that I looked her up online. Learning that she was heavily involved in charity work, I offered my services, although I've not told Mark the detail of what I do.

Right now, though, I need to ring her and apologise yet again.

'Hi, Harriet,' I say when she answers my call.

'Hello, Evie – how are you doing? We've missed you. How's the hand?'

Harriet sounds as brisk and efficient as always, and I imagine her looking at her watch, wondering how long this is going to take. She cares, but she has so many people to care about and not enough hours in the day.

'It's okay. The plaster's off, but I'm not quite up to coming in this afternoon. I'm supposed to be on duty at three, and I'm so sorry to let you down.'

Harriet's tone changes. She can hear something in my voice and suddenly she has all the time in the world.

'What's up? I can tell from your voice that something's wrong. What is it?'

'I'm okay, Harriet. Please don't worry about me.' I can hear the break in my voice and know that she heard it too.

'Do you want me to come over? Are you on your own?'

I sniff. 'Honestly, I'm fine. I've got Lulu here and I think I just need to be with her today.'

'Look, I'm not going to push you if you don't want to talk to me. But I'm used to keeping confidences. It goes with the job, so if you change your mind you know how to get hold of me. Night or day, Evie.' She pauses for a moment to see if I have anything to say, but my silence says it all. 'I'll call tomorrow to see how you are. Take care, Evie, won't you?'

I end the call feeling bad about Harriet, but knowing I had no choice. I couldn't let her see me today.

Lulu's having a nap and I'll hear her on the monitor if she wakes up, so I wander into the kitchen, looking for something to occupy my hands in the vain hope that by default my mind will be occupied too. I was supposed to be seeing Aminah for a quick lunch here, and then she was going to have Lulu for me this afternoon so I could go to the shelter. I've left a message on her mobile, telling her not to come. I wonder for a moment what she will make of that, and of my tone of voice. She won't have missed it, though. Like Harriet, she's too smart.

My mind drifts back to the night before. Mark had decided to go to bed and I promised to follow him soon. But that wasn't good enough – he wanted me with him. It was the night before a trip, and he said he wanted us to be close. He must have doubted that I would keep my promise, so he waited until I relented.

I knew he would want to make love – it is part of the ritual. Immediately before he leaves, and immediately he comes back from a trip, but I'm finding it increasingly difficult to comply and my withdrawal has become a serious issue between us. Before his last trip my refusal to surrender to his passion was painful for us both. But how can I? It's asking too much. It breaks my heart.

'Making love to you is something to think about when I'm away and on my own,' he said when I asked him why he has to be so predictable. 'I'm scared that when I come back you'll be gone, so each time it feels like it could be our last time together.'

It's not clear whether he thinks I will leave, or whether he thinks that – like Mia – I will die.

'When I come back,' he said, 'it's as if I'm repossessing you – claiming you back as my own. Then I feel calm again.'

I sometimes try to break him out of his routines, but I'm always met with obdurate resistance.

'Doing things a certain way gives me a sense of security. As long as I – no, we – stick to the rules, we'll be okay. That's how it feels.'

Trying to prove a point just before he leaves for a trip is guaranteed to do nothing more than wind us both up, so I let it go. Despite everything I strangely find myself understanding him. I know that his head is full of disconnected ideas that vie for dominance, and while most of us try to curb the excesses of our thoughts and manage our emotions, as an artist Mark feels he has to let them roam free. His need for rules is his way of keeping his feelings in check, and last night had been no different from the others.

He wrapped his arms around me and spoke softly. 'Evie, I want you to have something to remember me by when I'm away. You can't have it now, though. You'll have to wait until morning. Now all I want is you.'

I could hear the smile in his voice and knew he was excited about what was to come – another part of the ritual, and one that was supposed to fill me with anticipation.

The front doorbell rings fifteen minutes after I had expected Aminah to arrive for lunch, and in spite of the text I sent I know she's the one pressing repeatedly on the buzzer. She will have ignored my message telling her not to come because she'll want to know why I cancelled, and will want to ask me to my face. If I'm ill, she'll want to help.

But I'm not going to let her in.

She presses the bell long and hard, and I can imagine her irritation that I'm not answering. Then the phone rings and I don't answer that either. Any minute now she'll wake Lulu and I need her to stay sleeping. Maybe Aminah will go away, but I doubt it.

I stand in the kitchen by the tall, narrow window that runs from floor to ceiling. It looks out over the garden to the side of the house, and although not as spectacular as the sea view, I enjoy looking at the well-kept grass and the plants, especially the bulbs as they push their bright green heads through the sandy soil in spring or the roses as they burst with buds in the early summer.

The side garden is protected from public view by the house on one side, the sea on another and the high white wall that curves round in a semi-circle to enclose the land. Set into the wall and protruding into the garden is a garage big enough for three cars, its white walls covered with clematis and honey-suckle.

I continue to stare out of the window. I'm not going to answer the door however many time she rings the bell or calls my mobile.

After five minutes she stops and Lulu starts to cry. I need to go to her. But not yet. She might settle again.

I stare sightlessly out of the window, not focusing on anything as my mind takes me back to just before Mark left. It's a moment before I realise that Aminah is in the garden. She must have come through the garage and out through the garden door. She's gesticulating wildly at me, pointing at her phone.

I turn fractionally towards her and for once she is struck

dumb. She stops her march towards the house, and lowers the hand holding the phone. Her eyes open wide as she stares at me. After no more than two or three seconds I pull the blind down to hide my face from her.

I know she's seen it, though. Seen the blue and angry red skin around my right eye.

14

Cleo was in full flow, eulogising about one of Marcus North's latest local landscapes to a potential customer, when she heard the discreet ping indicating that someone else had come into the gallery.

She turned her head to smile at the newcomer and was surprised to see it was Aminah, and she wasn't returning the smile. Cleo's momentary lack of focus as she gave her friend a questioning look probably lost her the customer. His head swivelled towards the door too, following Cleo's gaze, and it diverted his attention away from the photograph.

'I'm going to think about it,' he said with a smile, placing his hand on his wife's waist as he guided her towards the door.

Cleo was frustrated. Another few minutes and she would have had him, she was certain. It wasn't Aminah's fault, though. She looked worried.

'Sorry,' Aminah said as the door closed behind the potential customers.

Cleo resisted the sigh that she felt building. 'Don't worry about it. It would have been great to sell a picture, though. I seem to have lost the knack somehow. Anyway, what are you doing here?' she asked. 'I thought you were going to Evie's for lunch and then having Lulu.'

Aminah was being unusually silent and hadn't interrupted Cleo once.

'What's up?'

'Can I ask you something?' Aminah said.

'Of course. I can't guarantee an answer, because it depends on the question, but ask away.' She smiled to let her friend know that she wasn't serious.

Aminah paused as if considering her question.

'Do you think Mark has anger issues?'

Cleo wasn't expecting that.

'Why the hell are you asking me that? Why would you even *think* that?'

'It's not a hard question.'

Cleo was quiet. There was something going on here – something Aminah wasn't saying.

'No.' She didn't feel the need to elaborate but she gave the word more force than it needed.

'Don't bite my head off, Cleo. I had to ask.'

'Why, though? Have you seen him losing it, or something? Has Evie been telling lies about him?'

Aminah's face was showing nothing, which was unusual to say the least. For a moment, neither of them spoke.

'That incident – years ago when you were kids. You always said Mark had nothing to do with it, but were you covering for him?'

Cleo knew straight away the incident that Aminah was referring to. It was long before the two fifteen-year-old girls had become friends but it had been a well-known story locally – one that Cleo refused to think about. She closed her mind to the sound of gulls screeching overhead, of waves lashing onto the sea wall and of a long piercing scream.

'Don't go there, Aminah. It had nothing to do with Mark, but you need to tell me what this is about.'

Aminah was silent again, biting the inside of her cheek as if pondering what to do.

'No,' she said. 'I don't need to tell you. I'm sorry I asked. Let's just forget it.'

'Absolutely not! You can't accuse my brother of something and then not explain where you're getting your ridiculous notions from.' Cleo knew she was over-reacting, and could see a puzzled look in Aminah's eyes. But she couldn't help herself. 'Has Evie said something? He should never have let her move in with him.'

Aminah gave her friend a half smile. 'I wasn't accusing him, and if I remember rightly Evie resisted the move for quite a while. She was six months pregnant before she finally relented.'

That was true. Evie said that Mark hadn't suggested a long-term relationship before she unexpectedly fell pregnant. Therefore she wasn't going to force him to commit to her and the child. In the end he'd had to convince her it was what he really wanted.

'Yes, but that was then. Look, if Evie's suggesting that he's hurt her in some way . . .'

'I haven't spoken to her, so she's suggested nothing.'

Cleo could see there was something that Aminah wasn't telling her, and she wasn't sure who her friend was trying to protect.

'Forget I said anything,' Aminah said.

'How can I do that?'

'Because I'm not going to say any more to you or anyone until I know the facts.'

'What facts? What the fuck are you talking about, Aminah?' Cleo could feel her heart rate increase. Even though she didn't know what had provoked her friend's suspicions, she knew exactly what Aminah meant and couldn't deny that a worm of doubt had popped into her own head recently – until she had forcibly rejected it. But there was no way she was going to admit to that. 'If she tells you he's hurt her in some way, I'll kill her myself.'

The expression on Aminah's face told Cleo that this time she had gone too far. She had to make Aminah believe that she hadn't meant it, but she was too late. Without another word, Aminah turned and walked towards the door.

'I didn't mean it like that, Aminah,' Cleo said quietly. 'I wouldn't hurt Evie.'

As she reached the door, Aminah cast a glance over her shoulder and Cleo could see that she didn't believe her for a moment. And why would she?

Cleo raised her hands to either side of her head and pressed hard, as if she could force the memory from her mind. A second was all it took – a moment of madness, a single push, a pair of eyes, round with shock, and a piercing scream that still haunted her nights.

15

It took Cleo all of thirty seconds to decide what to do after Aminah left. She flipped the closed sign on, grabbed her bag and her car keys, set the alarm and left the gallery at a run. She was cursing Evie under her breath, but she had to see her, to know what she had said to Aminah to make her react like that.

The drive took a matter of minutes, and Cleo's car skidded to a halt by the long white wall. She understood why there were no windows on this side, but right now it frustrated her. She would have loved to see Evie's face at the unscheduled visit of her partner's sister. Mark had asked Cleo some time ago if she would please call ahead before she visited, and since then she had never felt that she could drop by unannounced. But Mark would surely forgive her for this.

She leapt out of the car and marched towards the front door, banging hard on the wood and pressing the bell simultaneously.

Nothing happened. She tried again.

'Shit,' she muttered, knowing Evie wasn't going to let her in.

She glanced towards the garage, hoping to get through to the garden that way. She stomped over to the door and rattled it, but it was locked. Giving the door a last kick for good measure, she turned back towards the house. If Evie was going to ignore her there was nothing for it – she was going to have to let herself in.

Her mind was suddenly bombarded with images of the last time she had impulsively used her 'emergency' key. It had been the day that Mia died, and then she had used it not once, but twice. The first time she had entered in anger, as she was doing today, and the memory stopped her in her tracks. She needed to calm down. There could be no recurrence of that dreadful day and of all that followed.

She pulled the key from its place of safe-keeping in her bag and inserted it in the lock. She tried to turn it, but it wouldn't move. She tried leaning against the door in case the lock wasn't aligned properly, but it still wouldn't turn.

There could be only one reason for that. The locks had been changed.

She spun round and flung the key with force over the cliff edge onto the rocks below.

Climbing back into her car, Cleo picked up her mobile and punched in Mark's number, half expecting him not to answer.

To her surprise he picked up after two rings.

'Hi,' he said. 'What's up?'

It had obviously not occurred to Mark that she might have called for a chat with her brother, but on this occasion he was right to assume something was the matter.

'Have you spoken to Evie?' she asked abruptly.

'Not yet. I've only just got off the plane and I was going to

91

call her when I arrive at the yacht – which should be in the next half hour, according to the taxi driver. Is something the matter?'

Cleo paused for a moment. She didn't want to say anything that might affect his chances with this commission, and if he was worried he would be unable to focus. He might even turn round and come straight home. She forced herself to breathe more slowly.

'No, but I decided on impulse to call round to see her – see if she wants some company one evening while you're away.'

'Really? That doesn't sound like you.'

'Don't be mean, Mark. I'm trying to get on with her, and I adore Lulu.'

She heard a laugh.

'Cleo, you're not trying at all. But you don't have to ask my permission to go and see her, you know.'

'No, but she's not answering the door. I thought maybe she was out, so I was going to pop in to leave her a note but my key doesn't seem to be working.'

There was a moment of silence.

'No. It won't work. We had the locks changed.'

She felt a hot flush of tears. Her brother had locked her out of his house. 'Why would you do that? I'm the only other person with a key, for God's sake.'

'It's not personal, Cleo. When I started going away for commissions after Evie moved in, she suggested that we hire one of those security firms that comes round from time to time to check everything is okay. I thought it was a good idea, and the first thing they did was change the lock to something more secure. That's all it was.'

'And you didn't think to tell me?'

'Sorry – it never occurred to me. Evie dealt with it all, and I only knew the lock had changed because she presented me with a key and said the security company had insisted.'

Cleo wanted to ask him if he would give her a key now, but if he refused it would be too awful to contemplate.

'What's really going on, Cleo?'

She was going to have to tell him something, and it came to her in a flash.

'Aminah was supposed to be having Lulu while Evie went to do her charity work, but she cancelled. I thought that must mean there was something the matter, but maybe she's gone after all and taken Lulu with her. Do you know where this place is? You know, the place she volunteers?'

'No, and if I did I wouldn't tell you. Because of the type of charity it is, she's not supposed to let people know she's working there. Like the Samaritans, I suppose. If people believe they might get someone they know on the other end of the line, it puts them off calling. So I know she goes, and I know she hopes she's helping, but that's all.'

Surely she should be able to tell Mark? He was hardly likely to need to call a helpline, but it sounded typical of Evie to hide something that didn't need to be hidden.

'Anyone would think she was an MI5 undercover operative, not working for some poxy charity.'

She heard an irritated sigh from the other end of the phone.

'Sorry,' she said. She was letting Evie drive a wedge between her and Mark and she couldn't let that happen again. She had already let him down once this week – not because she hadn't had the time to do as he asked, but because she couldn't feel any commitment to it.

'I'm sorry, Mark. And I'm sorry too that I didn't manage to finish that silver piece for Evie – I had more on than I thought.'

'That's okay. Look, I've got to go – I think we're getting close to the marina. But don't worry about the jewellery. She never knew what I was planning. I gave her something else, so we can save it for another time.'

Mark rang off.

Cleo sat in the car for another ten minutes, wondering what she should do. Aminah seemed to think there was something wrong, even though she wouldn't be specific. Whatever it was, Cleo had to fix it. She might be happy if things between Evie and Mark were going wrong. But if Evie left, Lulu would be lost to her. And that couldn't happen.

16

Mark has been away for ten days now, which is longer than he had hoped. On his way back, he'd had to kick his heels for a couple of nights in London to talk to a gallery interested in including some of his pictures in an exhibition, and it made more sense to stay than to come home and go back two days later.

I've seen neither Cleo nor Aminah since that first day, although I know Cleo sat outside the house in her car for a while. There's a spy hole in the door and I watched her hitting the steering wheel with the palms of her hands in frustration. Both Cleo and Aminah have tried to call me, and even though I ignored them for a couple of days, I knew at some point I would have to pick up.

Eventually I spoke to Cleo. Mark asked me to explain to her why he was going to be away for longer, saying he didn't want to speak to her because she was being weird and he could do without her winding him up.

'Honestly, Evie, it's best all round if we keep her happy. She just worries about us all.'

By 'all' he means him and Lulu. There's nothing to be gained by my pointing that out though.

Mark isn't the same when he's away. Sometimes, depending how things have been between us before he left, we don't speak for the whole time he's gone. I don't know why he puts himself, and all of us, through it if he hates it so much. But I don't discourage him. In fact, I actively encourage him. I need him to be away for some of the time. It would be impossible if he was always here.

Today he spoke with what seemed to be genuine affection, saying how much he was looking forward to coming home and being with us. I try to respond, but sometimes it's difficult. I can feel him waiting, urging me to tell him that I love him. Sometimes the words come. Often they don't, and I know when he's home it will become an issue and I will regret my inability to play the game effectively. It's so very hard to let him get close when I think of the pain that is to come.

I did as he asked, though, and called Cleo. The conversation was short. She wanted to know what I had been saying to Aminah about Mark, and I told her I had said nothing at all – which was perfectly true. She asked if she could come round to see Lulu and I said it would be better when Mark was back. She didn't like it, but I think we've both given up pretending we can be friends. We have reached a point at which we manage to say all the right words to each other, but they are hollow – the fancy wrapping paper around an empty box.

It doesn't matter now, though.

Aminah, of course, is a different matter. She calls repeatedly wanting to know what happened to my eye.

'Ah,' I tell her. 'The black eye. I didn't realise you'd noticed. It was Lulu. I was fastening her nappy and she was having a bit of a kick with her legs when *boom*, her little foot went straight in my eye.'

'So why didn't you open the door when you saw me in the garden?' she asks, not unreasonably.

'Because I honestly didn't think you'd seen it, and I assumed if I let you in you'd take one look and think the worst – that either I'd had another stupid accident or I'd been punched.' I give a little laugh at the ridiculousness of this idea. 'It seemed better not to see anyone rather than try to make excuses. Nobody ever believes you, do they?'

Aminah is silent, and I guess she is deciding whether to ask me a direct question. But she knows, by what I have already said, that I will lie. So there is little point.

'Just remember, Evie. I'm your friend,' she says. 'If ever you need anyone, call me. Okay?'

That is the moment I realise that this has gone on long enough. It's time for it all to stop. It has to end very soon.

He's home. He arrived late this afternoon, walking into the house, dropping his bag by the door and flinging himself onto the sofa, his legs stretched out in front of him.

'Don't make me stay away that long again, Evie – it was hell.'

He hasn't noticed anything different about my face, but then he's been away for ten days and any black eye would fade in that time. Only Aminah knows, and she's unlikely to tell him.

Mark bathed Lulu and put her to bed. I could hear her giggling and him singing to her. She loves her daddy, which makes everything so much more difficult.

It's late now. We opened some good wine to have with dinner, and I decided 'to hell with sobriety'. When the first bottle had gone we opened another. Mark drank steadily but without a pause, and even I had considerably more than my occasional small glass. He told me all about his trip to Croatia.

'I wasn't too keen on the idea of the trip on the yacht, but actually it was good,' he said. 'And it did give me some ideas for the mural. But I missed you and Lulu.'

I know I was expected to say that we missed him, but I didn't.

'You know, Evie, I'm the first person to admit that I'm not easy to live with. There are some things about me that must drive you mad. But somehow you seem to manage to cope with me. I want you to know how much I value that. I'm going to try harder, I promise.'

'Were you the same with Mia?' I asked quietly.

'I don't know. It's difficult to see yourself through anyone else's eyes, but Mia was much more outspoken than you are. She thought she knew what was best for me.' He took a long gulp of his wine. 'I was bullied when I was a kid – I've told you that before. I swore I would never let anyone get the better of me again, so when Mia was telling me what to do I probably . . . Oh I don't know. I spent a year or so after she died wishing I'd been a better husband, I do know that.'

'But you still let Cleo tell you what to do. How's that any different?'

Mark looked puzzled. 'Do you think she's bossy with me?'

I gave a snort of laughter. 'Mark, you do everything she bloody tells you to!'

His face changed and I could see he was angry with me for

daring to criticise Cleo. I had to nip it in the bud before it became an argument.

'But that's fair enough,' I said, smiling at him. 'She's your big sister and all she wants to do is make sure you're happy. There's nothing wrong with that.'

The evening continued to go reasonably well until Mark received a call from Alain Roussel in Paris. I didn't even know he had our home phone number and couldn't believe Mark had given it to him. Maybe it was Cleo.

It seems that Monsieur Roussel wants Mark to go and see him in Paris as soon as possible. He's had some more thoughts about the pictures. Mark told him that it would be difficult right now because he has a number of commissions that need completing, but Roussel was adamant that he must come. Even from where I was sitting I could hear his broken English, telling Mark in no uncertain terms that, given what he was paying for these photographs, Mark should be ready to dance to his tune – or words to that effect.

The impact on Mark's mood was significant.

'I want to tell the bastard to go to hell,' he said as he slammed down the phone. 'I don't *need* this stress in my life.'

After that, the conversation dried up and now the mood is broken.

It's not long before Mark says he's tired and needs to go to bed. He's wired, though, and there is little or no chance of him sleeping. I know he wants me to go too, and despite everything I agree. I need him to keep in good spirits – or as good as I can make them – for the few days before he plans to leave for Paris.

But it's hard. Harder than I ever imagined.

17

The five days since Mark's return have passed quickly and reasonably harmoniously, although I'm struggling to keep my nerves under control. The thing is, I know what's going to happen. I have been picturing every single moment of the night before he leaves for Paris, and I haven't liked what I've been seeing. But now that night has arrived, and I'm scared.

I've bought Mark a present and it was delivered yesterday – only just in time for his departure. I want him to be happy and thrilled that I care so much about him. It's a telescope, something he's talked about buying for months because the view of the sky from the window in the sitting room is stunning. It's all wrapped and waiting for me to give to him tonight, as a parting gift. I'll tell him it's something to look forward to when he comes back from Paris. It's in our bedroom, though, and he won't see it until we go to bed.

I've arranged candles around the room, and I've changed the sheets. When it's this hot we only ever have a top sheet and no duvet. We never close the curtains in the bedroom. Nobody can see in. The moon keeps making a brief appearance from under the scattered cloud and floodlighting the room. Everything is perfect. My eyes are drawn to the photograph above the bed. It's a picture of me – Mark's favourite of the ones he took for my father. I look carefree, the wind blowing my hair across my cheeks and my eyes alight with laughter. The expression on my face conveys a sense of happiness that couldn't be further from how I'm feeling now.

I return to the sitting room to wait for Mark to say he's ready to go to bed, and when he does I whisper in his ear as he walks towards the stairs down to the bedroom. Mark has always been the one to arrange what he calls his little surprises before he leaves on a trip, but tonight it's my turn.

'I've got something for you.' I rest my hands on the back of his shoulders as I speak. He's ahead of me on the stairs, and he tries to turn round but I won't let him. 'It's in the bedroom.'

As we walk into the room, I reach out a hand to switch the light on. There's a tiny pop and nothing happens. The lights in the hall have gone out too.

'Bugger,' Mark says. 'It's tripped the circuit breaker for some reason.' He stands by the door, seemingly unwilling to enter the room.

I feel a flutter in my chest, but the moon is my friend at that moment and peeks out from behind a cloud just long enough for me to find matches and light the candles.

'This is better than a bright light, isn't it?'

He wasn't expecting that, and I see a flicker of interest in his eye. He's intrigued by this version of me. His present is lying on the bed, beautifully wrapped in black and gold paper with a huge bow.

I can see he's debating whether to open it now or come for me.

'You start to unwrap it. I'll go and get you some scissors. I think the packaging will need more than fingers to open it.'

I'm only gone for a couple of minutes, and the lights are still off.

'I was going to reset the lights, but I couldn't see which switch was down in the fuse box,' I say. 'But the candles are okay, aren't they? Let's not worry about it for now. I've brought you something to open the package with.'

Mark turns towards me and holds out his arms. 'You do know I love you, don't you, Evie?' he asks and I bury my head in his shoulder.

'Come on,' I say, gently pushing him away. 'Open your present.'

I hand him the long, thin boning knife that I picked up in the kitchen, and move to the other side of the bed.

Mark is looking at me with an expression I recognise. His eyes are glinting with excitement and it's not my present that's doing it. He holds the knife up and looks at the blade.

'I don't want you to forget me when I'm gone,' he says. 'You know that's my biggest fear. I've arranged something extra special for you in the morning, but maybe you should have it now instead.'

He walks round the bed towards me. It is happening. The moment is finally here.

PART TWO

The room is dark. It's the way he likes it. He knows exactly what he's doing: he can't bear to see eyes full of hatred staring at him. He likes the sounds, though — the crack of the whip cutting into flesh and the muffled screams.

18

Sergeant Stephanie King wished with all her heart that she hadn't been on duty that evening when the call for help had come through. From the moment she and Jason had opened the door in the windowless white wall, she had known it was going to be bad. But she hadn't expected it to be as bad as this.

Having sent Jason to find the crying child, Stephanie found herself alone in a room with at least one, if not two dead bodies. There had been nothing further to suggest that one of them was still alive since that faint moan a few moments after they arrived and she was beginning to wonder if she had imagined it. She couldn't take the risk, though. She had to be certain. Both bodies were entangled in the blood-soaked sheets, and she had no idea which of them might somehow have survived whatever atrocity had happened.

Knowing she was potentially destroying evidence, Stephanie nevertheless had a duty to preserve life so she shone her torch on the floor and moved as quickly as she dared towards the far side of the bed where the bodies were huddled, trying her best to avoid anything that might be vital to the investigation.

Only one face was visible, and this one was dead. There was

no doubt about it. The eyes were open – wide and unseeing. They didn't flicker when Stephanie aimed the beam of her torch straight into them.

The face of the second person was hidden beneath the jumbled mass of bloodied linen, and as Stephanie leaned forward and reached out a hand to touch a shoulder through the thin sheet, the upper body of a young woman suddenly reared up, the head shaken free from the bedding. Stephanie recoiled, startled, as a pair of eyes, wild with either fear or horror, stared at her and a deep cry of distress ripped through the silence.

Before Stephanie could do a thing she heard a shout and running feet. 'Sarge – are you okay?'

Stephanie twisted her head to the door. 'Where's the child?'

Jason didn't answer. He peered through the gloom at the figure on the bed, her slender body naked from the waist up, her skin covered with blood. Her initial cry had switched to sobs and Jason seemed rooted to the spot.

'Jason – the child,' Stephanie prompted.

'She's safe. She's too young to walk and she's in her cot.' He hadn't taken his eyes off the girl.

'We need to check the house – it didn't look as if anyone had broken in, but we can't be sure. If the child is safe, check the basement – there's a gym and a pool down there.'

Stephanie leaned towards the woman on the bed. 'Are you okay? Are you hurt?'

She could see some cuts on the woman's arms and chest, but these could not be the sole cause of the blood. The woman gazed blankly at her, tears pouring down her face. Stephanie reached out again and touched the woman's skin. Despite the warm evening, it was cool to touch and she realised she was in shock.

Stephanie looked over her shoulder.

'Why are you still here, Jason? Go – search the place now and don't take another step into this room. We need to do what we can to preserve any evidence I haven't already destroyed.'

She grabbed her radio and, without taking her eyes off the young woman on the bed, demanded that an ambulance be despatched urgently. She knew that within no time at all the place would be crawling with detectives, crime scene investigators and paramedics. She would be glad to hand this one over.

She glanced around her and saw a woollen throw on a chair close to the bed. She reached for it and put it around the woman's shoulders.

'Are you okay?' she asked again. 'Do you want to tell me what happened?'

The woman lowered her head, her body shaking, but at a cry from the child she raised her chin and her body stiffened.

'Lulu?' she asked, her eyes meeting Stephanie's for the first time.

'Is that your little girl?' The woman gave a quick nod. 'She's okay. She's in her cot and we'll get to her as soon as we can. But she's safe for now. Do we need to look for anyone else? My colleague's checking around, but it would help if you can tell me.'

But she already knew there would be no intruder hiding in the shadows. If someone had been there, he would have been long gone by now, and it was unlikely that he would have left his weapon behind.

Her eyes were pulled back towards the one piece of evidence that nobody must touch. Lying on the pillow next to the slashed throat of the dead man, the stainless steel hilt of an expensive boning knife twinkled in the beam of her torch, its blade covered in blood.

Stephanie didn't hear the paramedics arrive. The bedroom was on the sea side of the house, and although she had done what she could to comfort the woman on the bed, her sobs had not diminished and she had neither confirmed nor denied if anyone else had been involved. The baby crying in a room not too far away was distressing to hear as well, and Stephanie felt profoundly relieved at the clatter of heavy boots coming down the wooden staircase.

'Hey, Steph, how you doing?' said her favourite paramedic in a quiet voice. Like Stephanie, he had been to this house before. Only last time it was a broken body at the foot of the basement stairs they'd had to deal with.

'I'm okay, Phil. But it's a crime scene, so watch where you're going.'

'Can't we put the lights on?'

'They seem to be out. I don't want to mess with anything until the forensic guys get here.'

Stephanie followed Phil's gaze as he looked towards the bed.

'One dead, one in severe shock at a guess,' she said quietly.

'Okay. Leave it with us.'

Stephanie shook her head. 'I'd better stay so I can see what you touch. I really need to get to that baby, though. She sounds very upset but I haven't been able to leave here.'

'We'll be as quick as we can.'

Phil picked his way over to the bed, leaving his partner – a young woman that Stephanie hadn't seen before – by the door.

'Stay there, Lynne, in case we need something from the ambulance,' he said. 'No point two of us tramping around if we don't need to.'

He walked around to the far side of the bed and bent over the man. It was the paramedic's role to pronounce life extinct and he gave Stephanie a nod without speaking the words out loud. He leaned in towards the woman, still huddled up against the dead man's back.

'Right, love,' he said. 'What's your name? I'm Phil and I'm a paramedic.'

The sobs got louder.

Phil looked at Stephanie for permission to climb on the bed and she shrugged. They had to make sure the girl wasn't badly injured and she was so far from the edge that it seemed the only way. He shone his torch on her, looking for any serious wounds, but without delving under the covers it was going to be difficult to be certain.

'Are you hurt, love?' he asked. She said nothing for a second and then gave a sharp shake of the head. 'Okay, that's good. Can you shuffle over to this side a bit so I can take a look at you? You've got a few cuts and I need to see if any of them are deep.'

For a moment, Stephanie thought the woman wasn't going to move, but finally she leant on her left arm and dragged herself across the bed.

'Can you tell me your name, love?' Phil asked again, but there was no response. 'Okay. I'm going to check you over quickly and then we'll take you to hospital. I think you're in shock. Lynne, I don't think we'll be needing a stretcher, so can you go and see to the baby, please?'

'Lulu?' The woman gasped out the words as if she had forgotten the child.

'Don't worry,' Phil said. 'She's fine. Just needs a bit of a cuddle, so don't be worrying about her. Your little girl, is she?'

The woman nodded, and at that moment the sound of angry crying from the child's room reduced to a mild whimper.

'Lynne's got a magic touch with little ones. Don't you stress yourself.'

As he talked, Phil was checking the woman for signs of bleeding, but apart from some angry marks on her arms and chest where the knife appeared to have inflicted superficial wounds, she seemed okay. He looked across at Stephanie and nodded.

Stephanie knew they had to get her out of the room. The man's body would have to stay in situ until the pathologist had been, and goodness knew when that would be. But the young woman had to be removed.

She could hear Jason talking at the top of the stairs and that meant Detective Inspector Brodie had arrived to take over. Stephanie felt herself grow warm. She didn't want to see Brodie, but couldn't see how to avoid it.

She spoke to the paramedic quietly without moving from the doorway. 'I need a name, Phil.'

He nodded and spoke softly to the woman. Stephanie heard her respond, but couldn't make out the words.

'Evie Clarke,' Phil said as he helped her off the bed.

'Okay, Evie, can you tell me the name of the man next to you?' Stephanie asked.

This time Evie lifted her head. Stephanie couldn't see her eyes clearly in the deep shadows cast by the flickering candles.

'His name's Mark North.'

'And do you know what happened here tonight, Evie?'

Evie Clarke turned her head and looked Stephanie in the eye. For a moment she didn't speak and Stephanie waited. Evie closed her eyes for a few seconds.

'I killed him,' she said.

19

As the paramedic wrapped Evie Clarke in a thermal blanket, Stephanie heard a voice behind her.

'Stephanie, good to see you.'

She would have recognised that deep Scottish burr anywhere, and tried to act nonchalant, glancing over her shoulder at her superior officer. He'd grown a beard and his dark wavy hair was a little longer. It suited him.

'You too, sir,' she said, and was rewarded by a gentle snort. Angus Brodie knew her well enough to realise that she had to hide behind professionalism when she saw him. It would never do for the whole of the local force to know that barely an hour went by when he didn't invade her thoughts.

'So what's been happening here, then?' Gus was keeping his voice down so that Evie Clarke couldn't hear him.

Stephanie turned towards him. 'We need to send an officer with her to the hospital, and you need to talk to her.'

Gus didn't ask for the dots to be joined.

'She's very shaky,' Stephanie said. 'She hasn't been cautioned but she says she killed him.'

Gus looked shocked. 'Bugger,' he said. 'That makes it messy.'

'Sorry – she just blurted it out and it never occurred to me to caution her. I thought she was more badly hurt than she is.'

'It's not your fault, Steph. Let's hope she doesn't deny it later. If she does, the defence are bound to have it ruled out.'

Gus lifted a hand to rub the back of his neck – a gesture that Stephanie had seen often when he was thinking through a problem.

'So how the fuck do we play this?' he muttered. 'She's got to go to hospital, but God knows what else she might come out with.' He raised his voice slightly. 'Phil, you good to go?'

Phil nodded, and with one arm round Evie Clarke he guided her towards the door.

'Get her upstairs, sat down and warmed up a bit. I need to speak to her before you take her away.'

Phil nodded again as he slowly walked past Stephanie and Gus towards the stairs.

'I think the best bet is if I go up with her, caution her in case she says anything else and then arrest her,' Gus said, 'and hope I don't get a bollocking for making the wrong decision.'

He let out a long breath and reached for the torch in Stephanie's hand. She only just stopped herself from jumping as his thumb touched the inside of her wrist. He shone the torch on the bed first, and then worked his way around the room. Stephanie stood quietly and watched as he took in the details. He was always good at reading a scene.

'What's up with the lights?' Clearly the contact between his skin and hers had had no effect on Gus.

'We don't know. I didn't want to mess with the fuse box until the tech guys have checked it all out.'

'Do we know who they both are?'

'The woman is Evie Clarke. The man on the bed is Mark North – he has the studio in town. Calls himself Marcus professionally.'

'Sounds a bit bloody pretentious to me.'

Stephanie smiled. 'I think it was his sister's idea.'

'How the hell do you know that?' Gus asked.

'I've been here before.'

Gus turned back to face her and raised his eyebrows. 'Oh – that's the case you told me about. The dead American. Wasn't she his wife?'

'She was, yes.' Gus's face was blank, and Stephanie felt certain he hadn't remembered where they had been when she had shared that memory with him. It was the first time they had spent the whole night together, back when it had all seemed possible.

'Remind me.'

'Mia North – found dead at the bottom of the steps to the lower level about three and a half years ago. A loose shoelace was blamed for her fall. She was discovered by Mark North's sister, Cleo. No evidence of foul play and her husband was apparently on a plane at the time she died. I saw him just after he got back, and he seemed genuinely distraught.'

Gus nodded. 'Thanks. No obvious link, but two deaths in one house doesn't sit comfortably with me. Did Evie Clarke say anything else?'

Stephanie shook her head. 'No – she just said she killed him.'

'I'd better go and talk to her. Want to come?'

'No. One of the paramedics is looking after Evie's daughter

for the moment, but she'll have to leave with the ambulance. I'll take care of the child until we know what's going to happen to her.'

This time Gus turned completely to face her. He reached out a finger and gently touched her cheek.

'Are you sure you're okay with that?'

Stephanie brushed his hand away, ignoring the concern in his eyes. 'Course I am. Why wouldn't I be?'

She turned and left him standing in the doorway. She knew he was watching her, but she didn't turn around.

20

The house that had been so silent when Stephanie arrived was now full of people going about their jobs, speaking in hushed tones. The previously dark rooms were lit with bright arc lamps as the house lights were still out. Another female officer had offered to take care of little Lulu, although Stephanie found herself reluctant to hand over the child. But when she saw Gus's feet coming back down the stairs, she quickly passed her to the other woman.

Gus had reached the bottom step and Stephanie knew he was waiting to talk to her. The officer carried Lulu upstairs, muttering that she was going to find her something to drink, and Stephanie headed back into Lulu's darkened bedroom, knowing Gus would follow.

'Are you sure you're okay, Steph?' he asked.

Stephanie walked round to the other side of the cot to put a physical object between them.

'I'm fine. What did Evie have to say?'

'Exactly what you told me. I cautioned her and arrested her. But she confirmed that she killed him. She refused to say anything else without her solicitor.'

'Does she have one?'

'Harriet James.'

'*What?*' Harriet James was the most high-profile lawyer in this part of the country. A renowned advocate of women's rights, she had founded a charity that offered shelter to abused women and their children. Tough, feisty, she wouldn't take crap from anyone.

'That's what I thought,' Gus said. 'It's not going to be a clear-cut case if Harriet's involved.'

'Did you let Evie call her?'

'It was a tricky decision, and I hope I made the right one. I'd normally wait until she was in custody, but I couldn't see any harm in her making the call if I was standing by her side. Harriet knows the drill – Evie will have to be examined thoroughly, samples and photos taken and so on before she can talk to anyone. She says she'll wait, but as soon as we've got what we need, she wants to see her client.'

'Did Evie say anything else to you?' Stephanie asked.

'Only that the child can go to her aunt, Cleo North. I've got someone tracking her down.'

At that moment, Gus's mobile rang.

'Angus Brodie,' he answered, leaning back against the wall as if the events of the past half hour had worn him out. Stephanie took the opportunity to study him from her shadowy corner. Despite being officers in the same police force they were based miles apart and rarely saw each other, but right now the broad shoulders on which she had rested her head so many times looked just as inviting. Maybe the laughter lines round his eyes were a little deeper, but he looked good. Too good.

117

'Yes, sir,' she heard him say. 'No – I get it. Sergeant King is here with me now. I'll put it to her.' He was silent for a moment. 'Right. It's agreed then.' He rang off.

Stephanie realised that he looked slightly uncomfortable. 'What is it?'

'Apparently you talked a while ago about some career development and asked for a secondment to CID.'

'That was months ago. You know that.'

'I do. But it seems this is your moment. Lots of officers on holiday and we're a bit short-staffed to deal with a suspicious death. You're to report to me, starting now.'

Stephanie suddenly felt clammy. It was warm in the room, and she walked over and flung open a window. The sound of the sea pounding on the rocks below was both soothing and a reminder that some forces of nature couldn't be contained.

'That's shit, Gus, and you know it.'

He was quiet for a moment. 'What do you want me to do? Say I can't work with you because you're useless? Tell them that our relationship precludes us working together?'

'What bloody relationship?' she said without turning round. In her voice she heard the slight bitterness that she tried so hard not to feel.

She couldn't stay here in this room with Gus any longer. The cot between them seemed symbolic and Stephanie walked around it and headed towards the door. For a moment, as she got close to him, she thought he was going to reach for her, but just then one of the young crime scene investigators popped her head around the door.

'Sir, you're going to want to see this.'

Stephanie glanced at Gus's face and saw his mouth tighten fractionally, but he took a deep breath and turned to follow the girl out of the door.

'What am I looking at?'

Stephanie was standing outside the door to the bedroom where Gus was talking to the technician, but she could hear every word he said.

'This switch, sir.'

The girl had obviously unscrewed the cover of the light switch and tipped it, wires still attached, towards Gus.

'Sorry, but I'm no electrician,' he said. 'You're going to have to spell it out to me.'

'See this wire here,' she said. 'It's the live wire and it should go to this terminal, but it's been moved to here. When the light was switched on, it would have caused a direct short, and that would have instantly tripped the circuit breaker.'

'Are you saying it was deliberate?'

'It's not my job to say, but either someone was doing a bit of DIY and cocked it up, or it was done deliberately. The thing is, I can't see any reason why a person would need to fiddle with the switch – it looks quite new.'

Stephanie's attention was diverted by the sound of Jason's voice at the top of the stairs. For want of anything better for him to do, she had left him there to show any newcomers the way to the bedroom.

'It's down there, Miss,' he said. Stephanie assumed that 'Miss' would be the Home Office pathologist, Molly Treadwell. She smiled, knowing that being called Miss would amuse Molly. Her feet stomped down the stairs and she drifted into view. Never one to rush and always out of breath, Molly seemed to look the same whatever the time of day or year. Stephanie knew that under the protective clothing she would be wearing a black trouser suit, one size too large – 'for comfort' – and a white blouse that was half untucked. Her grey hair, as always, was scraped back into some semblance of a bun.

'Who's the joker at the top of the stairs?' Molly asked.

'Jason – he's a probationer,' Stephanie answered. 'You should be flattered that he called you Miss. You must have scared him.'

Molly cackled and ambled towards the bedroom door. 'Well, if it isn't the one and only Angus Brodie. Aren't I the lucky one?' she said under her breath, glancing towards Stephanie and raising her eyebrows.

Oblivious of the undertones, Gus turned.

'Glad you're here, Molly,' he said. 'We need to get the body moved as quickly as we can so that we can properly search the place.'

'All in good time – more haste, less speed, and all that.'

Stephanie stepped into the room and stood quietly in the doorway as Molly sauntered over to the bed.

'Oh dear. Poor chap didn't stand much of a chance, did he?' She started to hum tunelessly under her breath and Stephanie caught Gus's glance. In spite of everything they shared a brief smile.

This would take a while. But although Molly wasn't the fastest worker around, there was no doubt that she was thorough. Gus would stay with her until she allowed the body to be placed in a protective bag and transported to the mortuary, but Stephanie didn't need to be there.

The process of finding all the computers and telephones in the house would have begun and somehow they were going to have to unravel the story that had led to Mark North's death. Was it planned? Was Evie provoked? Stephanie had no idea, but as Gus had said, this house had now seen two terrible deaths, and that was too many in anyone's book.

21

Cleo had been restless all night, unable to settle. She thought it might be the unusually warm night, but somehow when the doorbell rang, it felt as if she had been waiting anxiously for this moment.

Grabbing a blue silk dressing gown and pulling it on as she ran down the stairs, she had no doubt this had to be bad news. It was the middle of the night, and nothing good could ever come from a visitor at this hour. She unlocked the door and was faced with a man and a woman in slightly crumpled clothing, looking as if they had jumped out of bed and dressed in the previous day's clothes.

'Miss North?' the young man said.

Both visitors held out their warrant cards and introduced themselves, but their voices blurred together into a dull mumble as Cleo's heart raced. She didn't care what they were called. She only needed to know what they had come to say. She could hardly breathe.

'What is it?' she asked. 'What's happened?'

'May we come in, Miss North?' the young woman asked. 'Better to talk inside, I think.'

There didn't seem any sense in arguing so she turned and marched into the sitting room, leaving them both to follow. With one hand she indicated the sofa, but she remained standing, pacing the floor.

'I think you might like to sit down,' the young man said.

'I'm fine. Just tell me.'

It was the woman who spoke.

'I'm very sorry to tell you that your brother, Mark North, died this evening.'

The woman was still talking, but her words washed over Cleo. Nothing else mattered. Not how he died, when he died, or where he was now. Her brother, the most important person in her life, was gone.

Cleo felt a scream build inside her. She lifted her chin and threw her head back, hearing herself shouting, 'No!' over and over again. She felt as if her legs were going to give way beneath her and she stumbled back into a chair. The man scurried from the room and the female officer stood up and moved towards Cleo, but she waved her away, trying to control her breathing, gasping for air.

How could it be true? She had spent most of her life protecting Mark – how could she have let him down now? Had something happened at the house? Was it an accident? A fire?

The police officer was quiet, giving Cleo time to register the devastating news. After a few moments, one word penetrated the fog that was enveloping her.

Lulu.

Her head dropped and she stared at the woman. 'Lulu's not hurt, is she?'

'No, Miss North. Lulu's fine. But her mother has asked if you could look after her for a while.'

'Why? Is she hurt too? This isn't one of Evie's stupid accidents, is it? Was it her fault? Tell me what's happened.' She knew she was shouting, but she didn't care. There was a wall of pain inside; any moment now it was going to burst, and she would be lost.

As the man came back in with a mug of tea she saw a nervous glance pass between him and his partner.

'I'm afraid Miss Clarke is in hospital,' the woman said.

Cleo stared at her. She hadn't felt a moment's concern for Evie.

'I knew it. I knew it would be something she did. *Jesus*. Mark, you can't be dead. You *can't!*'

Cleo had told Aminah that Evie's clumsiness was dangerous, but nobody had believed her, and now look what had happened. The tears couldn't be held back any longer, and she drew her knees up to her chest, wrapping her arms round her shins, trying to hold herself together.

'We don't believe it was an accident and we're treating your brother's death as suspicious. Miss Clarke's injuries are not severe, but she's suffering from shock.'

Only one word had sunk in. *Suspicious*. What the hell did that mean?

'What happened to him? Where's my brother now? Where's Lulu?'

'Your brother is being taken to the mortuary. We'll need to ask you to come to identify him, but not right now. Lulu's safe, please don't worry about her.'

There was something they weren't saying. It was there, in the room, and Cleo wanted to scream at them, make them tell her everything.

When the woman spoke again her voice was soft, almost hesitant, as if she didn't want to have to tell Cleo the truth.

'Miss Clarke will probably only be in hospital overnight, but Social Services will need to know if you can look after Lulu for a longer period. This is going to be difficult for you, Miss North, but I'm afraid Miss Clarke has been arrested. She claims she killed your brother, although as yet we have no means of knowing whether that's true.'

Despite the warmth of the night, Cleo felt her skin erupt in goosebumps. She stared at the police officer, wondering if she had heard her correctly, but knowing she had. She should never have trusted Evie. She'd had her doubts about her, so why hadn't she done something – persuaded Mark to kick her out, or somehow found a way to drive Evie away herself?

She had let Mark down.

She had promised him since he was a kid that she would look after him. She'd seen off the bullies, protected him from every bad thing that had happened, lied for him to keep him safe. And now this. How hadn't she seen trouble coming? How had she failed so completely to protect him?

Cleo rested her head on her raised knees, rocking to and fro, sobbing uncontrollably. The police officers gave her time, but her mind was chasing in every direction, making her dizzy. She thought she might be sick, and with trembling fingers she reached for the mug of tea and took a sip of the hot liquid. Her head was spinning again, the pain of losing Mark almost masking the shock at the news that Evie had killed him. She had suspected she was only with Mark for his money, but she had never thought of her as a murderer.

Suddenly Lulu felt like the only thing that mattered. At least Cleo could keep her safe, and loving the child might help to ease the worst of the pain.

'Where is she? Where's Lulu? I need her with me.'

She caught a glimpse of a frown forming between the eyebrows of the woman, but she didn't care. The loss of Mark was making her feel as if her body was being crushed in a giant vice, squeezing the breath from her body. Evie had taken his life, and Cleo would never forgive that, never get over it. But Evie had given her a reason to carry on living too. She had given her Lulu.

22

Harriet James strode through the maze of corridors, the click of her heels sounding unnaturally loud in the quiet of the hushed hallway. She had been called to this hospital in the middle of the night more times than she would care to count, usually by some poor soul who had been beaten to a pulp by her partner and wanted to be taken to the safety of the refuge. This time was different, though, and she ran through the questions that were crowding her mind.

All she knew was that Evie had been arrested and that she had killed Mark North. She didn't know why or how it had happened, and she had to keep an open mind. Had Evie lashed out in anger during an argument? Had she planned to kill Mark – and if so, why? Money? Revenge? Or was he hurting her and she had killed him in self-defence?

Speculation wasn't helpful, but there was a terrible suspicion at the back of Harriet's mind that she should have seen this coming. She had known there was something wrong when Evie couldn't make it to the shelter recently, and had made a mental note to talk to her about it the next time she came in. But there hadn't been a next time.

She also remembered hearing Evie talking to one of the women living at the shelter about coping with abuse. Her words reflected the advice they were all told to give, but there was a confidence in the way Evie spoke that had intrigued Harriet. Maybe she had been speaking from personal experience, but she had seemed so calm – so evenly balanced. If she had been a victim, how had Harriet missed it, knowing that it was almost always the least likely ones?

She needed to stop all of this second-guessing. She would find out the truth soon enough.

The hospital corridors seemed much longer at night, without the bustle of patients, visitors and staff. There was nobody about to ask where to find her client but she knew she was in the right place when she saw a policeman sitting outside the door to a private room.

'Evie Clarke?' she asked.

'Well, not personally,' he said with a grin.

Harriet gave him a withering glance. 'I'm her lawyer – Harriet James. I'd like to see my client.'

Flushing slightly at his misplaced sense of humour, the policeman pulled out his radio to call through to seek permission to let her enter and she showed him her driving licence to confirm her identity. With a sideways nod of his head, he indicated that Harriet could enter the room, but the door remained open. He would be able to hear every word.

Evie looked so insubstantial in the narrow hospital bed. Her face was unmarked, but where her arms rested on the surface of the bed Harriet could see several strips of gauze, some with signs that blood had oozed through. She looked at Evie's pale face, blotchy from crying. Walking over to the visitor's chair, she sat down.

'Evie, I'm glad you called me. I don't know what's happened, or why, but I'm going to do whatever I can to help you.'

Evie shook her head slowly from side to side, and when she spoke her voice was flat. 'I'm not sure you or anyone can help me, but thank you for coming.'

Harriet had seen this type of detachment from reality before, and knew it was a reaction to the events of the past few hours.

'I need to know what you've said to the police, but bear in mind that our conversation could well be being monitored.' She indicated towards the door with her head.

'I haven't said anything. Only that I killed him,' Evie said quietly. 'There was no point denying it. We were the only two people in the house, apart from Lulu, and Mark was dead. They've taken swabs from just about everywhere, photographed me, removed what I was wearing – which wasn't much.'

'I understand why you told them you killed him, but please don't say anything else to them unless I'm with you. They won't question you while you're in here, so let's do this by the book.'

'What's there to say?' Evie frowned. 'I killed him. Does it matter why?'

Harriet glanced at the open door and leaned closer to Evie, her voice low.

'Don't say that again. Until I have the facts and we've considered the options, say nothing. It's not necessarily as clear-cut as you think. I'm going to have to understand everything that happened tonight, and you need to tell me about your relationship with Mark – but we should leave it until you're out of here.'

Evie held up her bandaged arms. 'He was hurting me, Harriet. He had a knife. He was cutting me. I had to stop him.'

Evie didn't say anything more but it was enough. They should save the detail for the privacy of an interview room, but if she had killed Mark in self-defence and Harriet could make the police see that, Evie would walk free. Harriet was going to do everything she could to protect this woman from whatever charges were thrown at her.

'Had he hurt you before?' she asked, keeping her voice low.

Evie looked down at her hands, her fingers twisting and turning. She shrugged, and that said it all.

'You worked at the refuge, Evie, surrounded by women who have suffered in the same way. You could have come to us at any time, with Lulu too. We could have looked after you. Why did you stay with him?'

Evie looked up and Harriet saw the pain in her eyes.

'You know how it is. Nobody wants to admit they've allowed themselves to be abused. I was ashamed, and like a fool I thought it would stop. Mark was okay for most of the time, you see. I knew he was confused, conflicted, and he found life difficult. But he was a great dad and Lulu adores him.' Her voice dropped to little more than a whisper. 'Adored him.'

The use of the past tense seemed to break through Evie's reserve and her eyes filled with tears. She blinked them away and bit her top lip as if trying to pull herself together. Harriet couldn't imagine the trauma of living with a man who one minute was a loving father and the next a violent brute.

'I thought I could hang on until Lulu was older,' Evie said. 'I was sure he wouldn't hurt me in case she saw him. I tried to leave, but he said if I did he'd kill himself, and I didn't want that – although maybe it would have been a better outcome than this. Another time he said he would find me wherever I went and take Lulu somewhere I couldn't trace him. He had so much money, I'm sure it would have been easy.'

Harriet reached for Evie's hand and gave it a quick squeeze, looking into her eyes and expecting to see pain, guilt or possibly relief. What she saw, though, was confusion.

'I shouldn't have killed him, Harriet. I should have stopped it before it got that far.'

'What do you mean?' Harriet asked, her voice dropping to a whisper.

Evie closed her eyes and took a deep breath. 'It doesn't matter. I'm not making any sense to myself, let alone to you.'

'We both know it's not easy to make someone stop hurting you. You can't blame yourself for what he did.'

Evie shook her head. 'It only happened when he had to go away. It was as if something gripped him and took hold on the night before he left. I don't know if it's because of what happened to his wife when he was away.'

Harriet knew nothing about any wife. 'What *did* happen to her?'

'She fell downstairs and broke her neck.'

Harriet felt an icy trickle down her spine.

'Where was Mark?'

Evie's eyes met Harriet's. There was an intensity in her expression that Harriet couldn't read.

'He left shortly before she died. I know what you're thinking, but they investigated it thoroughly. Mia – his wife – spoke to

131

someone on the phone after Mark left the house. So it couldn't have been anything to do with him.'

'Who did she speak to?' Harriet asked.

'Cleo – Mark's sister.'

23

Stephanie pressed her finger briefly on Cleo North's doorbell. Gus had told her that Cleo already knew of her brother's death, but in Stephanie's new role as acting Detective Sergeant he wanted her to talk to Cleo to find out what she could about Mark North's relationship with Evie.

The door was answered by one of the two officers initially sent to give Cleo the bad news and Stephanie followed him through to the sitting room. She remembered Mark's sister from the inquest into the death of his wife three and a half years earlier, but the woman curled up on the sofa in a vibrant blue silk dressing gown bore little resemblance to the woman she had met then. Her hair had been longer and golden blonde, but her reaction to the death of Mia had been nothing compared to the anguish she was suffering now. The colour had leached from her skin – even from her lips – and her eyes were black with shock.

'Miss North, I'm Sergeant Stephanie King. Can I say how sorry I am for your loss and apologise for disturbing you at this time.'

Cleo glanced up, but there was no sign that she recognised Stephanie, which was a probably a good thing.

'Where's Lulu?' she asked, her eyes darting to the doorway as if the child was about to be brought into the room.

'We'll be bringing her to you as soon as we've had a brief conversation, if that's okay. Just so that you understand the process, Miss Clarke has said she is happy for Lulu to be placed in your care, but there will have to be an emergency case conference and Social Services will want to ensure that the child's welfare is taken care of.'

Cleo nodded slowly as though she had heard, but Stephanie could see she wasn't really taking anything in.

'Do you mind if I ask you about your brother's relationship with Miss Clarke?' she said.

Cleo's head snapped towards Stephanie at the mention of her brother.

'How did she kill him?'

She blurted out the question as if it had been building inside her since the moment she heard the terrible news, and there was little point in Stephanie trying to hide the truth. It would all come out sooner or later, but she wanted to avoid the worst of it until Cleo had become more used to the idea that her brother was dead.

'We won't know exactly what happened until we have the pathologist's report. But it would seem that he lost a great deal of blood after an incident with a knife. That's all we know right now.'

Stephanie thought it would have been impossible for Cleo to lose any more colour, but she was wrong. Her face had turned almost grey and Stephanie quickly moved away from the detail of his death.

'What can you tell me about your brother, Miss North?'

Cleo pulled her knees closer to her chest and sank her chin onto them.

'He was a kind, sensitive, thoughtful man,' she said, staring at nothing. 'But he had shit taste in women.'

'You don't like Evie Clarke, then?'

Cleo looked up sharply, a look of incredulity in her wide grey eyes.

'What do you think? She killed my brother – so no. I don't like her. I fucking *hate* her!' She took a breath and seemed to calm down a little. 'It was different to start with – it seemed she might be good for him. But something changed and I could tell she wanted me to be sidelined – she wanted me out of his life.'

Stephanie stayed quiet, giving Cleo time.

'Mark and I have always been close, and she resented it.' Her voice sounded as if her thoughts were far away, in a different time, a different place. But she snapped back to the present with a rush of words, tumbling over each other. 'Why did she kill him? *Why?* What reason could she possibly have?'

'We don't know the answer to that. We can't question her while she's in hospital, but when she's been discharged she'll go straight to the police station and we'll begin the process. As she's admitted to killing him, I expect she will be charged and go before the magistrates at the first possible opportunity.'

'And then she'll be locked up?'

'That's not for me to say. I imagine she will be remanded in custody, pending a trial. But it depends on the circumstances. Because of the child, the solicitor may apply for bail.'

'*What?* She's a killer! Surely they won't let her out? Surely she can't be trusted to walk the streets, let alone look after a child?'

'I'm sorry, Miss North, but until we know more I can't say how it will go.'

Stephanie knew she had to calm the situation down, but at the same time there were questions she needed to ask.

'Can you think of any reason why she would want to kill him – had they argued? Did they have a particularly volatile relationship?'

Cleo stared into the distance again, lost in thought. The other two officers had sat quietly throughout this conversation until now, but the young detective sat forward as if about to speak. Stephanie shook her head briefly to indicate he should say nothing.

'Whether I thought she was right for him or not, Mark loved Evie. Each time he had to go away – for work reasons, that's all – he told me he'd left her with something to remember him by. A small gift, I imagine. But Evie always engineered some situation that would make him feel guilty about the fact that he'd gone – some incident that might not have happened had he been there. She knew he had a fear of leaving her because of what happened to his wife, and she played on it. She was so manipulative. Mark wanted to marry her, the bloody fool – even though I warned him against it – but she always said no. That never made sense to me, although I was glad of it. His first marriage hadn't turned out too well as far as I could see, and I didn't want him to make another mistake.'

'You mean Mia?'

Cleo narrowed her eyes and looked at Stephanie. 'You remember that, do you?'

'Yes, I'm afraid so.'

There was an expression on Cleo's face that Stephanie couldn't read, but before she had a chance to ask any more questions, Cleo swung her legs to the floor and sat forward.

'Enough,' she said, her voice breaking. 'I just need Lulu here with me where she belongs, then I want us to be left alone.'

Fresh tears started to fall silently down her cheeks.

Stephanie felt a slight shiver down her spine at the words 'where she belongs' and wondered how Cleo would take it if Evie Clarke was granted bail.

She stood up to leave, knowing that she needed to unpick this conversation. She wasn't going to get any more out of the distraught woman now, but there was something in Cleo's words that Stephanie felt certain would provide a clue to what had really happened that night.

24

Harriet arrived early at the police station. She knew Evie was being discharged from hospital and that the police would bring her straight here. She wanted time alone with her before the formal interview so she could understand exactly what had happened, and why.

The sound of heavy footsteps broke through her thoughts and she turned to see the broad figure of DI Angus Brodie marching towards her down the corridor.

'Harriet,' he said with a curt nod.

She was probably one of the few women who hadn't succumbed to his charms, and he knew it.

'Angus,' she responded.

'Sergeant Stephanie King, who's been attached to CID for this case, has gone with one of the uniforms to collect Miss Clarke from the hospital. At a guess, you'll want some time alone with your client before the interview starts. She's admitted to killing him, though, so it should be quite straightforward.'

'I don't know why you're assuming that. I saw what could be defence wounds on her arms, so with any luck you won't charge her and I'll have her out of here today.'

Angus Brodie lifted his eyebrows and smiled. 'I'm not going to discuss this with you now. We need to interview her and then we'll inform the CPS of our recommendation. And before you ask, we'll resist bail,' he said, thrusting his hands into his trouser pockets as he spoke – a defiant gesture if ever she saw one.

'You're not going to win that one. She has an eleven-month-old baby!'

'Harriet, she killed him. She's not denying it. She could go to prison for life, and that's one hell of an incentive to try to influence witnesses or do a runner. Anyway, who's to say she won't go out and kill some other poor bugger? Do you want that responsibility?'

Harriet tutted at his posturing. He was trying to wind her up, but she wasn't going to let him. For now she had no intention of showing her hand. She needed to talk to Evie and then they would make a decision.

'Let me take you to an interview room,' Brodie said, holding out his arm to guide her. 'But once the custody officer has signed her in, the clock's ticking.'

Harriet hated police interview rooms with their melamine-topped tables, uncomfortable chairs and featureless walls. There always seemed to be an underlying odour of fear-induced sweat, and with no opening windows it felt as if the accumulated breath of hundreds of criminals still lingered in the walls.

Despite the surroundings, she loved her job. As soon as Evie arrived, everything other than the client and the case would become no more than a blurred background, but it was the waiting she couldn't stand and she had now been sitting here for half an hour. She tapped her fingernails in a drumbeat on the table and was beginning to wonder what the hold-up was, but as soon as Evie walked into the room Harriet could see she wasn't well.

'Evie – come and sit down,' she said, pulling out a chair. 'Have they discharged you too soon? You're terribly pale.'

'I was sick when I got here. But I'm okay now.'

'Are you sure? Can I get you some water?'

'No thanks, I've just had some. I think it's only now that the reality of what I've done has hit me. It was the handcuffs. Whenever I've seen criminals cuffed on the television I've always thought how degrading it must be, but nothing prepared me for the intensity of the shame.'

Evie wasn't the first person to feel like this, but Harriet was a little surprised at the strength of her reaction. She considered her client to be a self-possessed young woman, although based on her work at the shelter she suspected that beneath her smile there was a well-disguised degree of sensitivity. Several of the residents had commented that Evie was a good listener. She would sit with them for hours as they described the injuries – both physical and mental – they had suffered. Now it was Harriet's turn to listen.

'I need to understand in detail what happened last night, Evie. I know it will be painful for you, but you have to tell me everything. It's only then that we can decide how best to go forward.'

Evie raised her eyes. 'You know what happened. I killed him. I still can't believe I did it.' She lifted her hands to her cheeks and stared at Harriet in horror. 'I sliced into his neck with a boning knife, and then I lay in bed holding him close to me as he died.'

Evie put her arms down on the desk and rested her head there, her shoulders shaking with sobs. 'I'm sorry, Mark,' she whispered. 'You didn't deserve this.'

Harriet had trained herself to never show a reaction to anything her clients said, but the combination of the brutality of the death and the deep sense of intimacy in Mark's final moments was hard to understand.

'Evie, I'm sorry to push you when you are so upset, but I noticed last night that you had some wounds to your arms and chest,' she said, getting back to practicalities. 'Did Mark attack you first?'

Evie sat up and nodded, but her bloodshot eyes had glazed over and Harriet guessed she was reliving the moment, wondering if she'd had any other choice.

'Did you think he was going to kill you?' she asked.

Evie shook her head. 'I don't know what I thought. I was terrified. He'd never used a knife on me before and I had no idea how far he would go.'

'You told me at the hospital that there was a pattern to his abuse – that it always happened before he went away.'

'It was almost like he was claiming me as his own. He was scared of losing me, you see.'

Harriet had never understood the mindset of an abuser, and Mark North was no exception. The complexities of his personality weren't going to help much in the next twenty-four hours and all she cared about was getting the best outcome for her client. She needed to use her time with Evie wisely so she steered the conversation back to the events of the previous night.

'Where did you get the knife?' she asked. 'Did Mark bring it into the bedroom with the sole intention of hurting you?'

'No. I took it from the knife block in the kitchen. It was to open a present I'd bought for him, but once he had the knife in his hand the present was no longer the most important thing on his mind. I could see it in his eyes. That's when he started to cut me.'

Evie gently rubbed the dressings covering her arms and fell quiet again.

Harriet needed to think. This was not as straightforward as she had hoped, but Evie was intelligent and would perform well in court, if it came to that. It was a good case for Harriet and, she hoped, for abused women in general.

She could imagine Angus Brodie pacing up and down the hallway, getting increasingly frustrated at the delay. His team would be ready, prepared, their interview strategy in place, and as he had said, the clock was ticking. She had to decide what their defence was going to be, and for that, she needed Evie to give her more.

'How did you get hold of the knife? Did you fight him for it?'

Evie bowed her head, as if ashamed. Her voice was so low that Harriet struggled to catch what she was saying.

'He put it down on the bedside table.'

'He'd stopped cutting you? He wasn't threatening you any longer?'

'He wanted to make love to me. The cutting, the blood, had turned him on and that's when I lost it. As he lay on top of me it was as if I had no control over my own actions. I was terrified of what he might do to me next, and I could see myself picking up the knife – almost as if I was watching myself from above – and I couldn't stop it. The pain of the cuts on my arms and chest wiped all conscious thought from my mind. I couldn't go through any more.'

Evie started to sob quietly, and Harriet's heart sank. She had already suspected that Evie's injuries weren't defence wounds. They weren't deep and none of them had required stitching. She was certain that Brodie wasn't going to accept them either. These cuts were part of Mark North's ritualistic game – which didn't make it better, but did mean it wasn't a clear-cut case of self-defence. If Evie had fought him for the knife – a fight which it was difficult to imagine her winning – she would probably have had to grab the blade.

'I need you to listen carefully,' Harriet said, 'because this is critical to how we proceed. We have options, but it all comes down to what we can prove and what we can't. You're going to have to explain to the police what happened last night. You can say "No comment" but that's not going to go down well with a jury when it goes to court and your interview transcript is read out. If we plead self-defence and the police believe we have the evidence to support that claim, the CPS are unlikely to take it further.'

Evie narrowed her eyes as if she didn't understand what Harriet was saying.

'I know you believe you were defending yourself,' Harriet

continued, 'but the CPS will assess whether the use of force was necessary at that point, and whether it was excessive. They could argue that you were no longer in danger as Mark had put the knife down. Because of that I suspect that if we plead self-defence we might lose. We won't know for sure until all the forensic evidence is in, but I'm basing this on what you've told me.'

Harriet wondered whether she was making the right decision, but if a plea of self-defence failed there was no way back.

'I need you to think very carefully about this,' she said. 'It's clear that Mark's death wasn't an accident and that means, I'm afraid, that you need to prepare yourself for the fact that the police are going to want to charge you with murder.'

Harriet had asked for some water for Evie, who had taken the threat of the murder charge better than she had expected. Maybe she hadn't fully absorbed the reality of the situation and needed time to take it in. But that was a luxury Harriet didn't think they could afford.

'There's another option,' she said, her voice fast, urgent. She needed Evie to understand how important this was. 'We can plead loss of control. It's not as clear-cut, but based on everything you've told me I think it might be our best bet. It's a partial defence against a charge of murder, and if we can prove it, you will be guilty of voluntary manslaughter – which gives the judge far more scope in sentencing.'

She was about to launch into a further explanation of her plan when Evie finally spoke.

'I didn't plan it, you know,' she said. 'That will count for something, won't it?'

Harriet could offer few words of comfort, but she did her best to reassure her client.

'Of course, although the fact that you took the knife into the bedroom is undoubtedly going to be something we'll need to deal with.'

Evie frowned.

'Why?' she asked. 'I could have lied and said Mark had brought it with him. They would have no way of proving otherwise. Isn't my honesty a point in my favour?'

'They may well have been able to prove it, so you did the right thing. They would have checked for Mark's prints on the knife block, for example. They have all manner of forensic tools they can use, so it's far better that you told the truth. If you were caught in a lie as big as that, there would be nothing we could do. The important thing is that you killed Mark because you had a genuine fear of serious violence. You're going to have to hold it together when the police question you. The next few hours are going to be tough, and I know it seems harsh given everything you've been living with, but it's important that you don't suggest for one minute that you killed Mark as an act of revenge for all he had done to you. That would totally negate the loss of control defence. I'll be there, and I'll guide you, so you need to trust me.'

Evie nodded, but Harriet couldn't tell whether she had understood or not.

'I'll do everything possible to make sure you're not held in custody,' she said, 'and I'll suggest they release you on bail while they prepare their case. We might have a fight on our hands, but I'll do my best. I also need to warn you that, if we're

145

successful, Social Services are unlikely to allow you to have sole care of your little girl during the period of your bail for fear that you might lose control again.'

Evie gave a short laugh. 'As if I'd hurt Lulu.'

'I know, but I'm just telling you how it is.'

'It doesn't matter.' Evie leaned forward across the table. 'I don't want bail.'

Harriet stared at her, wondering if the shock of all that had happened had made her irrational. 'What do you mean? If you don't get bail, you'll be locked up in a remand centre for weeks, months, until a trial date is set.'

'I don't want bail.'

'Why on earth not?'

'Because of the impact on Lulu. I won't be able to function – the stress of what I've done and what's to come is bound to influence my behaviour, and you've already said I might not be given sole care of her. Lulu needs love and security. She's better with Cleo.'

For a moment Evie paused, as if uncertain, but when she spoke she once more seemed resolute.

'It's what I want.'

'Do you trust Cleo?' Harriet asked.

'With my child? Absolutely.' Evie paused. 'With anything else, not at all.'

25

Stephanie watched the monitor which was linked to the inter-view room. Evie Clarke was sitting opposite the two detectives tasked with interrogating her and she looked pale, her eyes lowered slightly, as if to avoid meeting the gaze of anyone else in the room. Next to her was her lawyer, Harriet James, whom Stephanie had heard of but had never met. She carried herself with confidence and a sense of cool efficiency, her back straight and her head tilted slightly to one side, as if she was prepared to listen to what the detectives said but was ready to rebuff any inappropriate questions.

The first detective, Nick Grieves, went through the formal-ities of introducing everyone for the purposes of the tape, and began his questioning. There was a stillness about Evie that was hard to correlate with the emotional woman of the night before, and Stephanie wondered at the thoughts and feelings that must have bombarded her overnight as she came to terms with what she had done.

Stephanie was unable to look at Gus as they sat side by side in the viewing room watching the interview unfold, but she sensed the tension in his body. He would be totally focused on every word, every nuance, but she was finding it difficult to be in such a confined space with him, feeling the warmth of his body, his thigh so close to hers.

She was glad not to be the one tasked with interviewing Evie, though – forcing her to reveal the gruesome details of all that had happened – but as she listened to the woman's account of her life with Mark North she felt a deep sympathy for her. Her voice was low and even but she barely hesitated before giving her answers.

'Tell me about the knife, Evie. How did it get to be in the bedroom?' the detective asked.

Harriet moved as if she was going to offer her advice, but Evie raised her hand slightly to signal her lawyer to say nothing. Harriet looked slightly taken aback, but remained silent.

'I brought the knife into the bedroom.'

'You've told us throughout this interview that Mark North seemed to enjoy hurting you. What was your intention in bringing a knife into the bedroom, knowing that?'

Evie's eyes had glazed over, as if she was reliving every moment of that evening.

'It was a stupid thing to do. I realise that now. I had bought Mark a present – a telescope – and he needed something to open it with. I went to get scissors, but the lights were out so I grabbed a knife from the block in the kitchen. I was so excited. Mark seemed different, and I thought the present had done the trick – broken the pattern, made this unlike any of the other nights before he went away. He'd never cut me before, you see, so I didn't think about the risk until I saw the look in his eye when I gave him the knife.' She spoke quietly, shaking her head as if in despair at her own actions.

'Evie, did you – even for a second – think of the knife as a weapon?' Nick asked.

'Not at first. Not until I saw the way he was looking at me. Then I knew, of course. But it was too late.'

Evie seemed to collapse a little in her chair, twisting her hair round her finger and tucking it behind her right ear.

'I think we need a break,' Harriet said, giving Nick the full force of her stern expression.

Evie's hand shot out to touch Harriet on her forearm.

'No, it's okay, Harriet. Let's get it over with.'

The detective paused for a moment as Evie took a sip of water. She closed her eyes briefly.

'I didn't mean a weapon for Mark,' the detective said. 'I meant a weapon for you.'

Evie opened her eyes wide and stared at him, her brow furrowed. 'Of course not.'

'Bollocks,' Gus muttered under his breath, leaning towards the video screen, his forearms resting on his thighs. 'I don't believe her, Steph.'

Stephanie said nothing and watched as the detective continued his questioning. She couldn't help comparing Evie's quiet composure with Cleo's raw emotion of the night before.

'Why did you set the scene so carefully? The attending officer said the room was full of candles – was it a seduction scene?' Nick asked.

'I told you. I wanted to break the pattern. Mark liked the room to be dark. I don't think he wanted to see my face when he was hurting me. I thought the candles might distract him – maybe they would give just enough light to stop him. It would

149

be harder to blow out a dozen candles than switch off a light, and I always felt that the darkness allowed him to imagine it was someone else he was hurting. Mia maybe.'

Stephanie felt a pulse of excitement. She had always been uncomfortable with Mia North's death. Had Mark been abusing her too?

'Why would he want to imagine he was hurting Mia?' the detective asked, earning himself a grunt of reproach from Gus, who of course he could neither see nor hear.

'Mark was carrying a weight of guilt around with him about Mia's death. I think he felt responsible in some way, as if he could have prevented it. But he blamed her too. Maybe he wanted to punish her for leaving him – I don't know. I've never understood how his mind works – does anyone understand an abuser?'

'Move on, move on,' Gus was whispering urgently. Stephanie tutted and he swivelled towards her. 'What?'

'Don't we need to understand if this was a pattern?' she said.

'Mark North's not the one on trial here. Neither he nor his wife are alive to tell us what happened in their marriage, so we need to focus on his death, not on something we can only make suppositions about.'

Gus turned back, and Stephanie hated to admit that he might be right. Her attention switched back to the interview.

'Let me get this straight,' the detective said. 'You wanted to change the atmosphere by lighting the candles. Very conveniently the lights went out. Are you telling me you had nothing to do with that?'

Evie stared back at him without flinching. 'Of course I didn't.

When the lights were on I was safe. When they were off I was in danger. Maybe Mark did something to the switch so it would be dark from the start. It was only because I'd put the candles in there that I was safe – or I thought I was.'

'So talk us through what happened with the knife.'

Evie sat up, leaning slightly forwards, a trace of irritation rising momentarily to the surface. 'I told you. I handed him the knife to open his present.'

'And what happened then?'

'He said he would open it later and asked me to get undressed, ready for bed. That's when I started to get scared, but I thought I could distract him. He got into bed next to me and I reached for him, but the knife proved too much of a temptation. For the first time he didn't seem to care that it wasn't fully dark.'

Evie lifted her bandaged forearms as if providing evidence.

'He laid me down on the bed and held both my wrists above my head with one of his hands. He got the knife and started to cut into my arms and my chest. I was crying, and he kept saying that he wanted to give me something to remember him by. Then he started to make love to me and he put the knife down on the bedside table. The hairs on his chest were rubbing against my open wounds and it was excruciating. I flung my arm out to the side as I screamed and in the candlelight I could see the lust in his eyes, the thrill of my pain. My hand hit the knife where it lay, and I picked it up, thinking I could cut him too – to see how he liked it. And then I don't know what happened. I don't remember – I just remember the agony of his sweat dripping into my open cuts, and I lost it. I didn't want to kill him. I only wanted to stop him, but I couldn't help myself

151

– it was all too much and I was certain that he was going to cut me again and again, now that he had a taste for it.'

After Evie's description of the last moments of Mark North's life, they had all agreed that a break was a good idea, and Evie didn't object this time.

Gus and Stephanie had escaped to grab a much needed cup of coffee, and as he stirred his drink Gus stared at the swirling liquid.

'I've seen so many sad cases of abuse over the years, yet I've never had a real answer to one question. What makes a woman stay with a man who is hurting her so badly?'

'I don't know,' Stephanie replied. 'People hurt each other in many different ways and I sometimes wonder if there isn't a hint of the masochist in all of us.'

'That's a bit cynical, even for a police officer,' Gus responded with a short laugh.

She hadn't meant it to be a dig at him, or at least not consciously.

'There's something I've been wanting to say to you since last night,' Gus said after a brief pause. He still wasn't looking at her. 'Actually, I've been wanting to say it for a long time, but given that you wouldn't speak to me . . . So I'll say it now, when you can't run away. I behaved like an arse, and I'm sorry I hurt you.'

'You didn't,' Stephanie replied. 'You disappointed me.'

'Whatever you say, Steph, but you need to let me apologise. We've got to work together, and I think we should clear the air.'

Stephanie felt her cheeks grow hot. She couldn't afford to let him get close again.

'Leave it, Gus.' She could hear the harsh tone of her own voice. 'We said everything that needed to be said months ago. Concentrate on Evie Clarke and Mark North.'

'Jesus, you're stubborn,' he said.

'And you're an obnoxious prick sometimes, Angus Brodie, but this is my chance at getting into CID, and I'm not going to screw it up because I've had the misfortune to be assigned to your team.'

He lifted his head to look at her and nodded briefly.

'Understood,' he said. 'I'm not going to make things difficult. You're an asset to the team, and I want you to do well.'

For a moment, neither of them spoke.

'What line are they going to be taking when they resume the interview?' Stephanie asked, and heard Gus chuckle briefly at her attempt to divert the conversation away from anything personal.

'They're going to push her on why she killed him, what other options she had, try to determine if it was revenge. We need to cover every angle before we charge her, but I've no doubt at all that we will do.'

'You don't think it was self-defence?'

Gus tutted. 'Of course it wasn't self-defence. She didn't wrestle the knife off him, we know that. Whether or not we believe the terrible stories of what was going on in that house, the fact is that she waited until he was distracted – making love to her, no less. According to the law, that makes it murder, Steph.'

26

'You're doing fine, Evie,' Harriet said. 'They're concentrating the questioning on last night, which makes sense, but they're going to want to know the background too. We should use this break sensibly – I need you to tell me how it all started. Has he always hurt you, because if he has, they'll want to understand why you ever moved in with him?'

Evie got that far-away look in her eyes again, as if she could see a clear vision of every detail of the events that had brought her here.

'Mark didn't start hurting me until after Lulu was born. He wouldn't have done anything when I was pregnant, but by the time it started I knew something wasn't right. I'd felt it brewing for days. He'd been looking at me and smiling, but there was a sense of madness in his eyes that I'd never seen before. I thought it was something to do with his work – an obsession with his latest project.'

Evie looked down and Harriet gave her a moment, but they couldn't afford to waste much time. 'What happened?'

'We were in the kitchen. I'd just put Lulu to bed and I'd gone to make a cup of tea. It was dark outside. I remember it as if it was yesterday. You haven't seen our home, but there's a vast window that looks out over the sea. It was one of those dramatic winter evenings when we could hear the waves crashing onto the rocks below, but we couldn't see much apart from thick rivers of rain running down the windows. I reached out to switch on the light, but Mark stopped me. "Don't," he said. "I love looking out on nights like this." I knew what he meant – if I'd switched the lights on, all we would have seen was the reflection of ourselves in the glass.'

Evie paused and looked down at her bandaged arms, rubbing the surface again. Harriet remained silent, knowing she was working up the energy to carry on with what had to be a painful story.

'I walked over to the kettle and switched it on. Mark was leaning against the worktop, watching me. I put tea bags in both mugs and the kettle boiled. I reached for it. "I'll do that," he said. "Give me your hand." I didn't know what he meant, but I held out my right hand to him. He clutched it in his left hand, stroking the surface of my skin with his thumb. I thought he was going to pull me towards him to give me a kiss, but he yanked my arm across the top of the sink and held it fast. He looked at me – his eyes were burning. Then he picked up the kettle and tipped boiling water over my arm.'

As Evie continued to list her injuries and the way they had been inflicted, nothing she said came as a shock to Harriet. She had heard it all, and worse, too many times. But there was something in the way Evie told the tale that chilled Harriet. It was as if she was talking about someone else, separating herself from the events so that they would no longer hurt so much.

'I think that's it,' she said, turning her blank gaze to Harriet. 'I've told you everything. Is it enough?'

'For me, Evie, any one of those events would be enough. We've got to go back in now, but as I said, you're doing fine. You really are.'

As Evie and Harriet walked briskly back into the interview room, Stephanie looked at the lawyer's face, and while Harriet was undoubtedly an expert at hiding her feelings, Stephanie was sure there was a touch more anxiety in her expression. Although previously her concern for her client had seemed real in a professional sense, there was something in the lawyer's demeanour that hadn't been there before. She seemed more attentive, and Stephanie wondered what had been said during the break.

The interview restarted slowly, going back to the beginning of Evie and Mark's relationship.

'When I first met Mark, he was a wreck – there's no other word for it. I don't think he cared about himself at all. He cleaned up his act a bit because Cleo told him to. But the closer Mark and I got, the more Cleo didn't like it. And when I became pregnant she was horrified.'

'Was the pregnancy planned?'

Stephanie felt her body tense and she kept her eyes firmly on the notepad in front of her. She could feel Gus watching her but she wasn't going to give in to the temptation to return his glance.

'Oh no. I had never thought for a moment that we would have a child together – it took a while for me to believe it was happening, but it was a total accident, although I'm not sure his sister believed that.'

'How did Mark react to the fact that you were pregnant?'

Evie half smiled. 'He seemed genuinely surprised – as if he hadn't believed he was capable of making a baby.' The smile changed to a frown. 'And then he went into denial. It couldn't be his baby, or maybe I had done it on purpose. He even asked me if I would have an abortion.'

'And what was your reaction to that?'

'I told him I was perfectly capable of bringing up a child on my own, without any man in my life. It was his loss. He came round eventually and apologised, saying it had just been such a surprise. He started to get excited and begged me to move in with him.'

'What happened then?'

'I said it was too soon to make that kind of commitment. Before I became pregnant, Mark had never shown any interest in us living together. He wanted me to stay over whenever it suited him, but I had always refused, and the last thing I wanted was for a man to be with me just because it was the honourable thing to do. He had to *want* to live with me, with or without a baby. It took him six months to persuade me.'

Stephanie tuned out. Images of the day she told Gus she was pregnant and his look of disbelief flashed in front of her eyes. The pregnancy had been an accident, but this was their *child* – created out of what she had believed to be love – and in her view his reaction had told a different story.

Sounds of quiet sobbing broke through Stephanie's memories and her eyes flicked back to the screen. Evie's head was bent and her shoulders were shaking, her words muffled and difficult to catch.

'I thought I'd given it enough time. I was sure that if there was any evil in Mark it would have come to light by then. I know there were questions over his wife's death, and there was no doubt that Mark had had problems with depression, but I loved him. I thought it was all going to be so perfect. How is it that women get that wrong so often?'

Evie wiped away her tears with the heel of her hand and raised her red-rimmed eyes to the camera.

'I was a fool. I should have known better.'

27

By the end of the day Evie's energy appeared to be fading. Gus seemed happy with the way things were going, but Stephanie was slightly uncomfortable with his conviction from the outset that Evie Clarke should be charged with murder, not least because Evie's solicitor, Harriet James, seemed equally confident that Gus was wrong. Her straight back and slightly raised chin spoke of a quiet assurance, and there was never a flicker of doubt in her gaze, no matter what the detectives asked. She had taken issue with them more than once when there was the merest hint of an assumption of guilt in one of their questions. Harriet was definitely someone Stephanie would want on her side if she was ever in trouble.

The lawyer was so slim that she looked as if she would snap in two, but it was clear she was a formidable lady. Although young for someone with such a powerful reputation, she gave the impression that nothing would faze her. There was something almost pristine about her, as if it would be impossible for her to look untidy. Her dark hair was neatly tied back, and her huge brown eyes glinted with fierce determination, the pupils slightly dilated as if she was fired with adrenaline. Next to

Harriet, Evie had looked drawn, her highlighted blonde hair having a faint yellow glow in the interview room lights, which did nothing to improve the pallor of her skin.

Stephanie ruffled her own hair with both hands. She had been on nights when she and Jason were called to Mark North's house, and had come straight into the incident room after leaving Cleo's home in the early hours of the morning. She had been on the go for more than twenty hours and knew that her short wavy bob would by now appear lank and untidy. She didn't have any makeup with her either. She felt like a pale shadow next to Harriet James, whose hair was darker, cleaner, tidier, and whose lipstick never seemed to dull throughout the hours of the interview.

'You look fine, Steph. Stop messing with your hair.'

She hadn't heard Gus approach, and she couldn't miss the amusement in his eyes. For a big man, he could move quietly when he wanted to. She hadn't got used to seeing him with a beard, and wondered how it would feel if he kissed her. She closed her eyes for a second, furious with herself for being so weak.

'I've been going through the phone records,' she said. 'Evie seemed to speak most often to a woman called Aminah Basra, and occasionally to Cleo North, but most of those calls were incoming. She called the shelter where she helped out a few times, but not often. There's one number that's interesting though. It seems she phoned the Samaritans on more than one occasion.'

Gus pulled out a chair on the opposite side of the desk and sat down.

160

'We'd better get a court order sorted so that we can hear what she had to say to them. Maybe we'll get lucky and find out she told them she was going to kill him.'

Stephanie grunted. 'I sincerely doubt that. I think you'll find people generally phone the Samaritans when they're thinking of killing *themselves* rather than someone else.'

'Do you think charging her with murder is the wrong call, Steph?' he asked, his face suddenly serious.

That was a difficult question. Evie hadn't claimed self-defence, which was just as well as there was little or no evidence to support that, but that didn't mean her actions had been premeditated.

'I'm a bit concerned that you seem to have a closed mind – that you've been determined from the outset to charge her with murder. I can't help feeling for her, given everything she'd been putting up with. But on the other hand it wasn't an accident. Did I hear Harriet tell you that she's unlikely to apply for bail when you've finally charged her? What about Lulu? It seems weird that Evie doesn't want to do everything she can to get home to her baby.'

Gus sat back and stretched his long legs out in front of him. 'I agree. I can't read Evie Clarke at all, but somehow I find it hard to imagine her letting North hold her down while he cut her. She seems more the type to have kicked him in the bollocks, although I accept it's rarely that simple.'

'She was probably terrified that if she fought back, he'd hurt her more. I would be, if I knew I was living with a sadist.'

'I get that, and I know that for a lot of women the only answer seems to be to grin and bear it, poor buggers. But Evie doesn't strike me as one of them. Look at the way she stopped Harriet intervening on her behalf a couple of times during the interview. Even when she's hit rock bottom – which must be how she feels right now – she's not a pushover, that's all I'm saying.'

'I just feel there's more to it than that. I was there, remember, and Evie was holding Mark close, her arms round him. She didn't seem to feel a scrap of malice towards him.'

Gus sighed and rubbed the back of his neck. They were both silent, lost in their own thoughts, for a few moments.

'I meant to ask – what did you make of the sister?' he said, changing the subject.

'She doesn't like Evie, that's for sure. I get the distinct impression that she adored her brother and thought that no woman was good enough for him. It seems she didn't think much of his wife either. We're going to need to look at the evidence around that case again. The defence will for sure. I'd like to take responsibility for that. Is that okay with you, sir?' she asked.

Gus looked around him. Nobody else was within earshot. 'Steph, you may think that calling me sir is appropriate, but most people around here are perceptive enough to hear the sarcasm dripping from your tongue. Just call me Gus. People will accept that we know each other well enough for that, without knowing the full story.'

Stephanie was ashamed of herself. She didn't want Gus to know he was getting to her.

'Sorry. Gus it is. I promise to behave, and no more acts of insubordination.'

She looked away and shuffled some papers on her desk. She

162

had almost convinced herself recently that, despite thoughts of him popping into her head at inconvenient times, Gus Brodie no longer mattered to her. That was all well and good when she never saw him, but acting as if he was just another senior officer right now was torture.

'Now, about the death of Mia North,' she said, her tone professional. 'There's something bugging me about it – but I'm not sure what it is. I was the first officer on the scene, you know.'

'I know you were, Steph. I haven't forgotten where we were when you told me about it.'

Stephanie couldn't meet his eyes. She picked up her bag and slung it over her shoulder.

'I'll see you in the morning, Gus.'

She couldn't be sure, but she thought she heard a sigh of irritation as she walked towards the stairs.

28

The minute the front door closed behind her, Harriet made for the kitchen and the fridge. She needed a glass of cold, crisp wine and was desperate to sit alone, in silence, in the garden so she could think.

Evie had answered all the questions the detectives had thrown at her. She had been calm throughout, only showing a moment of emotion at the memory of the life she had hoped for, but the police had needed more time. Evie was now in the cells, getting some badly needed rest while they waited for an extension to be granted.

Clutching her glass and a bottle of mineral water, Harriet opened the sliding door to the terrace. It had been a muggy day, but the air felt a bit fresher now. Sinking down onto a sun lounger she diluted the wine a little and leaned back, watching the condensation form on the outside of the glass.

Harriet's main concern following the initial interrogation was that Evie didn't have any evidence to support her claim that Mark had been hurting her, with the exception of the cuts on her arms and upper body on the night of his death. The police had made much of the fact that each time she had been injured she had told those who asked that her wounds were the result of an accident. How were they going to prove otherwise?

People were often too embarrassed to admit that they were being abused by a partner, so her secrecy meant nothing. Harriet had heard the same story so many times.

'You don't want to admit that you've made such a bad choice of partner – that your judgement is so flawed,' one woman had told her. Another said, 'It's because people don't understand why you let it happen – they think it's easy to walk away. They don't get it that you're made to feel it's all your fault, that he *had* to hit you, and every ounce of your self-confidence crumbles to nothing. Then he'll do something especially nice and you begin to kid yourself it's all going to be okay.'

The fact that one in four women from all walks of life suffered abuse at some time in their life – and an increasing number of men – was a thought never far from Harriet's mind. She was annoyed with herself for not recognising the signs in Evie. It was her job to defend women like her but for a moment she questioned whether her fixation on attracting attention to women's causes in general could be blinding her to the needs of the women closest to her.

She thought back to when she first met Evie. She had applied as a volunteer at the shelter and Harriet had agreed to meet her at a local café to explain how the charity operated. Evie had seemed to genuinely care about the plight of the people helped by the charity, and she didn't display any of the classic signs of abuse. She was relaxed, talked about her friends quite openly and Harriet had assessed that she was neither scared of nor isolated from others. She had arrived in a taxi and offered to pay for the coffee, so it was unlikely that she was being controlled financially, and Harriet seemed to remember that Evie received a call from someone – she had assumed her partner – while they were chatting. She hadn't seemed uncomfortable with him, and had asked him if she could call back later. She had even laughed at something he said. But then maybe it hadn't been Mark.

None of it had added up to Evie being an abused woman. Even Evie's call to cancel her shift at the shelter hadn't alerted Harriet. She had known there was something wrong, but it could have been an argument with a friend or a tough day with Lulu. She had made no assumptions, mainly because her initial impression of Evie had given no indication that she and Mark had a troubled relationship.

Harriet had asked about it during the break in the interview.

'It hadn't started then,' Evie said with a shrug. 'It was the trips away that precipitated it. I've always believed it was tied in to the death of his wife. I told you that happened when he was away, didn't I?'

The memory of that conversation struck a chord and Harriet jumped up from the sun lounger and dashed into the house for a notepad and pencil. Top of her list of actions was to look further into the death of Mark North's wife. If Mark had been into causing pain, it was unlikely to be new. There had to be some evidence to prove that he had hurt Mia, even if he hadn't been found to be responsible for her death. It was a starting point, but there was so much else to do.

She leaned back again and took a deep breath, trying to force from her mind the image of Evie lying on a hard bed in a police cell.

The thud of the cell door closing behind me resonates with the thumping of my heart. I shouldn't be here. I should be at home with Lulu, bathing her, singing to her, waiting for her daddy to come and kiss her goodnight.

Instead, I'm in a room with shiny pale green walls and a bench with a dark blue plastic-covered mattress on it. There's a toilet which is barely shielded from the spy hole in the door, and I don't want to use it unless I have to. And that's all there is. I'm told I'll be fed, but I don't want food. It would make me sick.

I walk over to the bed and resist the temptation to bend down and sniff the mattress to see if it's been wiped down since the last occupant. The room smells of disinfectant, so I take that as a good sign and lower myself gingerly onto the surface, hearing a sigh of air escaping through the plastic.

As I stare at the opposite wall I suddenly feel as if I'm not alone. It's as if all the previous occupants are in there with me, screaming in rage, crying in terror, or sitting numbly, wondering about the chain of events that brought them here – just like I am.

I see them pacing the floor, lying next to me on the bed, leaning their heads on folded arms against the wall in their despair. This cell will have seen the innocent as well as the guilty – the real criminals. But I suppose that's how the police think of me now.

I'm a killer.

167

The thought of Mark and how he died makes me gasp. I have to think of something else to stop myself from going over everything in my head – every decision, every step along the way. Did I get it right? Was there another way?

I think about the women I met at the shelter and the stories they told me of the brutality they had suffered. I listened because I wanted to learn from them, but I discovered that there was very little I didn't already know. The average abuser, it seems, is devoid of much in the way of imagination.

How many people will care that I'm here? Aminah, perhaps, but that's it. Lulu is too young to understand, and Cleo will be hoping it's as horrific an experience as possible. Now Mark's gone, there isn't anyone else, nobody to wonder whether I am coping with the police interviews and the persistent analysis of each moment of the past twenty-four hours.

Harriet cares, as I knew she would. If anyone can help me, she can. Right now, it feels as if she's the only person I have on my side. The interrogation today was hard in spite of her efforts because it forced me to question every action, but in other ways it was easy because I knew all the answers. I didn't have to make anything up. There's more to come tomorrow, and I need to rest so that I don't crumble under the pressure.

I want to find a way to tell Mark that I'm sorry. But I don't know if I am.

29

Harriet had barely slept, and when she had her dreams had been of the women she had defended in the past. She always attempted to file them away in her mind, trying not to dwell on the haunting images of their troubled eyes, but she doubted whether memories of Evie would ever fade completely. There was something different about her. Harriet's clients usually fell into one of two camps – those who nurtured their anger at the atrocities they'd had to endure, and those so psychologically damaged they were unable to utter a word in their own defence. Evie's responses and reactions didn't fit either profile, and despite the tiredness pricking the back of her eyelids, Harriet was determined to be at the top of her game for this case. Evie deserved the best she had to give.

When she arrived back at the police station, she could see that Evie looked exhausted too, but it was hardly surprising. In spite of the dark circles under her eyes, she seemed calm and Harriet wondered if she had prepared her client enough for what was to come. Her fears were heightened when she saw the expression on the face of the lead detective in the interrogation, Nick Grieves. He looked excited, and that was not good news.

The questioning began all over again and Evie was handling herself well, her voice calm, but there was a sense of anticipation in the room, as if everyone was waiting for some critical moment to arrive.

Finally, when it seemed to Harriet that there wasn't a single new question to ask, Detective Grieves asked Evie once again to describe how she killed Mark North.

'Nothing has changed since you asked me this yesterday,' she said. 'When my fingers touched the handle of the knife, something in me snapped. I was in such agony that I don't believe I was capable of rational thought, and it felt somehow that the pain was just beginning. I had never seen Mark in such a frenzy of excitement.'

'Which hand did you pick up the knife with?'

Evie was starting to look frustrated at the repetition, and Harriet reached out to touch her arm gently. She took the hint and calmed down.

'It was my right hand.'

'And what happened then?'

'I reached round his shoulders and cut him on the neck.'

Nick Grieves picked up a sheet of paper from the desk.

'Cut him, you say? We have now had the post-mortem report and the initial forensic report. It was clear from the height of the blood spatter above the bed that an artery had been severed in Mark North's neck. It has now been confirmed that he had only one cut to his body, and that was on the right side of his neck. That would appear to substantiate your statement that you picked up the knife in your right hand and, as Mark was lying on top of you, you wrapped your arm around him. Do you agree?'

Evie nodded. 'Yes, exactly as I said.'

'Your prints are on the knife, as are Mark North's. This is as we would have expected. According to the report, the knife, although reasonably sharp, would have required a significant amount of pressure to be applied to produce such a deep wound.' He paused, the significance of his comment hanging in the air. 'This was more than an act of retribution for your minor cuts, wasn't it? This was intended to inflict serious harm. The pathologist has confirmed that Mark North's neck was slit from under his chin to just below his ear, severing both his carotid artery and his jugular vein.'

Harriet maintained a neutral expression and resisted the temptation to look at Evie. She knew what was going to happen next.

'You do not deny that you inflicted this wound, do you, Evie?'

'No.'

'I am now terminating this interview and you will be returned to your cell temporarily.'

Evie turned her head towards Harriet, her eyes asking the question, 'Is this it?' Harriet had explained the procedure to her and gave a brief nod before Evie was escorted back to her cell.

It was now a matter of waiting, but Harriet knew it wouldn't be long.

They have come for me. I'm being escorted back to the custody suite and they're going to charge me. I knew this was going to happen – I've known all along, but it doesn't make it any easier. My teeth are clamped rigid in my mouth as I tell myself over and over again that I had no choice.

Another detective enters the room. I think he's the one who arrested me, but I can't be sure. The room that night was filled with shadows and it's only when he speaks and I hear his accent that I know for certain it's him.

'Evelyn Clarke,' he says. 'You are charged that on 17th August you did murder Mark North contrary to common law.'

That's it. I thought I was prepared, but it takes all my will-power to stay upright and to stifle a gasp of distress.

30

Four months later

Cleo was determined to get to the Crown Court early. She wasn't sure how long the thirty-mile drive would take, and she desperately wanted to watch the start of the proceedings, hear the charges read out, see the jury file in and witness the shame that Evie must surely be feeling. She was going to be called to give evidence and wouldn't be allowed into the court until after she had been questioned. Nevertheless, she wanted to get the lie of the land so that when she was released from the witness box she would know how to gain access to the public gallery.

Aminah had offered to take care of Lulu whenever Cleo needed to be at court, and although things between the two women were strained, Cleo would have struggled to get through the last few months without her.

The door from the street that led to the public gallery seemed to be locked, and a security guard in a yellow hi-vis jacket was standing outside beyond a barrier that Cleo assumed was there to control any queues. Would that many people be interested in the trial?

'Going into the gallery, are you, Miss?' the security guard asked.

'No – not yet. Hopefully later, but I have to give evidence first. Is this where I go when I want to watch the rest of the trial?'

'It is, but hang on a minute, Miss,' he said, holding his hand out to stop Cleo walking past. She looked to her left and saw why. Turning into a narrow drive leading to a shuttered entrance to the court building was a large white van with small reflective windows set high up, above Cleo's eyeline. The van waited as the dark grey shutter slowly rose, revealing a steep, unlit slope that led down deep into the bowels of the earth.

For a moment, Cleo felt a shudder run through her at the thought of how it must feel to be in that van, driven from view into the black concrete passageways below the building and brought up into court to be publicly accused of murder. The thought made her slightly queasy. How shocking and degrading it must be – especially for those who were innocent.

'Are you okay, Miss?'

Cleo couldn't bring herself to speak. She tried to smile, shook her head and made her way to the entrance he had indicated, suddenly more aware than ever of the horror of what was about to happen to Evie.

I've had plenty of time to prepare myself for today – four months on remand, and I'm told I'm lucky it wasn't longer. Four months in a prison full of women, many of them bewildered by how their lives ever came to this. Of course I'm not the only one in the prison who has killed her partner, but most of the others have already been given life sentences. Some of them had been abused for years before they took their revenge. But revenge is no defence in law, and sadly these women weren't fortunate enough to have a lawyer like mine who understands how a person might crack and do something wild in the heat of the moment, and who cares about the outcome of this trial possibly even more than I do.

It's the indignity that I have struggled with, and today has been the worst. The drive here in a prison van, being offloaded into the underbelly of the court, and finally being brought to sit in the dock, which is nothing like I expected or had seen on TV. It's not open, as I thought it would be, and I am isolated from the rest of the court by plate glass, as if I am suffering from a contagious disease, or I'm a dangerous animal. Perhaps I am.

In front of me are the two legal teams – an obscene number of people on each side for what, to me at least, seems a simple case. They have their backs to me as we are all facing the judge, a sombre-looking man with thin lips that turn down at the corners as if he has forgotten how to smile. I can't help wondering how he would look without his wig and his red gown. Ordinary, I suspect.

The jury are on my left in two rows. To the right is the public gallery and seats for the press. I'm not going to look there. I don't want to know who has come to watch, but Harriet has warned me that it will be packed with journalists. I'm fairly sure that nobody will be here to support me, so those watching will either be hating me for what I did, or curious to see a killer in the flesh.

I feel that my dignity has been stripped, and during the months in prison I've had time to think about all that happened. There have even been times when I have questioned my decisions, wondering if there could have been another way. And sometimes the moments of grief for Mark have been difficult to bear.

But I must never think like that. It would make a mockery of everything I have had to live with and the pain I endured. I have to believe in myself, even if nobody else does.

31

Harriet turned in her seat to watch Evie's face as the charges were read out. Evie confirmed her name, and the first charge was read by the clerk to the court.

'You are charged that on 17th August you did murder Mark North contrary to common law. How do you plead?'

'Not guilty.'

Evie's voice was calm and level. She seemed composed and having briefly taken in her surroundings she was now staring straight ahead, meeting the gaze of the judge full on. There was an air of certainty about her – as if she knew she had to be here, but believed absolutely in her innocence.

Although Evie had initially been charged on the single count of murder, Harriet had put forward her defence statement to the prosecution indicating that it was their intention to present evidence of loss of control. As a result the CPS had added a second count of manslaughter, to which Evie had no choice but to plead guilty.

Harriet almost smiled at the thought of Angus Brodie's displeasure at that decision. He wanted Evie to go down for murder, but the prosecution couldn't risk her being found not guilty on that charge and walking free. Given that she had admitted to killing Mark North, the lesser charge of manslaughter guaranteed them a conviction.

Her thoughts returned to her client as the manslaughter charge was read out.

'How do you plead?'

'Guilty.'

Evie hung her head, her remorse clear to see. She returned slowly to her seat and appeared to shake herself out of her momentary lapse of confidence, raising her head to fix her gaze on the prosecutor, who was about to make her opening remarks.

Harriet was pleased with her appointment of Boyd Simmonds QC to represent Evie. He was the perfect foil to the prosecuting barrister, Devisha Ambo, and based on Evie's account of the events of the night of Mark's death and all she had been forced to endure during the preceding months, he and Harriet had carefully worked out the structure of their defence.

'Our first priority is to make sure the jury finds you not guilty of murder,' Harriet had told Evie. 'It's never easy in a case like yours, and I would be lying if I said otherwise. But Boyd and I believe in you and we think we have a good chance.

'We need to demonstrate to the jury that Mark had been hurting you for some time, and that on the night of his death you lost control due to the risk of serious violence and a genuine fear of what he would do to you next. If we're successful in this you will be guilty of voluntary manslaughter instead of murder.'

Evie nodded and Harriet could see that she was absorbing every word.

'The second thing we need to bear in mind is the sentencing. There's no mandatory life sentence for manslaughter as there is for murder, but the judge can still impose life if he so wishes. So we need to devise a strategy that will allow him to be lenient. He must be in no doubt that you used the knife simply because it was available; that you did not carry it into the room for the purpose of killing Mark.'

At that, Evie's eyes had opened wide. 'But I didn't,' she said.

Harriet believed her. 'I know – and the fact that you demonstrated immediate remorse is in your favour. You suffered a high degree of provocation, and that's a good thing, as is the fact that Mark presented an ongoing threat. It's important that you understand all this, Evie, so you know what's happening in court and how our strategy is playing out. Have you any questions?'

Evie's eyes narrowed. She appeared to be thinking hard about everything she had been told, and Harriet almost smiled. Whatever the outcome of this trial, Evie's story was going to make national headlines, and it had the potential to represent a flagship case in her never-ending battle against abuse.

'No, I don't think I need to ask anything,' Evie said, shaking her head slowly. 'I know it's not going to be easy to convince the court that it was a spur-of-the-moment, impulsive act, but it's the truth, Harriet. I hope you believe me.'

Harriet trusted her word absolutely, but the CPS were determined that Evie would be found guilty of murder. They had presented their evidence to the defence team, and some of it didn't paint Evie in the best light. Harriet had been through it piece by piece with her client, knowing that defendants often came unstuck as they realised how exposed they were going to be in court, but once again Evie surprised her, listening carefully and giving valid explanations for every event.

The only time she seemed less self-assured was when the conversation moved to Mark's character and the dichotomy between a gentle, loving father and a brutal, savage abuser. She seemed to have the ability to separate Mark's actions from Mark the man, talking about her injuries without a flicker of discomfort, but she appeared far less confident when asked about his personality. It was almost as if she didn't want to denigrate him. But whatever her feelings for the father of her child, she was a victim, and it was Harriet's job, along with Boyd Simmonds, to prove that.

Harriet settled in her seat, the sense of nervous anticipation that she always suffered before a trial making her force herself to sit up straight and appear confident. She was determined that this case was going to go their way. It would validate everything she had been fighting for.

The prosecution and defence had both given their opening statements, and neither held any surprises. It was time for the first witness for the prosecution. Cleo North.

Cleo's hands felt sticky, her legs weak. She was first up, and that was good in some ways, because it meant it would soon be over. She didn't know how she would feel seeing Evie again, though. She had ignored her pleas to bring Lulu to the prison on the grounds that it would upset the child and it was too far to travel. So now she took the oath without lifting her eyes to the dock and instead focused on the prosecution barrister, a tall, well-built Afro-Caribbean woman with a wide smile that seemed slightly inappropriate for the occasion. Her voice was warm and persuasive and Cleo knew she was trying to make her feel comfortable. It wasn't working, though.

'Miss North, I know this can't be easy for you. Losing a family member to whom you were close never is. Can you tell us what sort of a man your brother was?'

Cleo understood she had two roles in court: to explain how Mark and Evie had met, and as a witness to her brother's character. She desperately wanted to make the jury care about Mark and what had happened to him so they would mistrust everything Evie said when it was her turn to give evidence.

'Mark was a gentle, sensitive man. Like a lot of artistic people, I suppose. But he cared deeply for those close to him, particularly Evie and Lulu, his baby daughter.'

'How did your brother and the defendant first meet?'

Cleo had still not forgiven herself for her role in their involvement and she stumbled over the words as she explained why she had introduced Evie to Mark.

'It was my fault, you see. Mark had been depressed for quite some time and I thought it would be good for him to take the commission.'

'The photographs were for her father, you say. Did you ever meet, speak to, or have any correspondence with Miss Clarke's father?'

'No. I didn't. Evie told us her father had died, just before the album was finished.'

'So there was no payment forthcoming at all?' the prosecutor asked.

'That's right.'

'Did you ask if there was money in his estate to cover this?'

'Yes, of course,' Cleo answered, puzzled that they were making so much of this. 'But Evie said her stepmother would get it all, and she wasn't going to inherit a penny.'

The prosecutor held out her hand to her assistant, who in turn passed her a document.

'I would refer the court to exhibit JC/9.' Devisha Ambo paused until the relevant papers had been found. 'This is a copy of Miss Clarke's birth certificate. As you will see, the space for the father is blank. She was born in Norfolk, and raised from a young age by her maternal grandmother. Although Miss Clarke claimed to have lived in an apartment at her father's home in London, that is a complete fabrication. She has never lived in any part of London, and there is no evidence to suggest that Miss Clarke knows either the name or the whereabouts of her father. She had, in fact, been living in a council flat in Leicester.'

There was a stunned silence. Cleo felt every muscle in her body tense, her breaths coming in short gasps. For the first time she lifted her eyes to Evie, staring at her through the plate glass, expecting to see some sign of remorse. Evie's expression was blank.

Devisha Ambo paused to give the court time to assess this.

'Can you think of any reason why she would have lied about this?' she asked.

Cleo was shaking her head, mystified. 'Only if she wanted to get the photographs for free, I suppose. But we wouldn't release anything other than a low-resolution image until payment had been received in full. So it doesn't make sense.'

'What was your brother's reaction to the fact that she couldn't pay?'

'Mark was wonderful about it. I told you – he was a kind man. He let her feel better about it all by allowing her to design a blog for him, and that's how she wheedled her way into his life.'

'So as far as you are aware, he never knew she had lied to him?'

'No. He would have told me.'

'What can you tell us about the relationship between your brother and Michelle Evelyn Clarke in the months before his death?' Devisha asked.

For a moment, Cleo was confused and glanced back towards Evie. She hadn't known her first name was Michelle; it was something else she had hidden.

'I didn't think things were easy between them. I noticed when he came back from a trip she shied away from him if he tried to hug her, and I could see how much her reaction hurt him. But he was so kind to her. He even asked me to make her an exquisite piece of jewellery to show how much he cared.'

'Was there a pattern of behaviour between the two of them that you noticed?'

'There was a pattern to Evie's behaviour, for sure. While Mark was away, she seemed to become clumsy – accident-prone – as if she was punishing him for leaving her. She was trying to control him.'

'He was away from home every time she had one of her accidents?'

'Yes.'

'And yet Miss Clarke claims that he was the one hurting her. How could that be, Miss North, if he was away each and every time she was injured?'

'I have no idea,' Cleo replied, turning to address her answer to the jury. They had to believe this – if they realised that Mark hadn't been hurting Evie there was no defence for what she did. 'Maybe she wants everyone to believe he was a bully, but he couldn't possibly have been the one to hurt her.'

'So you believe she's lying? Why do you think she's accusing him of this behaviour now?'

'Of course she's lying. She has to have some excuse for what she did to him. She's made it all up.'

'In your initial statement to the police, Miss North, you said that your brother had repeatedly asked Miss Clarke to marry him. Is that correct?'

'Yes. He couldn't understand why she refused him. He was doing all he could to make her happy.'

'And so in your opinion Mark had no idea that Miss Clarke is, in fact, already married and has been for some years.'

Cleo felt as if time had frozen. The buzz of the courtroom faded into the background as once more she looked at the impassive face of her brother's killer. Evie returned her gaze steadily and Cleo – just for a moment – felt uncomfortably as if she was the one in the wrong.

'You bitch,' Cleo said quietly.

32

The hubbub in the courtroom had finally died down after Cleo's reprimand from the judge. Her heart was still racing as the questioning continued, but she realised that by demonstrating that Evie was a liar, the prosecutor was aiming to undermine every part of her statement. Shocked as she was at the revelations, Cleo felt a tingle of excitement. The jury would never believe what Evie said about Mark now.

Finally, the prosecutor concluded her questioning and it was the turn of the defence QC, who she had been told was a man called Boyd Simmonds. Cleo hadn't been looking forward to this and had expected a sharp, aggressive character to be pleading on Evie's behalf. But the man lumbering to his feet, pushing his glasses back up his nose, seemed amiable enough and she felt herself relax a little.

'Miss North, as my colleague says, this must be a difficult time and I will try to keep my questions straightforward and to the point.'

He gave her a pleasant smile.

'Did you like Evie Clarke?' he asked, his head on one side as if asking her the time of day.

Cleo felt shocked at the abrupt and direct question, but took a steadying breath.

'No, I didn't. I did try, but we never really clicked and now I despise her. I always thought she might be a schemer,' she shot Evie a venomous glance, but it didn't appear to have any impact, 'and now I know she is.'

'Did you like your brother's wife, Mia North?'

'I don't see why that's relevant.'

The judge spoke. 'Answer the question please, Miss North.'

Cleo knew this was going to sound bad, but in truth neither of the women had been good for Mark and she wasn't sure how she could explain it.

'Then I'll have to say no – I didn't like Mia. But for different reasons.'

'Which were?'

'She didn't appreciate Mark's talent and she undermined him,' Cleo said. 'He lost his confidence when he was married to Mia. I told him she was a bad choice, but he swore that he loved her. I think she was too controlling.'

'Controlling, you say.' Boyd paused and consulted the piece of paper he was holding. 'I refer to your comments about Miss Clarke. "She was trying to control him," you said. Did you feel that anyone who became close to your brother was – by default – trying to control him?'

Cleo didn't know how to make them understand how it had been. She was trying to tell the truth, but this placid-looking barrister, however mild his manner, was making her sound stupid. He wasn't about to let up, either.

'You told the court that Miss Clarke had "wheedled her way"

186

into your brother's life. How long after she had met him did she become pregnant?'

'I don't know. A few months.'

'Was your brother pleased?'

'I think he was surprised – he told me there had been no discussion of having children and he had thought they had been careful. But he loved Lulu.'

'I'm sure he did. And what did you think about the pregnancy?'

Cleo felt decidedly uneasy. This wasn't going the way she had expected. 'I did wonder if maybe she had tricked him.'

'With what objective in mind?'

Cleo leaned forwards, resting her forearms on the edge of the witness box, trying to engage with everyone in the court.

'My brother was a very wealthy man. He was good-looking, kind, a brilliant photographer and lived in a stunning house. He was a catch for anyone – and I'm more convinced than ever that's what she wanted. To trap him.'

The barrister referred to his notes.

'You believe she wanted to trap him despite the fact that you described your brother earlier as depressed and a bit of a recluse.' The barrister paused for effect and once again Cleo felt flustered. 'So given that her principal objective was to ensnare your brother, at what point after she discovered she was pregnant did she move into his home?'

'A few months later.'

Boyd let the hand holding his papers drop to his side.

'A few months,' he said slowly, labouring each word. 'Two? Three?'

'Five.' Cleo's voice was hushed.

'I think, if you check back, you may find it was actually six. So in her attempt to trap your depressed brother, she refused to move into his house until she was six months pregnant? Does that sound to you like a woman on a mission to win a man, Miss North?'

Again he paused only momentarily before continuing his questioning. It felt like an attack, and Cleo was becoming increasingly uncomfortable.

'You give the impression that you and your brother, Mark North, were very close. Would you say that was true?'

Cleo nodded, a momentary stab of pain as she thought of the hole Mark had left in her life silencing her for a moment.

'Absolutely.'

'We know that Evie Clarke manipulated the truth a little when she spoke about her father . . .' he said.

'No she didn't.' The words burst from Cleo unrestrained. 'She lied.'

'. . . and we may learn in due course why she took that decision. Much is being made of the fact that she lied to your brother, but that is only an assumption, isn't it, Miss North?'

'What do you mean?'

'Just because *you* didn't know the truth doesn't in any way prove that *he* didn't, does it?'

'He didn't know – I'm sure he didn't,' Cleo said, her voice rising with her mounting concern about the line of questioning. 'He would have told me.'

'Why should we assume that Miss Clarke hadn't told your brother everything about her past? They became lovers – had a child together. Is it not probable that he was fully aware of her small deviation from the facts early on in their relationship, and that she had also told him she was married?'

'No. It's not possible. As I said, he would have told me.'

'He told you everything, did he?'

'Of course,' Cleo said, her voice catching. 'We were very close.'

Boyd Simmonds nodded, looking at her over his glasses. He gave her another of his pleasant smiles.

'Could you please tell us when you became aware that your brother was in a relationship with Evie Clarke?'

'I don't know precisely. They invited me round to dinner when they started seeing each other and told me then.'

The QC nodded slowly. 'They had just started seeing each other, had they?'

'Yes,' Cleo said. 'Evie had been doing some work for Mark on the blog she was helping him with, but it was purely platonic to start with.'

'Let me help you with some dates, Miss North. I believe your first dinner with Miss Clarke and your brother – as a couple – was the 21st of February. Does that sound about right?'

Cleo shrugged. 'It could be. I would have to check.'

'And when was your niece, Lulu, born?'

Cleo closed her eyes. She knew where this was going and she had no way of stopping it.

'August,' she said quietly.

'So this brother, who told you everything, had in fact had sexual intercourse with Evie Clarke on at least one occasion approximately three months before you became aware of the relationship, and they had very possibly been seeing each other

189

in secret, keeping the truth from you for all of that time. Because your brother chose not to tell you.'

Cleo stared at this mild-mannered, overweight man who she had mistakenly thought was going to be gentle with her. There was nothing she could say, because she knew he was right. Mark had hidden things from her, and she didn't understand why or how it had happened. It never used to be like that.

'We know you were not aware that Miss Clarke is, in fact, an orphan and has been since her childhood. She also never mentioned to you that she was married. But given the fact that your brother had a history of hiding the truth from you, I don't believe it's safe to assume that he was ignorant of it. Do you?'

Cleo had no answer. She knew how important it was for the jury to believe Evie was a liar – that all her evidence was suspect. And she could find no way of putting this right.

'In fact, it is possible that the only person who lied was your brother – to you. Do you agree?'

'It's possible, but I don't believe it.'

If this was true, what else had Mark hidden from her? For one second the image of Mia lying dead at the bottom of the basement steps leapt into her mind and she quickly blanked it. *Don't go there*, she thought.

The barrister leapt on her obvious confusion and launched into his next question.

'You said that Miss Clarke had a series of accidents when your brother was away. What happened?'

'She scalded her arm once. She said it was nothing, but I saw it. It was badly blistered. And then she caught her hand in the weights in the multi gym.'

'When did these accidents happen?'

'After Mark left for one of his trips.'

'And how, precisely, do you know the timing of the accidents?'

Cleo looked down. How could she answer? She had never seen Evie between Mark leaving and the accidents happening. She knew this was a hole in her argument, but at the same time she couldn't let the jury think there was any doubt.

'Evie told me. She phoned me when she had trapped her hand. Mark had been gone for over an hour – I don't believe she could have sat there for that length of time in so much pain if it had happened before he left. Why would she?'

Cleo glanced at Evie, wanting her to stand up and tell the world that it was all a lie and that Mark had never touched her.

'How many abused women have you known, Miss North?'

Cleo was confused at the line of questioning. 'I don't know. None that I'm aware of.'

'Precisely – and I've no doubt you are aware that statistically you probably know quite a few. I put it to you that you don't know which of your friends and acquaintances are abused because they don't want to admit it. Is it not possible that Evie Clarke didn't want you to know that your brother was hurting her every time he was about to go away?'

'No!' Cleo felt her throat tighten and was terrified that at any moment she would burst into floods of tears.

'When did Mark's wife die?'

Cleo stared at him. She knew he didn't mean what month or year. She knew where he was going with this questioning and she had to deflect him. Had he read her mind?

'That was different altogether,' she said, hearing the uncertainty in her own voice.

'You found her, didn't you? Am I not right in thinking that she fell to her death shortly after Mark North left for a business trip?'

'Yes – but I spoke to her after he left that day. She was fine then. We agreed to have lunch.'

'You agreed to have lunch with someone you have already told us you didn't like? We will have to take your word for that, Miss North. But when injuries started to be inflicted on Miss Clarke within hours of your brother's departure, did it never occur to you for one moment that they might be something other than accidents, and that they could have happened an hour or so earlier? When he was still in the house?'

Cleo hesitated for just a second. It was a second too long. Before she had time to respond, Mr Simmonds spoke.

'Let's get back to Miss Clarke's injuries. You say she "caught her hand in the weights" – weren't they your words? Isn't that a bit of an understatement?'

The barrister turned to the jury. 'I refer you to your screens. What you see is an x-ray of Miss Clarke's hand after she "caught" it. Even with no medical knowledge at all, I think you can see that she did rather more than merely "catch" it.'

The court was silent for a moment as the jury studied their monitors and Cleo looked at the QC. How could she have been so wrong about him? He had lost the avuncular expression and now looked like a bulldog about to attack.

'How did Evie Clarke say the injury happened?' Boyd asked.

The members of the public who had packed out the gallery listened in fascinated horror to Cleo's version of events, of how

Evie had accidentally let go of the bar when her hand was between the weights.

'I understand you are quite keen on fitness yourself, Miss North. Didn't it seem to you that this was a most unlikely accident?'

'Well it couldn't have been anything to do with Mark.' The words burst from Cleo. She had to stop them thinking like this. 'He never went down into the basement – not since his wife died down there.'

'Indeed,' Boyd said, leaving a space for those listening to draw their own conclusions.

Cleo was silent and Boyd moved on. 'And how did Miss Clarke scald herself?'

'She was pouring hot water from the kettle into her mug. Her hand slipped – I think she sneezed or something.'

Boyd turned to the jury again and asked them to consult the photographs now on screen, submitted by the hospital.

'Miss North, do you happen to know if Miss Clarke is right- or left-handed?'

Cleo thought about it for a moment. 'Right, I think. Yes, I'm pretty sure she is.'

'And yet she sustained these burns to her right arm. Does a right-handed person often pick up a full kettle of boiling water with their left hand? It's not impossible, but unlikely I would have thought. And at the first splash, would it not be normal to withdraw your arm as quickly as possible, rather than run the boiling water up and down the arm so that it scalded the skin from elbow to wrist?'

Cleo looked down. She suddenly felt as though she was the one on trial. And she had been found guilty.

33

Stephanie wasn't looking forward to being questioned. She had appeared as a witness many times, but it never got any easier. It was so important to get it right.

She and Gus were sitting next to each other in the witness waiting room and he reached out and gently took her hand in his. For once, she didn't pull away. She had become more accustomed to his occasional touch over the last months and knew he was trying to give her confidence. Her time working with him would soon be over, and she would have to decide then whether it was a good idea for the two of them to have their own post-mortem on all that had gone wrong between them, or whether to leave well alone. Now, though, she had to focus on accurately and succinctly relaying the facts relating to Mark North's death.

'Sergeant Stephanie King?' The court usher held the door open.

'You're on,' Gus said with a quick squeeze of the fingers. 'See you later.'

Stephanie walked into the courtroom, swore the oath and took a couple of deep breaths. She tried not to look at Evie.

As Devisha Ambo stood, Stephanie was reassured by her

wide white smile. The prosecutor eased her into the questioning by asking for facts – details of the call-out, how she and Jason got into the house, the role of the security guard. Stephanie's mind flooded with images of that night; of the moonlight, the candles, and the two bodies on the bed.

'What was your first impression when you entered the room?'

'There was blood. A lot of it. It was on the walls as well as the bed, and I immediately thought it was arterial blood. I've seen that sort of spatter pattern before.'

Stephanie's eyes flicked to the gallery, where she could see the bright hair of Cleo North, and she wished Mark's sister had left after giving her evidence. Her cheeks had a gaunt look about them and there were dark circles under her eyes. Surely she wouldn't want to listen as the prosecution attempted to prove that her brother had been ruthlessly murdered, while the defence claimed that he was a vicious brute and not the person she had believed him to be?

She dragged her attention back to her testimony, and tried to focus on describing those first minutes after she arrived at Mark North's home.

The prosecution questioning continued smoothly, but Stephanie's stomach tightened when Boyd Simmonds stepped up to the witness box.

'Sergeant King,' the defence QC said. 'When you entered the room – apart from seeing the blood – what was your impression of the individuals in that room?'

'I assumed they were both dead because neither of them was moving.'

'And then?'

'I heard a sound from the bed. I realised that one of them was alive and I needed to help them.'

'Can you tell me how their bodies were positioned?'

Stephanie had prepared for this question. 'They were tangled in the sheet so it was difficult to tell precisely, but they were both on one side of the bed.'

'Close to each other, you mean?'

'Yes, it seemed so.'

'And Miss Clarke's demeanour. Was she angry, aggressive?'

'Neither of those. She was upset. She was in shock.'

'You're an experienced police officer, Sergeant King. You were able to observe the scene, the condition of the defendant and her obvious distress?'

'Yes.'

'Drawing on your experience, did you form a view that the defendant had planned and executed a carefully thought through murder?'

Stephanie glanced across at Evie. She hadn't seen her since her police interview after Mark North's death and then all she had seen was a distraught woman with bloodshot eyes and hair scraped back from her pale, blotchy face. The woman she saw now was dressed smartly in a navy blue suit, but despite her attempt to wear a little makeup, she had the sallow skin of a person who didn't get out in the fresh air often. None of that counted to Stephanie. The fact was that when she looked at Evie Clarke, the only thing she could see was a victim.

She tore her gaze away. 'I didn't form a view. I had no basis for doing that and my only concern at that time was to ensure that the scene was preserved.'

She didn't look at Evie again but the intensity of Harriet James's gaze from the defence bench was disturbing, so Stephanie looked instead at the strangers crowding the public gallery. Her attention was grabbed by a man sitting in the far corner. His stare was firmly fixed on Evie in the dock, but she never once glanced his way. His brow was lowered, his mouth set in a grim line.

Who was this man? Stephanie had never seen him before, but he seemed too enthralled to be a thrill-seeking observer.

The rest of the questioning passed without incident, but throughout Stephanie found herself distracted as the man's attention never wavered from Evie. He looked neither at Boyd Simmonds when he asked questions nor at Stephanie when she answered.

Finally, she was excused and felt a sense of relief as she made her way out of the courtroom. She wouldn't be able to speak to Gus again until after he had been called, so she decided to head to the public gallery. There was something intense and very odd about that man and she wanted to know if he was still watching Evie.

She hurried to the gallery, hoping to find a seat that would give her good sight of the man, and quietly pushed the door open.

Glancing to her left she saw that he was still there, and she quickly took a seat next to one of her colleagues.

'Who's that man?' she whispered, indicating with her head. 'The one with the ginger hair.'

'No idea – never seen him before.'

The man pulled a single sheet of paper from his jacket pocket.

Even from a distance, Stephanie could see that it was starting to split along the creases as if it had been read and re-folded over and over again. It looked like a letter. Stephanie could make out the blue ink of something handwritten. The man looked down at it, then slowly, deliberately, started to rip it apart, allowing the pieces to fall like confetti around his feet.

With a final glance at Evie, he stood up and pushed his way past other observers and out of the gallery.

34

In Harriet's view, Boyd was doing an excellent job of damaging some of the prosecution's arguments and there was a reasonable chance that the jury would disregard the attempt to paint Evie as a liar. But the fact that she had invented a father who didn't exist was certainly a black mark on her character.

'I know what I did was wrong,' Evie had told her. 'But I saw Mark's photos in his gallery and I had to meet him. Have you seen the gallery, Harriet? It's amazing. I saw one photo hanging in the window from across the road. It was the only picture on display, blown up to about six feet tall – a woman's face, almost disembodied with all but her face in shadow, looking into my eyes, into my soul. I wanted so much for him to take my photograph – to see if he could make me look that incredible.'

Harriet looked at the passion in the woman's eyes, and didn't doubt her word for a second.

'I had no idea how I was going to pay him. I did try to make some money from blog commissions and a bit of bar work so he wouldn't need to know the truth, but it was stupid – I could never afford his prices. I told him what I'd done as soon as we became a couple and long before I agreed to move in with him.

He knew everything there is to know about me, and he forgave me. He decided not to share it with Cleo because she and I were struggling to be friends and he didn't want to make things worse than they already were.'

Boyd had made it seem far more likely that Mark had simply decided not to tell Cleo the truth about Evie, and it felt like a point to the defence. There were bigger obstacles to overcome, though, and it was too early to judge the odds.

Nick Grieves, the detective who had led Evie's initial interrogation prior to charging her, was called to the stand and read out the content of her interview. The words he spoke were Evie's words: her answers to the questions posed in her interview; her description of events on the night she killed Mark North.

Harriet risked a glance at her client. Evie sat motionless, her features clear of expression.

The crime scene technician was questioned and the prosecution made much of the tampering with the light fitting. But when pushed by Boyd, the girl admitted that it was impossible to say who had switched the wires. There were no fingerprints and Harriet knew that, despite a detailed check of all the computers in the house and their internet histories, no links to any useful sites explaining how to rewire a light fitting had been found. Evie's statement to the police had included her assertion that Mark only hurt her when the lights were out. So their argument was that it was far more likely that he had tampered with the lights to guarantee darkness.

The prosecution had moved on to the injuries that Evie had sustained on her arms on the night of Mark's death. The wounds had been carefully photographed and examined for Mark's DNA while Evie was in hospital and the findings confirmed that she and Mark had intercourse before he died, and that his DNA was found in her cuts.

As the forensic physician who had examined Evie was called to the stand, Harriet could see he was fidgeting and unable to keep his hands still. She checked her notes and it seemed he was new to the role. She had to hope he was good enough at his job.

Once the doctor had been introduced to the court, Devisha pulled up an image of Evie's inner arms and chest on the screen.

'Would you describe these as defence wounds?' she asked, smiling broadly in spite of the subject.

'I think it's unlikely because of the pattern of the cuts. If the defendant had been holding her arms up to protect her face or head, the angle of the cuts would be different. Also, when someone is protecting themselves against a serious knife attack, the wounds would typically be a lot deeper and would be on the outside of the arm. These are quite superficial and those on her arms are all to the soft skin between wrist and antecubital fossa – that's the inside of the elbow.'

Harriet had been sure from the outset that it would be a mistake to plead self-defence, and now she was relieved she hadn't recommended it to Evie.

'And those on her chest?' Devisha asked.

'Again, superficial. If he had been slashing at her with a knife, I would have expected the wounds to have different depths, depending on how successful each stroke was. These are fairly consistent in their depth – measured, almost.'

201

'Doctor Moore, given that these cuts were unlikely to have been sustained as Miss Clarke defended herself against an attack, is it possible that she could have inflicted these wounds on herself?'

'It's not impossible, although very painful, I would have thought. But there is nothing to suggest that self-harm should be ruled out.'

Devisha consulted her notes. 'The forensic evidence tells us that Mr North's body came into contact with the cuts at some point. We know that when the victim was found, the defendant was holding him, lying close, her chest against his back, her arms around his upper body. Would this have been sufficient for the DNA to be transferred into the cuts?'

'Yes.'

'And the fact that a chest hair was embedded in one of the cuts?'

'We know that intercourse had taken place and it's very possible that chest hairs were on the bedding. There is no way of telling precisely how they were transferred to Miss Clarke's injuries.'

'So what you're saying, if I understand you correctly, is that it is possible Evie Clarke cut herself, that the DNA was transferred to the wounds as she lay with her chest against Mark North's back, and that the hair could have come from the bedclothes?'

The doctor nodded. 'Yes, that's all perfectly feasible.'

Harriet resisted the temptation to look at Evie. It could appear to the court that she was sharing a moment of doubt, so she remained straight-backed and attentive.

Devisha concluded her questioning and thanked the witness. Boyd pushed himself slowly to his feet.

'Doctor Moore,' he said. 'You have told the court that there is no way of telling how the chest hairs and DNA were transferred to Miss Clarke's cuts. So that assumes, I would imagine, that her statement claiming they were transferred as they made love *after* he had cut her could equally be true?'

The doctor's gaze moved backwards and forwards between Devisha and Boyd. 'Yes, I suppose that's right.'

'As you know, Miss Clarke has never claimed that she killed Mark North in self-defence. She never accused him of wielding a knife with the intention of killing her, either. It was more complicated than that, and as we will see when I call witnesses for the defence, there was a pattern of physical abuse in their relationship. So are these wounds consistent with cuts that could have been made as a form of punishment, or maybe just for the sheer pleasure of causing pain to another?'

Harriet looked at the jury and saw one or two of the women wince at the thought.

The doctor was silent for a moment, clearly thinking about the question. 'If someone had stood behind Miss Clarke and held her hands above her head, he could have cut the inside of her arms by reaching round from behind, and cut her chest too. Or he could have laid her flat on the bed and secured her hands above her head, exposing the inner arms and holding them out of the way of her chest. That would make sense, if the wounds were inflicted by someone else.'

'Thank you, Doctor Moore. I have no further questions.'

To Harriet's surprise, the doctor carried on, although he

203

appeared to be talking to himself. 'The same could be said of the other scars on her body, too, I suspect.'

Harriet leaned forward in her chair and at the same time she saw Devisha's head snap up. She hadn't known about any other scarring. Why hadn't Evie mentioned it?

'You found evidence of previous scarring on Evie Clarke's body?' Boyd asked.

'Yes, I'm sorry.' The doctor's eyes flicked around the court-room, from judge, to jury, to defendant. 'I probably shouldn't have mentioned it. I realise it's not relevant to the case. I was just speaking my thoughts out loud.'

'Where did you find this scarring?'

'On her abdomen. I'd been asked specifically to report on the recent cuts only, so I didn't examine the rest of her body. I noticed the other scars as I was treating those on her chest.'

Harriet was suddenly desperate for Boyd to stop. Evie had said in her interview that Mark had never cut her before – the court had just heard that, and it was her whole justification for not being worried about taking the knife into the bedroom with her. Boyd needed to stop this line of questioning now. But Harriet had no way of interrupting him, and he was standing in front of her so she couldn't catch his eye.

'And would you say the previous scars were a result of similar injuries?'

'Very possibly. It's hard to say, though.'

'Why would that be, Doctor Moore?'

'Well, many of the scars had faded considerably. They were completely healed.'

Harriet's head was spinning. What did it mean? She should

have known about this – Evie should have told her. She knew what was coming – what line Devisha would take – and Boyd clearly realised that they were in uncharted territory too. He tried to close it down.

'Thank you, Doctor. That's very helpful. No further questions.'

Devisha was immediately on her feet, asking to re-examine the witness.

'Doctor Moore, when you say the scars had healed, how old would you say they were?'

Whatever the answer, Harriet feared this could be a gift for the prosecution.

'Impossible to say with any certainty. People heal at different rates and it can depend on all sorts of factors. After the scabbing process, the scar usually remains brown or pink for quite a long time. I didn't study the scars in much detail but given her age and fitness I would say that the scars I saw were a few years old.'

'By a few, does that mean two, or more than two?' Devisha asked, her smile widening.

'A minimum of two, I would say. In reality the injuries could have dated back a long time – even back to adolescence.'

'So given that Evie Clarke didn't meet Mark North until two and a half years ago, and moved into his house as recently as eighteen months ago, are you saying that it is unlikely that these injuries could have been – in terms of time – inflicted by Mark North?'

The doctor blew out a long breath and paused for a moment. 'In view of the timescales, he'd have had to inflict the injuries more or less from the day they first met, and even then, I would say that they were older. I would need to take another look to be certain.'

'And could they, like the other cuts, have been self-inflicted?'

'I would prefer to take another look before committing myself.'

It didn't matter. The damage had been done. Harriet once more resisted the temptation to turn to look at Evie. Instead, she looked confidently around the courtroom as if she had known all along about these scars.

'Why didn't you tell me about the other scars?' Harriet asked Evie. The judge had granted a brief recess, and the timing had given her a chance to talk to her client. 'Honestly, Evie, you have to tell me everything.'

She tried not to show her frustration, but she knew that the chances of Evie being found not guilty of murder hung in the balance, however well Boyd was performing.

'I'd forgotten they were there,' Evie said. 'They're just part of me now, and I never think about them.'

'Was it Mark?' It had been fairly clear from the doctor's statement that this wasn't the case, but she had to ask.

'There's no point trying to pin this on Mark. The doctor would re-examine me and I would be proved to be a liar. So no, it wasn't Mark. It was before him.'

'Your husband, Nigel?'

Harriet knew that some women were addicted to abusive relationships. Their own sense of self-esteem was so low that they were attracted to people who treated them as worthless. If she put Evie on the stand and this came out, it might increase the jury's sympathy for her, but only if she was prepared to explain it.

'It wasn't Nigel – he never touched me.'

It seemed Evie's husband, Nigel Clarke, was proving difficult to locate. Evie hadn't talked about him much, saying he was irrelevant. All Harriet knew was that they had married when Evie was in her late teens, and Nigel had treated her well.

'It's a dreadful thing to say,' Evie had told her, 'but I left him because I was bored. We weren't going anywhere, and I felt there was more to life. I'm not proud of it.'

Harriet could sympathise. She had never had time for a man in her life, and having seen the devastation some of them were capable of causing she hadn't been interested in any relationship that lasted more than a week.

The prosecution had tried to track Nigel down, but Evie had told Harriet that she thought he had left the country, and claimed she had no contact with him.

'The truth is, Evie, that if you have other old wounds, you are going to have to explain where they came from. The prosecution is already trying to suggest that your cuts were self-inflicted, and it's essential that we can demonstrate without doubt that Mark was hurting you. It's your only defence, and unexplained scars are not going to help with that. You have to tell me, Evie. I don't want any more surprises.'

Evie stared at her and didn't speak for a few seconds. Harriet was about to ask her again when to her surprise Evie stood up and took off her jacket. Turning her back on Harriet, she started to unbutton her shirt.

She spoke over her shoulder without turning round. 'The

doctor only examined the fresh wounds on my arms and chest. I didn't realise he had seen the scars on my stomach.'

She dropped the shirt to her waist and Harriet stared, speechless, at the criss-cross pattern of white scars on her back.

'Seen enough?' Evie asked, pulling her shirt back on after a few moments. 'Do you think I could have done that to myself?'

Harriet was silent while Evie dressed, waiting until the young woman sat down again.

'What happened?' she asked quietly.

'If the doctor wants to examine me again, I think he'll find that on closer inspection these marks were made by something other than a knife. They were in fact made by a leather bull-whip.'

'Jesus, Evie – who did that to you?'

'It doesn't matter now. It's got nothing to do with any of this and I'm not going to talk about it.'

Harriet had seen every type of abuse – or so she thought – and there was sadly nothing that unusual about a woman being whipped.

'Evie, this might help your case. I need to think about it, but it might be something we can use to our advantage.'

Evie pushed herself up from the chair and leaned on the table separating her and Harriet.

'No!' she said, snapping out the word. 'You want everyone feeling sorry for me – the victim who has been abused not once, but twice in her life. This trial is about me and Mark, and I don't want anyone to know about this. Understood?'

Harriet nodded slowly, although she didn't agree. 'I think that on the evidence of the doctor the prosecution will try even harder to find Nigel – whether he's the one who hurt you or not.'

'Well, wish them luck with that,' Evie said, a lopsided smile lightening her bleak expression. 'Even I don't know where he is.'

35

I wish I hadn't been forced to show Harriet my back. Why did that doctor have to mention the other scars? He wasn't asked the question, so he shouldn't have volunteered the information.

Harriet's face became pinched when I refused to tell her how I got them. She doesn't like me holding anything back but the only way I will tell the story is as a very last resort.

Thinking about it makes me want to curl up into a tight ball and hug my knees close to my chest. I can still feel the leather bindings digging into my wrists and ankles as I am stretched on the bed, face down, naked. I only showed Harriet my back – I spared her the rest.

The memory of his voice, raspy with too many cigarettes and too much booze, and the stink of his skeletal, unwashed body, nearly makes me gag.

'You think you're something special, don't you?' he asked, his lips close to my face. I twisted my head away from him so that I couldn't smell his sour breath or feel the spittle spraying from between his rotting teeth.

I don't know if it was the first lash of the whip that hurt the most, or the last. The first was a shock, the pain ripping through me, the skin splitting open. I tried to block all feeling from my mind as I had done so many times before as he experimented with new ways of hurting me. The whip was his latest idea – and when the thin nylon cord of the cracker hit the open sores of the previous lash I had to bite the pillow to stop myself from screaming. I knew he wanted me to beg for mercy, but I wouldn't give him the satisfaction.

But it's over. He's dead. He can't hurt me any more. Nobody can.

36

Cleo felt as if she had been spun in a washing machine and hung out to dry. Her body ached with the tension of holding herself taut throughout the day, and every ounce of energy had leached from her body. It had been a struggle to force her way through the hordes of press outside the court, trying to block out cries of 'Cleo!' or 'Miss North!' as hungry journalists vied for her attention, demanding a comment on the revelations about her brother. Her head throbbed and she longed to lay it down on a cool, soft pillow, but she was going to have to raise some energy for Lulu.

She drove like an automaton along the busy dual carriageway, noticing nothing and almost forgetting to turn off onto the narrow country lanes that would take her home. How she managed to avoid knocking down a cyclist who crossed in front of her as he signalled to turn right she didn't know, but without conscious thought she swerved around him and ignored the gesticulations and abuse that followed her.

Finally she pulled up in front of Aminah's house. She sat still in her seat for a few minutes, taking deep breaths and trying to calm herself until she saw the face of one of Aminah's children at the window and knew she had to make a move. She wearily forced herself from the car and walked slowly up a path strewn with children's toys to the front door.

Aminah opened the door. 'Are you okay, Cleo?'

'Not really.' Cleo fought to control the urge to cry. Everything she had heard in court had almost felt worse than hearing that Mark was dead. She could hardly bear to look at Aminah, but when she finally raised her eyes she felt a brief stab of surprise at the sight of her friend. There were dark smudges below her eyes, and two deep lines between her brows.

'Look, love – I'd like to ask you to come in, but it's difficult. I don't mind having Lulu for you, but you know we can't talk about the case.'

Cleo felt her concern drain away to be replaced by anger. Maybe Aminah's obvious stress was the result of a guilty conscience.

'How are you going to be able to bring yourself to stand up in court and speak in Evie's defence? It's beyond me.'

'We've been over this a hundred times, so don't let's fall out. I'm so worried about you, Cleo, and I can't bear the thought of hurting you. But I don't think that telling the truth indicates that I'm siding with either the defence or the prosecution. I'm only answering the questions I'm asked, and I will answer honestly.'

'It's all bollocks, you know that. Mark wouldn't hurt a fly. She's saying that he always hurt her in the dark – but Mark's afraid of the dark!'

Aminah's lips settled into a tight line.

'For God's sake, Cleo – I don't need to know any of this.

213

And apart from anything else, Mark wasn't a small child. I find it difficult to believe that a man of thirty-seven was still afraid of the dark. You really never stopped thinking of him as a child, did you?'

'You don't understand,' Cleo said, the anger draining from her. Nobody could understand what she had done for Mark.

'Anyway, I'm pleased to hear that you're keeping Evie alive in Lulu's thoughts.'

Cleo said nothing but avoided Aminah's gaze.

'She's been chuntering on in that language that only she understands today, but there's one word that she seems to have grasped. Mummy. Or Mumma as she says. Well done, Cleo. I'm proud of you for that.'

'Where is she?' Cleo asked, suddenly needing to get out of there and away from Aminah as quickly as possible.

'She's playing with Anik. Zahid's watching them. Are you going back to court tomorrow?'

'Of course,' Cleo said. 'I'll sort something for Lulu, though. I can see that it's difficult for you, and it's probably best if we keep out of each other's way until it's all over.'

'Don't be ridiculous. We're happy to have Lulu whenever you like. She's a cute kid and she's no trouble.' Aminah's voice softened. 'Cleo, you and I have been friends for a long time. We may not see eye to eye on this, but it's separate to our friendship, isn't it? I'm only going to tell the truth – not make any judgements – surely you can understand that?'

Cleo was saved the trouble of replying as Zahid walked into the hall carrying Lulu.

'She must have heard your voice, Cleo,' he said. Zahid wasn't

214

smiling, and that was unusual for this normally relaxed, cheerful man. 'I think she was calling for you.'

Cleo held out her arms for an excited Lulu.

'Mumma,' Lulu said, reaching towards her.

It seemed to take forever to get Lulu into her car seat. Cleo had felt Aminah and Zahid watching her, but she had made no excuses. It was none of their business. She had avoided Aminah's shocked stare and had simply turned and walked back down the path, stepping over a small bicycle lying in her way.

'Cleo, come back and talk to me about this,' Aminah had called after her, but she had ignored her.

There was no way she could explain her decision so that Aminah would understand. What was she expected to do? Lulu wouldn't even remember her mother, and Evie was going to prison, locked up until Lulu was a teenager. Surely it was better for Lulu to believe Cleo was her mother? They would move away from here to a town where nobody knew them. Cleo would change her name. She wouldn't be able to change Lulu's without Evie's permission, but if she wouldn't give it Cleo would change her own surname to Clarke so that everyone would believe Lulu was hers. Evie had insisted that her daughter was a Clarke and not a North until such time as she and Mark were married. She had always said that if their relationship didn't work out, she didn't want her child to have a different name to her own. Well, if she was so concerned about her daughter's well-being she could hardly object to Lulu believing she was the child of a loving mother, as opposed to someone rotting in prison for murder.

She would be glad to get home. The dark had descended early tonight. It was December, but the unseasonal warmth of the last few days had turned and a storm was brewing.

As Cleo swung the car into her drive, her headlights briefly illuminated the sitting room.

She felt a jolt of shock, but the image was gone as the lights swung to the right to glare on the garage door. She hadn't imagined it, though.

Just for a second as she had spun the wheel she was certain she had seen the silhouette of a man standing in the window.

37

Stephanie was glad the day was over. Unfortunately it meant it was one day closer to the time when she would be back in uniform, but she was sure she had done a good job as a detective and hoped she might be able to apply for a permanent post in CID with Gus's backing.

Of course when the trial finished she and Gus would have no reason to see each other. He kept talking about going for a drink and a chat before she left, but maybe it would be better for both of them if she got him out of her life completely and moved on. There were another couple of command units within the force that she could apply to without moving to a completely different part of the country. That had to be for the best.

As she headed out of the court, Stephanie was dismayed to see that it was starting to drizzle. She put her head down and ran through the streets back towards where her car was parked, but the rain was getting heavier, and she had forgotten her umbrella. There was nothing for it; she had no choice but to dodge into the wine bar and wait out the rain. Either that or ruin the new green silk shirt she had bought especially for the court appearance.

She pushed through the door into a virtually empty bar. It was that strange tranquil time before the onslaught of people popping in for an after-work drink to noisily celebrate the end of another day – people who probably didn't have anyone to rush home to. Much like herself, really.

She let the door swing to behind her, but before it clicked shut it was pushed open again. For some reason it came as no surprise to Stephanie to see Gus come striding in.

He hadn't been on the stand for long that day. He only had to give evidence about the arrest, but she had enjoyed listening to his confident voice and watching how well the jury responded to him. She had felt a stirring of pride, as if he was still hers.

'I thought it was you,' he said, following her to the bar.

'You stalking me?' she asked with a slight smile.

'Yeah. You got me. What are you drinking?'

Gus put his hand under Stephanie's elbow and guided her away from the bar and towards a quiet corner at the back. She looked at him and raised her eyebrows, but he merely grinned.

'Well, as you're buying,' she said, 'I'll have a large glass of Malbec please.'

Gus turned back to the bar and she watched him from behind. She had always thought that he walked like an Italian man – that slight swagger that came from the innate sense of confidence bred into them by their adoring mothers. There was a looseness about him that usually made others feel comfortable around him. It had the opposite effect on Stephanie, putting her on her guard.

She heard him laughing with the barman over something –

he always knew what to say. But she also knew that this was his affable side. Anyone who had seen Gus angry would think twice before they crossed him. His face would freeze and those soft brown eyes – laughing now with relaxed ease – would turn hard, black and frankly terrifying.

Those were the eyes he turned on Evie Clarke each time he looked at her. There was something he could see that Stephanie couldn't.

38

Cleo was still sitting in her car, not knowing what she should do. She was certain there was a man in her house – standing in the window. She'd *seen* him. Or had she imagined it?

For one wild, ridiculous moment, she had thought it was Mark, and the quiver of pleasure she felt for those milliseconds before logic kicked in left her weak with longing for her brother.

She wanted to call Aminah to ask if Zahid would come to her aid, but it would be a while before she forgot the look of dismay on her friend's face as she left earlier, and Zahid had looked appalled when Lulu had called her Mumma.

Should she call the police? She had seen the silhouette only for a second. It could have been the shadow of a tree reflected in the glass, and she would look such a fool. What if they thought she was becoming unhinged by the trial? She didn't want to give any indication that she was emotionally unfit to look after Lulu. They could take the child away from her, and that didn't bear thinking about.

She had nobody left to fall back on. She had to face this alone.

Much as she hated the thought of leaving Lulu in the car

even for two minutes, she couldn't risk walking into the house carrying a small child if there was someone in there.

'Lulu, darling, Mummy's going to leave you in the car for a minute.' She turned round to look at the child she now thought of as her own, safely strapped into her seat. Her little head with its fine covering of wispy dark hair was resting on the wing of the chair and in the gloom Cleo could see she was asleep. Good. Lulu wouldn't know she was alone.

She opened the car door and got out as quietly as she could, pressing the key fob to lock all the doors. Keeping herself close to the wall, she slid her door key into the lock and turned it slowly. Should she switch the lights on, or should she walk in the dark into the sitting room, to see if the man was still standing there? Perhaps she should pretend she hadn't seen him and stroll confidently into the house, switching the lights on and going straight to the kitchen, leaving the front door open. If he was there, it would give him an opportunity to escape.

Her heart felt as if it was coming up through her chest and into her throat. Every inch of her body seemed to be beating in time to its fast thud – she could hear it as well as feel it.

Cleo couldn't bring herself to do as she had planned. She didn't want to see his face, whoever he was, because he would become the face of her nightmares.

She opened the door quietly. If she stayed where she was and shouted, maybe he would come to her.

With the door still open behind her so she could run out into the street and scream if it came to that, Cleo shouted, 'Hello? I know you're there. I saw you. Who are you? What do you want?'

For a moment there was nothing. Then she heard a thump coming from the sitting room. It sounded as if he had walked into the coffee table.

'I'm going to go back out to my car. I'm going to lock myself in. You can leave then. Take anything you want.'

She had started to reverse up to the door when she heard a voice speaking softly – little more than a whisper. 'Cleo?'

Cleo stood still, frozen to the spot. She knew that voice – she would know it anywhere.

39

Stephanie had never imagined that she would end the day having a drink with Gus, but he was being relatively well behaved and had talked only about the case. He hadn't yet strayed into personal territory.

'The defence are putting up a good fight. I've come across Boyd Simmonds before, and he fools everyone into believing he's benign, then he floors them – like I hear he did with Cleo North. But despite his cunning, I still say that Evie Clarke is going down for life.'

'I get it that charging her with murder was our only option given that she clearly didn't kill him in self-defence, but would it be the end of the world if her partial defence is successful and she's sentenced on the voluntary manslaughter charge? Don't you think you're being a bit harsh, wanting her to be convicted of murder? Mark was abusing her for months, Gus. It's not surprising that she lost it.'

Gus took a sip of his beer and shook his head slowly.

'Steph, you know full well that I think abusers are the scum of the earth. They should be locked up – every last one of them. It sickens me when I hear of the shit some women have

223

to put up with. But that's not the point here. We're not arguing about whether she was or wasn't abused. We're arguing about her state of mind when she killed him. There's something about Evie and I just think there's more to it. She seems too emotionally controlled to have lost it. Too smart to have put herself at risk of going to prison for life.'

Stephanie sighed. She found it hard to believe that Gus was so intransigent; it was unlike him. He'd really got a bee in his bonnet about Evie Clarke.

'You see Evie as a controlled, intelligent woman, Gus. I see someone who's suffered enormously. And anyway, being smart doesn't preclude her from being in an abusive relationship – it's not a situation that's confined to the weak and needy.'

Gus put his beer glass down on the table and leaned back in his chair. 'I know that. That's not what I meant. But Mark North's not the one on trial here, although that's not how it feels. You're saying that effectively his guilt proves her innocence. But that's not true, and he's not here to speak for himself. We're trying to determine if she planned to kill him – if it was murder. Think of the consequences if Evie is found not guilty. Will it persuade other victims of abuse to plan a murder and say it was a rush of blood to the head?'

It was pointless arguing. It didn't matter how many times they discussed it, because Gus was adamant that Evie didn't fit into his idea of a woman who would lose control.

'There's something about her, Steph. A kind of quiet assurance that doesn't sit comfortably with a person who could lash out in a moment of madness.'

Stephanie understood what he was saying, but Gus hadn't

been the first officer on the scene to see the broken body of Mia North less than four years previously and she knew her discomfort about the coroner's verdict on that death was influencing her judgement on this one. She had always believed there was more to it.

Stephanie clearly remembered that day. She had been at the house since the body was discovered, and it was several hours later that she heard Mark burst through the front door, shouting for his sister.

'Cleo – what's happened to Mia? What is it?'

Mark had been recalled from his business trip, but by the time he arrived home Mia's body had been removed from the scene. Stephanie had watched the interaction between brother and sister, and had felt then that something was slightly off. There was nothing she could put her finger on, but it had felt odd. Cleo had been the one to discover Mia's body at the bottom of the basement steps and she seemed agitated rather than upset.

'I'm so sorry, Mark,' she had said, putting her arms round him and hugging him close to her. 'I did check her pulse – I didn't know if I should or not, but I had to be sure.'

In Stephanie's view there was nothing to be unsure about as Mia's eyes were wide open, staring unseeing at the ceiling. Then Stephanie had heard Cleo begging Mark not to talk to the police until he had spoken to a solicitor. She remembered glancing into the master bedroom and seeing him with his head bent, his shoulders shaking, and Cleo pacing anxiously, telling him repeatedly that it was okay. She was there for him.

Mia's death had been ruled an accident, but as part of the

pre-trial investigation in the Evie Clarke case Gus had given Stephanie the go-ahead to take another look. If Mark had been abusing Evie, he could have been doing the same to his wife and they needed to be aware of anything the defence might bring to court. When she finally acknowledged that there was nothing to find, Stephanie realised she had been hoping to discover evidence of a succession of injuries to Mia North before her death, and she'd had to admit to herself that there was only one possible reason for her disappointment. She wanted to believe in Evie's innocence.

'I know you weren't in court when I was giving my evidence,' she said, deciding it was time to steer the conversation on to a less controversial subject, 'but there was a man in the gallery who caught my eye.'

Gus raised his eyebrows.

'Oh not like that,' she said with a tut. 'He was staring at Evie as if he wanted to burrow inside her head and extract whatever was lurking there. It was intense. I went up to the gallery for a closer look, but I've no idea who he was. Something rattled him, though, and he ended up tearing up a sheet of paper and scattering the pieces all over the floor.'

She fished the paper scraps from her pocket and dumped them on the table.

'You picked them up? How very tidy of you. Do you want me to find a bin?' Gus asked.

'No. I wondered if there was anything on there that might be interesting.' She ignored Gus's withering glance. 'When someone behaves like that, I want to know why. Call me nosy.'

Unfortunately, the rain had soaked through the pockets of

her jacket, and as Stephanie started to separate the soggy pieces while Gus went to get another drink, she realised that it was going to be difficult to make any sense out of them.

'They got wet in my pocket,' she said as he put the drinks down on the table. 'The writing's all run together. I can't send them to the lab, though, because I've no idea whether they're relevant or not. It's just that if he knew Evie, he might be someone else to talk to.'

Gus picked up a few of the scraps that Stephanie had successfully separated. The blue ink had been reduced to little more than a series of disconnected smudges.

'Obviously a letter of some type. But we've got no proof this man has got anything to do with the case, so I don't think you should worry about it.'

Stephanie ignored him and tried to match the pieces together. The letter had been folded when he had torn it, so several of the pieces were identical shapes. It was hard to work out how they fitted together with the smudged ink blurring the letters.

'Listen to this, Gus. It starts, "My darling," although there is no name after it, which isn't helpful. It then seems to say something about someone dying. I can just about read the words "already dead".' Stephanie peered closer to the paper. 'Don't you think that makes it interesting?'

'Let's have a look,' Gus said, moving round to look over her shoulder. 'You've got these two pieces in the wrong place. See – here.' He moved two scraps around.

Stephanie stared at the rearranged pieces. 'That bit now says, "I am already dead." That's a bit weird, isn't it?'

227

Between them, they managed to pick out a few words and phrases, but it still wasn't clear.

'It's obvious that this is a farewell message from someone who was expecting to die. But I can't see why it matters,' Gus said. 'The signature is "With love always, S x." Sorry, Steph. I admire your detecting skills, but I don't think this is going to lead you anywhere.'

Stephanie couldn't help feeling disappointed. She gathered up the scraps of paper and pushed them back in her pocket.

40

Cleo was still reeling from the shock of hearing that voice – the voice that had once meant the world to her.

She stood still, waiting to hear if he would speak again – maybe the stress of the day was causing her to imagine things.

'Cleo, it's me,' he said.

This time, she saw a shadow emerge from the sitting room and stand in the doorway, clearly uncertain of the reception he would get.

'Sorry if I scared you.' His voice was quiet, almost nervous.

'*Scared* me – I was bloody *terrified*,' she said, her voice coming out as a high-pitched squeak. 'What are you doing here?'

Cleo glanced over her shoulder towards the car. Now that she knew there was no danger, she should go and get Lulu.

'I was in court today, sitting in the gallery, behind you. I needed to see if you were coping, and I'm not sure you are.'

She sighed and leaned against the wall by the front door, ready to run for Lulu if she woke and started to cry.

'Joe, we agreed not to see each other again. It's good of you to care, but this isn't helpful.'

'I wrote to you, though. Pen, paper – the whole shebang.'

229

She could hear the slight smile in his voice. She had always loved to receive letters – they could be kept safe to reread in the future, unlike the more transient emails and texts. But she also wasn't stupid and knew why Joe had chosen to write. Anything committed to his phone or his computer could easily be tracked by his wife.

'I got your letter, and I appreciate it. But I could hardly respond, could I?'

She heard him breathe out slowly. 'I suppose not. Can we talk though, now that I'm here? I want to be sure you're okay. I can't stand to see you suffering.'

Joe had no idea. How could she explain to him that she felt as if her body was in a vice, the pressure no less than it was four months ago? There was only one thing keeping her going.

'You know I've got Lulu, don't you?'

'Of course. Just because I don't see you any more doesn't mean I don't know what's happening in your life.'

Cleo felt a vague shudder of unease. Had he been watching her?

'Do you want me to get Lulu out of the car for you?' he asked.

'She doesn't know you – she'd be scared. Look, go in the sitting room, shut the curtains and put the lamps on. I'll take her straight up to bed. She's been playing with Aminah's kids all day so she'll be shattered. I'll be with you in a minute.'

She could almost feel Joe's body tense as he forced himself not to look at his watch. Throughout all the time they had spent together, it had been the one thing that had driven her mad. He was forever checking the time to see if he was supposed to be home, or whether it was still safe to continue peddling the myth that he was working late.

It shouldn't matter to her any more, but it did. She turned her back on him and ran out to the car, the rain now falling heavily. Leaning in to unstrap Lulu she felt the cold drops hit her back and slither under the waistband of her skirt.

'Come on, baby girl. Let's get you inside.'

Lulu started to object to being woken, grizzling and saying two of the few words she could manage. 'No, Mumma, no.'

Cleo kissed her soft cheek and lifted her out, protecting the top of her head with her hand. She ran up the couple of steps and in through the front door. She could see the sitting room light was on now, but she didn't pause, continuing up the stairs with Lulu, who was starting to nod off again.

Making sure Lulu was dry, Cleo decided that no harm could come to her if she laid her in her cot for a while. She would undress her when Joe had gone. He wouldn't be staying long, unless things had somehow changed at home, and anyway, she didn't think she wanted him to. He was another reminder of something that she had lost.

Slowly she walked back down the stairs, wondering what she was going to say to him.

'Do you want something to drink?' she asked – always a safe opener – as she pushed open the door to the sitting room. Joe had taken a seat on the sofa, but he had perched right on the edge, hands clasped between his knees, as if ready to take flight at a moment's notice. He wasn't a big man, but tonight he seemed smaller, thinner than she remembered.

'No – but if you do, go ahead.'

'Don't you have to get back?' she asked, ashamed at the slightly bitter tone in her voice. She didn't need to be like this.

Joe had the sense not to answer and waited for her to come back in with a large gin and tonic. After the day she'd had, she needed this.

'Tell me how you are,' he said. 'How you *really* are.'

She couldn't do it. If she opened her mouth to talk about the pain of losing Mark she would fall apart, and she mustn't do that in front of Joe. The temptation to give in and let him comfort her would be too great.

'I'm doing okay. But you shouldn't be here. How did you get in?'

'I still have a key. You never asked for it back.'

Joe used to come round to her house whenever he could safely get away. He would call her at the gallery and she would stop whatever she was doing and run to him. It had started when Mark had begun to spend more and more time with Evie, and their budding relationship had created a huge gap in Cleo's life.

To start with, time with Joe was little more than a filler for her lonely hours, and she knew that for him it was something of an adventure. He was the type of man who never took risks, but when he had come into the gallery to find a piece of jewellery for his wife he swore that he had been completely bowled over by Cleo.

'You were – no, are – so vibrant,' he had told her. 'Everything about you from your shocking cropped white hair to your vivid clothes was mesmerising. I thought you were exciting, different, dangerous. You represented everything that I had never experienced in my life.'

For Cleo, Joe became the person on whom she depended. Despite the fact that he was being unfaithful to his wife, something that he had always found difficult to believe about himself, in every other way he was steady, reliable.

He told her that more than anything he wanted to be with her permanently – to live together, maybe have children together. But they would have to leave the area.

'It's not fair on Siobhan if I'm still around,' he'd said. 'But if we moved away, not so far that I couldn't get back to see the kids at the weekend of course, but far enough so that she didn't have to witness our happiness, we could start again from scratch.'

Mark was the only person who knew about Joe. She had told him she had ended the relationship because she had no right to steal another woman's husband – that was how she felt and truly what she believed. But it wasn't the only reason.

The minute Joe had suggested moving away – away from Mark, away from the baby that was growing inside Evie and was now lying upstairs in her cot – Cleo had known she couldn't do it.

In all truth she didn't believe they would have lasted as a couple either, and recognised that they had both fulfilled a temporary need in each other. She had needed someone to care about her, and he was looking for excitement. Would it feel the same when someone had to go out in the pouring rain to put the bins out, or when one of them was lying in bed with a streaming cold? She doubted it.

She made a virtue out of her decision to end the relationship before Siobhan found out, but her apparent self-sacrifice was only half the truth.

41

The trial had reached a critical point. The prosecution had rested its case and the defence was due to begin. The jury had heard from forensics, from the pathologist, and from a string of other experts, and for Harriet there had been no surprises other than the additional scars on Evie's body. Right now the jury would probably be feeling most inclined to believe the prosecution, and so it was up to the defence team – and in particular, Boyd Simmonds – to change their perception.

They had yet to decide whether Evie should take the stand. It would be the obvious thing to do, but Harriet was concerned about how the jury would see her. She could appear aloof, distant, and although Harriet was certain this was Evie's way of protecting herself against all that was happening in her life, she needed to appear to be the victim she undoubtedly was. She would have to convince the jury and the judge that when she took the knife into the bedroom she had no intention of hurting Mark – that there was no premeditation and it wasn't an act of revenge. One unintentional slip, one unguarded word, and the case could turn on its head. But they had time to decide. Until then, they would see how the defence developed.

Boyd Simmonds called his first witness.

'Doctor Chaudhry, I believe you treated Miss Clarke when she came to the accident and emergency department at the hospital at which you work. Is that correct?'

'Yes, that's right. She was in considerable pain.'

'Can you tell me what her injuries were?'

'She was suffering from a severe crush injury, and had broken the proximal phalanges of three fingers.' The doctor held up his hand and indicated the bone above the knuckle. He then grasped the end of the middle finger. 'She had also damaged the distal phalanges on two fingers, and two metacarpals. Fortunately there didn't appear to be any long-term nerve damage.'

'Can you please describe to the court what you mean by a crush injury, Doctor?'

'A crush injury occurs when a compressive force is applied to the tissues. At the site of the injury the tissues experience several forces simultaneously. Imagine, for example, getting a hand caught in an old-fashioned wringer.' The doctor, who clearly enjoyed giving demonstrations, held one hand flat while the other turned an imaginary handle. 'There can be all kinds of implications but it seems Miss Clarke was able to extract her hand quite quickly, which probably saved her from damage to the blood vessels.'

'And did Miss Clarke explain to you how she had suffered this injury?'

'She did. She said she had trapped her hand between some weights in their home gym.'

The doctor described in detail how Evie claimed the injury had been caused, complete with further intricate hand movements.

'Did you believe her?'

'The injuries were consistent with the accident that she described, yes.'

'Did you believe that she had been holding onto the bar that lifted the weights, and that it had slipped out of her hand?'

The doctor gave a small shake of the head. 'It's technically possible that she did that, but highly unlikely. I didn't believe her, if I'm honest.'

'Apart from feeling it was an unlikely accident, was there any other reason to disbelieve her?'

'Yes. I checked her medical history and she had been in to see us before. The last time was with a particularly wicked scald on her right forearm, and prior to that her ribs had been x-rayed for a possible fracture, although none was found, and she had broken a couple of toes on one occasion – apparently from kicking a coffee table. There were a few notes in her GP records which gave me cause for concern too.'

Boyd stopped him. The next witness would be a nurse from the GP's surgery, and it would be far more powerful to hear her evidence directly.

'From what you had read in the notes, Doctor Chaudhry, did you feel there was a pattern to these injuries?'

'I'm sure you'll understand that we see a lot of people – not just women – who have been subjected to abuse. The red flag was definitely waving for me in this case.'

The doctor looked towards Evie and gave her a sympathetic half smile. Evie dropped her head, as if too ashamed to face the doctor or the court.

'Did you ask Miss Clarke if she was being abused?'

The doctor gave a slight nod. 'I did, but she kept shaking her head and denying it. I was not convinced by her response.'

The questions for the defence were complete, and as Boyd took his seat, Harriet glanced up to the gallery. Cleo North was sitting right at the front, practically hanging over the rail. Her eyes were bleak, her face white, and once again Harriet felt deep sympathy for the woman. How awful to realise that someone you loved had done such terrible things to another person.

She turned back as Devisha Ambo stood up for the prosecution.

'For the sake of clarity, Doctor Chaudhry, when Miss Clarke presented herself at the hospital telling you the damage to her hand was the result of an accident, could she have been telling the truth?'

The doctor's mouth settled into a tight line. There was only one answer he could give, although clearly he didn't like it.

'Yes,' he said.

'And when you asked if she was being abused, according to you, she said no. Is that correct?'

The doctor looked uncomfortable. 'Yes,' he said quietly.

'So, if I have interpreted your answers correctly, you decided not to believe what she was telling you purely because of an expression in her eyes and because you have had to deal with abused women in the past. In other words, you made an assumption, didn't you Doctor Chaudhry?'

Harriet glanced at the gallery and saw Cleo North fold her arms and lean back, a fraction more colour in her cheeks.

42

I'm letting everything that is happening in court wash over me, because one thought, one image, pushes everything else into the background. In my head it's as if I'm looking at one of Mark's photos – the centrepiece brightly lit and in sharp focus, everything around it dark, blurred, indistinct.

Central to the image in my mind is my daughter – Lulu.

It's so long since I've seen her and I missed her first birthday. I've tried not to think of her too much, not to miss her, but I've been away from her for four months, and what happens in the next few days is going to decide whether I see her any time soon.

Since I've been on remand I have contacted Cleo time and again to ask if she will bring Lulu to see me, but she says it's too upsetting for such a young child. And of course Cleo doesn't want to see me. I killed her brother – whether justified or not, it's all the same to her. If I killed him because of the way he treated me, she will assume it was something in me that made him behave the way he did. Cleo could never allow herself to believe that Mark would abuse anyone, and whatever the courts say, she never will. But she does think that he is capable of lashing out in anger. I know that.

I could probably demand to see my daughter – maybe appeal to Social Services. But I know what Cleo will say. She just repeats the same excuses over and over: it's too far to travel; it will unsettle Lulu; she's too young. If I force the issue she will do all she can to turn my daughter against me. What do they call it? Parental alienation, I think. Cleo wouldn't have to do much to make the visit unpleasant for Lulu. Just making sure that my little girl was tired before she arrived so she was grumpy and tearful would be enough to make her dread a return visit.

If I'm out of here in a few weeks, I'll be able to get Lulu back – eventually. If I'm found guilty of murder, it might be best for her if she doesn't have to visit me in prison week after week throughout her childhood. It's not a great place to be and it will be so hard to explain – as soon as she's old enough to understand – why I'm in here and not at home with her.

And what would I say? 'I'm in here because I killed your daddy.'

Should I say, 'He had it coming to him,' as if we were all part of a bad TV drama?

The sad thing is that Lulu is going to have to learn the truth some time, and it's not what I want for her. Which would be worse in her mind – that she had an abusive father or has a mother who is a killer? I can see no happy outcome for my daughter, and that's not the way it should be. I know instinctively that she would be no happier with Cleo either – whose twisted version of the truth and bitter hatred of me would be bound to colour my daughter's life.

Whatever Cleo chooses to believe, I find it hard to accept

that for the six months before I killed Mark she didn't suspect anything was going on. She must surely have noticed how nervous I became each time Mark went away, and how withdrawn I was when he returned, how I flinched from his touch? I was sure she would see there was something wrong.

I did everything I could, short of saying outright that her brother was hurting me, to make her believe what I wanted her to believe. But she was blind. Perhaps I should have come right out with it; spoken the words out loud.

Surely by now she must have some doubts? She has to believe he was a bully. I *need* her to believe that.

She's been in court all day, but I can't see her unless I turn my head. I know she's there, though. Every now and again when someone makes a comment about Mark that she doesn't like, I hear a little gasp. Nobody else in the gallery would care that much about what was said, so it has to be Cleo – probably sitting right at the front, wishing there was no glass between us so she could throw a rope around my neck and strangle me. I had originally thought the glass was to protect the court from violent defendants. But perhaps it's the other way round.

For most of this session, with a parade of witnesses recounting the dreadful things that I suffered, I will hang my head in shame. Nobody wants the world to know that they allowed themselves to be abused, and I don't want anyone to see my eyes or what is lurking behind them. I don't want to look at the people who are having to stand up in court and talk about my injuries.

Of course, they don't know the half of it.

No matter what anyone says in this court, whatever injuries they describe, they will never understand the pain I have suffered or experience the hatred I feel for the person I hold responsible. Maybe justice has been done now. Maybe I can let it go, and carry on with the rest of my life.

But for that to be possible, Harriet and her worthy QC are going to have to perform a miracle, and at this moment I'm convinced it's not going to happen. I may be in prison for a very long time.

43

Stephanie stole a sneaky look at Gus. His jaw was tight as he listened to the evidence presented in support of Evie's not guilty plea. It was hard on the senior investigating officer; there was always the sense of the unknown – some fact or other that the defence could pull out of the hat which might knock the carefully constructed prosecution case sideways. She wanted to reach out to him, to show her support. But she resisted the temptation.

The previous evening it had almost felt as if they were a couple again, but when they had exhausted talk of the case Stephanie had begun to feel uncomfortable. If she had stayed any longer the conversation would have become too personal and they would have had to expose all the unspoken truths about their relationship, so she had made her excuses and left. Now, watching him lean forward as the next witness took the stand, she wondered if that had been a mistake.

The defence had called a nurse from the local GP practice to the stand. A tall, cheerful-looking woman with a frizz of curly hair and a big smile, the nurse didn't seem at all fazed by the occasion.

'Mrs Gifford, you are the practice nurse at Church Street Surgery, is that correct?'

'Yes, that's right.'

'And you saw Miss Clarke for a routine smear test a few months after she gave birth to her daughter?'

'Yes. I think the baby was about seven months old when she came to see me.'

'Had you met Miss Clarke before?'

Mrs Gifford turned to give Evie a smile, but Evie's head was lowered, as it had been for most of the day.

'I've seen her a few times. She came in with the baby once or twice, and I'd replaced the dressings when she scalded her arm the month before. That was nasty – I thought she was very brave.'

'Yes, thank you, Mrs Gifford. We know about the scalding. On the occasion that she came in for her cervical smear test, did you feel there was anything of particular interest about Miss Clarke's behaviour?'

'I thought she was a bit nervy – but then nobody likes having a smear test.'

'What happened when you began to examine her?'

Mrs Gifford again glanced at Evie, and this time Evie looked up and gave the nurse a tight smile, as if in apology for what she had put her through.

'I could see the poor lass was badly bruised,' she said. 'The soft tissue on the insides of her thighs was discoloured – some reddish purple bruising, which suggested it was fairly recent, and some signs of older damage, maybe a few days.'

'And did you comment on this to Miss Clarke?'

243

'I did. I wanted her to tell me how the bruising came about, because sometimes it can indicate other problems or illnesses, and if she had no explanation I would want to run some tests or ask the doctor to take a look at her.'

Boyd Simmonds nodded his head, as if this was all news to him. 'And was she able to provide a reason?'

Mrs Gifford nodded eagerly. 'Yes, but she wasn't telling the truth. I could see that because she wouldn't look me in the eye. She said she'd fallen off her bike.'

'And what did you think of that?'

'I asked her if she'd fallen off twice, because she had two sets of bruises, and she said the road to the house she lived in was covered with gravel and it was easy to slip. But the bruising was on both thighs and she'd have had to roll around a few times with the bike between her legs for that to have happened.'

'Did you draw any conclusions of your own?'

'I've been a nurse for a long time, sir, and I would say these bruises were the result of fairly violent sex.'

'Thank you, Mrs Gifford.'

Boyd Simmonds made his way back to his seat as the prosecutor stood up.

'Mrs Gifford, did you ask Miss Clarke if she had been raped?'

For the first time, the woman looked slightly uncomfortable.

'Not in so many words, no. But I did say to her that if someone was mistreating her, she could tell me.'

'And did she?'

'No. She repeated that she had fallen off her bike. Twice!'

Devisha gave the witness one of her most glowing smiles.

'In your experience as a nurse, would you say that there are some people – both men and women – who enjoy rough sex?'

'Well, yes. I suppose so. Each to their own.' Mrs Gifford gave a slight shudder.

'And is there any reason to suppose Miss Clarke could not have been one of those people – that in fact the bruises were the result of rough sex, but that she had been a fully active participant?'

'I can't say, obviously. But she didn't look happy at what I'd seen.'

'Thank you, Mrs Gifford. I have no further questions.'

Stephanie glanced sideways at Gus again.

'Well?' she asked.

'Too close to call.' He pushed himself up from his seat and headed for the exit.

He was right. She had no idea which way this was going to go either.

44

Cleo had been dreading the moment when Aminah took the witness box. It was still hard for her to believe that her friend was being called by the defence, and she wondered if their friendship would ever recover. She tried to imagine a life without Aminah in it, and it was nearly impossible. She had already lost Mark, and if she lost Aminah too she would be completely alone.

For a moment last night she had seriously considered re-kindling her relationship with Joe, but whatever she had felt for him in the past, she was certain he wasn't her future.

She no longer felt particularly sad about him. She had no room for any other grief. The agony of losing Mark rippled through her body constantly, sometimes building into great waves of sorrow that threatened to engulf her and drag her down into the depths of a despair from which she might never surface. It was hard enough to lose her brother – but to lose him like this, with the publicity and the accusation that he was an abusive bully, was unbearable.

And now, suddenly, her best friend was being sworn in to give evidence against him.

The questioning started, the QC's apparently affable manner suddenly becoming the focus of Cleo's anger. What right had he to drag her brother's name through the mud over and over again?

'Mrs Basra, I'd like to take you back to the afternoon of 7th July, if I may.'

Cleo watched Aminah's face. Usually so cheerful, today she looked as if she was struggling not to cry. She glanced up to the gallery and met Cleo's eyes just as Cleo felt someone slip into the seat beside her and reach for her hand. Aminah was looking at the newcomer and trying to smile. Cleo turned her head. It was Zahid.

'Aminah wanted you to have someone with you,' he whispered. He gave her hand a squeeze between his two palms and held it there, his attention turning to his wife.

Cleo felt a huge surge of emotion for her friend. Even after the way she had behaved yesterday, Aminah and Zahid's big hearts weren't going to let her go through this alone.

'You went round to Mr North's house to see Miss Clarke. Is that correct?'

'Yes. She had originally invited me to lunch, but then she cancelled.'

'But you went anyway?'

'I was concerned about her. She sent me a text message and I tried to call her, but she didn't answer.'

'Why did that concern you? Surely it's not so unusual for people to cancel arrangements?'

'I'd been a bit worried about her for a while. I'd only recently taken her to the hospital to have the plaster cast taken off her hand, and I wondered if she was coping okay. I knew Mark had gone away the night before, you see, and if she was struggling a bit – her hand was still sore, I'm sure – I wanted her to know that I was there for her.'

'And what happened when you arrived at the house?'

'I rang the doorbell over and over but she didn't answer. I called her on the house phone and on her mobile, and she didn't pick up. So by now I was really worried, and was tempted to phone Cleo – Mark's sister – when I noticed the garage door was open.'

Cleo sat up straight. That couldn't be right. It didn't make sense.

'And does the garage lead straight into the house?'

'No, but there's a door at the back that lets you through into the side garden that runs level with the top floor of the house. So I went through. Evie was in the kitchen, by the window. She was staring into thin air. I don't think she noticed me.'

'And what happened then?'

'She turned towards me. She looked shocked, and I only saw her for a minute before she pulled the blind across.'

'Even though she had seen you, she closed the blind?'

'Yes – I don't think she wanted me to see that she had a black eye. The whole of one side of her face was swollen – purple and red. It looked very sore.'

'Did she let you in then?'

'No. I tried to get to speak to her for a couple of days after that, sending her texts, calling, dropping round unannounced. Finally she answered.'

'And did you ask her about the black eye?'

248

Aminah gave an uneasy smile. 'Yes, of course. She said Lulu had kicked her while she was changing her nappy. That's why she had been confined to the house for the last few days. She hadn't wanted anyone to see her.'

'And you find that excuse unconvincing?'

'Look, I've got four kids and I've changed more nappies than I can count. And I've had feet in my face – of course I have. But have you seen Lulu, Evie's little girl? She's a skinny little mite, and even my infinitely more hefty brutes would never have made a mark like that on my face. She was making it up.'

Cleo wasn't listening any more. The prosecution barrister had stood up and was asking one or two questions, but none of them mattered. She let go of Zahid's hand and leaned forward, her head lowered so she could think. She quickly turned her head. Were the detectives still in the courtroom? Yes – the woman who had come to see her, Sergeant King, was sitting at the back of the gallery.

As Aminah was dismissed from the witness box, Cleo jumped up and pushed past Zahid and the other people in her row. She heard Zahid call her name, but she was heading for Sergeant King. There was something wrong with this story.

Stephanie had noticed Cleo's agitation, and the fact that she had turned around, searching the gallery for someone. It was clear to Stephanie that she was that someone, and now as Aminah Basra left the witness box, Cleo came scurrying towards her and leaned across two spectators who were whispering to each other.

'Can I talk to you?' she asked, her speech fast and her voice breathy.

Stephanie excused herself as she pushed past the couple to reach the aisle. The judge was about to announce a break, so she wasn't going to miss anything vital.

'Let's go and chat outside,' she said, touching Cleo gently on the arm in a small gesture of sympathy. It felt to her that in this case there were no winners. Only losers, and Cleo was one of them.

There were signs everywhere in the court advising people not to discuss cases, and so Stephanie steered Cleo out of the building. Fortunately it was a fine, if chilly day, and they found a bench that was capturing some of the sun's weak rays.

'What can I do for you, Miss North?' she asked.

'There's something wrong about what Aminah said in there.'

'You mean you don't believe her?'

Cleo shook her head quickly. 'No. Aminah wouldn't lie. It's not that. It's the garage door.'

Stephanie gave Cleo what she hoped was an encouraging nod, but she had no idea where this was going.

'Why was the garage door open?' Cleo asked.

Stephanie shrugged. 'I've no idea. Why do you think it's important?'

'Look, I happen to know that Mark went to the airport by taxi that morning, so he had no need to open the garage. I bet if you ask Aminah she will tell you that Mark's car was there.'

'You're going to have to explain your thinking here, Miss North. I'm sorry if I'm not getting it.'

'They always kept the garage locked, because it was the only way anyone could get into the grounds, other than through the house. It was the only weak spot in their security. So it would have been closed for sure when he left that morning. Why was it open when Aminah went round? Evie must have opened it, but why would she do that, unless she wanted Aminah to see her?'

Stephanie gave a small shrug. 'Maybe Miss Clarke went out?'

'No, no. That's not right. You heard Aminah – Evie told her she was housebound because of the eye. I can't see any reason why she would have opened the garage door.'

Cleo had grabbed Stephanie's arm, as if to make her listen more carefully, but much as she wanted to help this woman, Stephanie couldn't for the life of her think of any way in which this might benefit the case for the prosecution.

'And when I went round later,' Cleo continued, her tone urgent, 'the garage was closed and I couldn't get through. Look – they were so security conscious that they had changed the locks on the doors and even *my* key no longer worked. It doesn't make sense.'

Stephanie spoke softly, not wanting to increase Cleo's agitation. 'If Evie knew that Mrs Basra had got in through the garage it might well have reminded her to close the door. That would explain why it was closed when you arrived. And there could be any number of reasons why she had opened it. I'm not sure we can go anywhere with this.'

Cleo tutted with frustration. 'Will you do something for me? *Please.*' She paused and waited until Stephanie spoke.

'I'll do my best, but I don't know what I can do.'

'Will you ask the prosecution barrister to question Evie about why the garage door was open?'

Cleo's eyes were pleading with her, and Stephanie tried to give her a sympathetic smile, but Cleo turned away as if in disgust.

'I'll pass it on to her. Of course I will. But there's no guarantee that the defence will put Miss Clarke on the stand.'

Cleo's head spun back towards Stephanie, her mouth slightly ajar. 'What? Are you telling me there's a chance that she might not be called to account for what she did – that she doesn't have to explain herself to the jury?'

Stephanie looked at the woman's white face, the black circles under her eyes. She didn't want to add to her distress, but she couldn't set false expectations.

'We interviewed her when she was arrested, and we've told the court everything she said. I suspect the defence will only call her if they need some part of her testimony to convince the jury of the truth of her story.'

'Well can't the prosecutor call her?' Cleo's voice was rising, and Stephanie touched her arm again.

'I know this must be terribly upsetting for you, Miss North, but the only way she will be brought to the stand is if her solicitor and barrister think there's something to be gained. If I had to guess right now, I would say they won't.'

Cleo leapt up from the bench. 'She's got to be *made* to speak. The jury have to see through her. They have to know that my brother wasn't the bully she says he was.'

She turned on her heel and marched quickly back towards the courtroom.

45

The last witness for the defence was about to be called, and Harriet was still not sure whether they had done enough. Surely the jury would believe by now that Mark had been hurting Evie? The rest of it, though, was so much harder to prove. How could you demonstrate conclusively that someone lost control, rather than planned to kill? There were points in Evie's favour – and Boyd would use these in his summing-up – but even if the defence was successful they would need to be sure the evidence of brutality was strong enough to limit the custodial sentence, and that decision was down to the judge.

The prosecution were going to play heavily on the fact that Evie took the knife into the bedroom, but until now they hadn't been able to make much of it, other than to state the facts. They'd had nobody to ask. If Evie took the stand, that would be their chance. So she and Boyd had to balance the risk against the gains of hearing her explanation of all that had happened. So much of the court's perception of Evie might rely on her testimony.

Harriet stopped thinking about the pros and cons of putting Evie on the stand. They had the weekend to prepare, but before that they were about to call one witness who might do their job for them, at least in part. She was introduced as Deborah May, and she looked as if a gust of strong wind would blow her away. She stared around the room as if not entirely sure how she came to be there.

'Mrs May,' Boyd said. 'Can you please tell the court in what capacity you know Miss Clarke?'

The woman's eyes flicked quickly to the dock and then away.

'I work for the Samaritans. I spoke to Miss Clarke on several occasions on the telephone.'

'We all know that anything said to the Samaritans is confidential, so can you please explain to the court why you're here today.'

'We can pass on information if we have consent from the person concerned, or if we receive a court order. In this case, the court order wasn't necessary, because Miss Clarke gave her permission.'

'Can you tell us about these phone calls?'

'I volunteer one night a week, usually a Tuesday, and Miss Clarke called when I was on duty. She told me her name was Evie and she knew me as Debbie. She called again the next week and asked for me.'

She was speaking quickly, apparently anxious to get her words out. Boyd gave her a moment as he consulted the document in his hand. Harriet saw her take a deep breath and blow it out slowly through pursed lips.

'Is that normal? To request the same Samaritan?'

'It's not a good idea for callers to become dependent on a single Samaritan, because if they reach a crisis and the person with whom they've formed the relationship isn't there, it could be catastrophic. But Evie worked out the times I would be on duty and tried to call then.'

'Did you always take her call?'

'Unfortunately there were times when I was already on a call with another person, so one of my colleagues tried to speak with her. But Evie always chose to call back.'

'How many times did you speak to her in total, Mrs May?'

'Six times.'

'And what can you tell us about the nature of the conversation?'

Debbie May glanced at Evie, her brow furrowing as if she was saying something she shouldn't. 'Evie was upset because the man she was living with was violent. Suddenly, for no reason that she could think of, he would do something so shocking, so painful that she simply collapsed.'

Boyd turned to look at Evie and the eyes of the jury followed. He shook his head slightly to indicate his sympathy.

'Did she ever say she had challenged him about why he was hurting her?'

'I think she tried. But she said it was as if he didn't know he'd done anything and he always expressed horror and surprise that she'd had an accident.'

Debbie May's lip curled slightly at the thought of Mark pleading ignorance.

'And what was Miss Clarke's state of mind when she called you?'

'It was strange because she sounded bemused to start with, like she couldn't understand what was happening and why. She said his bursts of violence seemed to be triggered by the fact that he was having to go away and she started to dread his going while at the same time being glad he was gone, if that makes sense. It's not our job to give advice, but I wanted to tell her to get the hell out of there – as fast as she could.'

Boyd nodded and reordered his papers again. Harriet knew he was waiting to see if Mrs May said anything else without being asked.

'Nobody should have to put up with that,' she said, as if to fill the silence, and Harriet almost smiled.

'Did she ever suggest that she was thinking of leaving him?' Boyd asked.

'I think it was on about the third occasion. She was crying and I could hear the baby crying in the background. He had just left and she wouldn't tell me what he had done, but she said it hurt so much. "I should leave him," she said. "But I've got nowhere to go and I don't have any money of my own." I told her there were shelters she could go to.'

As she very well knew, Harriet thought to herself with a momentary flash of irritation. When Harriet had asked Evie why she hadn't come to the shelter, she had said she was too ashamed and she worried about what the women that she had been helping would think of her if she was no more able to sort out her own life than they were.

'But she stayed?'

'Yes. He threatened her with everything if she left – from killing himself to killing her. He even said he would abduct the baby and leave the country.'

'Did she know why he was so anxious about leaving them when he had to go on business trips?'

'She thought it could have something to do with the death

of his wife. Evie had been doing some research and thought he might be suffering from Separation Anxiety Disorder – something to do with experiencing panic attacks when forced to be separated from someone close, perhaps because of a fear that something might happen to them. But I'm not an expert.'

Harriet sat up straight. This was the first time this had been mentioned. If Mark had been suffering from some psychological disorder would it help their case? It might, if they could prove it. Evie hadn't said anything to them about it, but abused women were often so traumatised that they couldn't remember the finer details. They needed to understand this better. Thank God they had the weekend.

Devisha Ambo stood up.

'Mrs May, in all your conversations with Miss Clarke, was there any point at which she suggested that she wished to harm Mr North?'

'No. Absolutely not. She just didn't know what to do to make him stop hurting her.'

'So she was trying to come up with a plan to stop him?'

Mrs May glared at the prosecutor. 'That's not what I said.'

'You've already told us that she had tried talking to him, so what else could it be but a plan?'

Mrs May looked uncomfortable, and Devisha didn't give her a moment to recover.

'Did Miss Clarke at any point suggest that she wanted to seek revenge on him for all he had done to her? Perhaps use phrases that might suggest that he would "get what was coming to him" or similar?'

Mrs May's eyes opened wide. 'She didn't, but I wouldn't have

257

blamed her if she had. I couldn't understand it – she was so nice about him. She tried to be fair and to explore with me whether it could be her fault. I told her that it was no such thing. There was no excuse. None.'

Devisha studied her notes and Mrs May glanced anxiously at Harriet, who tried to give her a reassuring nod.

'Mrs May – you say you suggested that if Miss Clarke wanted to leave Mr North, you could provide her with a list of shelters, is that correct?'

'I wasn't trying to push her – I just wanted her to know that there were options.'

'That's okay. Nobody is accusing you of saying anything inappropriate. But did Miss Clarke mention to you at this point that she in fact was a volunteer at exactly the sort of shelter you were recommending?'

Mrs May's eyebrows drew together and she glanced at Evie. 'Well, no. I don't remember her saying anything about it.'

'Don't you find it odd that someone who worked at a shelter for abused women should call the Samaritans when she had a host of well-qualified people to whom she could turn?'

Debbie May's face cleared and the corners of her mouth lifted. 'Not at all. When people are in trouble, they like anonymity. For some there's an unwarranted sense of shame attached to their mistreatment. They've already probably been made to feel worthless by their partner, and the thought of the pity of others is too much for them to bear.'

Harriet sat back with relief. *Well said, Debbie.* The prosecutor had had a reasonable chance to strike a blow there, but she'd missed.

46

Cleo made it to the ladies' bathroom just in time. There was nothing much to come up from her stomach – only the cup of coffee she'd had when she arrived at the court. She had hardly been able to eat since the trial started, but today had been the worst day by far. The knowledge that Evie had been calling the Samaritans for months somehow hit her harder than any of the other evidence. In her own mind she had been able to find explanations for everything else that had been said, dismissing the allegations as lies. But the thought that Mark had been traumatised each time he went away was devastating. She had been the one to persuade him – every single time – to go.

Was all this her fault? Did it mean that what they had been saying about Mark might be true? That he *did* hurt Evie? No. *No!* She still refused to believe it. Every niggle of doubt that crept into her mind was vigorously pushed away, and she would never give up the fight to prove his innocence.

She collapsed onto the floor of the cubicle, her back against the door, trying to suppress the sobs that were ripping her apart. She pulled up her knees and rested her forehead on them, her hands clasped behind her head, pushing her face down to muffle the sounds she was making.

'Cleo?' She thought she was hearing things when someone said her name. But the voice came again, stronger. 'Cleo, it's Aminah. Come out, love – let me look after you.'

'Go away, Aminah. I can't bear to look at you after what you said. How could you tell the court that Mark hit Evie? You've known him for *years!*'

She heard a deep sigh. 'I didn't say he'd hit her, Cleo. I said she had a black eye, and she tried to hide it from me. I never said it was Mark.'

'You didn't need to, did you? Who else could it be? And why couldn't you say that she might very well have been kicked in the eye by Lulu? Not everyone is as adept at changing a nappy as you are.'

'Cleo, stop this. I told the truth. I made nothing up, and even you have to admit that if Lulu really had given her the black eye she wouldn't have felt she had to hide it from me. She would have let me in and we'd have had a bloody good laugh about it. I know how much all of this is hurting you, love. It must be unbearable and I don't know why you're forcing yourself to listen. Come on, get yourself out of there and let me give you a hug.'

Cleo didn't want to get off the floor. Somehow, with her back against the door, cramped into a small space with her arms and legs protecting her, she felt safe. But she couldn't stay here all night, and she had no idea what time the court building would be closing.

'I'm not going anywhere until you come out,' Aminah said,

and Cleo knew she meant it so she wearily started to push herself up off the floor. She got one foot beneath her and suddenly had to reach out for the toilet bowl. The room was spinning and she closed her eyes and gasped for air.

'What's going on? Cleo, are you okay?'

She steadied herself and risked opening her eyes. The walls were staying in the same place.

'I'm okay. I felt a bit light-headed. That's all.'

'Jesus, when was the last time you ate anything?'

Cleo opened the door to find Aminah rooting in her handbag. 'Here, have these,' she said, thrusting a half-eaten packet of chocolate buttons into her hand.

Cleo opened her mouth and upended the packet.

'Bloody hell – now I know you're not yourself,' Aminah said, putting her arm round Cleo to pull her close. 'Come on. Let's get you sat down with a cup of tea or something and then I'll take you home. Zahid and I will come back to pick your car up later. You can't drive like this.'

For a moment Cleo rested her head on Aminah's comfortable shoulder.

'It's all bollocks, you know,' she said.

Aminah said nothing and Cleo pulled away slightly, twisting her neck to give her a fierce look, hoping she could get through to her friend. 'I've told the police officer that there's something odd about the garage door being open when you went round – I don't know if they'll do anything about it, though.'

She saw Aminah bite on her bottom lip, her brows drawing together. She obviously thought Cleo was making too much of this. Cleo could hear the urgency in her own voice and tried to bring it down a notch to convince her friend that she was thinking logically.

'It's not just that, Aminah. It's all the other stuff. I can't imagine Mark doing any of those things. When I listened to the evidence about the light switch, it was all so wrong. Mark wouldn't have wanted it to be dark. He never *liked* the dark.'

'Oh come on, Cleo! We've had this conversation before, and I think you're exaggerating.'

'No,' Cleo said, pushing herself away from Aminah and going to lean on the wash basins. 'I don't mean he was scared. He always said that when it was completely black he felt as if he was alone in the world, and he hated that. The stuff about him wanting to hurt Evie in the dark is crap.'

She had to convince Aminah. She needed just one person to believe she was right, one person who didn't believe Mark was the devil.

'Please, Aminah, I'm telling you the truth. When Mum left us, Mark's sense of isolation became worse. And then with the bullying he had to put up with at school – just because he was a bit different – he began to feel that home was the only safe place, with those who loved him. Well – me, I suppose. He couldn't even bear going on a school trip or staying overnight at a friend's house.'

'Surely that all ties in with what the woman from the Samaritans said. If he was suffering from this separation disorder, or whatever it was called, wouldn't that make his trips away from home all the more difficult? If he had a fear of bad things happening to people he loved when he was away, how much worse must it have become since Mia died when he left her alone?'

Cleo didn't want to think about Mia.

'Typical of Evie to find some disorder to clutch onto. Even if it's true, can you honestly imagine Mark doing the things that have been described? Come on, Aminah. Can you? *Really?*'

Aminah folded her arms and took a deep breath. 'In all honesty, I can't imagine anyone committing half the horrors that go on in the world. The truth is, Cleo, that however close we are to someone, we never truly know what's in their heart.'

Cleo felt her chest tighten. She knew Aminah was right, but she couldn't admit it. There was one secret that had loomed large between her and Mark, both of them too scared to admit to the other what they had done. And now it was too late.

47

Harriet and Boyd are worried – I can see it in their faces. I know they have done an excellent job and Boyd has torn some of the witnesses to pieces. Especially Cleo. But they can't predict the vagaries of a jury, and there is a fine balance here between indisputable facts and conjecture.

I thought I was resigned to whatever was going to happen, but thoughts of Lulu have weakened me. I can't let them know that, though. My hands are clasped tightly in my lap, hidden from view, and I dig my thumbnails into my palms to keep me focused.

'What do you need me to do?' I ask them, my voice level.

'We've always known that to have the best chance of convincing the jury of your innocence, you might have to take the stand,' Harriet says, her voice brisk and business-like as ever. 'If you do, you will have to account for why you told Mark your father was paying for the photographs. In my opinion it's not relevant to his death, but it serves to demonstrate your overall reliability and honesty. If you lied about that, what else have you lied about? Do you see what I mean?'

I nod at them, knowing exactly what I'm going to say and how I will excuse myself.

'Then we have to prove beyond any shadow of a doubt that you lost control as a result of a fear of extreme violence. I believe there is ample proof of Mark's cruelty, but there must be nothing to suggest your actions were either premeditated or an act of revenge. I can't stress that strongly enough.'

'So you've decided it's necessary for me to give evidence?' I ask, knowing what she will say.

I can tell Harriet cares about what happens to me, even when she's being brusque. I am something of a flagship client for her. She believes strongly that not enough is done to help abused women, and if she wins this case, she will have an even bigger platform to shout from.

'We would have preferred to rely on your police interview transcript rather than giving the prosecution a chance to question you, but we need the jury to believe in you. And the judge has to be convinced of your honesty, because whatever the jury says, the sentencing is ultimately under his control. Nobody else can win their hearts and minds, Evie. Only you.'

I know, of course, that the knife is going to be a big issue. But then I've always known that.

'The fact that technically the marks on your chest and arms could have been self-inflicted is a worry and I'm certain Devisha will want to go to town on that. But we know – although the jury doesn't – that you have old scars on your back that were highly unlikely to have been made by you. We're going to need to see them. That's another reason why we want you to take the stand, because there is no other way of bringing that evidence to court.'

'What do you mean?' I ask, thinking for a moment I'm going to have to expose my back in court.

'We'll show them a photograph of your back. And I'm afraid you're going to have to say how it happened. You still haven't told me, and before we put you on the stand, you're going to have to. I can't defend you and neither can Boyd if we don't know the truth, Evie. You've got to tell me.'

I'm going to have to unearth so many memories that I would prefer to stay buried but I mustn't let them weaken me. I need to be strong – to ensure I don't make any mistakes.

'Okay, take my picture and Boyd can ask me about the scars. Ask me about other injuries too, why not? I can give you a list.'

Harriet leans towards me. 'This isn't Mark we're talking about, is it, Evie?'

'No. Long before Mark and nothing to do with Nigel – my husband – either.'

Part of me wants to hold it back, because I don't want to have to say it more than once, but I know they're not going to go for that. They need to know everything so they can ask me the right questions.

I've never told anyone before. Mark knew about the scars, of course, as did Nigel. But neither of them got the truth, and I'm terrified that telling my story might burst the dam holding it all in – and then God knows what else I might reveal.

But I have no choice. I stutter over the words and my skin feels clammy with sweat, but I tell them. Every last detail. And I see Harriet's eyes grow wide with shock and disbelief.

48

Stephanie had decided that she was going to give herself a few treats over the weekend. She had been stressed for too long; working with Gus and not being able to fully commit to his conviction that Evie Clarke had committed a carefully staged murder had taken its toll.

To take her mind off things, the next couple of days were going to be full of self-indulgence. She loved to cook but rarely found the time, so she was going to make her favourite winter dish – a hot, spicy chilli – and while the meat was simmering in the oven she was going to soak in a scented bath, surrounded by candles. And she wasn't going to think about Gus. Not for one minute.

The water for her bath was running and she had just tipped in a good helping of oil when the front doorbell rang.

'Damn it,' she said. She wanted to ignore it, but somehow in her job it never felt like the appropriate thing to do. Grabbing an old towelling bathrobe off the back of the bathroom door and turning off the tap, she made her way downstairs.

She could see his wide shoulders outlined through the frosted glass of the front door. What the hell was he doing here today?

Surely it couldn't be anything to do with a case? They had all agreed that they were due a quiet weekend.

With a tut, she opened the door. 'Gus,' she said by way of greeting.

'What is that *delicious* smell?' he asked, barging past her into the house, sniffing the air.

'Erm – I don't remember inviting you in?' she said. 'I'm busy. What do you want?'

'I want some of whatever you're cooking, that's for sure.'

'Well you're not having any – so bugger off.'

'Come on, Steph. You know we need to talk, and not about work. You avoid being on your own with me. Even when we got stuck in that bar together you scurried off as soon as I mentioned anything slightly personal. Obviously getting soaked to the skin was preferable to talking to me.' Gus's tone softened. 'A conversation is well overdue, I think. Can we talk?'

Stephanie stayed by the door, her arms folded. 'Well go on then.'

'Come and sit down, or go and have your bath and I'll watch the telly until you've finished. Look – we've got on well enough over the last few weeks, haven't we? I'm prepared for anything you want to fling at me, but it feels like we're both swirling in a spin dryer, pinned to opposite sides of the drum.'

Stephanie felt herself begin to give a little. Maybe Gus was right. Maybe she was stubborn.

Gus carried on into the house and plonked himself down on the sofa in exactly the spot where he always used to sit. Stephanie felt a strange sensation in her chest – almost as if she was finding it hard to breathe. She walked across to the seat opposite him and perched on the edge.

'Relax, Stephie,' he said. 'Shall I open a bottle or something?'

She almost twitched when he called her Stephie, a name he used rarely and only with affection.

'No – you won't swan around here as if it's still your second home. Say what you want to say, and then go.'

Gus tried and failed to hide a smile. 'You're determined to make this as difficult as possible, aren't you? Okay – first things first.' He breathed deeply and looked straight into her eyes. 'I am so very sorry that I wasn't thrilled when you told me you were having our baby. It was a huge surprise. I didn't know if I was ready to be a parent, and up until then I had felt fairly certain,' he held his hands up to ward off the defence he was going to get, 'that you weren't either. I realise now that I was wrong. But if you'd given me a moment to think about it, I genuinely believe I would have been delighted. But you didn't wait. You took control. Your resilience, strength and determination are some of the things I love most about you, but you're so quick to make decisions, and some of us just need a beat or two longer.'

Stephanie couldn't speak. She was stunned by the realisation that Gus had totally misunderstood what had happened.

'Why did you chuck me out, Steph?' he asked gently. 'We should have talked about it, made the right decision – whatever that was – together. It must have been hell for you to do what you did when you were all on your own.'

'What did I do, Gus?' Stephanie said quietly.

'I don't blame you for having a termination – it was your decision to make. But why kick me out?'

269

Stephanie was still. She didn't know whether to laugh or cry.

'For a policeman, you can be unbelievably thick,' was all she said.

'What does that mean? I loved you – I still bloody love you. But you are so determined to do things your way that you don't allow anyone else to have an opinion. I would have got used to the idea – welcomed it. I would never have let you go through any part of it alone.'

'Got *used* to the idea? Jesus. It was a *baby*. You make it sound like I swapped your posh car for a skanky one without telling you.'

'You know I didn't mean it in a negative sense. Stop being so bloody difficult. You refused to speak to me, and when I cornered you because it was obvious that you weren't pregnant any longer you told me that the problem had gone away. I had nothing to worry about. But I *was* worried. I was worried about *you*.'

'You ripped me in two, Gus. You made me feel that I had created that life inside my body all by myself, or that maybe I'd tried to trap you.'

'I'm sorry. I've said it a thousand times in my head, and as often as I could to you – when you'd listen. I was in the middle of the case from hell, stressed beyond belief, and I behaved badly.'

She couldn't do this any longer. The anger had evaporated, leaving her weak and vulnerable. She struggled to control her voice.

'I didn't have a termination. Our baby – he, if you must know – chose to leave my body when I was sixteen weeks pregnant.

A month after you left. I was already three months pregnant when I told you, because I was afraid of your reaction and I knew the case was getting you down.'

Gus's mouth had dropped open, and she could see so many emotions flash across his eyes. Guilt, sorrow, shock. She realised that in her own pain she had failed to consider his, but somehow the only way she had been able to cope with the loss of her lover and then her tiny baby boy was by trying to savagely thrust all feelings for Gus from her mind.

'Steph, come here.' He held out his arms, and she pushed herself off the chair and went to kneel on the rug in front of him. His arms came around her and he held her gently as her tears started to flow, only to turn into sobs. He bent down and lifted her onto his lap, and she buried her head in the warm hollow of his shoulder.

49

Harriet had spent the whole weekend working. She couldn't keep still. She had pushed Evie to tell them about her scars, and the picture she had painted was enough to break the heart of the toughest lawyer.

Nothing Evie had said was new, but it was the chilling way in which she had told it and the obvious damage it had done to her that Harriet couldn't drive from her mind.

More than ever she felt she owed it to Evie to make sure she was found not guilty of murder; that the judge and jury would understand why and how she had totally lost control and deliver a lenient sentence.

As she took her seat in court – glad that the weekend and the waiting were over – Harriet posed the same questions that she asked herself every day. *Have I done enough? Have I accomplished everything I set out to achieve? Have I given this case everything I have got?* It never felt like enough, no matter how hard she drove herself, and in Evie's case the questions seemed more forceful and insistent than ever.

One of the most difficult aspects of the case had always been proving that Mark was routinely – almost ritualistically – hurting

Evie. If they were unable to convince the court that this was true, the question of why she killed him was irrelevant. If he wasn't hurting her she had no defence.

It had been hard to understand why the abuse only seemed to happen immediately before Mark left for a business trip – it appeared inconsistent and irrational. If he was suffering from Separation Anxiety Disorder, though, that gave credibility to his behaviour and added strength to the evidence of his abuse.

Devisha Ambo's closing statement was bound to rely heavily on the fact that Mark North wasn't on trial. There was no hard, irrefutable evidence of wrongdoing, and wasn't it just as likely that Evie's injuries were self-inflicted? But if the jury believed that the SAD syndrome was affecting Mark's mental state, they would have less reason to question Evie's testimony. Half the battle would be won.

They had one additional witness to call before Evie would take the stand, and Boyd rose heavily to his feet, explaining to the judge and jury why he had been invited to give evidence. He turned to the eager-looking young man, who seemed to be moving constantly from one foot to the other, pushing his glasses further up his nose and casting his smile around the courtroom.

'Doctor Perkins, what can you tell me about Separation Anxiety Disorder?'

'Oh, quite a lot,' the doctor said, his speech fast and clipped. 'Basically, someone suffering from this disorder will experience extreme anxiety and fear when separated from a major attachment figure – often a spouse. They worry that harm will come to those close to them if they're not there.'

'Is this a common disorder?'

The doctor smiled again, clearly enthusiastic about the subject.

'It's actually more common than you might think. It's possible that somewhere between six and seven per cent of the adult population may suffer at some level.'

He nodded, as if this was good news.

'Can you explain to us, Doctor Perkins, how this disorder might present itself?'

'Yes, of course. Some sufferers feel excessive distress when separated from the person – or place – to which they feel attached. Others find it hard to be alone, and that can be very difficult for their partners, who may be unable to go out and leave them in the house. Sometimes they find it hard to sleep alone.'

'Would any of these symptoms explain why Mark North repeatedly attacked the defendant, Miss Clarke, before he went away for a period of time?'

'No. Not on their own, no. I don't think so.'

Harriet saw Boyd momentarily stiffen. This was clearly not what he had been expecting.

'When you say "not on their own", Doctor, that suggests there may be other, related issues?'

'Well yes, but without meeting the sufferer, I couldn't say. It's true that ASAD – sorry, that's Adult Separation Anxiety Disorder – does often occur along with other psychiatric conditions, phobias, OCD, but there's also a high probability that people with ASAD will experience some kind of mood disorder.'

Boyd appeared to relax a little.

'And are any of those mood disorders linked to violence?'

'Well, if a person also suffered from Intermittent Explosive Disorder, for example – and the two have been linked in some cases – then it's not unlikely that the stress brought on by the separation could cause them to lose their temper.'

'Can you please explain to us what Intermittent Explosive Disorder is, although the name is itself a very clear indicator.'

'Basically it's the inability to resist aggressive urges. The attacks might be brought on by tension, or sometimes by arousal. The action of aggression gives them an immediate sense of relief, and it's over as soon as it's begun.'

'Do they feel remorse for their actions?'

'People react differently. Some appear to genuinely regret their actions, others are embarrassed and might try to pretend it never happened.'

Boyd nodded and his glance took in the jury.

'And what does research indicate about the life of someone living with a sufferer of either of these disorders, let alone both?'

Dr Perkins shook his head and lost his smile for the moment. 'Oh goodness, that wouldn't be pleasant at all. ASAD is extremely hard on relationships. Sufferers are very needy and it can be extremely difficult to handle. If that same person suffered from Intermittent Explosive Disorder it would force those closest to them to be constantly on their guard, making sure they do nothing that might tip the sufferer over the edge.'

'And in your expert opinion, Doctor, would that level of pressure be sufficient for someone close to the sufferer to have moments when they find that combination of behaviours impossible to bear?'

'Absolutely. There would be times when they would be at their wits' end.'

'Thank you, Doctor Perkins. I have no further questions.'

Devisha Ambo rose quickly to her feet.

'Doctor Perkins, at what age do either of these two disorders tend to present themselves?'

'Separation Anxiety Disorder wasn't recognised as an issue in adults until about twenty years ago. It often starts in childhood. Similarly, Intermittent Explosive Disorder usually presents itself in late childhood or adolescence. But not exclusively.'

'So you would expect this issue to be noticed by someone close to the sufferer – someone, for example, like his sister?'

'It depends how close they are and how often they see each other. Certainly if they are close in age she will have seen it as they grew up.'

'So would you expect her to describe her brother as,' she consulted her notes, 'gentle, sensitive?'

The psychologist shook his head. 'He was her brother. He's dead. I'm sure she'll be wanting to remember the best bits of him. It's what we all do, isn't it? And if she wasn't his major attachment figure it's possible she never experienced his anxiety on separation.'

Harriet wanted to punch the air. The perfect answer.

But Devisha hadn't finished.

'Did you ever meet or see Mark North as a patient?'

'No.'

'So all of your comments today are purely hypothetical?'

Dr Perkins frowned at the prosecutor.

'I was asked to talk about the two disorders and how they might present themselves. I was not asked to diagnose someone I've never met. Whether he suffered from either or both of these disorders I can't say. All I can do is tell you what they are.'

'In other words, your testimony and Mark North are not in any way related?'

'No, they're not.'

The prosecutor turned to the jury and then back to the doctor.

'So we have no evidence at all that Mark North suffered from either of these disorders. All we have is the testimony of a Samaritan to whom Evie Clarke – the woman accused of his murder – passed on her suspicions based on an internet search. Is that correct?'

'I wouldn't know, I'm afraid. I don't know the details of the case. I'm here as an expert witness in psychology.'

'Thank you, Doctor Perkins. You've been most helpful.'

Shit, Harriet thought. They could have done without that. They just had to hope the jury didn't disregard Dr Perkins's testimony. She couldn't lose this case.

Harriet felt her chest grow tight. All they had left now was Evie. It would all come down to her testimony.

50

Cleo wasn't sure if she had the strength to sit through Evie's testimony. It would all be lies. Evie wasn't even going to be questioned about the garage door, according to Sergeant King, because apparently the prosecution didn't think it was significant. They felt certain that she would offer a plausible reason for why it was open when Aminah had turned up. To them it seemed like a small thing, but to Cleo it had felt like a beacon of hope.

All she wanted now was the verdict, and even if the jury let her down badly by finding Evie not guilty of murder, she hoped and prayed that the judge would have the sense to lock her up for years to come for manslaughter. She didn't deserve to be free after depriving Cleo of a wonderful brother and Lulu of a loving father. If Evie was sentenced to life, Cleo would make sure Lulu grew up understanding what had happened and how wonderful her daddy was.

Aminah had asked if Cleo wanted company during the final stages of the trial, but she didn't. She wanted to be alone. If she felt the merest waft of sympathy for Evie coming off Aminah, she would lose it.

Evie was being sworn in, and Cleo looked at her with disgust.

She was dressed in a dark blue skirt which sat well on her slender hips without being too tight, and she had chosen a white silk blouse that hung loosely but nevertheless managed to hint at the woman underneath. She had pulled her long fair hair into a small neat bun and wore minimal makeup. It seemed to Cleo that she had managed a look that couldn't offend anyone, but at the same time spoke of a balanced, neat woman. Clever.

The defence barrister's opening surprised Cleo.

'Miss Clarke, there has been a great deal of evidence provided to the court relating to your more recent horrific injuries – the result of which was the loss of control that resulted in Mark North's death. The prosecution has suggested that these, together with the older injuries noted by Doctor Moore at the hospital, could have been self-inflicted. Would you please explain to the court the origin of the old scars that the doctor noticed?'

She saw Evie swallow hard. She breathed in deeply and appeared to be holding her breath as she spoke.

'It was my uncle,' she said.

Cleo almost laughed out loud. Evie clearly habitually found someone to blame for things that had happened to her. Surely the court weren't going to be taken in by this?

'And the scars weren't confined to your chest and stomach – those the doctor saw and commented on. They are in fact on your back too, aren't they?'

'He inflicted many wounds on my body.' Her voice was so soft that Cleo strained to hear.

The QC referred the judge and jury to the screens in front of them and gave them time to study the photographs. From where Cleo was sitting, she couldn't see the detail of the images, but she could see looks of concern on the faces of the jury, some of whom gave Evie worried glances from beneath lowered brows – almost as if they didn't want her to know they were staring at pictures of her body.

'How, exactly, did your uncle inflict these and other scars?' the QC asked eventually.

'The scars you can see on the photograph and the ones the doctor spoke of on my chest, stomach and arms, were inflicted with a bullwhip.'

There was a small gasp of horror from the woman to Cleo's left.

'For the sake of the court, a bullwhip is a single-tailed whip, originally designed for use on livestock. The main part of the whip – often called the thong – is typically made of braided strips of leather. At the end of this is a flexible piece of leather, which in turn is attached to the cracker – a piece of string or nylon cord or any number of other materials. The length of the overall whip could be anything from three feet to twenty feet.'

The QC handed some papers to the usher for distribution.

'We asked a doctor to examine Miss Clarke this weekend, and in his report – of which you now have a copy – he has confirmed that the scars on Miss Clarke's body could have been made by such a weapon. He is available for cross-examination, should the court require it.'

The jury were given time to read the documents before Boyd continued.

'It is abundantly clear from this evidence that these older scars were not self-inflicted, and therefore there is no reason at all to believe that the more recent ones were either, as was previously suggested.' He paused to allow that statement to register. 'Miss Clarke, I understand these aren't the only injuries your uncle inflicted. Can you talk us through the others, please?'

'He broke my left ulna and on another occasion my clavicle. I had broken ribs twice, and broken bones in my foot.'

Evie spoke with an air of detachment, as if she was talking about someone other than herself, and Cleo stared at the woman she thought she knew. Could this be true? But Evie couldn't lie – at least, not about the broken bones. An x-ray would prove immediately if she was making it up.

'Can you please tell us the circumstances under which this happened, Miss Clarke?'

'I was in care from the age of nine. My mother was an alcoholic and she died about a year after I was taken from her. Social Services contacted my grandmother. She and my mother hadn't spoken since my mother left home just after I was born, but they wanted to know if she would take me in. Of course, she was only interested if she could be classed as a foster carer so she got the money for looking after me, rather than acting as a concerned grandparent. On the basis of the cash, I was probably worth having – just about. My uncle was her youngest – my mother's half-brother.'

'And did he live in the family home?'

'Not to start with. He was married, but his wife kicked him out – threatened to go to the police about his behaviour – so he came back to live with my grandmother.'

'Did the physical abuse start immediately?'

Evie shrugged. 'In a way, but it wasn't too serious to start with. It began with small acts of cruelty – a foot outstretched,

281

a cry of pain as my knee hit the ground. He developed a taste for it. He pushed me, slapped me, took great joy in tripping me up so I went sprawling on the floor. That kind of thing. But he seemed to get more and more angry as the years went by.'

'Why do you think that was?'

'He was angry with life. Women didn't find him appealing – I don't think anyone did because he had a permanent snarl on his face. He was so belligerent that he rarely managed to keep a job for more than a week or two, so in the end he gave up and took to stealing instead.'

'And when did he start to beat you?'

Evie closed her eyes momentarily as if the pain of what she was about to say was too unbearable. Cleo saw her bite down on her bottom lip.

'I was about thirteen. He made me strip to the waist, then he whipped me.'

The QC gave her a moment, but the silence in the court was taut, as if every person in the room had become rigid, scared of breaking the tension.

'Was the abuse sexual as well as physical?' The QC's voice was quiet and Evie's matched his.

'Only in his mind. Beating me, or causing other harm to me, seemed to offer him some sort of release.'

The lawyer peered at her over his glasses.

'I'm so sorry to be putting you through this, Miss Clarke, but as the scars have been mentioned and were being suggested as evidence of self-harm, it was necessary to get to the truth.' Evie dipped her head in acknowledgement and he continued. 'What was your grandmother doing while all of this was going on?'

'She pretended she knew nothing about it. She told me, just once, that if ever I told a soul she would take me to the edge of a cliff, suspend me by my hair, and drop me off. I believed her. She had taken me in for the money, and she wouldn't kick my uncle out because his thieving was proving lucrative too. I only went to hospital twice – when I broke my arm and my collar bone. The ribs and foot were left to heal themselves. She took me to two different hospitals and gave the names of some other kids at my school so there was no paper trail.'

'One last question, if I may, Miss Clarke. When did you manage to escape the tyranny of your grandmother and uncle?'

'I tried to run away several times, but I had no money and I wasn't good at it. In the end I told a friend and she gave me fifty pounds out of her own savings so that I could get away. I left just before my fifteenth birthday.'

At that point, the QC asked for a recess, claiming that Miss Clarke needed a break before he continued with his questioning, and Cleo felt almost a sigh of relief run around the court. That hadn't made good hearing, and for one moment she had felt a paradoxical sympathy for Evie. Cleo's own childhood had been far from perfect, but it had been nothing like Evie's, and if she herself felt like that, how would the jury feel? They had to see that, in spite of their empathy with Evie the victim, none of it mattered. Evie had killed Mark – that was the only thing they should be interested in.

She pushed herself up abruptly from her seat. For a moment she couldn't help wishing that Evie's grandmother had carried out her threat and dropped her off that cliff.

283

51

The recess was short, and before long Evie was once again in the witness box. Her cheeks were pale, but she appeared to be under control. There was a quiet certainty about her, as if she knew she was in the right. One never knew, with Evie. The more Harriet got to know her, the more private a person she realised she was.

Boyd took to his feet.

'Miss Clarke, I'm sorry to have to ask you more questions, but there are a few matters we need to clear up. Can you explain to the court why you pretended your father was funding the series of photographs that you commissioned from Mr North?'

Evie dropped her head. 'I'm ashamed of this now, although I did explain it to Mark and he understood. He forgave me.'

Harriet heard what sounded like a faint hiss from Cleo in the front row of the gallery.

'I was visiting the area. I was wandering through the town one day and I saw a stunning photograph in the window of the Marcus North gallery. He was such a wonderful photographer and seemed capable of making anyone look beautiful. I had been told all my life that I was ugly, and I wanted to know if

Marcus North could take a picture that would allow me to change my perception of myself.'

Evie cast a pleading glance at the jury.

'It was my uncle, you see.' She pressed her lips together, her words harsh. 'He told me I was an ugly little shit and nobody would ever want me. I needed some evidence for myself that I wasn't totally hideous. When your confidence has been shattered all your life, it's hard to explain.'

She turned to the front again, shaking her head slightly.

'I could never afford Mark's prices, but I thought if I tempted him with my well-connected father, he might be persuaded. That's why I made him up.'

'Was that the only reason?' Boyd asked.

'No, I also wanted to use the experience to learn from Mark. Basically it was a very cheeky way of getting free lessons, because I love photography but I'm not very good at it. I'd hoped to make myself so useful, such good company, that maybe he would take me on as an assistant.'

'And you told Mr North all this?'

'Not straightaway, no. When I knew there was no way I could raise the money to pay him, I thought I would just have to say that my father had died, and then apologise and disappear. But I really liked Mark and thought he liked me, so I stayed and did what I could to repay the debt. When he started to become interested in me as a person – a girlfriend – I felt I had to tell him the truth. He understood. Mark had his problems, but when you stripped away the evil side, he could be kind.'

Harriet heard another hiss and this time just made out the whispered words 'Lying bitch.' The judge was too far away to hear what was said, but he glared at the gallery, uncertain of exactly where the disturbance had come from. If Cleo wasn't careful, she would be thrown out of the courtroom.

Boyd continued with his questioning, seeking clarification on some of the content of Evie's original statement, but Harriet was confident he had done a good job. Devisha, though, wasn't going to be so kind.

Devisha Ambo rose quickly to her feet and stood looking at Evie for a few seconds. Harriet recognised this as a ploy to unnerve her client, but it was too brief to cause comment from the judge.

'I only have a few questions for you, Miss Clarke. Cleo North told the court that Mr North had a strong aversion to going into the lower level of the house – the basement where the gym was – as that was the site of his wife's accident. She said he refused to go down there. Yet you claim that Mr North trapped your hand between the weights of a multi gym that was situated in that same basement room. How could that happen if Mr North never went into that part of the house?'

Harriet watched Evie's face, concerned that this question might throw her. But she should have known better. Evie was totally in control.

'It was before Mark went on one of his trips. I was sure he was going to hurt me, so I hid in the basement – certain he wouldn't follow me. Cleo is right that he almost never went down there, so I thought I was safe. I relaxed and made the mistake of dozing off while I waited for him to leave. When I woke up, he was standing there, fully dressed and ready to go.'

The whole court was hanging on Evie's every word. This wasn't helping the prosecutor's case and Harriet knew she would be keen to take the sting out of it.

'Thank you, Miss Clarke. I imagine this is when you claim he injured you.' Devisha rustled some papers, as if about to move on.

'He had tears on his cheeks. "Not here, Evie. Not again," he said. I didn't know what he meant by "Not again."' Evie lifted her hand and stared at it. 'He dragged me onto my knees, used his other hand to pull the bar that lifted the weights, thrust my hand on there, and then he let it drop.'

The last words were almost whispered and the courtroom was totally silent.

'So why, knowing that he was – according to you – a violent man, did you take a knife into the bedroom on a night when you knew he was most likely to hurt you – the night before he would be separated from you?'

'I had bought him a present! I thought it might be a game-changer. I had set the scene with candles, so that he wouldn't have the darkness he seemed to prefer when he was hurting me. I was excited because he seemed so pleased about the present, and in my haste I brought the knife instead of the scissors. It was easier to find in the dark – the lights had fused in the whole house, not only in the bedroom.'

'Miss Clarke, I put it to you that you used the present as an excuse to bring a knife into the bedroom and that you had planned from the start to kill Mark North. You never intended to bring scissors – maybe you had even caused the lights to fuse so that Mark wouldn't be able to see that you had a knife in your hand.'

Evie didn't rise to the bait. 'I wouldn't know how to fuse the lights, and the last thing I wanted was darkness. Why would I have lit the candles if that were the case? I can only imagine Mark fused them because he had something worse in store – he must have wanted to start hurting me straight away and needed to guarantee the dark.'

There was a cry from the gallery and Cleo jumped to her feet. 'That's not true – he didn't even *like* the dark!'

Before the judge had a chance to exclude her from court, Cleo pushed past everyone and ran out of the courtroom.

The prosecutor continued as if there had been no interruption.

'Miss Clarke, we know you have provided evidence of your more recent injuries and you want us to believe that it was Mark North who hurt you. But we have no evidence other than your word that he was the perpetrator, do we?'

Evie met Devisha's gaze. 'No, you don't.'

'And we have no evidence, other than your word once more – and let's not forget that we know you have lied before – that you took the knife into the bedroom purely to open the present.'

Harriet was shocked by the coldness of Evie's eyes and prayed that she wasn't going to lose control.

'If I had been going to lie about that, I would have said that Mark brought the knife into the bedroom. Instead I told the truth.'

Devisha was not to be deterred.

'Even if it could be proven that Mark North hurt you, which it can't, I put it to you that you decided you'd had enough, and you sought revenge against Mark North for the harm he had caused you. You carefully planned an attack on him in a darkened room with a knife that you took there for that very purpose.'

Evie's face changed. Two hot spots of colour flashed angrily on her white cheeks and her eyes glittered. Harriet wanted to signal her to calm down, but Evie was staring at Devisha Ambo.

'*Revenge?* Do you seriously think that killing someone is any form of *revenge?*'

The barrister looked taken aback, but Evie hadn't finished.

'If I'd stabbed Mark for revenge, he would have suffered nothing more than a moment or two of pain. That's not revenge. Revenge is seeing someone suffer for a lifetime in retribution for what they've put you through. If I had wanted revenge on Mark, he wouldn't be dead. He'd be feeling the kind of pain that I have felt every single day for a long, long time.'

52

*R*evenge. Such a powerful word, and one that covered a multitude of sins. Stephanie thought about the word and its implications. She had to wonder if she had been exacting revenge on Gus by refusing to talk to him about their relationship. Was she really protecting herself from further heartbreak, or was she making him suffer as a form of retribution?

She had been finding it difficult to concentrate for the last couple of days. Saturday night had confused her so much, and she was furious with herself for giving in to her emotions.

In the end, after her outpouring of grief, Gus had stayed for dinner. She had loved having him there, sitting opposite her as he had so many times in the past, and he had been enthusiastic about the chilli. But to Stephanie it hadn't tasted of much. She had been too confused by her emotions: the renewed sadness about the baby she had lost and the pleasure of being with Gus had been tying her in knots. The truth was that when she'd told Gus she was pregnant she'd interpreted his reaction as one of horror, while he now claimed it had been one of surprise and confusion. She had been angry with him and devastated at their breakup, and then she had lost the baby. More than anything, she had needed Gus with her to share her grief. She'd wanted to be held close as her heart shattered into pieces for their child. But she'd had to bear it alone.

She had said none of this to Gus, but he knew her too well.

'Steph – I'm so sorry I wasn't there for you. You deserved better, and if I'd known – if I hadn't thought you despised me – I would have done anything to try to help you through it. Can we not forgive ourselves and each other?'

She knew he was right, but she had been storing up the resentment for so long that she wasn't sure she could let it go; when he asked if he could stay, she had said no.

Even before she had closed the door behind him she was regretting her decision, momentarily fooling herself into thinking that she could have at least enjoyed a single night with him. But she was vulnerable, scared of loving him and losing him. There was no way their relationship should be nurtured back to life.

Gus had turned at the front door as he left, seemingly unwilling to let her shut him out of her home, and her life.

'I love you, Stephanie. You're a stroppy, strong-willed woman and that's one of the things I admire most about you. But I made a mistake. Given a chance I would have welcomed our child.'

'You mean it's my fault,' she said, her pain hidden under cover of an aggressive scowl.

'There you go again.' Reaching out a hand, he rested it on the back of her neck, and for a moment she was sure he was going to pull her back into his arms. But he must have thought better of it. 'Look, people hurt each other in relationships. They don't always respond the way their partner wants or expects them to. It shouldn't mean the end.'

Logic was Gus's strong point. Stephanie's reactions were always instant, emotional, inflexible. And right now she was retaliating – making him hurt as much as she had – and Evie's words about revenge kept piercing her thoughts.

She dismissed the words from her mind as her attention was drawn back to the last stages of the trial. Devisha Ambo was on her feet addressing the jury, and was in the middle of her closing speech when her words penetrated Stephanie's consciousness.

'Miss Clarke claims that she was systematically abused by the deceased and there is no doubt that she sustained injuries. But do you believe it was Mark North who hurt her? At no time did she inform anyone other than the Samaritans that this was happening to her. Why was that? Maybe because it wasn't the truth. There had been no calls to the police prior to the final incident – the time of Mr North's death. We have no evidence other than that of Miss Clarke that it was, in fact, Mr North who was inflicting these injuries on her. Similarly we have heard statements about two disorders that may, or may not, have affected Mr North and caused these apparent outbursts. But he had never been diagnosed as having either syndrome, and there is no evidence whatsoever to suggest he did. And although Miss Clarke's testimony about her uncle was compelling, once again we have evidence of injuries, but no proof of how these were sustained.'

The barrister turned to her notes, then gave the jury one of her fierce stares.

'We know that Miss Clarke took the knife into the bedroom, by her own admission. Is that something you would expect a woman who was being abused to do, given that it could be used as a weapon against her? I don't think so. The knife injuries to her arms were superficial and she was in no immediate danger of being killed, so did she take the knife with her because she was out to avenge herself for the previous acts of violence against her? I put it to you that this was carefully staged – that Miss Clarke planned every last detail of the murder of Mark North.'

Stephanie watched the jury. She knew this was going to be a difficult decision for them, and as the prosecution barrister continued, Stephanie moved her attention from one juror to the next in an attempt to deduce their thoughts. She had been late to court that morning, and so was seated right at the back. Gus was towards the front, and she could see his wide shoulders hunched as he leaned forwards, focusing every ounce of his mind on the prosecutor's words.

She switched her gaze back to the jury, and could see one or two of them were giving slight nods of their heads, jotting down notes. There were no signs of complacency, of people leaning back with arms folded as if to say 'I've already made my mind up', and to a person they were focused.

If Devisha could convince the jury that Evie took the knife into the bedroom with the specific intention of killing Mark North, she would be found guilty of murder. She would never see her little girl grow up, and once again Stephanie felt sympathy for a woman who had been brought up for the first part of her life by an alcoholic, for most of her teens by a woman who allowed her son to physically abuse her, only to find herself living with a man who ritualistically hurt her.

53

As I sit in the dock waiting for Boyd Simmonds to make his closing speech, I feel my legs shaking. I've had plenty of time to prepare myself and I've always known this moment would come, but as I look at the jury I can't help but wonder if I have behaved the way they might have expected. How should a woman who has killed her partner in a moment of total madness look? Should I seem repentant? Should I be sad? Or should I be terrified? I'm surprised that I feel anything at all, but I would be a fool not to consider that I might be found guilty of murder. It's always been a possibility, and one that I believed I had accepted.

Harriet has been working hard to convince me that it will all be fine in that fierce way of hers. She told me that on average two women are murdered each week in the UK by their partners or ex-partners, so surely the jury must believe that ultimately I might have been one of that number if I hadn't acted? I know Harriet hopes the judge and the majority of the jury will understand that although I hadn't been with Mark for long, the fact that I had been abused throughout adolescence – and I have the scars to prove it – might explain why I couldn't take it again.

Boyd starts to speak. He has a strange cadence to his voice, with the tone rising at the end of each sentence. I feel mesmerised by the sound, if not his words, which wash over me.

'Here is a woman who has suffered abuse before in her life and who emerged scarred, but strong, and determined not to be tormented by another man. And yet she tried to live with it. By her own admission, Mark North wasn't all bad, and like many women she clung to all that was good about him, hoping that the bouts of irrational anger would stop. It seems clear that he needed to be certain she would remain in the family home during his absence, and wouldn't be free to go out without him – or run from him. Was that his concern? That she might find another, better life elsewhere? We will never know what drove him to cause such pain to the woman he claimed to love – the mother of his child.'

Boyd put his notes back down on the bench as if he no longer needed them. Perhaps he didn't. He spoke with passion.

'Evie Clarke never planned to kill Mark North. Maybe – and we can't ignore this – thoughts of the death of his former wife gave her cause for concern. The coroner stated at Mia North's inquest that in the absence of any other evidence, he had to declare her death to be accidental, but we need to consider the phrase "in the absence of other evidence" very carefully. Whether Mark North was innocent of his wife's death isn't the point here. The point is that if Evie Clarke was troubled by the thought that he *might* have been involved, she may well have been terrified by the thought that the brutal attacks she suffered could escalate. She could, quite reasonably, have gone into her bedroom hoping that the present she had bought might have turned things around. But then she realised how wrong she was as he started to cut her. With her head full of fear of what might be coming next, what plans he had in store for the future, she reached the point where her terror took over.'

I know my QC is making the points well. We have discussed over and over how Boyd planned to conclude the case, and Harriet has told me repeatedly that he is the best. I have to believe her, so I have to trust him. And I know she wants to win as much as I do.

'Evie North has the scars of previous injuries on her body – some caused by North, some by her uncle. Imagine, if you can, how it must feel to believe that you have escaped a life of violence, and now – through no fault of your own – you are plunged back into a similarly impossible situation. Do you not believe that, rational as you may consider yourself to be, you might for just one moment lose control? Imagine your arms and chest have been cut, small slices into your flesh, and as you heard from Miss Clarke's statement to the police, the hairs on your partner's chest are rubbing into them as he moves over you, making love, excited – thrilled, maybe – by the pain he has caused. The knife is still there in the room. Imagine a partner saying to you that he is about to give you something to remember him by, and all you can see is the blood from the injuries he inflicted running down your arms and your chest.'

Boyd takes a sip of water, and I want to look at the jury, but I can't. If I meet their eyes, what will they see there? A guilty person, or one who was forced to kill this man? I don't know, so I keep my eyes either fixed on the high point of the wall, or on Boyd. I don't want to look down. It might signify shame, and I shouldn't be ashamed. I'm not ashamed, but neither do I feel the way I expected to.

'Evie Clarke has never denied killing Mark North. She called the police – initially to ask for help – and then she stayed in the bed with Mr Clarke, holding him as he died. She was sobbing, distraught, failing to understand how she had so completely lost control. She showed clear remorse for her actions. Only the crying of her child – a child who would soon be old enough to walk in and witness her father hurting her mother – brought her back to reality, and immediately she admitted to the police that she had killed him.'

I've stopped listening. I have to block this out of my mind and imagine myself somewhere else before I shout out something inappropriate about how Mark wasn't a bad man. Confused, struggling with his own demons, but not bad. And I can't tell them that. I mustn't.

Instead I imagine myself with Lulu, playing on the beach in the winter when it's deserted and the sand is clean, swept free of all footprints apart from ours. I don't know when – or even if – that will happen. But once, just once, is all I ask.

Harriet has warned me that when I am allowed to go free – whether after this trial or when I have served whatever sentence is imposed – I will have to be assessed before I am allowed to keep Lulu, to make sure that I am a suitable parent. But I know that anyone who sees me with her will never doubt my love for her. I need Lulu to know it, to feel it, to remember it.

Cleo has sneaked back into the gallery after her earlier outburst, and I can sense her eyes piercing the glass that separates me from the court, wishing she could send poison darts to my heart, praying that I am jailed for life for what I have done so that she can keep Lulu.

Was it worth killing him? Did I do the right thing?

My brain suddenly explodes with a memory – the sea pounding on the rocks, the cry of a gull as it skims the surface of the water. And a child's scream of terror.

And then I know.

Yes. It was worth it.

54

Harriet was summoning up every ounce of her positivity. Each muscle in her body was taut and she prayed that the jury would see sense. This *had* to go Evie's way. It was such an important case for women. It was time the world woke up to the fact that anyone could crack when placed under enough pressure, and while she would never condone cold-blooded murder, there were times when a normal, rational person would lash out as the dam broke and all the pent-up fear, pain and anguish exploded.

Now that the trial was over and the judge had completed his summing-up, explaining to the jury that the onus was on the prosecution to prove the case and it was not up to the defendant to prove her innocence, Harriet had to trust in the process and believe that the jury were capable of understanding the trauma Evie had endured.

The judge had summed up the key points fairly, giving no indication of his personal view in relation to the charges. He had explained the two counts against Evie, the first being the murder of Mark North, the second a count of voluntary manslaughter.

'You need only decide whether you believe Michelle Evelyn Clarke to be guilty of murder. Miss Clarke has pleaded guilty to manslaughter, and there is no doubt that she killed Mark North. She has never denied it.' The judge's deep voice resonated throughout the court, and not a soul moved. Neither a rustle of clothing nor a discreet cough intruded as they hung on his every word. 'It is also clear that Miss Clarke suffered painful injuries, although it cannot be proven that these were caused by any act of the deceased. You, the jury, need to consider what prompted Miss Clarke to kill Mr North. Was it planned? Even if not, did she decide on the spur of the moment to kill him as an act of revenge for the pain he allegedly inflicted on her? Or was the fear of further injury the trigger that caused her to lose control?'

Finally the judge concluded his remarks and the jury retired. His points had been succinct, and Harriet knew it was never sensible to second-guess a jury. The next few hours – or maybe days – were going to be hard as they waited for the verdict.

Evie was returned to the cell of the courts, and Harriet made her way to meet with her client. The sound of her heels clicking on the concrete floor seemed to reverberate around the corridor, and she walked with her head high. There was no way that Evie should see any signs of concern. She needed confidence, and Harriet was determined to give it to her.

As she pushed open the door she saw Evie standing with her back to the door looking upwards, out of the high window at the cloudy sky, her arms tightly folded. Harriet forced her voice to sound upbeat.

'That all went well, Evie. Didn't you think so?'

'It doesn't matter. I'll do my time, if I need to.' There was a hint of resignation in the low, modulated tone of her voice.

'Come on, let's be positive about this. The judge had to say there is no absolute proof that Mark was hurting you, but those jurors have listened to the evidence and they won't be in any doubt. We have to trust them.'

Evie turned round and the light hit one side of her face, the other remaining in shadow. The one visible eye glinted with something that Harriet took to be determination and there was no sign of the weakness she had suspected.

'You don't get it, Harriet – and why should you? Even if I get a life sentence, I'm in no doubt at all that I did the right thing – the *only* thing. I'll accept my punishment, whatever it is.'

There was something going on in Evie's head and right now Harriet didn't know what it was, nor was she sure she wanted to.

'I think it's admirable that you're taking this attitude,' she said, although inside she was confused.

'It's not admirable. I killed a man. I don't think I had a choice, but there are many who would disagree with me, and maybe twelve of them are out there right now in that jury room.'

Harriet felt a shiver run down her arms to the tips of her fingers.

She turned to Evie to offer more reassurance, but she had shut down. She had closed her eyes, and Harriet had the feeling she would get no more out of her until the jury returned.

55

Cleo felt sick. This couldn't be happening. Twelve people were about to walk back into the courtroom and pass judgement on the woman who had killed Mark. How could anyone in their right mind believe Evie Clarke's wicked lies?

For a moment, a worm of doubt wriggled itself into Cleo's mind. She'd been doing her best to ignore it since the trial began, but there had been one moment – just one – when she had wondered about Mark and Evie. It had been after Evie hurt her hand. There was something about the way she had related the story of her accident to Cleo that hadn't rung true, and for just seconds Cleo had experienced a sick feeling in the pit of her stomach as if she was being dropped from a great height. But back then she had dismissed the thought as quickly as it came, convincing herself that Evie's slightly odd behaviour was down to embarrassment at being such an idiot.

She pushed the other thought from her head too, the memory of a time before she knew Evie. She didn't want to lose faith in her brother – she had to believe in him, as she always had. He was a good, kind man. Yes, there were times when he had been slightly obsessive and lacked confidence, perhaps acted impulsively, out of fear. But she blamed that on their childhood.

She focused on the man she knew. The man who had wanted Cleo to make a beautiful present for the mother of his child, who had seemed deeply concerned when he saw how seriously Evie's hand had been injured. None of this was the man that Evie had described.

Who or what had the jury believed? Evie, or the truth?

Evie was back in the dock, and the jury had moved to their seats. The court rose to its feet as the judge entered.

Cleo looked away. She couldn't bear it. She rested her elbows on her knees and buried her face in her hands.

Finally the foreman of the jury stood, clutching the piece of paper on which the verdict was written.

'Have you reached a verdict on which you are all agreed?' the judge asked.

'We have, Your Honour.'

'On the count of murder, do you find the defendant guilty or not guilty?'

Cleo held her breath and whispered, 'Please, please.'

I've been told to stand. The jurors have made their decision. I have closed my mind to the verdict, just as I have closed my mind to any feelings of remorse for Mark's death. I don't know where my thoughts will go to when this is all over. For so long I have had only conviction – one all-encompassing goal – and I'm not sure what I will do with the empty space that will be left behind. Maybe I will grieve – for Mark, for Lulu, for my life. But there will be nothing left to cling to, to aim for.

The chairman of the jury is looking at me. He slowly unfolds the paper and prepares to respond to the judge.

It feels as if the whole court is holding its breath, and I drop my gaze so that I don't have to see the look on his face as he announces my fate.

'Not guilty.'

I don't move. I don't react, but I can hear a sound from the gallery, a soft scream of distress, and I know it must be Cleo. I don't turn to look at her, but I hear a scuffle. She must have pushed past other spectators and run from the gallery again, not waiting to find out more.

I should feel relief. But I feel nothing – not even the sense of satisfaction that I was hoping for.

Maybe I'm not done, after all.

Harriet felt a huge rush of pleasure, and threw an unresponsive Evie a wide smile of satisfaction. Boyd turned to her and raised his eyebrows a fraction – his signal to say that it had gone the way he had always known it would, even though they both knew that wasn't entirely true.

This was the right result. Harriet wondered whether any abusers reading about this trial in the newspapers or watching it unfold on the rolling news channels would quake in their boots, thinking twice before doling out their brutal acts. She had to admit that it was a personal success too, and hoped a rather sombre-looking Evie was more pleased than she appeared to be.

Evie's future would ultimately come down to the sentence, and if the judge believed the jury had made the wrong call he could still impose life imprisonment for manslaughter, so in real terms she would be no better off. All they could do was hope that he would take into account the mitigating factors that Boyd had tried hard to demonstrate.

There was no point in trying to predict the outcome, though, so for now Harriet was going to focus on a sense of elation that justice had been done.

For Stephanie, it was all over. Not just the trial, but her brief stint in CID. She would return to uniform immediately and say goodbye to Gus. What a day to choose. He'd had a face like thunder since the verdict was read out, and unless Evie was given a significant custodial sentence, he was going to be even more frustrated.

He hadn't said a word when the foreman uttered the words "not guilty" on the count of murder, and had remained seated until the court had emptied.

'It's the wrong decision, Steph. I know you don't agree with me – but I'm sure it's wrong.'

He sounded discouraged rather than irritated, and Stephanie didn't know what to say. She knew Gus felt that there was rarely an excuse for one person to take another's life, except in a clear case of self-defence. Even then he asked why a serious wounding wouldn't have been more appropriate than death. She blamed his Presbyterian upbringing, but she could see from the tight line of his mouth that he was anything but happy.

'What more could we have done?' he asked. 'It had all the hallmarks of a premeditated attack to me.'

She didn't want to end their time working together with an argument, but this was ridiculous.

'Oh come on, Gus. We've been over this so many times, and still you're obsessed with her guilt. The man committed ruthless acts of violence on her.' Stephanie could hear her voice rising, and struggled to get it back on a level. Gus was so adamant, and so bloody bull-headed. 'Mark wasn't drunk, he wasn't on drugs – so what kind of a psychopath holds their partner's hand over the sink and tips boiling water over her arm? Jesus, if you had ever done that to me I would have beaten the shit out of you.'

That brought the ghost of a smile to his face.

'Don't I know it, although I very much doubt you would have brought a fucking knife into the bedroom! It's not that. I'm still struggling with the fact that we never had cast-iron evidence that Mark *did* hurt her. There's something that doesn't feel right to me. If I could have put my finger on it, nailed it for the prosecution, I would have done. I'm just bloody frustrated that I didn't.'

Gus stood up and shoved his hands into the pockets of his trousers and turned to look at the empty courtroom. Stephanie pushed herself up from the chair.

'I'm going to go now, Gus. I don't agree with you and whatever you say, somehow or other domestic abuse has got to be curbed. But I don't want to argue with you. Not today.'

He turned back towards her. 'I know you think I'm a dinosaur, but I'm not. Over a million women reported incidents of domestic violence last year and we're still not doing anything like enough to help. So if Mark North really did everything that Evie says he did, then he was a monster and should have been locked up for it. I know it has to be stopped, although not necessarily by killing any bastard that raises his fist. We can't open the floodgates to everyone thinking it's okay to kill in order to make it go away.'

'I said I didn't want to argue, but you're making it bloody difficult. My final say on this: you fear that Evie being found not guilty could pave the way for other women to feel they have the right to fight back. I say that making her serve a life sentence for murder means that abused women – and men – have to lie back and take what's being doled out. I'm not entirely disagreeing with your view, but you're going too far.'

'Okay, I accept there are two ways of looking at it,' Gus said, lifting a hand to touch Stephanie on the shoulder. 'Although personally I'd rather not attend too many more scenes like Mark North's death again. But we're confusing two things. I don't want to argue the rights and wrongs of fighting back. It's not the issue here. It's whether that's what actually happened. I can't help thinking that there is something staring me in the face, and I just can't see it. Ignore me, Steph.'

Stephanie tried her best to smile, and took a step back. Gus's hand fell back to his side.

'Well, that's not going to be difficult from now on, is it? Look, I'd better be off. I've got a couple of days' leave and then I'm back in uniform, so thanks for everything. It's been good working with you.'

She turned and started towards the door. Gus shouted after her.

'Is that it, then? Is that all you're going to say?'

Stephanie held her breath. 'What do you *want* me to say?'

'I want you to say, "Come to dinner on Saturday, Gus – I'd love to see you." How about that for a radical thought?'

Stephanie carried on walking and raised her hand. She couldn't let him see her face.

'Bye, Gus,' she said as she let herself out of the courtroom.

PART THREE

Every cut, every broken bone, every second of pain stokes the fire of revenge. The more brutal the attack, the deeper bores the canker of hatred.

56

'Come on, my little love,' Cleo said as she picked Lulu up from where she was sitting on her play mat and kissed her soft cheek. 'There's a lady who wants to talk to me and she wants to see what a good girl you are too.'

The lump in Cleo's throat was growing bigger by the moment. This was it. The judge had given Evie a two-year prison sentence, but he had suspended it and she was free. Cleo had been certain Evie would come racing round to collect Lulu on the very first day she was out, but she hadn't. For days Cleo had been waiting, dreading the knock on the door, knowing it had to come sooner or later. It felt as if Evie was making her suffer by not letting her know when the axe was going to fall.

Finally Social Services had explained to her that it wasn't quite as simple as Evie picking up her daughter. She was guilty of manslaughter and it was their job to assess her, to be certain she wasn't going to have any further episodes of loss of control – this time affecting her child. Their evaluation up to now had been very positive, so Cleo had to accept the fact that Lulu would be returned to her mother soon. She had considered inventing stories of Evie's poor mothering skills, but it didn't make sense to alienate either Social Services or Evie. Cleo was going to have to bite the bullet and pretend to be supportive. She couldn't lose Lulu completely – not after the months they'd had together – so Evie had to see Cleo as a caring aunt who could be relied on to look after the child, perhaps while Evie worked. Surely everyone would benefit from that arrangement?

Today wasn't the first time Social Services had called round. They had seemed happy with the way Lulu responded to Cleo, although they had registered surprise when Lulu had called Cleo Mumma.

'Oh, she did that of her own volition,' Cleo said, smiling cheerily. 'She's far too young to understand why her mother isn't here with her, and given that I could have been looking after her until she was fifteen – or even older – I didn't think it did any harm.'

'Maybe it would have been better to discourage her,' the social worker had said, without any hint of recrimination in her tone. But Cleo could see what she was thinking.

'Yes, I suppose so. I show her photos of Evie and say, "That's Mummy," and encourage her to repeat the word. But she's only a baby and no doubt she was confused.'

The social worker had just looked at her and said nothing. Cleo felt she could see right through her.

And now the day had come – the day when Evie was going to be seeing Lulu again for the first time. The social workers had suggested they choose a neutral location, and that Cleo didn't need to be there, but apparently Evie had disagreed.

'Cleo is the one who has given Lulu stability. Lulu probably won't recognise me, and I don't want her confused and upset the first time we meet again. She hasn't seen me for months, and she was only eleven months old when I was separated from her. Unless you think it's a problem, I'd rather Cleo was there too.'

Cleo had been stunned. Maybe Evie would see how happy Lulu was and decide she was best left where she was – at least for a while. She knew this was no more than a hollow dream, though.

She carried Lulu through to the sitting room from the play room she'd decorated in those first dreadful weeks after Mark's death. She'd had to keep busy and wear herself out each day so she fell into bed exhausted at night, ready for sleep – in theory, at least. The truth was that sleep had rarely come easily and she hadn't wanted to take any medication for fear that Lulu would need her during the night. She had lost weight, lost the muscle tone she had spent years building up, and her once attractive pallor was now closer to uneven shades of grey than its former creamy smoothness. She had done her best with her appearance for this meeting, though. Nobody else needed to know how she was feeling inside, and as she carried Lulu into the sitting room she gave the social worker a wide smile.

'Hello, Lulu,' said the lady sitting on the sofa. She had told Cleo her name, but Cleo couldn't remember it for the life of her. Lulu smiled and buried her face in Cleo's shoulder. 'Does Lulu know who's coming today?'

Cleo shook her head. 'I thought it might confuse her.'

The woman was looking at her intently. 'Cleo, you do under-stand that Evie's assessment has been very positive. There is no reason why Lulu can't return to her mother – today, if that's what she wants.'

Cleo had been blocking this thought from her mind. 'Surely that wouldn't be fair on Lulu?' she said, hearing the quiver in her own voice.

'Evie's her mother. Unless we see signs that the child is scared of her, we have no reason to be concerned about her returning to live with her.'

'But she's been mine for six months – that's nearly as long as she was Evie's!'

Cleo realised immediately that claiming possession had been a bad move. It was written all over the woman's face. There was a pause before she spoke again.

'My colleague Suzanne has gone to collect Evie,' she told Cleo, who finally remembered this woman was called Paula. 'Are you going to be okay seeing her, Cleo?'

She wasn't, but she couldn't admit it.

'Of course, why wouldn't I be?'

Paula sighed. 'Because she killed your brother, and I have little doubt she will be taking her daughter back. I can see you've become very attached to Lulu.'

Cleo frowned. 'It would have been unfair to take the child on and *not* become attached, I would have thought.'

Paula's gaze was intense and Cleo didn't like the idea of what she might be able to see. 'Would you like a cup of coffee?' she asked.

'Why don't we wait until Evie arrives. Once we've all had a few minutes, you could go into the kitchen to make us a drink, and we can see how Lulu copes.'

Cleo felt small tremors running through her body. Surely Lulu would panic if she was out of the room? Apart from Aminah and Zahid, Lulu had barely seen anyone else for months and was rarely left in the care of another adult. But Cleo was out of time. The doorbell rang and she looked at Paula. She didn't know what to do.

'Are you going to get that?' Paula asked. 'Why don't you leave Lulu with me? It's the first time you've seen Evie, and if there's any tension between the two of you it's better that it's out of sight of the child, don't you think?'

Cleo stood up. Her legs seemed weak, as if they wouldn't hold her up, but she had to be strong. She kissed the top of Lulu's head and passed her to Paula, expecting but not getting a cry of protest. She made her way into the hall. Through the frosted glass she could see the outline of two women, and could just make out the sound of their voices.

There was a light laugh.

Evie. Obviously she wasn't affected by the same nerves as Cleo, who forced herself to take a deep breath and open the door.

She stared at the woman on the other side, barely recognising her.

Evie's hair had been cut short. Not quite the crop that Cleo had worn for the last few years, but just below ear length, wavy and stylishly messy. It had been bleached a pale blonde – not the bright platinum white of Cleo's, but a cool ash colour. She looked so different. Lighter, happier, and unlike Cleo – who had dressed as if she was about to attend an interview – Evie was wearing dark blue jeans and a loose t-shirt.

315

Evie looked straight into Cleo's eyes and smiled. 'Hi, Cleo. It's good to see you.'

Suzanne, the social worker, was staring at Cleo watching for her response, so only Cleo could see Evie's eyes. Her mouth smiled, but her eyes burned Cleo's flesh where they touched.

57

The look that Evie had given her had left Cleo feeling distracted and unsettled. She had expected Evie to be the one feeling the pressure – the one who felt guilty for what she had done to Mark, perhaps embarrassed at having to face her victim's sister. But she had never seen her so comfortable with herself, and both Suzanne and Paula seemed to sense Cleo's confusion as they all took their seats in the sitting room.

Paula kept hold of Lulu, and although Cleo's immediate instinct was to walk over and take the child from the social worker, she managed to restrain herself.

Evie didn't rush to Lulu either, but sat down and started to speak softly to the others in the room.

'Why did you change your hair?' Cleo blurted out, unable to stop herself. 'Lulu won't recognise you, so I don't understand why you would do that.'

Evie gave a sad smile and Cleo could see the sympathetic glances of the social workers.

'She's not going to recognise me anyway, is she? It's been almost six months now. I left an eleven-month-old baby, and now she's a toddler. I don't think she would have remembered my face. If she has any memory of me, it's going to be something else.'

Lulu was watching Evie as she spoke, and she started to wriggle in Paula's arms.

'Okay if I put her down?' Paula asked. Cleo started to answer, and then realised she wasn't the one being consulted.

'Of course,' Evie said. It was hard to understand her. Why didn't she rush in and pull the child into her arms? But as Lulu was placed back on the rug, she couldn't take her eyes off her mother, who smiled at her but sat quietly.

Cleo wanted to get up, to make some noise, to break the tension. But she was strangely mesmerised, watching mother and daughter looking at each other.

'Hello, Lolula,' Evie said softly, and Cleo nearly jumped. She had never heard Evie call Lulu that before. In all the time she had spent in their house, it was a name that had never been used, so it had to have been a private name between Evie and her baby. Lulu's little face lit up in a smile and she toddled towards her mother.

Every woman in the place was tense – waiting to see what would happen. Lulu reached her mother and rested both her hands on Evie's knees as if to hold herself up. Evie reached out a finger and delicately stroked the dimples on the back of Lulu's hand.

'How's my baby girl?' she whispered, and Lulu started to bounce up and down until Evie gently reached down and picked her daughter up, both of them now smiling. It was as if the room relaxed with a sigh.

'Right,' Cleo said, her loud voice breaking through the serenity of the scene. 'Who would like some coffee?'

She didn't wait for an answer, but fled from the room, certain she would cry if she had to witness any more of this. She should be pleased for Lulu – but she wasn't. Mark's child was going to be returned to his killer, and it shouldn't be allowed to happen.

She had to do something. Evie had been given a suspended sentence, so if she broke the law again she would immediately go to prison. Cleo had to think of something – anything – to make her go away and leave them in peace.

She thrust the kettle under the tap, forgetting to watch it until the water overflowed.

'Shit!' she muttered, tipping some of the excess back in the sink. She slammed the kettle back on its stand and leaned back, her arms folded.

She hadn't realised that anyone had come into the room until she turned round.

'Jesus, Evie – where did you come from?'

'I could see you were upset, so I asked Suzanne and Paula to look after Lulu for a moment so I could check if you were okay.' Evie reached behind her and closed the door.

'What do *you* think?' Cleo said.

'Do you know what Lulu said when you went out of the room?'

Cleo laughed. 'No, but she only says about three words that are comprehensible, so it can't have been much.'

'She looked at the door and said, "Mumma." She meant you, didn't she?'

'Oh, don't start. I've been through all of this with the social workers.'

319

Evie leaned against the door as if to prevent anyone from coming in, and for a moment Cleo felt a moment of fear. She was stuck in here with a murderer – whatever the jury said.

'Look, I didn't know you were coming home. It never occurred to me for one minute that the judge would be so stupid as to let you out without a lengthy prison sentence. But he did. I wanted Lulu to have as normal a childhood as possible. Surely that's what you want too?'

Evie shook her head. 'Normal? With you as her "Mumma"?'

Cleo wanted to scream at Evie, but the women in the other room would hear and that wasn't going to help anyone.

'What happens now, Evie?' she asked.

'I'm going to take Lulu home with me.'

Cleo felt her hands begin to shake again. 'I haven't packed her stuff yet.'

Evie shook her head. 'It doesn't matter. I've bought enough to keep her going.'

'Well, when can I see her? Can we set up some kind of access arrangement?'

There was a soft laugh. 'I don't think so, do you?'

From down the hallway Cleo heard the sound of a door opening; obviously either Paula or Suzanne was coming to check up on them.

'Please, Evie – can I come round tomorrow and see her, bring her favourite toys?'

'No.'

'So when?'

Evie moved away from the door as they heard the social worker's footsteps on the hardwood floor of the hall. Suzanne's

320

call of 'Everything okay in there?' almost covered Evie's response. But not quite.

'Never,' she whispered, her tone fierce. 'And don't bother arguing. Unless you want me to tell them about Mia.'

Evie turned towards the door with a welcoming smile for Suzanne.

58

Cleo stood back from the window. She didn't want Evie to know that she was watching, and she didn't want her to see the tears she had tried so hard to control running down her cheeks.

Evie had returned to the sitting room from the kitchen as if everything was fine, and when the social workers had asked if she was ready to leave, she had hung on for a while, saying she didn't want to rush Lulu away too quickly.

It had been agony. It would have been so much easier if she had just gone, and in the end as they had all stood up to leave with Lulu held firmly in Evie's arms, it had felt almost a relief.

'Thank you so much, Cleo. What you've done for Lulu has been more than I could ever have expected or asked. I'll never forget that you treated her as if she was your own.'

The two social workers couldn't see Evie's face as she turned towards Cleo. Nor did they notice when Evie held Lulu forward so that Cleo could kiss her, turning the child's face at the last second as if adjusting the weight on her hip, so the kiss landed on the back of Lulu's head. Only Cleo saw the malice in Evie's eyes.

She felt as if Evie had thrust a hand deep into her chest and slowly dragged out her heart. Not a short, sharp pain, but a long-drawn-out agony. Evie had taken Mark first and now Lulu, leaving nothing but an abundance of love building day after day in Cleo's chest, with no outlet.

As the car carrying Lulu away from her turned the corner and disappeared from view, Cleo made a snap decision. She was going to go to the gallery, lock it from the inside and pull down the blinds to avoid the unwelcome interruption of customers. She had to do something to take her mind off everything she had lost.

As she pushed open the door she felt the resistance of a mountain of post. It was weeks since she had been here and the gallery felt like a cold place now, devoid of the hope she'd had for it when it first opened. She would never again look up from her work to see Mark rushing through the door, excited by his latest stunning photographs. She craved one more opportunity for the two of them to prop up his remarkable pictures around the room, trying to decide on the best position and lighting.

Cleo's eyes burned. She needed a distraction from her desolation at the loss of Lulu and from thoughts of Evie's last comment. What did she know about Mia? What *could* she know? Cleo had never told anyone what had happened that day, not even Mark, so there was no way that Evie could know anything, surely.

For a moment, Cleo was back in the gallery on the morning of Mia's death.

'Mark, it's Cleo,' she'd said, calling him on his mobile. 'Just checking that everything's okay for your trip. Is there anything you need me to do while you're away?'

'No, I'm fine.'

She could tell from the clipped tone of voice that he was unhappy about something.

'What's up? It's a pretty straightforward commission, isn't it?'

'Yes – just some photos of a very bad-tempered-looking child. I have to attempt to make her look angelic, or at least interesting. It'll be fine.'

'So what's winding you up?'

She'd heard a sound as if he was blowing out hard through his mouth. 'It's Mia. She's driving me mad, saying I shouldn't be going, why was I bothering, all that kind of crap. You know what she's like. She thinks I should live off her generosity, and tempting as it sometimes is, I don't enjoy feeling like a kept man. I hate going away, you know that. I'm wound up enough without her making me feel like a fool.'

'Is that what she does?'

Maybe the condescension that Cleo had witnessed was more serious when the couple were alone. Mark was making it sound as if it bordered on derision.

'She pays for everything, and when I want to spend any money I have to ask her. I hate it, Cleo, but she loves it. She calls my photographs my "silly pictures" and if she says one more negative thing before I leave, I'm going to flip.' Cleo heard another sigh. 'Look, forget I said all this. I need to go. The taxi will be here in about twenty minutes. I'll see you when I'm back.'

Mark had rung off without saying goodbye and Cleo hadn't liked the sound of it at all. She remembered pacing up and down the gallery for a while before coming to a decision. She had to talk to Mia and make her understand how unhappy she was making Mark.

She had picked up her keys and run from the gallery, in her rush almost forgetting to lock the door behind her. She had thought of driving, but given her mood it made more sense to walk in an effort to release some of her pent-up anger at Mia. She had taken the shortcut, across the common, through a small wood, and up the cliff path.

There was nobody about. It was February, and a cold wind on this side of the bay persuaded Cleo to break into a jog – up the path and out onto the track that led to the long white wall of Mark and Mia's house.

She had hoped that some of her outrage at the way Mia was making Mark feel would have abated by the time she got there, but it hadn't and she had hammered on the front door with her fists. Nobody answered. She glanced towards the garage door, but as usual it was closed so there was no way to get round the back. She could only have missed Mark by minutes, but it was perhaps as well. He wouldn't have been happy at her interference.

Cleo fingered the bunch of keys in her pocket. She was sure Mia would know who was at the door and was probably being difficult – especially if she knew Mark had spoken to his sister just before he left.

Selecting a key from the keyring, she held it up and looked at it for a long moment. This was an invasion of their privacy

325

and Mia would be furious if Cleo simply marched in. It was, after all, her house and not Mark's, as she frequently reminded everyone. She probably didn't even know Cleo had a key. But what could she do?

Cleo made her decision. Mark would be well on his way to the airport and was probably miserable because of everything his wife had put him through that morning. She was going to sort it for him. It was what she had always done when he had a problem.

With determination she put the key in the lock and turned it.

59

Stephanie was back in uniform and not enjoying being out on patrol in the squad car with Jason the probationer. It seemed he hadn't moved on much in the months she had been on secondment to CID, and was intent on grilling her about life 'on the other side'.

'Can we talk about something else, Jason?' Stephanie asked, knowing she was taking out her grumpy mood on the poor guy. 'I enjoyed the investigative side – it was a great experience, in spite of working on a particularly tricky case. But it's over, and given the crap we're going to have to deal with today I'd rather not dwell on the delights of being a detective. Okay?'

Jason lifted one corner of his mouth in an unattractive snarl, but stopped talking for a few minutes.

Stephanie felt in limbo. She loved being a police officer, but her time in CID had convinced her that it was where she wanted to be. The only way it could happen – unless she was prepared to work for Gus – was if she moved. Gus still wanted them to talk, but as she was no longer seeing him every day she was giving herself a bit of space to try to work out whether the current low-level ache of loss was better or worse than the piercing pain of a broken heart if they split up again. She still hadn't worked it out, but she missed him. Gus was exasperated by her stubbornness, but if they were going to give their relationship another chance, she had to be one hundred per cent sure of herself and of him.

She shook the thought from her head as she noticed a short, wiry man with ginger hair scurrying along the pavement, turning his collar up against the thin drizzle that seemed to be hanging in the air rather than falling to the ground. There was something familiar about him, and she couldn't think for the life of her what it was. He dodged into a coffee shop on the high street, and then she got it. She pulled the car over to the kerb.

'Just going to get coffee, Jason. Flat white, as usual?'

Jason looked slightly shocked at the fact that she was going for the coffee instead of sending him, but she didn't give him a chance to answer as she jumped out of the car, slammed the door and ran across the road.

The windows of the café had steamed up and she couldn't see where the man had gone, so she pushed the door open and found him giving his order to the surly-looking waiter at the counter.

'I'll be sitting over there,' the man said, pointing to the furthest table.

'If you hang on, your coffee will be ready in a couple of minutes,' the waiter said. 'You can take it with you.'

The man raised his eyebrows, slammed a few coins on the bar and walked over to the table.

The waiter tutted and muttered something that sounded

remarkably like 'tosser', before turning his sullen face to Stephanie.

'Yes?'

'A flat white and a large espresso to take out. I'm going to join your customer for a chat.'

The waiter looked as if he was going to object to her sitting down without buying anything to drink in, but then took in the uniform and thought better of it. The young girl making the coffee put a cappuccino on the bar.

'Take him his coffee, then,' the waiter said, which only served to remind Stephanie that she wouldn't be back in this particular café for a while.

Picking the cup up from the bar, she walked over to the table and placed the coffee in front of the man. He didn't look up from the newspaper he was reading, but muttered his thanks.

'Mind if I join you?' Stephanie asked.

For that, he did raise his head. He gazed around at the empty tables and chairs and then back at Stephanie, not showing any surprise that a police officer wanted to sit with him.

'As you wish,' he said, returning to his paper.

'Can I talk to you for a moment?' she said.

With a sigh, he folded his paper and placed it on the table. 'What about?'

'I saw you a few weeks ago at the Crown Court. The trial of Evelyn Clarke. You were in the gallery.'

'And?'

'I wondered about your interest in the case. Do you know Evie?'

329

'I'm just nosy, okay? I saw there was a big trial on, so I decided to check it out. I'm interested in people, that's all.'

Stephanie took her hand out of her pocket and stretched her arm across the table. 'Sergeant Stephanie King,' she said.

'How do you do,' he answered, raising a heavily freckled hand to shake hers, but saying nothing more.

'And you are?'

'Is there any reason why I might be compelled to give you that information?' he asked. 'As far as I'm aware, I haven't broken any laws and I haven't witnessed any crimes. So I'm not entirely sure why you need to know.'

'Just call me nosy,' she said, echoing his words.

The man lifted his coffee cup and took a long drink. 'Well, I'm leaving. Nice to have met you, Sergeant.'

As he rose to his feet, Stephanie remembered the torn scraps of paper.

'While you were listening to the trial, you were tearing up a letter.'

Suddenly, she had his attention. He stopped and looked at her.

'I have the pieces. I picked them up.' She omitted to tell him that the scraps were a soggy mess and illegible.

To Stephanie's surprise, the man leaned in towards her, his voice low and urgent.

'Look, it doesn't mean anything – okay? She must have had her reasons. Forget it.'

Before Stephanie could ask him what he meant, the man turned and hurried out of the coffee shop.

60

Throughout the remainder of her shift, Stephanie hadn't been able to put the face of the man in the café out of her mind. She had deliberately mentioned the note to try to get a reaction, and sure enough his rather sarcastic manner had changed to one of minor panic. He hadn't liked the thought that she might have read whatever was on the paper, and now more than ever she wished she had taken more time drying it out and piecing it all together. But she hadn't, and she had no legitimate reason to start nosing around now. The case was closed. On the other hand, going strictly by the rules had never been her forte.

In truth, she hadn't stopped thinking about Evie Clarke. She had heard that Evie had rented a cottage facing the sea wall, and wondered if anyone had warned her that from time to time waves could crash right over the top. It might put Lulu at risk. Stephanie had thought often about Evie's baby and how the enforced separation from her mother during the remand period might have affected her. She had never understood why Evie had voluntarily chosen prison over bail – denying herself precious time with her child. It was none of her business, though, and it would be entirely inappropriate for her to seek Evie out to warn her about the possible danger from the sea. She had to forget it.

The rest of the day held few surprises. She introduced Jason to the delights of teenage shoplifters and their cockiness, although their lack of remorse shocked even him, but in truth, Stephanie couldn't wait for the day to be over so she could get home and check if she still had what remained of the soggy scraps of the paper torn up by the man in court. They had been in the pocket of her jacket, but her whole suit had been such a mess after the rainstorm that she had sent it off to the dry cleaner's. She always emptied her pockets into a bowl on her dressing table but she couldn't remember whether she had thrown the paper away, believing it was no good to anyone.

At the end of her shift she hurried home and, taking the stairs to her bedroom two at a time, rushed over to the dressing table and sighed with relief. The scraps were still there. She should have known, really. Housework of any description wasn't her thing, and the paper would undoubtedly have remained in the bowl until the next time her conscience struck her and she got a duster out. But for now, it was where she had left it.

Grabbing a pair of tweezers from her mug of oddments next to the bowl, she made her way downstairs and sat at the kitchen table. The scraps were dry now and quite brittle, but easier to separate than when they were nothing more than a sodden mass.

Carefully and slowly, Stephanie tried to pull each piece of paper away from the next, using the tweezers to grasp the edge of the scrap and damping it slightly with a cloth to stop it from ripping.

The ink seemed even more badly smudged than before. The pieces had torn where they had become frail and slightly crumbly, and she couldn't work out how they might join together. Gus may have been able to help, but he already thought this was a wild goose chase so she had no intention of giving him anything to tease her about.

She was ready to give up when she saw two pieces that looked as if they might be in the wrong place. If she swapped them around she could see a word starting on one scrap and finishing on the one next to it. There was an 'L' and a smudge on one piece, and on the other the letters 'ester'. Could the missing letters form the word 'Leicester'? Wasn't that where Evie had lived before she came here?

Stephanie leaned back, lifting a hand to massage the stiffness from the back of her neck. She rotated her head a few times, hearing some slightly alarming clicks, and decided it was time to stand up and move around. She walked across to the kettle and switched it on. Why was she wasting her time on what was undoubtedly a fool's errand?

She poured boiling water over a tea bag and swished it about a bit, staring sightlessly at the darkening ripples. She should throw the scraps of paper into the wood burner and forget about them. But somehow she knew the letter would continue to bug her.

She took the cup of black tea back over to the table and sat down again. All she had was a suggestion that the letter had something to do with Leicester. And it told her precisely nothing.

61

The days were dragging slowly by, merging into each other, and Cleo was struggling to motivate herself to get out of bed every morning. At night she lay awake, tossing and turning, trying to lie still and relax each part of her body deep into the mattress in the futile hope that her taut limbs would finally succumb to exhaustion. The only thing keeping her going was the belief that at some point Lulu would come back to her. Evie was bound to slip up, and she would finally be seen for the monster she was. Cleo had to at least keep herself alive, if not healthy, so she could enjoy that day to the full.

The threat of what Evie might tell the police about Mia still hung over Cleo's head, and she needed to understand what Evie knew – or thought she knew. She couldn't risk having the enquiry into Mia's death reopened. It was four years ago now; four years of wondering whether she had done the right thing.

The memory of that day had burst into her dreams every night for months afterwards, and it was only by exercising herself to the point of collapse that she had been able to make it through a whole night without waking up screaming.

That dreadful morning, just minutes after she had let herself into Mark and Mia's house with her own key, she had found herself tearing back down the cliff path and into the gallery, locking the door behind her and flipping the closed sign to discourage customers. Her heavy breathing had been nothing to do with the run along the uneven sandy surface of the path. It was pure fear.

Mia was dead.

Cleo hadn't hesitated. She had known exactly what she had to do. Thank God she hadn't taken her mobile with her. The police would have been able to check and would have placed her at the scene. She picked it up now, though, and dialled a familiar number.

'Hi, you've reached Mia and Mark North but we're not in right now. Leave us a message and we'll call you back.'

Cleo hadn't said a word, and after several minutes of silence, she hung up. All she had to do was erase the silent message on the answering machine in the house so that her phone records would prove that she had spoken to Mia long after Mark had left. That way no suspicion would be cast on him. She needed the police to think that Mia had answered when she called and that they had chatted on the phone.

She knew she would have to go back to the house very soon, that she would have to be the one to discover Mia's broken body, lying at the foot of the basement steps. Cleo's DNA might be at the scene, so she had to touch Mia again, ostensibly to check if she was still alive. But she already knew that she was dead.

She dialled another number. 'Aminah, hi,' she'd said, trying to sound as normal as possible. Fortunately the cry of a new-born baby disguised any unsteadiness in her voice.

'Sorry, Cleo – it's a bit hard to hear you. What can I do for you?'

'I've just spoken to Mia. We're going into town at lunchtime for a quick bite to eat. With Mark away, I thought it would be a nice thing to do. Anyway, she seemed happy with the idea, so I wondered if you'd like to join us.'

'Bloody hell, Cleo – I can tell you've never had a baby! He's only two weeks old, so unless you want me to bring him with me and have him attached to my left breast throughout our lunch, because trust me he's not happy to be put down for more than five minutes at a time, I will have to decline your kind invitation.'

Cleo had known she would say that.

'Okay, well maybe next time.'

Aminah chuckled. 'What's the lunch in honour of anyway? You don't even like Mia.'

'Course I do. She's Mark's wife, and I know sometimes I have a moan, but that's normal, isn't it? You moan about Zahid all the time!'

'Ah, but he's my husband so he's fair game.' There came a louder wail. 'I'm going to have to go, but say hi from me. I like Mia. She makes me smile with her "I'm so rich it hurts" attitude.'

With another laugh from Aminah, the call was ended. But Cleo knew that her friend would remember the conversation.

Next she called Mark. 'Hi – are you at the airport now?'

'Yes, we're boarding in five minutes. Why?'

'I wondered if you'd sorted things out with Mia before you left? Maybe you should give her a call before you get on the plane.'

Mark had gone very quiet on the other end of the phone, and Cleo wished she could read his thoughts.

'Maybe you're right,' he said softly. 'Maybe that would be a smart move.'

When he had rung off, Cleo put her head down on the workbench and sobbed. This couldn't be happening. She had to get herself together, though, because she knew that Mark would call her back any minute.

'Cleo, she's not answering. I've left her a message, and I'll call again when I land. I might need you to go to the house. Would you mind?'

'Of course not. Shall I go now?'

Mark's voice had sounded shaky. 'No, best not. Let's give it the hour of my flight.' He paused. 'I'm a fool, Cleo. I'm pathetic.'

'You're not, Mark. You're wonderful and I love you. You know I'd do anything for you, don't you.'

'I know, and sometimes I ask too much. Look, I've got to go. I'll call you later.'

Cleo hadn't moved from her seat in the hour it had taken Mark to call back with the inevitable request that she go to the house and check on Mia.

'I think she was feeling a bit wobbly this morning. Obviously I wouldn't normally ask you to check on her after a couple of hours of no contact, but I thought she looked a bit pale when I left.'

Cleo had kept a smile in her voice. 'Of course, and when I see her, I'll tell her how concerned you are. Don't worry.'

How she had stopped herself from crying or giving away what she already knew, she had no idea. As if in a trance, she locked the gallery again, but this time drove to the house, waving to a couple of acquaintances as she passed along the busy high street.

She had sat outside the house for ten minutes before she had been able to force herself to go through the door and do what needed to be done.

The priority was the answer machine. It was showing two messages and she knew the other one would be Mark. His would be the second message, and although she dearly wanted to listen to what he said, she had to leave that one intact. She selected the first message and deleted it.

It had been so very hard to find the strength to go back to the top of the basement steps. She stood there and stared down at Mia's body, her eyes staring straight at Cleo in accusation. It probably wasn't necessary to go back down the stairs. She had already felt for Mia's pulse, but just in case there was something different – some fragment of clothing or anything which could prove that Cleo had been down there earlier – she made herself go through exactly the same motions again, forcing the sick feeling from her stomach as she touched Mia's wrist, now cold.

And that was when she saw the watch – its face shattered – its hands showing a time that must never be seen. Finding a tissue in her bag, she altered the time to five minutes after she was supposed to have spoken to Mia.

And then she turned and walked back upstairs, pulling her phone from her bag, preparing herself to call the police.

62

Her recollections of the day that Mia died had left Cleo feeling weak. What could Evie possibly know? Even Mark didn't know that Cleo had been to the house twice. So how could Evie? She had to talk to someone about this. Not about what really happened, but about what Evie might think she knew.

She grabbed her coat and made her way out into the wet and windy streets. It was freezing outside, and there were reports on the news of heavy snow in some parts of the country. But not this far south, especially on the coast. She could hear the distant boom of a fierce sea hitting the sea wall, and wondered if it would be coming over, into Evie's cottage. Would Lulu be safe? She hoped Evie would have more sense than to take her outdoors on a day like this.

There was no point taking the car. The trip to Aminah's would take fifteen minutes on foot, and she needed the exercise. Maybe this stormy weather would blow away the thick mist that seemed to have settled in her brain.

Head down, she battled against the wind, welcoming the sharp shards of rain as they lashed her uncovered face and head.

Aminah's house was lit up like a Christmas tree even though it was the middle of the day. It looked warm and inviting through the window, in sharp contrast to the murky day outside.

Running up the last few steps to the front door, jumping over a puddle in her path, Cleo pressed hard on the doorbell. She heard Aminah inside shouting at one of the children to watch the baby. She was surprised by that. Anik was the youngest and he could hardly be classed as a baby. She hadn't expected all the children to be at home, and realised belatedly that it was probably a school holiday.

Hoping that Aminah would at least be able to spare her an hour for a chat, she pasted an expectant smile on her face as her friend opened the door.

She was not prepared for the look of shock and embarrassment on Aminah's face.

'Oh. Cleo. I wasn't expecting you.'

Cleo was confused. She had never had to make an appointment to come round here before.

'Can I come in?' she asked, hating the pleading sound in her voice.

'Oh shit, Cleo, I'm sorry but you can't.'

Rain from the small porch was dripping into the puddle and splashing the back of Cleo's legs. She could feel the water seeping through her already wet jeans. She knew she should speak, but she was shocked and hurt by Aminah's response.

'Look, this is dreadful and I never wanted to be put in this position. But we've got Lulu here.'

Cleo felt a leap in her chest. 'Can I see her, Aminah? Please – I've missed her so much.'

Aminah's usually cheerful face looked drained and Cleo sensed pity in her friend's words and tone.

'I'm so sorry. God, this is awful. Evie brought Lulu round this morning because some of the sea water has come into the house. She needs to keep on top of it and brush it out until the tide turns.'

'I get that, but why does it mean I can't come in?'

Cleo knew the answer, but surely Aminah wouldn't side with Evie?

'She doesn't want Lulu to see you. Look, Cleo, I just think she wants Lulu to know who her mummy is and to avoid her getting confused.'

Cleo felt her cheeks burn and the hand in her pocket balled into a tight fist. How could Evie do this after the care Cleo had taken of her child?

'I can see how this is making you feel, but it's not my decision to make. I'm just helping a friend.'

'But *I'm* your friend.' Even to Cleo's own ears she sounded pathetic but, bit by bit, Evie was stripping her of everything that mattered in her life.

'Of course you're my friend – but so is Evie. She's had a tough time over the last year and I'm simply trying to be supportive.'

Cleo wanted to grab Aminah and shake her to try to make her understand. She felt her throat tighten and her words came out as a hiss.

'She killed my *brother!*'

'I know, love, and I realise how devastating it's been for you. We all do, and I understand why this made you more possessive of Lulu than was really acceptable. But he was hurting her, Cleo. I know that must be a hard thing to come to terms with, but I can see both sides. Look, I can't let you come in now, but as soon as Lulu's gone why don't I give you a call and we'll have a glass of wine or two when the kids are in bed?'

Cleo could see the compassion in her friend's eyes but she didn't care. She didn't want her pity. She wanted Aminah to understand how devastated she was by all that had happened and fight for her – for her right to see Lulu. But she could see that wasn't going to happen. She took a step back, straight into the puddle. The cold water washed almost unnoticed around her feet.

'Forget it. I can see where your loyalties lie. Just forget it.'

Cleo turned and walked down the drive, her head held high. She wasn't going to beg, but the truth was that Evie had taken Mark, Lulu and now Aminah. Cleo had nobody left.

63

Relieved that it was her day off, Stephanie was still wandering around in her dressing gown at ten o'clock in the morning. She had slept badly and had planned to have a lie-in, but once she woke up she found it impossible to settle again. So with a sigh of irritation she had thrown back the covers and got up. She had wasted far too much time trying to piece the letter together last night, and in the end had gone to bed determined to forget it. But she couldn't. Instead she went over and over in her mind the man's behaviour in court in the hope that it would give her a clue.

He was fixated with Evie. The letter mentioned Leicester. It was clearly written to someone special, because it began 'My darling' and she could only assume that referred to the man. It was signed by someone with the initial 'S', and it seemed to be saying that S would, by the time he was reading it, already be dead.

'Right,' she muttered to herself. 'Let's do this.'

She was certain that if Gus found out what she was doing he would tell her to stop wasting everyone's time, but with a bit of luck he would be hiding in his office and wouldn't know she had called the team responsible for checking on Evie's background.

'Azi, it's Stephanie. Can I pick your brain on the quiet, do you think?'

She had chosen Azi, a young Nigerian man, because she knew he had a soft spot for her since she had helped his mum – a neighbour of hers – when she had been ill. She paced the room as she spoke.

'Sure. Fire away.'

'You were one of the team that looked into Evie Clarke's life in Leicester, weren't you? What can you tell me, in addition to the information that was shared in court?'

'Sorry, Stephanie, but not very much. We were looking for her husband, Nigel Clarke, but although neighbours told us he'd left the country, nobody seemed to know where he'd gone.'

'But Evie didn't go with him?'

'Apparently she was supposed to follow a couple of months later, after she'd sorted out their flat, got rid of their stuff, that kind of thing. But of course, she never did.'

'Did she get rid of everything – or was anything left behind?'

'Not a thing. They rented, so she terminated the lease and apparently had a massive garage sale. Sold anything that wasn't actually nailed down, by all accounts.'

Stephanie thought for a moment.

'Did you find out anything about friends, other family, anyone they were close to there?'

Azi laughed. 'Absolutely the opposite. Everyone we spoke to said they were a very self-contained couple. I think that was a euphemism for anti-social. Especially her – she hardly passed the time of day with the neighbours. They only knew the husband was leaving the country because he asked them to keep an eye on her. He was worried about leaving her alone, but he couldn't delay his departure for some reason. Work-related, I expect.'

'Okay, thanks, Azi. It was a long shot. One last thing, if I may. I don't suppose you spoke to or came across anyone whose name began with S, did you?' Stephanie said, without either hope or expectation.

'Not that I recall. Other than Shelley herself, of course.'

Stephanie stopped pacing. 'What did you just say?'

'Evie – you knew her first name was Michelle, didn't you? Well, the husband – Nigel – apparently always called her Shelley.'

Oh my God, Stephanie thought. It all made sense.

'Thanks, Azi, and if you could avoid mentioning this until I've checked a few things, I'd be forever grateful.'

She pulled out a chair and collapsed into it. All her efforts had been worth it, if what she suspected turned out to be true.

The letter was from Shelley, aka Evie, to someone she called 'My darling' – could that be Nigel? That would explain why he had been staring at her in court, possibly unable to believe his eyes. That's why he had ripped up the letter.

Because he believed his wife was dead.

It was only later, as she was hurriedly taking a shower and getting dressed, that another thought occurred to Stephanie. Was the real Evie Clarke dead? Had the woman in the witness box somehow gained her identity? But surely if that were the case and the man in court was Nigel Clarke, as she suspected, he would have said something?

Somehow or other, Nigel must have heard about the trial and come along, suspecting it was some other woman with the same name. And then that day, as he sat in the gallery staring at the wife who had deserted him, he must have felt so dreadfully betrayed. Why would she do that? If she had wanted to be rid of him, why not just leave?

It was all too confusing, and it felt as if only Nigel held the key.

Stephanie walked over to the window to stare out at the wet and windy day, wondering what she should do next. She was tempted to call Gus to tell him what she had discovered, but then decided it would be much better to see if she could track down Nigel Clarke first, provided he hadn't already left the area. Gus had never trusted Evie, and now Stephanie may have found further evidence of her lies. But maybe there was an explanation and she wasn't prepared to share her doubts until she knew more.

How was she going to find Clarke on her own? She could start with the assumption that he was staying around here, but there were so many hotels locally. This was a holiday resort and he could be in any of them. Their background research hadn't suggested that he was wealthy, and when she saw him in the café he had been neatly dressed but he wasn't flashy. She decided to start by calling the mid-priced hotels and the better bed and breakfasts. It was going to be a hell of a job, but she couldn't justify asking for help from her colleagues. The trial was over. Evie was free. Gus would probably tell her to leave it, and then she would have no choice. She logged onto her laptop and pulled up a hotel directory.

The list was pages long. It was going to take hours, and she had to find a way to narrow it down. Gambling on the fact that Clarke would have chosen a hotel where he could get a hot meal each night, Stephanie refined the list and started making the calls. On her seventh call she punched the air. She had found him – or at least, she had found where he was staying. He was out, according to the receptionist, but had booked a table for dinner in their tiny restaurant for seven pm, and was due to check out the next morning. Stephanie gave the receptionist her details and asked her not to inform Mr Clarke that she had been enquiring about him.

The thought of going out into the stormy night didn't thrill Stephanie, but this might be her only chance, and so she kicked her heels until she was sure Nigel would be safely ensconced in the dining room and made a dash for her car.

She pulled up in front of a small, respectable-looking hotel and raced through the rain. The reception area was small, but had a cosy feel to it, and Stephanie shook the water off her shoulders and held out her warrant card to the receptionist.

'I called earlier, looking for Nigel Clarke. Is he in the restaurant?'

The girl nodded and asked Stephanie if she needed someone to show her which table. She declined the offer. She would recognise him, she was in no doubt of that.

The dining room had a utilitarian feel to it, with no cloths on the dark wood-veneered tables, and it was a bit too brightly lit to feel as welcoming as the reception area had promised.

Only a couple of tables were occupied, and Nigel Clarke was sitting at the back of the room, facing the door. He was casually dressed in a dark jumper and he was studying his iPad as he forked pasta into his mouth. As she walked towards him, he lifted his head and stared at her, clearly startled by her presence and even more shocked by the fact that she seemed to be making a beeline for him. He wiped his mouth on his napkin and pushed his plate of food away, as if preparing to stand up and leave the room.

'Sit down, Mr Clarke,' Stephanie said. 'I assume from your expression that you recognise me?' She carried on without waiting for an answer. 'Don't look so worried. You're not in any trouble. I just want to check up on a few things, and to understand exactly what's been going on. Do you mind if I join you?'

He didn't look impressed, but he no doubt felt he didn't have much choice.

'Technically, I'm off duty – so I'm going to have a glass of wine. Would you like one?' she asked.

'Red, please,' he said quietly. 'I'm not fussy about what sort. What do you want with me? I haven't done anything wrong.'

'I know. But I also know you believed Evie – Michelle, Shelley, whatever you prefer to call her – to be dead. What's going on, Mr Clarke?'

His eyes had a hollow look as if he didn't know what to say, or even think. He shook his head.

'Why don't you just go? There's nothing going on. Nothing that would interest you, anyway.' The words were clipped, laced with pent-up emotion.

349

'Does Evie know you're here?' Stephanie asked.

'*No!* She'd be livid.'

Stephanie looked at the thin, fox-like features of the man opposite and understood why he seemed so angry. He had discovered the wife he thought dead had been living with another man, and had his baby.

'Listen, Nigel – you don't mind if I call you Nigel, do you?'

He shrugged and lowered his eyes to his half-empty plate.

'I'm not here to cause you any bother – but I want to understand what made Evie pretend she was dead.'

His shoulders slumped.

'She obviously didn't want me any more. I had outlived my usefulness – isn't that what people say?' He gave a lopsided grin, but his eyes were desolate. 'I don't blame her for dumping me. I'm not much of a catch, and Shelley – that's what I called her – seemed to get more beautiful with every passing year. She told me she was on a mission to be drop-dead gorgeous. But then she always was to me.'

'How did you meet her?' Stephanie asked.

'She was living rough – had been since she was a teenager after her grandma died. I used to pass her sitting in a shop doorway on my way to the factory where I worked. I bought her a coffee one day and it went from there. She wanted to be someone different, she told me. I didn't know what she meant, but in the end I asked her to marry me – said I'd help her fulfil her dreams. Maybe I was just one rung of the ladder.'

Stephanie felt for this man. His rude, aggressive demeanour had gone. All that was left was a sense of hopelessness.

'My cousin sent me a clip from the paper with an article

about the trial of Evie Clarke,' he said. 'I had to go to court to see if it really was my Shelley. I thought someone was pulling a fast one – using her identity. I've been out of the country for a few years now, but I decided I had to come back, just to check.'

Stephanie said nothing. The shock of seeing Evie in court must have been profound.

'Talk me through it, Nigel – about the letter and what you believed.'

He looked at her for a moment, and sighed. 'She was supposed to be following me. I'd always dreamed of travelling, and Shelley said she had too. I got a job abroad, but she said someone needed to stay and sort things. She would join me when it was all done and dusted. I thought she was stalling a bit, but she always had a good excuse for why she hadn't left yet. And then I got the letter.'

'I didn't manage to read all of it. Can you tell me what it said?'

'What, you want it verbatim? Because I can remember every last word.'

'No – just the gist will do. How she explained herself.'

He let out a long, slow breath. 'The letter was one she wrote when she knew she was ill. She gave it to someone and asked them to post it when she was dead. She thanked me for being such a loving, wonderful husband and for changing her life. She said she had taken care of everything – there was nothing for me to come back to. Her ashes would by now have been scattered according to her wishes, and any possessions had been given to the hospice where she'd been living.'

'Do you know where that was?'

'I guess it was London. That was the postmark, anyway. She

351

told me in her letter that her grandma had died of the same thing, so once she knew what kind of cancer it was she realised she wouldn't have more than a few weeks to live. That's why she didn't ask me to come back.'

'Did she say which grandmother?'

'She only knew one – her mum's mother. She went to live with her when she was about nine. They were very close. She said her death had been devastating, and it was after that that she ended up on the streets.'

Stephanie couldn't decide whether to tell him the truth – that the grandmother was still alive, had never been diagnosed with cancer as far as they knew, and from what they had learned in court was a monster. He must have stayed away from court after that first day. He couldn't have heard the stories about Evie's adolescence.

'During the trial there was some evidence relating to scarring on your wife's body. Were you not in court for that part of the proceedings?'

'No. One day in that place was enough for me. I didn't know what to think and I just wanted to get away.'

'How did she explain the scars to you?'

Nigel Clarke looked to be on the verge of tears. 'It was the worst story I've ever heard. When she was about thirteen she was abducted by a gang – something to do with revenge on her poor uncle, who had spoken out against this bunch of thugs. They beat her, broke several bones in her body, and then dumped her back in the street outside her house.'

Stephanie nodded sympathetically. 'Did the police ever catch the guys who did this to her?'

'No. The family decided not to report it. Shelley didn't want the world to know she had been brutally beaten and raped, and they were concerned about further retribution. This was gang warfare, and her uncle had been trying to do the right thing. After that, I think they moved to get away from it all.'

On balance, Stephanie thought she believed Evie's courtroom version of events rather than the abduction story. But who knew?

'Why did she concoct this elaborate lie about her death, though? Why didn't she just leave you?'

Nigel's eyes opened wide. 'Oh, I understand that totally. She didn't want to hurt me.'

He must have seen the confusion on Stephanie's face. 'If she'd left me, I would have known I wasn't good enough for her. She knew me well, you see, and it would have destroyed me. I would have followed her wherever she went, begged her to explain what I could do to fix things, tried to make her come back to me, promised to change. All that stuff. Of course I was devastated that she was dead, but I was left believing that she loved me, like she said in the letter.'

Stephanie had to accept that there was some weird logic to it, but suspected it was more a case of Evie not wanting her husband to know where she was living. Had she merely left him, he seemed like the kind of man who would forever be checking up on her to see if she was doing okay.

Nigel sighed and leaned back in his seat, as if worn out by the conversation.

'I still didn't believe it was really her on trial for murder until I got to court. She looked so skinny, so different from the lovely plump lass I married. I was mad at first that she'd lied to me. I decided to go back home – to New Zealand, as it happens. But when I read what had been going on, what that bastard had been doing to her, I was horrified. I thought she might need me, you see. So when I heard she was out of prison, I came back. I thought I'd hang around here, close to where she grew up, thinking this is probably where she would choose to live. I haven't plucked up the courage to see her, though. I've been waiting for the right moment. The anger's gone, but now I'm terrified that she won't be pleased to see me, so I've changed my mind. I'm leaving.'

Stephanie had barely taken in the last part of Nigel's comment. She leaned forward, across the table.

'What do you mean, where she grew up?' She tried to keep her voice even. She didn't want Clarke to know this was news to her.

'She was born in Norfolk, but her mum ran away from home when Shelley was born and came here. Shelley lived here with her mum and brother as a kid. She was always obsessed with this place. She had the local paper delivered to us all the time we were in Leicester and she would read it from cover to cover. I never understood why she bothered, because sometimes she would get so cross at the articles – especially those about people or places she used to know. I asked her a few times what was winding her up, but she said I wouldn't understand.'

Stephanie was still struggling to absorb the fact that Evie had lived here and yet that fact had never come to light. But they'd had no reason to look so far back.

Nigel Clarke rested his chin on an upturned palm. 'Once or

twice I pulled the paper out of the bin to see what was bugging her, and after one of her strops I saw there was a story about some guy who had married a rich American. I realise now that must have been Mark North, but I didn't take much notice at the time. It didn't mean a thing to me. I didn't ask her about it because I knew she'd have yelled at me and told me to mind my own business. She could be quite fiery.' He smiled fondly at the thought.

Stephanie could feel her heart rate increasing with every sentence. Why would Evie have taken the local paper when she was living in Leicester? Why would she have been angry about Mark and Mia's wedding?

'We understand her mother died, but you mentioned a brother. Do you know what happened to him?'

Nigel Clarke nodded.

'I think it was because of him – Dean, he was called – that she was so fixated on the place.'

'Why? Where's Dean now?'

'There was an accident when she was about nine and sadly she witnessed the whole thing. Her brother died quite tragically.'

64

Cleo had succumbed to a sleeping tablet the night before, but it hadn't worked so she had taken another one. All she had wanted was oblivion, but now, as a harsh banging on the front door slowly dragged her back from a state of stupefied semi-consciousness, she wanted to hide her head under the pillow until whoever it was had gone away.

Sadly, they didn't seem to be going anywhere and the banging continued. She heard a voice she didn't recognise shout her name, and if this carried on the whole street would be out. Mark's death and the news of his abusive behaviour had made her something of a pariah around here, as if she was responsible for his actions. Maybe she was. Maybe she had protected him from the harsh realities of life for too long.

'I know you're in there, Cleo North, and I'm not going away.'

It was a woman's voice.

Cleo tried to look out of the window, but whoever was making all the racket was standing underneath the porch by the front door. She was going to have to go down and let this woman in, but she had no idea what she might want.

She grabbed a dressing gown and dragged her fingers through her hair. Fortunately it was so short that it never needed much attention. Her face, however, was a different matter. As she passed the mirror she couldn't fail to see the dark hollows around her eyes and the blotchy appearance of her otherwise pallid skin. Well, it wasn't a beauty parade and if this woman was determined to see her, she would have to deal with her frightful appearance.

She walked down the hall and pulled the door open as the woman raised her fist to start hammering again. Cleo looked at her, and felt a twinge of recognition. The woman standing in front of her was tall and slender with short auburn hair. She would probably have been very attractive if it hadn't been for the straight line of her clenched lips and the wild look in her eyes. Cleo was sure she had never met her, but maybe she had seen a photograph, or perhaps she had been one of the nosy parkers who'd come along to watch the trial.

'What do you want?' Cleo asked, with little grace. She didn't feel it necessary to be polite to someone who was banging on her front door first thing in the morning.

The woman stared back, looking slightly puzzled.

'I'm coming in,' she said after a moment, taking a step forward.

Cleo was about to try to close the door when she noticed someone standing behind the woman who had previously been shielded from view.

It was Joe, and suddenly Cleo knew where she had seen this woman's face before. When she briefly believed that she and Joe had a future together she had parked outside his house when he was away on business because she wanted to see his wife – the woman whose life she was about to tear apart.

This was Siobhan, and there could only be one reason she was here.

Cleo stood back and Siobhan stormed in. Joe shot Cleo an anxious look, but followed his wife down the corridor. She had found her way to the sitting room and was now standing in the centre of the room, her face a picture of disgust as she looked at Cleo, who could guess what she was thinking. Why on earth would Joe have been interested in this mess of a woman?

But she hadn't been a mess – not then, at least.

'Sit down, if you like,' she said. 'I'm going to put some clothes on.'

'Don't bother on my account,' Siobhan said. 'And no doubt Joe's used to seeing you in all stages of undress.'

Cleo felt slightly nauseous at the misery in the woman's voice, but ignored her and fled up the stairs. She could hear angry whispers behind her, and wished Joe would follow her and explain what was going on. But clearly he couldn't do that.

She nipped into the bathroom to clean her teeth, pulled on a pair of jeans and a bright coloured shirt and dabbed some tinted moisturiser on her face. She would have felt much safer behind full makeup, but she had the feeling that if she delayed too long, Siobhan would come marching up the stairs and drag her back down to face the music.

When she returned to the sitting room, Siobhan was exactly where Cleo had left her but Joe had seated himself on the arm of the sofa with his head bowed. As Cleo looked at him she realised what an insignificant little man he was. She had never wanted to tear his family apart – but he had seemed to sway with the wind, clearly glad to be told what he should do. And then he had turned up during the trial to suggest they could take up where they'd left off. She was well out of it.

Cleo had no time to speak before Siobhan launched into the attack.

'I want to know why you've been shagging my husband, for how long, and when you're going to stop.'

Cleo took a deep breath. She felt this woman's pain and didn't want to hurt her more than she already had been. But she had no idea what she knew, or how.

'Why don't you ask Joe, Siobhan?' she said.

'Oh, you know my name! Excellent, so my weasel of a husband bothered to tell you at least that much about me, did he?'

Cleo didn't answer, but looked away from Siobhan's torment.

'Apparently everyone's talking about the fact that my husband is shagging the sister of that wife-beater. It seems I'm the only one that didn't know.'

Cleo jerked her head round and glared at Siobhan.

'He wasn't a wife-beater.' The one thing Cleo would not take, from anyone, was the lie that Mark was an abuser. The fact that Evie wasn't his wife was irrelevant.

Siobhan scoffed, and Cleo thought how strange it was that even the most attractive people turned ugly when they were hurting. Her own anguish faded momentarily at the sight of the woman's distress, and she felt ashamed of herself and of Joe. She had been sure Siobhan would never find out. Nobody

359

had known about their affair. Only Mark, and he wouldn't have said a word.

'I don't know how it's taken me so long to find out about you two.' The contempt dripped from Siobhan's tongue. 'But the word is that it's a full-on affair, and that Joe is going to leave me – you've talked him into it, against his better judgement.'

She suddenly seemed to crumple and finally she walked over to a chair and sat down.

'That's not true, Siobhan,' Cleo said quietly. 'Joe's not going anywhere. At least, not with me.'

'I didn't believe it to start with,' Siobhan continued as if she hadn't heard Cleo. 'Some woman in the park was talking about you – you're quite the celebrity these days. She knew so much about you, Cleo, and she seemed to hate you every bit as much as I do.'

'Do you know who she was?'

'Does it matter?'

'Yes. At least, it does to me.'

'I don't know who she was. Shoulder-length dark hair, red lipstick, black raincoat. I don't really care. To start with, I decided it was ridiculous gossip, but I started to check up on Joe – and that's when I saw the email.'

Cleo flicked a puzzled look at Joe, but he couldn't meet her eyes. He hadn't spoken a word in defence or support of either of them. What had she ever seen in this man?

'What email?'

'The one you sent late last night – and don't be coy with me. It's not the sort of email you would forget writing, trust me.'

'I didn't send any email to Joe – not last night, not *any* night, come to that.'

Communication between Joe and Cleo had always been via a pay-as-you-go phone that Joe kept hidden in his car.

Siobhan reached into her pocket and pulled out a crumpled sheet of paper. '*It's our time now, Joe,*' she read in a tight voice. '*I need you more than ever. My world is falling apart, and I have nobody left. Please, Joe – change your mind.*'

Cleo stared at Joe to see if he could cast any light on it, but he shrugged as if he had no more idea than she did.

'Siobhan, I promise you that email did not come from me.'

Siobhan jumped up from the chair and walked over to Cleo, pushing the piece of paper under her nose. 'And that's not your email address, I don't suppose?'

The email address was *cleo.north.1979* and it was a Hotmail address.

Siobhan snatched the piece of paper back from Cleo's hand.

'I don't have a Hotmail account. Anyone could have set that up.'

'Oh, right. And they knew the year of your birth, did they?'

Cleo looked at Joe, even more confused. She wasn't born in 1979, but Mark was . . . Of course! There was one person who might do that – who might use Mark's year of birth as a calling card. *Evie.* Why would she want to do this? Hadn't she caused enough pain already?

'Tell me one thing, Cleo. Do you want my husband, or don't you? If you do, I'm warning you that I'm going to fight for him. Not because I think he's worth it, but sadly his children do. So what's it to be?'

361

Cleo felt nothing but a deep sense of sadness and shame. Just the day before she had been wondering whether to get in touch with Joe. Not because she wanted him, but because right now she had nobody else.

She didn't look at Joe, but leaned forward and stared straight into the other woman's eyes.

'I'm deeply sorry for any hurt I've caused you, Siobhan. I didn't send the email, which suggests someone is out to make trouble for me, but that's not the point. I've behaved badly, and there's nothing I can do but apologise. And I can tell you categorically that I don't want Joe. He's all yours.'

65

It's nearly time. I'm glad I've got this day with my lovely Lulu – Lolula, my private name for her. She's so pretty, so delicate, and today we're on the beach. It's deserted, as I knew it would be at this time of the year, and our footprints are the only ones in the sand. I show them to Lulu – I let her walk right to the edge of the sea and run back ahead of the gentle wave that fills the holes made by her wellies. She laughs with joy.

The weather has been dreadful all week and far too rough to take a child onto the sand, but today is different, and everywhere appears to have been washed clean by the storms. I have to have this day with her, before everything changes. It's only when I'm with Lulu that I feel calm. The rest of the time I'm filled with a sense of inevitability. I had expected my thirst for retribution to have been slaked, but the anger and hatred still disturb my nights and haunt my days.

I think about my journey to this place – the years of wondering how it would feel to be back in these streets, on this shore. But I never came. Not until I saw that Mark had married Mia. Only then did I venture here, disguised with my dark hair and over-the-top makeup. I even saw Cleo a few times, knowing she would never recognise me when I returned, fresh faced, slim and blonde.

Nobody would see any similarity to the child I used to be either — fat from too many chips, mousey hair that was rarely washed hanging limply to my shoulders, scruffy clothes that were usually stolen from the charity shop. It meant I was able to mingle, listen to the gossip and find out everything I needed to know about Mark: how he had met Mia; where he liked to eat; what his life had been like before her.

Lulu deserves so much more in her life than I had – and I can't give her that. I'm not sure if I'm famous or infamous – I suspect it depends who you ask and which side of the fence they are on. The truth is something I can't afford for Lulu to know if I want her to grow up without making all the mistakes that I've made, and if I'm part of her life the truth will inevitably be revealed. She will be better off without me.

I was so sure I was doing the right thing – the only thing. So very certain. There was a burning inside me that I thought could only be extinguished by my own actions.

But it's still not over. I'm not done.

For now I want to enjoy these moments with my daughter, as if I'm an average mum on an average winter's day. But it's not true. I know I have demons inside me, just waiting to get out and devour everything in their path, sweeping obstacles out of their way, like the sea sweeps the beach clean of footprints.

I need to protect my little girl and there's only one thing I can do to make sure that my Lolula is safe from harm.

66

Stephanie felt a bubble of excitement. She couldn't wait to see Gus to tell him what she knew, and how it changed everything. Nothing was how they had imagined it, but finally it all made sense.

She had to find him. She had spent the morning researching the information she had gleaned from Nigel Clarke and, deciding to take the evidence she had unearthed directly to Gus rather than speaking on the phone, she jumped into her car and set off to CID headquarters.

She burst through the door into the squad room and several faces looked up from their computer screens and smiled at her.

'Hey, Steph – you coming back to join us?'

She shook her head. 'No – just looking for the boss. Is he here?'

Eyes went back to monitors with nobody apparently keen to answer that question, simple though it was. In the end, one of the guys she had worked with closely during the investigation came over to her.

'Fancy a coffee?' he said, leading her towards the drinks machine. He seemed to be stalling for time.

'What's going on?' she asked.

He looked uncomfortable, and Stephanie realised that although she and Gus had never behaved as if there was anything between them, everyone knew.

'I probably shouldn't say anything, but DI Brodie is apparently in Leeds today.'

'*Leeds?* What the hell is he doing there – is it a case?'

'We're not supposed to know, but there are never any secrets in this place. It seems he's gone for an interview.'

Stephanie felt as if she'd been punched in the gut. He was leaving. She didn't doubt for a second that he would get the job – he was always destined for somewhere with a bit more action than here and she had often wondered why he stayed.

She did her best to look interested rather than devastated.

'Any idea when he'll be back?'

'Later on today, we think. He went yesterday.'

Swallowing a lump in her throat she started to explain what she had found, but realised it wasn't going to work. The explanation would take too long, and this wasn't Gus she was talking to – a man she knew would pick up the implications immediately.

'Look,' she said. 'If Gus comes back can you tell him I've gone to find Cleo North. There's something I need to ask her.'

Without waiting for a response, she turned and ran from the room.

67

'Aminah, it's Cleo.'

'Yes, that's right. This is Aminah Basra speaking.'

Cleo was puzzled at the response until she heard a slight puffing sound which suggested that Aminah was on the move, and she realised that for some reason she didn't want anyone to know who was on the line.

Cleo waited.

'I'm so glad you've called, Cleo,' Aminah whispered. 'We've been worried about you. I didn't want you to think I'd taken sides with Evie against you. I was just trying to be fair on everyone – and Lulu in particular. Please, let's get together soon and sort this. Please, Cleo. I miss you.'

Cleo felt choked. Aminah had a soft heart and would never intentionally hurt anyone.

'Why are you whispering?'

'Oh lordy – Evie's here again. She's acting a bit weird to be honest. I heard her talking to Lulu. She said, "You're going to be amazing, Lulu, and it's all for the best." She told her she was going to be okay – but why wouldn't she be?'

'*Is* Lulu okay?' Cleo asked, with a sudden thud of fear for the child she missed so much.

'She seems fine. Anyway, I didn't want Evie to know you were on the phone, but I do want to see you. And I know you haven't called me for nothing, given our last conversation, so what's up?'

'Do you remember a few months ago you asked if I was seeing someone and I said no?'

'Yes – of course. And I knew you were lying, but that was your prerogative. Why – is there a problem?'

'He was married.'

'Of course he was. Why else would you not have told me. I sensed that it was over, though – so is he back on the scene?'

Cleo would have laughed if she'd had a laugh in her.

'No, but his wife came to see me first thing this morning. All the time I was seeing Joe, nobody knew about it except Mark, but Joe's wife says someone has been spreading gossip, and someone faked an email from me. Aminah, I know you think of Evie as a friend, and I know how hard this is. But I don't know who else to speak to, and I can't think of anyone else who would do this to me.'

Aminah was quiet, and Cleo thought maybe she had over-stepped the mark.

'Look, I'm sorry I said that. Forget it. Joe probably told a mate or something. That would explain the gossip, but not the email. I'm clutching at straws.'

'I'm not sure you are, my lovely,' Aminah said, her voice even quieter. 'There's something calculated about all this. I know she doesn't want to confuse Lulu by seeing you, but she let her child get really close to you and then dragged her away. Lulu asks for you sometimes, you know.'

Cleo's eyes filled with tears, but before she could say more, Aminah's tone changed.

'Okay – lovely to speak to you.' It sounded as if she was going to hang up, but then Cleo heard another voice in the background. 'Sorry, Cleo. I forgot to mention that Evie's here, and she'd like a quick word, if that's okay.'

Aminah's theatrics had clearly failed to fool Evie, and Cleo didn't know how to respond. But she was left with no choice.

'Cleo.' Evie's voice sounded friendly enough. 'I'd like to talk to you about Lulu – and about the future. I'm going up to the house soon to get more of my things. Are you free to meet me there in, say, thirty minutes?'

Was she going to relent? Was she going to let her see Lulu?

Cleo didn't hesitate.

'I'll be there,' she said.

Stephanie left the CID squad room and headed for her car. She wanted to ask Cleo about everything she had discovered and get her side of the story. But she needed a moment to pull herself together. Gus was leaving, and she felt a fool for being upset. After all, she was the one who was refusing to see him. Somehow, though, it was different when it was her decision.

'Stop being so bloody pathetic,' she mumbled. Taking a swipe at the steering wheel, she switched the ignition on and rammed the car into gear. This was getting her nowhere. She needed to do something.

It was about a fifteen-minute drive back to town and to Cleo's house, and when she arrived she was disappointed to see no car on the drive. She walked up to the door in case Cleo was in, but wasn't surprised when there was no answer.

'Bugger,' she muttered, uncertain what her next move should be. The sensible thing would be to leave it until she'd had a chance to tell Gus what she had found, but it felt like an anticlimax. She had wanted to present him with a fully fleshed-out story of what had happened all those years ago, and for that she needed to talk to Cleo.

Thrusting her hands in her pockets, head down, she set off back to her car but was only halfway down the drive when she heard a car horn. She looked up to see a people-carrier that appeared to be stuffed with kids. The window on the passenger side came down, and Aminah Basra, who Stephanie recognised from court, leaned across the child strapped into the front seat. The cacophony coming from the car drowned her words – the radio was playing and the children were all singing along to 'Firework' at the tops of their voices. Stephanie could just make out Lulu in one of the two car seats in the back, and she seemed to be laughing at the antics of the other children.

'Pipe down, you lot,' Aminah said, turning the radio off to shouts of 'Aw, Mum!'

She jumped out of the car.

'Sorry about that,' she called to Stephanie. 'Are you looking for Cleo? You're one of the police officers, aren't you?'

'That's right. Are you looking for her too?'

Aminah screwed up her eyes. 'Shit. Has she already left? I

was hoping to catch her but it took me a week to get all these kids into the car.'

Stephanie hurried towards the parked car. 'You know where she is, then?'

'I think so. Evie asked her if they could meet up at the house, but I came here to try to stop Cleo from going. There's something not right. I don't know what it is, but Evie doesn't seem entirely rational. There's an intensity about her that I've never seen before. She doesn't look well, and she asked me something strange before she left. She said she'd named me as Lulu's guardian, if anything should happen to her. She wanted to know if it was okay.'

Aminah's bottom lip was firmly clamped between her teeth, her hands clasped together.

'When you say they're meeting at the house, do you mean Mark's house?'

'Yes. I don't know what to do now. I was sure I'd be in time to catch her.' She shook her head. 'I'd go there, but if Evie and Cleo are both there I don't think I should take this bunch with me.' Aminah waved her arm to indicate the children, several of whom seemed to be engaged in some sort of noisy play fight right at the back of the vehicle.

'Leave it with me,' Stephanie said. 'You take the kids home and I'll go and check that everything's okay.'

Aminah paused for a moment as if uncertain. 'If you're sure . . .'

Stephanie nodded and, with a final worried frown, Aminah got back into the car.

Waving goodbye to the enthusiastic children, Stephanie fixed a smile on her face. But the minute they turned the corner her smile disappeared and she ran for her car. She didn't like the sound of this at all.

Hastily she made a call to Gus and left him a message. She needed to tell him what she believed had happened, and it was quicker to explain to him than anyone else.

As she finished her brief account she thought of where he had been that day. There was something she had to say.

'By the way, I know about Leeds, Gus. I want to wish you luck, but . . .' She paused. 'Oh bugger it, I wish you weren't going.'

She hung up and pushed the car into gear.

68

Cleo parked the car by the door in the long white wall of what had been Mark's house. She wasn't sure she was ready to go in there again, to see his home without him in it, but if it meant she could persuade Evie to let her see Lulu, she would try anything.

She pressed the doorbell and waited. Nobody came. She pressed again, and banged on the knocker.

There were no windows to look through but as she spun round in frustration to return to the car she noticed the garage door was open. Evie must be expecting her to come in that way.

Making her way slowly past Mark's car, covered with a fine layer of dust and still parked there all these months since he died, she opened the door that led through to the garden. There was no sign of Evie. She was either in the house or on the other side of the shrubs, where rough ground led to a rocky cliff that plunged steeply into the sea. Cleo remembered Mark saying they would have to fence the area off before Lulu was walking and Cleo hoped Evie had more sense than to bring her here. She moved quietly towards the tall beech hedge and peered round.

A woman in a black raincoat with shoulder-length dark hair was standing right at the edge of the cliff. She had her back to the garden, but it seemed she knew Cleo had arrived. She called out, but her words were whipped away by the wind. Cleo moved closer.

'Sorry – who are you? I'm looking for Evie Clarke.'

The woman turned round slowly and Cleo gasped. The person staring back at her had sunken cheeks and red-rimmed eyes, but despite the hair, Cleo knew who it was. Gone was the confident, attractive Evie who had come to take Lulu away just a month ago. In her place was a woman who Cleo could have passed in the street without recognising – except there was something familiar about this version of Evie, something tugging at Cleo's memory.

She felt a jolt of unease, and walked slowly forwards as Evie watched her. The ground was sodden from the recent rain, and Evie looked perilously close to the edge.

'Evie, move away from the cliff,' Cleo said, her initial apprehension at seeing Evie again suddenly turning to concern. 'You're too close. It's dangerous.'

Evie stared at Cleo, her eyes burning with some inner torment that Cleo didn't understand. She said nothing, and she didn't move.

'You wanted to see me,' Cleo shouted over the sound of waves crashing onto the rocks below. She moved a little closer, wanting to be near enough to hear what Evie had to say, but not too close to the edge.

'It was all for nothing,' Evie called out, shrugging her shoulders. 'For so long, I wanted only one thing. I thought I could make the pain go away, but it hasn't worked. It hasn't made me better.' Two deep grooves appeared between her eyebrows as if she was puzzled by her own words.

Cleo had no idea what she was talking about.

'How about you, Cleo? What about your part in all this? How do you feel about everything you've done?'

'Me? What did I do? Except take care of your daughter for months – loved her like my own. And now you won't even let me see her.' She hadn't wanted Evie to know how much that hurt, but her voice cracked. Evie had taken everything.

'Ah, my beautiful Lulu. We need to talk about her – but not yet. The poor child – to have a mother like me and an aunt like you, both riddled and twisted with hatred. Yes, I know how you feel about me, Cleo. You can say the words out loud if you like – shout it to the heavens.' Evie opened her arms and leaned back, shouting, 'I hate you, Evie! I hate you!'

A well of bitterness rose up like acid, burning Cleo's throat. It was true that she loathed Evie for what she had done, but this might be her only chance of seeing Lulu, so she shook her head and dropped her gaze to the soggy ground at her feet.

She didn't hear Evie approach, didn't know she was standing so close until the toes of two black boots came into view in the mud just inches from Cleo's own.

'Wouldn't you like to push me over the edge of this cliff? No-one would ever know,' Evie whispered.

Cleo's head snapped up and she leaned back, away from the feel of Evie's warm breath on her cheek. 'I'm not going to push you. Why would I do that?'

'You pushed Mia, though, didn't you?'

Cleo felt her body jerk, but was silent. Evie had claimed all along that she knew something about Mia, but she couldn't possibly know what really happened.

'I didn't push her. You've got that wrong.'

Evie shook her head. 'Come on, Cleo. There's only the two of us here now. Why not admit it?' She inched closer.

What did Evie think she knew? Cleo felt her heart racing and fought to keep calm.

'Well, I'll tell you, shall I,' Evie said, her lips almost touching Cleo's ear as if she was sharing a secret. 'You see, the timing was all wrong. None of it made sense – and I wasn't the only one who worked that out.'

A cold gust of wind forced its way through the narrow gap between them, and Cleo shivered. She was scared of saying the wrong thing, but Evie didn't give her a chance to speak.

'I forced Mark to come down into the gym with me one day, and he cracked, Cleo. He broke down, because he couldn't hold it in for a moment longer. He told me everything – what you did, and how that knowledge was destroying him.'

'What do you mean, he told you everything?' Cleo said softly.

Evie was so close that Cleo could see a pulse throbbing in her neck. What had Mark said? He knew she hadn't pushed Mia, so what had he told Evie? Had he admitted what he'd done? Was Evie playing with her?

'He told me you pushed her,' Evie said.

She was watching Cleo, testing her reaction.

'He couldn't have told you I killed Mia. Because I didn't – honestly I didn't.'

Evie laughed – a harsh sound that ripped through the space

between them. She stepped away, back to the edge of the cliff, but Cleo's relief was short-lived.

'Mark knew what you'd done, Cleo. Mia had already gone down to the gym before he left for the airport. He'd stormed upstairs after their argument to wait for his taxi. If she'd fallen, it would have been then. But the time on her smashed watch was all wrong. According to Mark she would have finished her workout and would have been in the pool by then. She was a bit like him, you see. Always stuck to a schedule.'

Cleo swallowed. Why would Mark say any of this to Evie?

'He said there was only one reason she would have come back upstairs before her swim,' Evie continued, 'and that would have been if she heard someone upstairs, and there was only one person apart from Mark who could get into the house. You, Cleo – you, who insisted on having a key to your brother's home. How does it feel to know your brother died believing his sister was a murderer?'

Expecting to see triumph in Evie's eyes, Cleo dropped her gaze.

'I didn't kill her, Evie. She was dead when I got there,' she said quietly.

It was the truth. Mia had been lying at the bottom of the stairs, staring straight into Cleo's eyes. She hadn't known what to think, but Mark had told her about their argument, so Cleo had faked the phone call and persuaded him to call Mia and leave a message. Then she had come back to 'discover' the body. That was when she saw the broken watch. She remembered her horror at realising the hands were pointing to the time when Mark would have been about to leave the house. She'd had to

377

change it to make her story work and protect her brother. She couldn't see him accused of murder.

Evie pushed her hands deep into her coat pockets and stared up at the sky for a moment. 'I'm sick of the games, Cleo. Tired of the battle. There are no winners, you see, even though I thought there would be.'

She was talking in riddles again. What games?

'I know you didn't kill Mia, but Mark was convinced you did and he felt responsible for that. He knew you would never have called his wife to suggest lunch, so why else would you go to the trouble to fabricate such a story? None of it made sense – the timing, the call, the insistence that he should phone Mia to apologise. You had to be hiding something, and as he hadn't killed Mia, it had to have been you.' Evie's voice cracked. 'God, that poor man. I let him believe it, even though I knew it wasn't true.'

'How did you know?'

It was as if Evie hadn't heard her. Her eyes were staring into the distance, remembering something that seemed to hurt.

'When I made him go down there he told me that every time he stood at the bottom of the stairs he didn't see Mia's body. He saw you, at the top, pushing her. It tormented him, and you never knew. And I let him suffer.'

Cleo barely caught the last sentence. Evie whispered it, as if to herself. Could it be true? If Mark thought she had killed Mia . . .

'That's right, Cleo. In spite of the police concluding that Mia had fallen, Mark thought you had killed his wife. And all along you thought *Mark* had killed her. You did, didn't you? And you covered for him.'

378

The last sentence was spoken slowly, forcefully, and Cleo stared at the woman in front of her – the woman whose stories of abuse she had refused to accept in spite of what she believed Mark had done to Mia.

'Do you know, Cleo, all the time I was suffering from my injuries, I thought I might just once have seen some compassion in your eyes. Some understanding of what I was going through. But I never did. Maybe everything would have been different if I'd thought you cared. Why couldn't you accept that he was hurting me when you thought he had killed his wife?'

'It was different. Completely different. Mark would never have killed her on purpose. He might have given her a little push or something – he seemed so confused when I spoke to him. That would be very different from the kind of cold-blooded cruelty that you described. It would have been a mistake – a moment of madness.'

Evie stared at her, and Cleo knew what she was thinking. A moment of madness – just as Evie had claimed as her defence for killing Mark. She couldn't read the expression in Evie's eyes. They seemed sad, defeated, and for a moment Cleo wanted to run. To get away from here. But her feet wouldn't move.

'You thought you were so close to your brother, but you never really understood him, did you?' Evie shook her head slowly. 'Mark was confused that day because he had been horrible to Mia and she didn't deserve it. Afterwards he had to live with the fact that you had killed her before he'd had a chance to apologise. It ate him up. He loved you, fool that he was, and he could never ask you what happened, because if

379

you'd admitted to killing his wife he would have had to cast you out of his life. It was unbearable for him.'

Cleo didn't know what to say, what to think. Evie took a step towards her again, and instinctively she moved back. Thrusting her head forwards, Evie spoke quietly.

'You're right about one thing, though. Mark wasn't capable of cold-blooded cruelty.'

Cleo heard the words, but they didn't make sense. She stared at Evie, and was surprised to see what looked like tears in her eyes. Or perhaps it was the wind.

'What do you mean? *Evie* – tell me what you mean!'

Evie didn't take her eyes from Cleo's, as if waiting for her to work it out. Then she spun round and retreated to the edge of the cliff again. Cleo couldn't believe what she had just heard – or what it meant.

'What about all those things you said he did to you?' she shouted, her voice breaking. 'Was everything a lie? All of it?' She felt a stab of intense pain as she looked at her brother's killer. 'I *knew* he wouldn't have hurt you! I *knew* you were a lying bitch – but why? How did you hurt yourself if it wasn't Mark? Was it someone else, or were they all stupid, careless accidents?'

Her voice was rising, increasing in both volume and speed, and she watched in horror as Evie started to make tracks in the grass with her right foot. What was she doing? Cleo tried to take another step back, away from this woman whose pale, drawn face was so unlike the Evie she had known. But the hedge blocked her retreat.

Evie stopped moving and held her windswept hair back off her face.

'No, Cleo. None of them were accidents. But it's true that Mark never touched me.' Her sunken eyes seemed lifeless. 'I did it all to myself.'

'You did *what*? Why the hell would you do that? *How* could you inflict so much pain on your own body?'

As Evie lifted her face to the wind and dropped her hand, the dark wig fanned out again like a black halo. She didn't look at Cleo as she spoke. Her words were flat, emotionless, her shoulders slumped as if she was carrying a burden that was too much for her.

'Pain ceased to have any meaning to me years ago. Every word I spoke in court about my uncle was true. He was a vicious brute but I learned to accept that the pain would soon be over. You see, the thing that makes pain so dreadful is the memory of it. The agony is over in moments, but the mind recalls the sensations and replays them over and over. I know a lot about pain.'

'Why did you lie about everything? Why did you kill Mark?'

'Haven't you worked it out yet?' She tutted and shook her head slowly from side to side. 'It was revenge, Cleo.'

'For what, if he didn't hurt you?'

For a moment Evie's gaze softened.

'Mark would never have hurt me. That's why I've not found it easy to accept what I did. I thought killing him would make me feel better, after all these years of planning. But it hasn't. The hatred inside me is still there, burning just as fiercely. It's part of me now and it won't let go.'

Cleo fought the urge to rush at this woman and watch her tumble down the cliff, bouncing off the rocks until the cruel swell of the tide dragged her down into its depths.

'I'd been preparing the ground for years,' Evie said, 'getting myself ready to be the kind of woman that Mark North would fall in love with – just so I could exact my revenge.'

'But you said in court that it *wasn't* revenge – Evie, you're not making sense.' Cleo could feel her feet advancing towards Evie almost of their own volition.

Evie's eyes were like granite, her mouth a thin, hard gash in her pale face.

'I wasn't taking revenge against Mark, Cleo. It was you. It's always been you.'

69

'Shit, shit, *shit!*' Stephanie shouted as the queue of cars in front of her remained at a standstill. She had totally forgotten about the road closures and now she was stuck, hemmed in on all sides by bloody traffic. If she was in the squad car, she could switch on the siren, but she wasn't, so she had to sit here like every other driver, most of whom seemed to be frantically beeping their horns – as if that would make any sodding difference.

She was working on a hunch, but she had a bad feeling about Evie and Cleo being alone together. Since her conversation with Nigel Clarke she had been sure everything was tied to Evie's brother, so she had searched through old records to discover the awful truth about his death. That morning she had tracked down a retired social worker who had filled in the last of the details.

'It was a complicated case,' the lady said. 'The family was a total mess – the mother an alcoholic with no money coming in. Dean – the brother who died – had managed to keep everything from us, and essentially he was the main carer for both his mother and his sister. As we discovered later, he stole food for them because anything that came in through benefits went straight down the mother's throat.'

The woman shook her head, and Stephanie could see how sad she found this story. Even sadder, probably, because it wasn't unique.

'Once the brother was dead and we discovered how sick the mother was, the girl – Michelle – had to go into care. Her grandmother took her, but unfortunately not without some financial persuasion. So the poor kid had lost the one person she trusted: her brother. Her mother died shortly afterwards – from the booze, of course. Dean was a little toe-rag, it has to be said. He was always in trouble, but then the poor kid was carrying the weight of the world on his young shoulders.'

As Stephanie knew, that was only half of the story. The files had told her the rest. She needed to get to that house on the cliff, and quickly. If her hunch was right, there would be no good ending to this meeting.

70

Cleo is crying now. The words bursting through her sobs are wild and uncontrolled, but I haven't finished with her yet.

'You'll have to spend the rest of your life without the person you loved most. Your brother. And all the world, except you, believes he was a bully. I don't need to ask you how that feels, Cleo. I already know.'

She doesn't seem to understand what I have just said. That I, like her, lost my brother and that she's always been the one I blamed. I have been nursing my hatred of Cleo since the day Dean died and I had to make her suffer the way I had suffered. She had to lose her own beloved brother, and the world had to think he was evil.

In the end, killing Mark proved far more difficult than I had expected. He didn't deserve to die. He was a good man, and I think he loved me. I know he loved Lulu, but I couldn't see any other way. I had closed my mind to everything but my plan. Like a storm out at sea, it was coming – and it would destroy whatever was in its path. Only Lulu penetrated my armour, and now I must protect her. She must never suffer as a result of the sickness that has driven me for so long and is still eating away at me from the inside.

I didn't know how to stop it – stop myself – so I wore my disguise and used the computer at the library to learn how to rewire a light switch, and then I carefully set the scene. Cleo was right about Mark not liking the dark, but I wouldn't have been able to kill him with the lights shining brightly on his slender, handsome face, reflecting off his trusting eyes. I see them when I go to sleep. They haunt me, and I can no longer bear the long, dark winter nights.

Making love that last time was such a bittersweet experience. Mark couldn't have been more loving, more relieved that I wanted him after months of shutting him out. But the knife was there, lying by the side of the bed. This was my chance – what I had lived for, dreamed of, for years, through every lash of that bullwhip, every broken bone. I felt the pain of killing Mark far more acutely than anything I had suffered at either my uncle's hands or my own, though.

The worst of it was that for my plan to work, I'd had to phone the police and scream that I needed help, and then I had to take the same knife and cut my own flesh. Each incision felt as if Mark was making the cuts – each slice into my flesh a question. *Why, Evie? Why?*

I pulled Mark's naked body back onto mine so that the hairs from his chest would rub into my wounds, catching there, ready to be analysed, proving conclusively that we had made love after he had cut me and not before, and then I had waited, lying close to him, my arm round his waist, sobbing – begging his forgiveness.

Cleo will never know any of this. No-one will. She's still babbling and it's hard to make out her words.

'Who . . . don't know . . . brother?'

I know what she's trying to say.

'Remember Dean Young, Cleo? The eleven-year-old boy you persuaded to climb onto the sea wall in a storm? I saw you. Remember me now?' I pause and watch her face. Has she got it yet? 'Do you remember little Shelley Young? I was standing at the entrance to the alley across the road, but I was too scared to come out. You were yelling at him, calling him a coward. Then you rushed at him and pushed him over, just as a huge wave washed over the top of the wall. I can still hear him scream now – every day I remember. You killed him, and you got away with it. Then you told the whole world what a bully he was – how he had tortured Mark.'

'No!' Cleo's cry is clear. The wind has risen and her anguished words are being blown towards me. 'He *was* a bully – a nasty kid who made Mark's life a misery. But I didn't kill him. It was *Dean's* fault – not mine. Not Mark's. When I found Dean and Mark at the wall your brother was trying to push Mark up there – to get him to "walk the wall" as he called it. The sea was wild and there was no-one to help us, so I told Dean that if he was so brave he should get up on the wall himself. He laughed at me, but he did it. He was showing off, and I was goading him.'

Memories of Dean haunt me. I know he wasn't perfect, but he was doing his best to hold our sad little family together and was the one person in my young life that I could trust. Cleo took him from me.

'Why did you push him?' I ask, keeping my voice calm. The time for shouting is over. 'He was just a kid.'

'I *didn't* push him. I could see over the wall – he was looking at me, and I was screaming at him to get down. I could see a big wave coming from way out at sea and I ran at him to grab him. He toppled over backwards as I ran towards him. I reached for his legs, but it was too late.'

This time I can't help myself. I see the truth hiding in her eyes and I scream at her, 'You're lying. I saw it all. I saw your face when you turned round. You didn't even look over the wall to see if he was okay. You turned your back, Cleo – and you smiled. You fucking *smiled*! Even after everything I've done to hurt you it's still not enough to make up for everything I suffered because of you – the life I had to lead, the torture I had to endure.'

As I stare at Cleo I feel the last reserves of energy drain from my body. I have always believed that killing Mark would be the end of it – the finale. But the pain is still there, burning me. Cleo hasn't suffered enough. Or maybe I haven't. I no longer know. But I need to finish this.

71

Cleo couldn't take it in. Evie had killed Mark. Murdered him in cold blood. All the lies she had listened to in court, all the evidence of Evie's injuries – none of it was true. So many people believed her, and now the world thought that Mark was evil.

She had been certain that her brother was incapable of such brutal acts, but felt sick at the memory of those tiny moments of doubt. If only she could speak to him, beg his forgiveness for questioning – even for a second – that he was a good man.

Evie wasn't looking at her now. She was focusing on her foot, twisting it around again on the muddy ground. She was inches from the edge of the cliff, and Cleo had no idea what she was doing. In spite of the cold, wet day, she felt her jumper sticking to her clammy back.

'I had one good thing in my life, you know,' Evie said, lifting her head to stare at Cleo. 'My beautiful sweet Lulu. And I've got to let her go – all because of you. She needs to be the first of us to lead a clean life, untarnished by the past.'

Cleo took a step towards her. She hated Evie with every

ounce of her being, but what was she saying about Lulu? If Evie was going to let her go, could it mean . . .

'Come away from the cliff, Evie. I don't know what's going on in your head, but you're going to slip on all that mud and fall if you're not careful. Step back here and we can talk about Lulu.'

'I don't want to discuss my daughter with you. She's not your concern and she never will be.'

'I love Lulu,' Cleo cried as her momentary hopes crumbled. 'You're not fit to be her mother. And I loved Mark. You're twisted, Evie. I don't know what you want me to do or say, but you're not going to get away with this.'

The corners of Evie's mouth turned up, but it wasn't a smile. Her body was slumped as if her spirit had flown, leaving behind an empty shell. But her eyes continued to burn, and Cleo knew that she was building towards some terrible finale.

'I can see why you might think that, but you see,' Evie said, 'one of us is going to die here today. The other is going to prison for life – for murder. Which would you prefer, I wonder – death or captivity?'

She barked out what should have been a laugh, but the high-pitched note floated away in the wind. The sound made the small hairs on the back of Cleo's neck stand on end.

'What the hell are you talking about?'

'I think death would be too good for you – but years rotting in a cell would be a perfect ending. Plenty of time for you to regret what you did. Or maybe you're the one who should die. I can't decide.'

It was as if something had snapped in Evie, and with a burst of energy she ran towards Cleo, who stepped sideways – but not fast enough. Evie rushed at her and grabbed her arms, holding her tight, her fingers pressed hard against Cleo's wrists.

'Get off me, you mad bitch,' Cleo shouted. '*Shit!* What did you do that for?'

Evie had let go of one wrist and scored her nails down the side of Cleo's face before jumping back and retreating to the edge of the cliff again, her face a pale mask.

'It's evidence – I struggled, you see, before you pushed me to my death.'

'But I'm not *going* to push you. I would love you to jump, but I don't think even you are mad enough to do that.'

'You think?' Evie put her head on one side as if considering Cleo's words. But she shook her head slowly. 'It would be so very easy for me to leap off this cliff and die. I'm not afraid, you see, and Lulu deserves better than either you or me – the blood on our hands. So I have to let her go – to be with a family who'll shelter her from all of this. From us. And you'll never see her again, because if I decide to jump, you'll be my murderer. Aminah knows you were coming here – there's evidence that we fought. I killed your brother, and how else would I have died unless you pushed me?'

'You're evil – you're sick,' Cleo cried. 'Why did you let me have Lulu for all that time if this is how you feel?'

Evie stopped trampling the ground. She stood still and looked at Cleo. When she spoke, her voice was flat, even.

'I wanted you to get close to her so that when you lost her it would be all the more unbearable.'

Cleo heard every word, but although her heart ached at the

loss of Lulu, a loud voice was shouting in her head and she opened her mouth so the words could escape on a scream.

It's nearly over. I wish it felt as good as I had always believed it would. But it doesn't. I can't let go yet – I can't let my mind spin out of control. Not until I know. Not until Cleo tells me the truth.

'I want you to die a little more each and every moment, Cleo, and that's what will happen if you kill me. You'll spend your days paying for it. I have no more use for this life, not now I have accepted that I can only bring Lulu harm. Your guilt, your life imprisonment, will give my death meaning. You're covered in fibres from my clothes, there are scratches on your cheek, bruises on your wrist, and signs of a scuffle in the mud. And I've left a trail of other evidence – I'm good at that, I think you'll concede. Everyone will believe it – I killed your brother and I stopped you from seeing Lulu. I've made Aminah her legal guardian in the event of my death, and anyway, you won't get her back if you're in prison, will you?'

'It was so long ago,' Cleo cries. 'Please, Evie. Stop this.'

'Not until I hear the truth.'

She's crumbling. And she knows I won't stop until she says the words I've waited so long to hear.

'Okay, I pushed him,' she screams. 'I didn't plan it. I rushed towards him to *save* him, but then he shouted at Mark – said he'd get him later and called him a puny little twat – and it just happened. Dean was a monster.'

I expect to feel a rush of relief as she admits it. But I feel nothing. I always knew what she'd done, so perhaps it makes no difference. Shall I tell her about the hours of planning? The years of transforming myself from a chubby, spotty teenager into a sleek, sophisticated young woman, using all Nigel's hard-earned cash that he so willingly gave me? The years of learning skills that I thought might allow me to get close to Mark North – just so that I could kill him?

I'm surprised she hasn't mentioned the wig, but I'm sure I saw a fleeting moment of recall in her eyes when she first arrived. Does she remember the young woman with the black hair and bright red lipstick who lived close by for months, finding out everything possible about Mark and Mia – working out the finer details of my plan? I hope so.

I move away from the cliff towards Cleo and she takes a step back.

'Come on,' I dare her. 'Come and get me. You want to, don't you? I know you're good at pushing people to their death – I've seen you in action. But then I'm pretty good at it myself.'

Cleo is staring at me again, wondering what I mean. I've thrown so much her way, I don't know if she will work it out, and I no longer have the strength to tell her.

I'm talking about Mia, of course. She was in the way – coming between me and Mark just as I was ready for him – so I had to get rid of her. I had been watching the house for a few weeks, looking for an opportunity. And then I saw it. I waited for Mark's taxi to disappear down the drive and then posed as a pool maintenance girl, turning up a day early to add the chemicals that Mia was too lazy to add herself. She buzzed me in, but came to the top of the basement stairs to meet me and escort me down to the pool. I had taken a knife, but I didn't need to use it.

'After you,' I'd said, allowing her to go in front of me.

She'd shrugged and moved to go ahead. The technique was well known to me, of course – God knows, my bastard uncle tried it often enough – and I quickly edged my foot between her leading and trailing ankles. I remember the momentary look of surprise on her face, but it didn't last long as she tumbled head first down the stairs and onto the tiled concrete floor below, her neck snapping as she hit the ground. I didn't expect it to be so easy, and then all I had to do was to untie one of her trainers.

But I'm not going to tell Cleo all this.

It's getting cold on the cliff now, and while I've been deciding how much to reveal, I haven't taken my eyes off her face. It's taken a while for her to understand what I meant about my expertise in pushing people to their deaths, but finally she gets it.

'Mia?' Her voice is hoarse, worn out with emotion. I raise my eyebrows and nod.

'I was there, Cleo – hiding in the boiler room when you stormed into the house itching for a fight. I heard what you said when you saw Mia's body. "Jesus, Mark, what have you done?" Why did you make that assumption, I wonder? Did you think "Like sister, like brother?"'

I can see she's had enough. It's all become too much, and if I push her further she will collapse in a heap. That's no good.

'As I said – today one of us is going to die. Who is it going to be?'

Cleo stood her ground as Evie walked towards her. For days she had thought she had nothing left to live for, but now she didn't want to be the one to die. She needed to live, to tell the world that her brother was an innocent victim.

'Come on,' Evie dared her. 'Come and get me. You know you want to.'

Evie was right. Cleo wanted her dead, and nothing would give her more pleasure than to rush at Mark's killer, drag her to the edge and force her over the cliff. What did she have to lose? Mark was gone, Lulu was lost to her – even if she lived out her days in prison, the world would be rid of the evil that was Evie Clarke.

She took a step forward, her heart thumping.

Jump, Evie. Jump, she begged silently.

She took another step. Then another.

So this is how it ends.

It is clear to me now: one of us has to die.

And with a roar, she charged.

72

Finally, after half an hour stuck in traffic, Stephanie raced up the track to the white wall of the house where Mark North's bloodied body had been found, shards of stone flying sideways as her tyres skidded over the rough surface.

Cleo's car was there – parked outside the door. Stephanie knew the whole story now. Cleo had been a witness to the death of Evie's brother. She had tried to save him, the report said. Had Evie believed that, or had Gus been right to think there was more to Mark's death than a bad ending to an abusive relationship?

She slammed on the brakes and felt the back end of the car slide on the gravel. She didn't care. This meeting might be entirely innocent, but Aminah Basra had been worried – and Stephanie couldn't ignore what her instincts were telling her.

Running towards the door, uncertain whether her knock would be answered, she saw the garage door standing open, and remembered a distraught Cleo telling her it was possible to get into the house this way.

She sprinted to the garage and stopped. Everything might be fine. She couldn't just charge in there – she had to be calm.

She took a deep breath and moved towards the open door leading to the garden.

There was no-one to be seen, so Stephanie walked towards the window of the house, expecting to see signs of life in the kitchen or living room. But it was empty and had a look of desertion about it, as if – like its owner – the beautiful room had died too.

Above the thunder of the waves and the call of gulls circling overhead she heard the sound of high-pitched laughter, and she breathed out. If they were laughing, it was all going to be okay. She had panicked for nothing.

She walked quietly across the lawn, and peered around the corner of a tall beech hedge towards the cliff edge.

A woman stood there alone, looking down at the sea pounding on the rocks below. A burst of spring sunshine reflected off her bright bleached hair and she raised her hands up to the heavens, tipping her head back as if giving thanks.

Epilogue

The boy is standing on the sea wall. He's showing off, pretending it's dangerous even though the top of the wall is flat and wide. He doesn't see the danger when it comes rushing at him with such violence. All that is left is the dying echo of his scream.

As I wait for my visitor to arrive, knowing what she is going to say to me, I look around my new home, at the four walls that crowd me, seeming to grow ever closer, crushing me between their shiny surfaces. I presume the gloss paint makes them easier to clean, but it glares harshly in the over-bright lights.

I will have plenty of time to think – to consider everything I have done. I'm sure I am supposed to feel remorse, but I feel nothing.

I've told the police it was an accident. I have repeated it time and again, but I know the odds are stacked against me.

I have been charged with murder, and I doubt I can prove otherwise, but for now I have no more time to wonder what is going to happen to me. I can hear the sound of footsteps coming towards me, and the door to my cell is opened to reveal the sour face of my prison officer.

'Your visitor's arrived,' she says, flicking her head to the right to indicate I should follow her. The officers don't like me because they believe I'm a killer. I don't much care what they think.

I'm taken to a private room – the room reserved for inmates and their lawyers – and as soon as I sit down the door clicks open again. Harriet James strides into the room. Her face is a mask and I've no idea what she's thinking. It's not long before I find out.

'I'm not going to ask how you've been, because frankly I don't give a shit,' she says, spitting out the words. I realise now that her features are being held steady as part of a strategy to ensure that her anger doesn't erupt.

I say nothing. I doubt she will act for me. She sees me as the enemy, but she's good so perhaps it is worth a try.

'I've come to see you because you asked for me, but I have no intention of defending you. What you did was monstrous. You killed an innocent woman.'

I return her gaze, refusing to flinch beneath the force of her anger.

'She wasn't innocent. She murdered my brother.'

'I'm not even going to waste my breath trying to convince you that you're wrong.'

I consider telling Harriet about the confession on the cliff top, but I know she wouldn't believe me, so I remain silent. Harriet hasn't even sat down and it's clear she won't be staying.

She leans forward, her hands grasping the back of the chair, her knuckles white. 'Nothing to say?'

'Nothing that would mean anything to you, no,' I answer.

She gives a tut of disgust. 'Do you have any idea of the damage you have done? Somewhere out there is a woman being abused who might genuinely lose control and kill her partner. The fear of what might happen to her may have been lessened slightly by the famous "Evie Clarke case" – but the press are going wild with delight at the latest developments.'

I sympathise with her anger. This was supposed to be her moment to bask in the glory of all she had achieved, but given how things have turned out I expect clients might be more hesitant about seeking her services. The news is full of speculation and nobody knows what to believe.

I've seen to that.

'So,' she says, picking up the briefcase that she put down only a couple of minutes ago, 'if you've nothing more to say, I'll leave you to it.'

She turns and walks towards the door.

'She fell, Harriet,' I say, without raising my voice. 'It was an accident.'

Harriet spins round and walks back towards the table. 'That's not true and we both know it. The evidence is too strong – the churned-up ground, the fibres on her clothes and yours, the scratches, the bruises. She fought back. But she lost.'

The plan had worked well, it seemed. Too well. And she's right not to believe me, of course. The end, when it came, wasn't as simple as I have claimed.

For a while it had seemed as if nothing was going to happen. We stood staring at each other, both waiting for the other to make a move. She killed my brother. I killed hers. Which of us should die?

She decided it had to be me. First I saw confusion in her eyes – then indecision. But in the end the hatred and fury that had been festering within her burst free and she made her move.

Harriet reaches the door and opens it.

'Goodbye, Evie,' she says. 'I hope you rot in this place for the next twenty years.'

It doesn't matter to Harriet that I had intended to die that day. She would be sorry I failed, I'm sure, because then her reputation would be intact, everyone continuing to believe that I was a victim. But I didn't die, and the world now believes I am – and probably always was – a killer.

The irony is that I didn't murder Cleo. She charged at me, and I simply stepped out of the way, an instinctive act of self-preservation that I neither wanted nor expected. As the ground slid beneath her feet she reached for me and grabbed a handful of my hair. The wig came off in her hand as she tumbled to her death on the rocks below.

The carefully prepared grounds for her conviction – the blood under my fingernails, the fibres on my clothes – are now evidence of my guilt.

I hadn't been lying when I told Cleo I was ready to die that day. I didn't think I would ever be free of the memories that sicken me, and my carefully planned revenge had done nothing to lessen the bitterness that had poisoned me for so long.

Strangely, though, I feel as though Cleo's death has set me free. Maybe I am destined to spend the rest of my life in here, but I dream of days on a winter beach with my beautiful Lolula, watching the waves wash the sand clean of every mark, every memory of those who walked there before us.

Nobody saw Cleo die. There are other possible interpretations of the evidence.

Maybe this isn't the end after all. Maybe it's just the start of something new. Maybe one day I'll look back and I'll know: This is where it all began.

Acknowledgements

I am always staggered by the generosity of people when it comes to answering book research queries, and with this novel I needed more expert advice than for any other.

In particular I would, as always, like to thank my wonderful police advisor, ex-DCI Mark Grey, who somehow seems to cope with questions that range from the most mundane to the most complex. He never lets me down.

I also needed specialist help with the court scenes, and criminal lawyer Cheryl Dudley's guidance was vital. Thank you, Steve Rodgers, for recommending her. Together with Jane Britton, Steve was also good enough to spend New Year's Day listening to my ideas for this story and making valuable suggestions. It helps that he is a judge, I suppose!

Colin Lawry at Truro Crown Court was so accommodating and informative, as was David Earl, whose technical knowledge can always be relied on for accuracy.

One very special person who never lets me down is my agent, Lizzy Kremer. Together with the whole team at David Higham Associates she has supported me on this journey and offered encouragement and invaluable advice. I genuinely couldn't have done this without her. Harriet Moore, Olivia Barber and Clare Bowron also gave wonderful editorial input.

I have been overwhelmed by the enthusiasm and expertise of the Wildfire team, particularly Kate Stephenson, Alex Clarke and Ella Gordon, and the wider Headline team – including Becky Hunter, Jo Liddiard, Caroline Young, Louise Rothwell and Becky Bader – are a joy to work with.

My special thanks to Tish McPhilemy who joined me three years ago to look after the necessary administration involved in being an author, but who now does so much more – including making me laugh when things don't go to plan and providing me with inspiration in so many ways.

Finally, I couldn't do any of it without the support of my family – especially John, who makes sure I am fed and watered when I can't think of anything that exists outside the world of my imagination, and who listens – with apparent interest – when I talk about a group of people who I know so well but who he will never get to meet, other than on the pages of my book. That takes a special kind of person.

Rachel Abbott began her career as an independent author in 2011, with *Only the Innocent*, which became a No.1 e-book bestseller, topping the chart for four weeks. Since then, she has published five further psychological thrillers, plus a novella, and sold over 3 million copies. She is one of the top-selling digital authors of all time in the UK (published and self-published), and her novels have been translated into 21 languages.